THE UNICORN CHRONICLES

BOOK I
INTO THE LAND
OF THE UNICORNS

BOOK II
SONG OF
THE WANDERER

BOOK III
DARK
WHISPERS

THE
UNICORN CHRONICLES
III

THE
UNICORN CHRONICLES
BOOK III

DARK
WHISPERS

BY
BRUCE COVILLE

SCHOLASTIC PRESS
NEW YORK

Text copyright © 2008 by Bruce Coville

LIBRARY OF CONGRESS CATALOGING-IN-PUBLICATION DATA

Coville, Bruce.

Dark whispers / Bruce Coville. — 1st ed.

p. cm. — (The Unicorn Chronicles ; bk. 3)

Summary: Seeking to unravel the secret of the long enmity between unicorns
and delvers, Cara travels through a strange underground world to the court of the
centaur king, while on Earth, Beloved and her hunters make final plans to jump to
the fantasy land of Luster and drive the unicorns to extinction.

ISBN-13: 978-0-590-45951-8

ISBN-10: 0-590-45951-1

[1. Unicorns — Fiction. 2. Fantasy.] I. Title.

PZ7.C8344Dar 2008

[Fic] — dc22

2007031053

10 9 8 7 6 5 4 3 2 1   08 09 10 11 12

Printed in the U.S.A.

First edition, August 2008

Map by Katherine Coville copyright © 2008 by Scholastic Inc.

The text was set in Adobe Garamond Pro.

The display type was set in Mantinia.

Book design by Phil Falco.

To Jean Feiwel, who
opened the door to Luster for me.
I am eternally grateful.

ACKNOWLEDGMENTS

This book has been a long time in the making, and I have been helped by good eyes and even better ears of many friends, including Daniel Bostick, Cara Coville, Katherine Coville, Kelly Lombardo, Naomi Miller, Tamora Pierce, Michael Stearns, and the late and much-missed Paula Danziger.

I also owe thanks to Pat Brigandi, my editor for the first book, and Zehava Cohn, who guided me through the second. Both helped me shape the world and the story that continues to evolve. For this book the editorial reins were taken up by Dianne Hess and Lisa Meltzer, ably assisted by the wonderful Grace Kendall.

This book would not exist at all, had not Jean Feiwel invited me to write a unicorn series back in 1991. She could have had no idea, when she did so, that it would take me this long to reach book three!

Additionally, my beloved writer's group — Tedd Arnold, MJ Auch, Patience Brewster, Cynthia De Felice, Robin Pulver, Vivian Vande Velde, and Ellen Stoll Walsh — listened patiently in and out of eight years, trying to keep track of the strands of the story even when I would return to it after leaving them hanging for six months or more. Their patience was monumental, and their contributions invaluable.

But most of all I must thank the fans who urged me (with varying degrees of patience!) to finish the darn thing. Many who started reading the Chronicles as children have grown up while I have been trying to write this third volume, and I am both chastened and heartened by their continuing emails letting me know they are still eager to read it. If I hadn't been so painfully aware that so many people were waiting for this story, I might have given up at any number of points along the way. So thanks, dear fans. I literally could not have done it without you!

— Bruce Coville

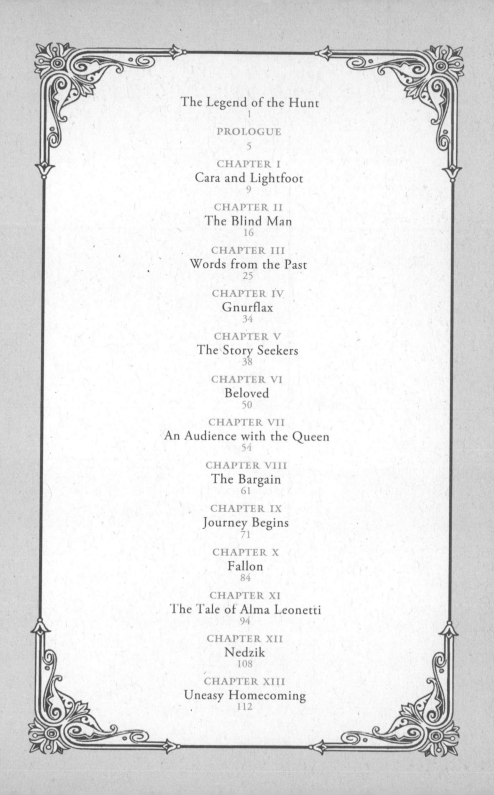

The Legend of the Hunt
1

PROLOGUE
5

CHAPTER I
Cara and Lightfoot
9

CHAPTER II
The Blind Man
16

CHAPTER III
Words from the Past
25

CHAPTER IV
Gnurflax
34

CHAPTER V
The Story Seekers
38

CHAPTER VI
Beloved
50

CHAPTER VII
An Audience with the Queen
54

CHAPTER VIII
The Bargain
61

CHAPTER IX
Journey Begins
71

CHAPTER X
Fallon
84

CHAPTER XI
The Tale of Alma Leonetti
94

CHAPTER XII
Nedzik
108

CHAPTER XIII
Uneasy Homecoming
112

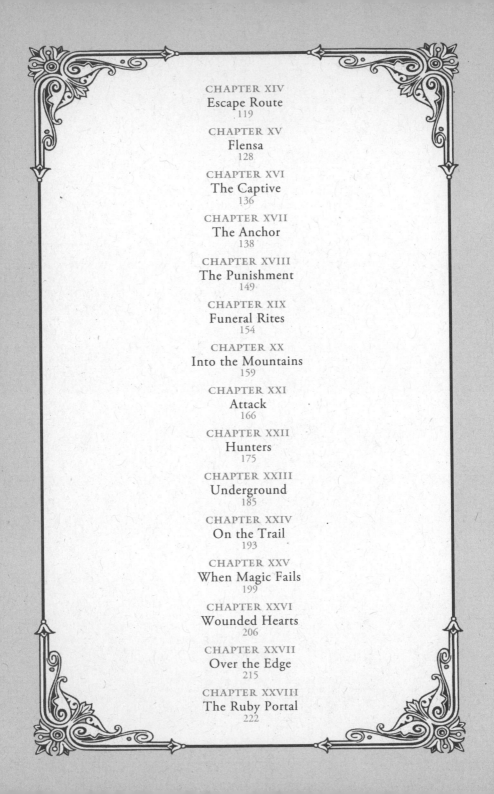

CHAPTER XIV
Escape Route
119

CHAPTER XV
Flensa
128

CHAPTER XVI
The Captive
136

CHAPTER XVII
The Anchor
138

CHAPTER XVIII
The Punishment
149

CHAPTER XIX
Funeral Rites
154

CHAPTER XX
Into the Mountains
159

CHAPTER XXI
Attack
166

CHAPTER XXII
Hunters
175

CHAPTER XXIII
Underground
185

CHAPTER XXIV
On the Trail
193

CHAPTER XXV
When Magic Fails
199

CHAPTER XXVI
Wounded Hearts
206

CHAPTER XXVII
Over the Edge
215

CHAPTER XXVIII
The Ruby Portal
222

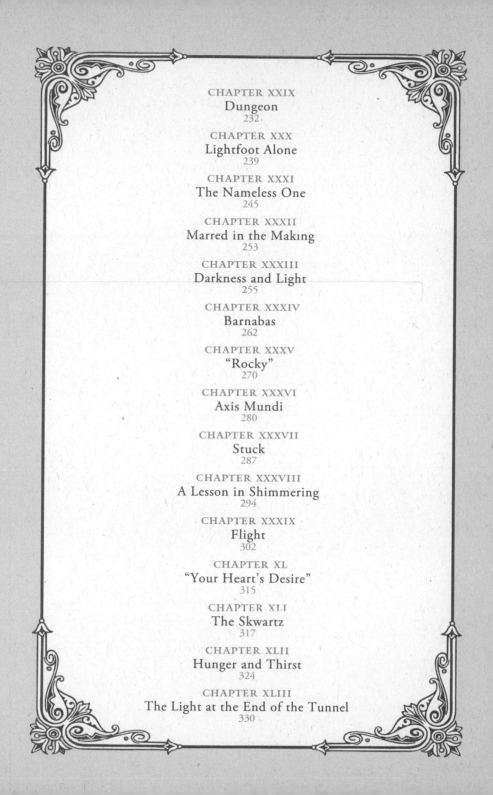

CHAPTER XXIX
Dungeon
232

CHAPTER XXX
Lightfoot Alone
239

CHAPTER XXXI
The Nameless One
245

CHAPTER XXXII
Marred in the Making
253

CHAPTER XXXIII
Darkness and Light
255

CHAPTER XXXIV
Barnabas
262

CHAPTER XXXV
"Rocky"
270

CHAPTER XXXVI
Axis Mundi
280

CHAPTER XXXVII
Stuck
287

CHAPTER XXXVIII
A Lesson in Shimmering
294

CHAPTER XXXIX
Flight
302

CHAPTER XL
"Your Heart's Desire"
315

CHAPTER XLI
The Skwartz
317

CHAPTER XLII
Hunger and Thirst
324

CHAPTER XLIII
The Light at the End of the Tunnel
330

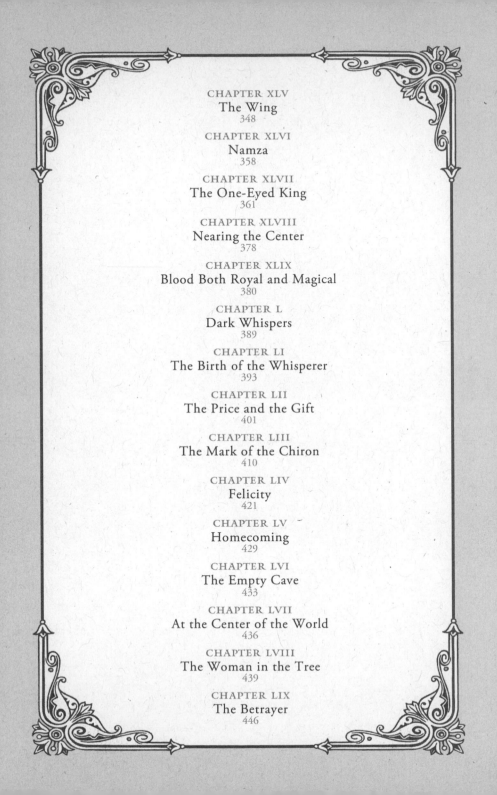

CHAPTER XLV
The Wing
348

CHAPTER XLVI
Namza
358

CHAPTER XLVII
The One-Eyed King
361

CHAPTER XLVIII
Nearing the Center
378

CHAPTER XLIX
Blood Both Royal and Magical
380

CHAPTER L
Dark Whispers
389

CHAPTER LI
The Birth of the Whisperer
393

CHAPTER LII
The Price and the Gift
401

CHAPTER LIII
The Mark of the Chiron
410

CHAPTER LIV
Felicity
421

CHAPTER LV
Homecoming
429

CHAPTER LVI
The Empty Cave
433

CHAPTER LVII
At the Center of the World
436

CHAPTER LVIII
The Woman in the Tree
439

CHAPTER LIX
The Betrayer
446

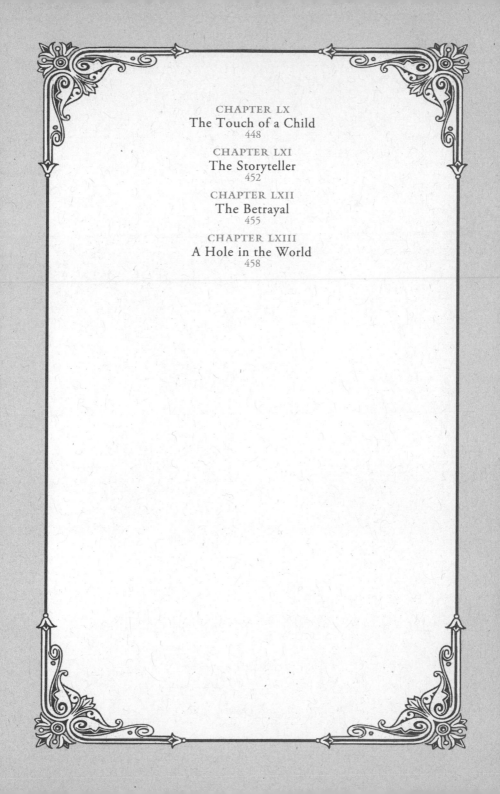

CHAPTER LX
The Touch of a Child
448

CHAPTER LXI
The Storyteller
452

CHAPTER LXII
The Betrayal
455

CHAPTER LXIII
A Hole in the World
458

LUSTER
THE WORLD
OF THE UNICORNS

Forest........
River..........
Swamp........
Hills..........
Mountains....
Water........

Here There be Merfolk

AUTUMN~
GROVE

0   25 mi.   50 mi.   75 mi.   100

THE
LEGEND OF
THE HUNT

For the seventh time I, Grimwold, Keeper of the Chronicles, take pen in hand to record the story of how the Hunt began. This has been done once every ten years by each Chronicle Keeper since the unicorns first came to Luster. We do this because from this story flows all that has happened to the unicorns in the centuries since, and this is our way of keeping the story fresh in memory.

*   *   *

Where the unicorns came from, no one knows. But there is no question that their appearance on old Earth made it a sweeter, richer place to be. In that time humans and unicorns lived largely apart from one another. However, they were not enemies.

Now, while unicorns live very long lives, they are not immortal. And the day finally came when the first of the

1

unicorns passed away. Alas, his horn — which was all that was left of him, for his body dissolved, as is the way of unicorns — was found by a man who soon discovered that it still held powerful healing magic. This should have been enough for him. But seeking to make himself seem brave and bold, he boasted that the unicorn, who had died before the man even saw the horn, had been a fearsome foe, and that he had battled it to the death.

Lies being what they are, this tale of the fierce unicorn spread — as did the truth of the way its horn could heal.

So it was when a man, who was a true hunter, found himself with a daughter sick and in danger of dying. Deciding to go in quest of a unicorn's horn to cure her, he prepared himself to face a terrible beast. As his wife was already dead, he took to carrying his child (whom he called Beloved, for his entire heart was filled with her) into the forest on his back.

One fateful day the hunter left Beloved to rest in a clearing while he continued his quest. That afternoon an ill-fated breeze caught the scent of the child and her illness, and carried it to a unicorn named Whiteling. Wanting to help, Whiteling came to the clearing. Approaching with care and tenderness, the unicorn knelt and pressed the tip of his horn to Beloved's chest, piercing her flesh in order to heal her.

The hunter returned at that moment and cried out when he thought he saw a unicorn trying to kill his daughter. Swiftly he loosed an arrow. It pierced the unicorn's heart, in the very same moment that the unicorn's horn pierced the heart of the ailing girl.

Whiteling snapped his head up in shock and pain, a movement so sharp that it broke off the tip of his horn, which lodged in Beloved's heart.

The hunter charged, and before the girl's horrified eyes, man and unicorn fought unto the death. As she watched both of them die, her father's words about the evil of unicorns seared their way into Beloved's heart, which had now become the most unusual heart in the world. For in every moment it was being wounded by the shard of horn that was lodged there, and at the same time healed by the horn's powerful magic.

Fueled by pain and anger, and kept alive by this strange magic, Beloved became the fierce and eternal enemy of the unicorns. She sought ever to destroy them in vengeance for her father, and also as repayment for the never-ending pain of her ever-wounded, ever-healing heart.

Thus began the long hunt, which has stretched across centuries as the immortal Beloved continues to seek the destruction of the creatures she blames for her misery.

Grimwold

Fourth Keeper of the Unicorn Chronicles
The Queen's Forest, Luster

PROLOGUE

The Dimblethum stopped, looked around, sniffed the air. For a moment the huge creature thought he had caught the scent of something unpleasant . . . something dangerous. Holding himself as unmoving and silent as the silvery-blue trunks of the eldrim trees that surrounded him, he stood and listened intently.

Nothing.

He waited another moment, then moved on. The shambling creature had parted from the gryphon, Medafil, only two days earlier. Now he was making his way back to his own territory.

Though it had been many years since he crossed this particular stretch of Luster, the manbeast was guided by powerful instincts that pointed him to his home ground. It was a good thing, for the long journey to help his friend Cara find her grandmother had taken him farther afield than he usually wandered. Now he longed for the comfort and familiarity of his own cave, which was the center of his world.

An hour or so later the Dimblethum stopped again, this time to gather sunberries from a low-growing bush. Savoring the sticky-sweetness of the bright yellow fruit, he remembered how much Cara had liked the taste of them, and wondered how she was faring with the unicorns.

Without realizing it, the creature curled his upper lip in something between a sneer and a snarl. Save for Lightfoot, the Dimblethum had little use for unicorns. Nor they for him. There was a reason for this, but he could not remember it. It was lost in the haze that clouded so much of his memory.

With a growl, the Dimblethum shoved the thought aside. He would have no more cause to deal with unicorns for now. Trying to think of more pleasant things, he decided he would catch a fish for dinner that evening, maybe one of those sweet-fleshed silvery ones with blue stripes.

The sun, hot against his shaggy hide, was making the creature drowsy. He yawned, opening his great muzzle so that the ferocious teeth were on full display. Then he shook his head and rubbed his paws over his odd face, which looked like nothing so much as that of a bear who had begun to turn into a man and been stopped halfway through the process.

Insects droned in the trees above him, their slow hum lulling him further into drowsiness. He wanted a nap, but decided he wanted to be home even more. He pressed on.

The Dimblethum was passing beneath a quilpum tree when a familiar voice whispered, "I know what you want."

The Dimblethum stopped. He looked up, but could see no one. Even so, the voice spoke again. "I know what you want."

"Go away!" growled the Dimblethum. He shook his head and started forward.

The whispering continued, the voice soft and sweet as honey. "I can go a world away, and I would still be close by. And no matter where I go, I'll always know what you want. The question is, do you know what you would give to have it?"

"Go away!" roared the Dimblethum.

"As you wisssssh," sighed the voice.

The Dimblethum heard a rustling sound, then nothing. He waited in the silence for a long moment, then leaned against the tree, covered his face with his paws, and began to weep.

CHAPTER
I

CARA AND LIGHTFOOT

"It's the waiting that makes it so hard," complained Cara.

She and Lightfoot were walking beside the bank of a stream that bordered the eastern edge of Autumngrove, one of the four great resting places of Luster's unicorns. Cara had her hand on the unicorn prince's side so they could speak mind-to-mind.

At her words, Lightfoot shook his head. His mane rippled over his shoulders like silver water. "Now that the Hunters have gained one of the Queen's amulets, we know they're going to try to invade Luster. But when? And where? We don't even know how many of them there are!"

"We should have asked my father about that when we had the chance," said Cara rucfully.

At the mention of Cara's father, Lightfoot shook his head again. "Your family is such a strange tangle!"

"It's your family, too," replied Cara, a trifle sharply. "We are related, after all."

"I never thought I would have a human for a cousin!" answered Lightfoot, his bemusement more clear to Cara because of the way they were connected.

"And I never thought I would find out that my grandmother is a unicorn who had been trapped in human form! I still don't know what to think about it — what to think about *myself*! I mean, what *am* I?"

They had come to a place where the stream widened to form a pool. Without a word passing between them, they decided to stop. Lightfoot stretched his neck to nibble some late-ripening fruit that hung from a *gualpa* vine. Cara pulled off her boots and waded into the sparkling water, enjoying the feel of the mud as it squished between her toes.

"We should go back soon," she said after a while, forced to speak aloud now that she no longer had her hand on her companion's side.

"I'll let you ride when we do. We'll get to court faster that way — which means we can stay a little longer now."

"I'd like that." Though she loved riding Lightfoot, Cara would never actually request the privilege. The idea felt presumptuous somehow. So she always waited for the Prince to invite her.

She was still amazed at the fact that the young

unicorn — young by unicorn standards, for in truth he was over a century old — was a prince. When she had met him in the wilderness, the day he came to the Dimblethum's cave to heal her, he had seemed more like a rebellious teenager. Of course, that was shortly after she had first jumped into Luster, back when she knew nothing of unicorns, least of all that her own grandmother was one of them. Then again, even her grandmother had not known that startling truth until a few days ago, when she had been returned to her true shape.

Cara stripped off her shirt — a comfortable, handwoven garment given to her by the Geomancer — and tossed it onto the bank. She dipped her face into the stream. The water was so clear she could have counted the tiny silver minnows swarming around her legs, if they had only been willing to hold still. As she began scrubbing at her brow and cheeks, the minnows flashed away, moving in such tight formation it was as if they were one creature instead of many.

Cara lifted her face, shook the water from her hands, then waded back to the edge of the pond. Plucking her shirt from the bank, she used it to dry herself. She loved being in Luster, but it was not always easy to keep clean in a place where there were no washing machines or hot showers, or any of the other conveniences she had taken for granted in her life back on Earth.

On the other hand, the unicorn world was also free of the noise and crowding and pollution she had learned to take for granted on Earth — free, too, of the teasing and bullying she had come to accept as the price you had to pay for being a slightly dreamy kid with bright red hair.

After pulling her shirt back on, Cara wandered beneath the drooping branches of a lacewillow; they overhung the pond, forming a kind of blue curtain. The sun dappling through the fluttering, blade-shaped leaves cast a pattern of light and dark on the water. Idly, Cara began braiding three of the slender branches, thinking — as she did so many times a day — of her mother and wondering how they would ever find a way to free her from the Rainbow Prison. She had given her father the great scarlet gem, originally a gift from Grimwold, that had first let her see her mother's imprisonment. Now he was off doing what he did best: hunting. Only this time he was not hunting for unicorns, but seeking his own lost wife.

Cara longed to know where he was, how his quest was proceeding. Much as she loved being here in Luster with the unicorns, she longed even more to have her family back together.

So lost was the girl in her thoughts that she didn't notice the rustling in the branches above her until a furry creature dropped from them onto her shoulder. Cara gasped in terror, then rolled her eyes as a high, squeaky voice cried,

"Hotcha gotcha! Bad girl long gone without Squijum. Stinky, hidey girl! Squijum found you good!"

When Cara had first met the Squijum his chatter was little more than random sounds to her. But since she had been given the gift of tongues by the dragon Firethroat, she could understand and speak to any creature in Luster that had language. Now, her heart still pounding from the surprise, she snapped, "Squijum, don't *do* that."

"Be nice!" cried the Squijum, swatting at her with a three-fingered paw.

"You be nice!" she replied sharply, lifting him from her shoulder so she could look him in the face. His thick gray fur — dark on his back, lighter on his underside — felt good beneath her fingers, and the bright blue pupils of his eyes seemed to glow with mischief. He looked a little like a squirrel, a little like a monkey, and entirely like himself. "Stinky girl!" he chittered. "Put Squijum down!"

"Squijum, listen to me," she said firmly, not letting go of him. "With everything that's going on right now — with all of us waiting for the Hunters to attack — you can't act like that. Someone's going to poke a stick through you if you're not careful."

"Hotcha stinky pokey girl," muttered the Squijum sulkily. But he stopped squirming. She returned him to her shoulder, where he tugged her hair once to let her know that he was vexed with her, then settled into a crouch. She sighed, but didn't say anything. Despite how annoying he could be, she was deeply fond of the little creature.

"Don't be too angry," said a mellow voice. "The Queen *did* send us to fetch you."

Cara turned toward the voice, crying happily, "Finder! How did you know we were here?"

The big unicorn — the tallest Cara had met since she came to Luster — was standing beside Lightfoot. "Why do you think they call me Finder?" he replied with a gentle chuckle. His face grew serious. "I would gladly have left the two of you in peace. But something has come up, and the Queen wants you both back at court. We need to hurry."

"Is it bad?" asked Cara nervously.

Finder shook his head. "I don't know. I only know that your grandmother asked us to gather the inner circle immediately. Everyone was close by except Lightfoot and you. I don't have to tell you that Moonheart made some comments about *that*."

"Is there anything I do my uncle *doesn't* make comments about?" replied Lightfoot, somewhat sourly.

Finder laughed — a deep, musical sound that Cara found both soothing and beautiful. "He wouldn't fuss so much if he didn't care."

"It would be fine with me if he didn't care at all!" replied Lightfoot. He sighed. "All right, let's go see what this is all about. At least it's not an attack. Climb on, Cara."

Not having time to dry her feet, Cara tied her bootlaces together and slung the boots over her right shoulder. With the Squijum still clinging to her left shoulder she climbed onto Lightfoot's back and wound her fingers into the silk of his mane. They started toward court.

CHAPTER
II

THE BLIND MAN

"This way, sahib. This way!"

Ian Hunter followed the slender figure of the boy named Rajiv as he wove his way through the crowd that surged along the narrow, cobblestoned street. Ian's mind was divided, part of it eagerly seeking the next clue that would lead to his quarry, another part on high alert for danger, especially for any sign that he was being followed. Still another part — a part he tried to force into silence, because he could not afford distraction right now — was thinking of his daughter. Where in Luster was Cara at this moment? What was she doing?

Ahead of him, the boy slipped through the knots of people as easily as a minnow gliding among strands of seaweed. Ian, larger and clearly foreign, could not move so fast.

"Hurry, sahib," urged Rajiv, coming back to grab his hand.

The two made an odd contrast: Rajiv, little more than four feet tall, had dark brown skin set off with a mop of jet-black hair and eyes like obsidian; Ian, a solid six feet two inches of lean muscle, had close-cropped reddish-brown hair and piercing hazel eyes.

As near as Ian could make out, Rajiv's desire for speed at this moment came strictly from a longing to pocket as quickly as possible the rupees he had been promised for helping locate a certain address.

Ian had come to India in search of a clue to the secrets of the Rainbow Prison, where his wife was being held captive by Beloved. It was not his first trip to the sub-continent; some of the training he had received after Beloved first recruited him to join her war against the uni-corns — training in how to still the busy brain so that deeper parts of the mind could offer their wisdom — had taken place here.

That was back when he had believed in Beloved and her crusade, before his daughter's courage had opened his eyes and caused him to turn against the Hunters and their quest to destroy the unicorns. Despite his change of heart, he still valued the training he had received from Beloved. Though arduous — there were times when he feared he would not survive it — that training had given him strength and skills he had never thought to have in his old life, back when he was a teacher. Even more, it had given him connections to a world he had never imagined to exist, a network of people who worked with secret knowledge and arcane lore.

It was through one of these contacts that he had learned of the man he was seeking now, a mysterious blind man who, his source claimed, had a great deal of unusual knowledge.

Were his quest not so urgent, Ian would have been filled with delight at returning to India. Nowhere else in all the world — and he had seen much of it since becoming a Hunter — had he felt such a sense of ancientness, such a presence of something sacred, a presence unmistakable even in the mad riot of color and sound and smells that filled the streets of Old Delhi.

He had picked Rajiv out of the crowd of clamoring boys who accosted him when he climbed out of the taxi that had brought him here to the Chandni Chowk, the fabled market district in the old section of the city. He chose the boy by instinct as much as anything, sensing a lively intelligence behind those dark, flashing eyes. Though the child was dusty and ragged, he spoke good English — not that that was unusual in India. With hundreds of local dialects, the country had fallen back on English as the national language, perhaps the most useful relic of the days of the Raj, when the entire subcontinent had been held under the control of Great Britain.

A motorbike roared past, weaving its way through the crowd of shoppers in the narrow alley. To the right, a stairway led down to a basement shop that sold saris made of gorgeous, vibrantly colored silks. On a roof overhead, Ian noticed a monkey glaring at them. It made him think of the odd little creature called "the Squijum" that had befriended his daughter.

Again his thoughts had come back to Cara, as they did a hundred times every day. She had only been three when she was stolen from him — abducted by his wife's own mother. That had been the darkest day of his life, and the loss had set him on a path that had changed his way of being beyond his wildest dreams.

Through all that had happened since Cara's kidnapping he had vowed to find her again, and less than three months ago he had succeeded. But when he did finally locate Cara, he had been an entirely different man than the father she had been stolen from, and he had lost her again — lost her heart, this time — because he held to his allegiance to Beloved and the Hunters while she sided with the unicorns.

Ian's thoughts after that second loss had been bitter indeed. Then, only a week ago, he and his daughter had come face-to-face once more. This time, Cara's courage and need had forced him to see past the ferocious training — *brainwashing*, he now angrily considered it — that he had received from Beloved. But though the two of them had reconnected on a deep and powerful level, Cara had returned to Luster, as she felt she must, to take her place with the unicorns. So he had lost his daughter yet again.

No, he corrected himself. *I haven't lost her. Not this time. Our hearts are linked once more.*

Still, it was difficult to have her in Luster, since the unicorns did not trust him. Not that he could blame them. Unfortunately, the Hunters, knowing he had betrayed their cause, no longer trusted him either. In fact, they were likely in pursuit of him at this very moment — even as he himself was searching for his wife.

Or, more specifically, for his wife's spirit. He knew where her body was.

The final result of all this was that Ian Hunter felt more alone than he ever had in his life. Oddly enough, at the same time, he felt more hope than he had imagined possible.

His thoughts were interrupted by Rajiv grabbing his hand. The boy's slim, brown fingers were strong and urgent as he hissed, "This way, sahib! This way!"

They turned down an alley even narrower than the one they had been traveling. A cow brushed past, serene in her knowledge that she could walk the streets unmolested.

The alley was lined with nondescript doors. But at the

end, it opened into a little courtyard made brilliant by a thousand flowers, each a burst of crimson or gold. The blossoms surrounded a door that was larger than the others. Beautifully carved, it was framed by ornate and colorful tiles.

"That is the place you asked for," said Rajiv, sounding a little nervous.

"Thank you." Ian pressed some rupees into the boy's hand — a larger amount than was called for, really, but with his daughter again in his mind he could not help but overpay the boy.

"Do you want me to wait for you, sahib?" asked Rajiv, his dark eyes eager. "Only fifty rupees more."

"I can find my own way back," said Ian brusquely.

"Probably. Even so, it is never bad to have a friend when you are in a new place," replied Rajiv, masterfully combining sage advice with an edge of pleading.

"I'll be fine," said Ian, who had dealt with too many street urchins in the years since he became a Hunter to be moved by these tactics. Even so, another part of his heart — the part that remembered his years as a teacher — could not help but respond to the boy. He clamped down fiercely on that response, telling himself he had a job to do. Without further notice of Rajiv, he stepped forward and pulled the bell handle.

A moment later an old woman opened the door. She was dressed traditionally, in a worn but beautiful sari, and had a bright red dot — a *bindi* — in the middle of her forehead.

"You are Mr. Hunter?" she asked, then smiled slightly as Ian's eyes widened in surprise. "We are expecting you. Come in, come in."

He stepped inside. Noticing her disapproving glance at his feet, he slipped out of his shoes.

The woman nodded in satisfaction. "Follow me."

The house was pleasantly cool, surprising after the outside heat. Ian padded silently after the woman, intrigued by the mix of modern and ancient artwork that covered the walls. They passed two or three doors before she ushered him into a dark room, sweet with incense. She bowed slightly, then backed away, closing the door behind her. At once the room was plunged into complete and utter darkness.

Ian resisted an urge to leap toward the door and wrench it open. Holding still, he waited, listening with ears trained to the Hunt. On the far side of the room he could hear breathing, slightly labored.

"You are Ian Hunter?" asked a man's voice.

Holding his own voice calm, Ian replied, "Yes, that is me."

"Forgive the darkness. As I am blind myself, it seems a bit of an . . . equalizer."

"It would be more equal if I had had years to get used to it and knew the layout of this room."

"Ah, not a hint of pity. That is good. I do not like to be pitied. Nor do I like to waste time. So, let us move forward. I understand you are interested in the Rainbow Prison. More specifically, in the Ruby Portal, which will allow you entrance to the red shaft of that prison."

"How do you know that?" asked Ian, realizing at once that the source who steered him here must have alerted the blind man that he would be coming, and why.

His host confirmed as much when he made a tutting sound and said, "Come, come, Mr. Hunter. How did you know to seek *me* in order to find out about it? We both have our sources."

Ian did not answer for a moment. The pause was natural enough, as if he were thinking of his response — which, indeed, he was. But he was also listening intently for the sound of anyone else breathing. No, it was just the two of them here in the darkened room. Even so, he had an uneasy feeling and could not help wondering if he had been led into a trap of some sort. He did not panic — he had been trained not to. What he did do was try to gauge the distance to the voice and remember the thickness of the door he had just come through. He was certain he had not heard the snick of a lock after the woman closed it. Assuming the lock was not so carefully oiled as to be completely silent, that was a good sign.

"Well?" asked the voice.

Ian made a quick decision. Adopting a student-to-teacher tone he said humbly, "You are correct. I have come seeking instruction about the Rainbow Prison."

"And why should I offer this?"

"Because knowledge is sweeter when it is shared."

This earned him a chuckle. "Sweeter knowledge does nothing to put rice on the table."

"Tell me, then, what fee might be appropriate."

"How much do you wish to know?"

"As much as possible. Where did the Rainbow Prison come from? How big is it? How does one enter it? Once there, how does one find someone? Most important, how does one leave it?"

"All good questions. But it is a great deal of information that you seek, Mr. Hunter. Such knowledge does not come cheaply. It did not come cheaply to me."

"What did you pay for it?"

The answer, when it came, made Ian's blood run cold.

"I gave my eyesight. So tell me, Mr. Hunter, what are you willing to pay for this precious treasure of knowledge?"

CHAPTER
I I I

WORDS FROM THE PAST

Whenever the unicorns stayed in Autumngrove, the Queen's Council met at the base of a small waterfall, where the stream widened to form a pool about twenty yards across. The moist rocks glistened in the afternoon sunshine, their reddish surface dotted here and there with patches of blue-green moss. To the left of the waterfall, the land sloped up in a gentle curve, like the sides of an enormous shallow bowl. That slope was now populated with nearly a hundred unicorns and about ten humans, an unusually large gathering of the latter for Luster. Among the humans, Cara saw several she knew, including Jacques, the old man who had once been married to her grandmother and who might or might not be her grandfather. His face drooped in its familiar lines of gloom, and Cara wondered if he, too, had been frustrated in his attempts to have a private audience with the Queen.

Standing near Jacques, unmistakable in his multicolored patchwork coat, its front adorned with numerous gold watch chains, was Thomas the Tinker. Thomas was the first human Cara had met in Luster. Though she had not, in fact, known him that long, they had been through so much together that he felt like an old friend. Over the last few weeks he had been teaching her how to use her sword, a gift of time and knowledge that she deeply appreciated. She had been surprised to discover how much the cheerful man knew about deadly combat.

At the edge of the water stood her grandmother. During the years she had been trapped in human form, she had been known both as Ivy Morris and "the Wanderer." Now that she had been returned to her true shape, she was revealed as Amalia Flickerfoot, granddaughter of the recently faded Arabella Skydancer and new Queen of the unicorns.

To the Queen's right stood Grimwold, the old dwarf who was Keeper of the Unicorn Chronicles. He wore a coarsely woven, earth-colored robe. At the Queen's left, and nearly twice as tall as Grimwold, was M'Gama, also known as "the Geomancer." The elegant, ebony-skinned woman was the master of earth magic. In contrast to Grimwold, her garments were bold and vivid with color. Golden rings encrusted with sapphires, rubies, emeralds, and other precious gems sparkled on the long fingers of her left hand. Her right hand was bare of all ornament.

Cara, Lightfoot, Finder, and the Squijum entered at the top of the bowl. The Queen nodded when she saw them and said in a clear voice that carried easily above the sound of the falls, "The last of our members have arrived. We shall begin."

Only a few of the unicorns looked back. One of them was Belle, the fierce warrior unicorn who had accompanied Cara on her journey to fetch her grandmother. Belle was standing near Lightfoot's uncle, Moonheart. Cara expected Moonheart to look back, too, but he remained rigid and alert, staring at the Queen — who was also his sister.

"I do not need to tell you all that we face great danger," began the Queen. "Now that Beloved has gained one of the amulets, it is only a matter of time before she and her Hunters enter Luster. We must prepare and guard against that, which will not be easy, because we do not know where their invasion will take place. Until recently, we did not know *when*, either. Fortunately, M'Gama has solved part of that riddle for us."

She turned to the tall woman, who nodded slightly and stepped forward, joined by a unicorn who slipped from the shadows.

The hint of a breeze rustled M'Gama's red and purple robes. When she spoke, her voice, rich and deep, rang out across the bowl. "I have consulted the stones and soil, questioned the bones of the world, and I am confident that Beloved cannot open a new gate before the next full moon."

M'Gama spoke in a human language. She paused as her words were repeated by the unicorn who had come to stand beside her. Though she and Grimwold could both speak the language of unicorns, when they had a lot to say, and needed to say it to a large group, a translator was a great help.

"She's talking about the Blood Moon," murmured Lightfoot with a shiver.

Putting a hand on his shoulder so they could talk mind-to-mind, Cara asked, "What do you mean, '*Blood* Moon'?"

"We have a name for each full moon of the year. The next one is called the Blood Moon."

"What an awful name!"

"Well, it's not called that without reason. Two reasons, in fact. First, it often has a red cast over it. Second, it falls closest to the day when Whiteling and Beloved's father fought and killed each other." He shivered again. "It is not my favorite night of the year."

The Geomancer was still speaking. "That our enemy cannot try until then is the good news. The bad news is that I am almost certain she will make her attempt on that night. This gives us three weeks to prepare. One of our problems — one of many — is that if she does succeed in creating such a gate we do not know *where* she will enter

Luster. It could be hundreds of miles from where we stand now, which would gain you even more time to prepare. On the other hand, it could be right here in Autumngrove. My work now will be to discover where the gate is most likely to appear. I will bend all my efforts to that task. Alas, I cannot guarantee success."

She made a slight bow, then stepped back beside the Queen.

"Important as this news is, it is not the main reason I have called you together," said Amalia Flickerfoot. "Another matter, mysterious and possibly also urgent, has arisen. While we know that the piece of horn lodged in Beloved's heart has kept her alive these many centuries, some of us have suspected that there must be more to her obsession with us than that. This is a long hatred, and nothing has dimmed its passion through the years. What keeps her anger so alive? What gives it such strength and fire? Is it only the pain? Or is there something more?" The Queen shook her head. "I do not have an answer. However, Grimwold has discovered something that may offer a clue."

She nodded to the dwarf beside her. Cara noticed now that he was clutching a piece of paper.

Grimwold stepped forward. He took a moment to look across the bowl, as if drawing each unicorn into what he was about to tell them, then said, "While Cara and the others sought the Wanderer, I was combing through the

Chronicles. In one of the earliest of the scrolls, written not long after the beginning of Luster, I found this passage."

He held up the paper, unrolled it, and read:

In the darkest hour
Of their darkest day
The unicorns must face
Their own darkness.

What was their crime?
For what must they pay?
That is the riddle
The white-horned ones
Must unravel.

Have they forgotten the night?
Fled from the deed?
The Whisperer knows,
But not the Whisperer alone.
So, perhaps, do the delvers.

When he had finished, Grimwold rolled up the paper and tucked it into the front of his robe.

Cara heard the unicorns muttering uneasily to each other.

"What does it mean?" asked Moonheart at last. His deep

voice, rising clearly above the others, sounded scornful. "What crime have *we* committed? What have *we* to do with the delvers? Or any of this with Beloved?"

The very mention of delvers made Cara uneasy. One of the vicious creatures had attacked her only minutes after she first entered Luster, and nightmare replays of that assault — of cold fingers clutching her throat, of the little monster's bulging eyes and clammy skin — still sometimes caused her to wake, trembling and terrified, in the middle of the night.

"I do not know the answers to your questions, Moonheart," said Grimwold. "But messages such as this do not end up in the Chronicles by accident."

Moonheart tossed his head impatiently. "I still don't see what this has to do with Beloved!"

The Queen turned to Grimwold. "Read those opening lines again, please."

The old dwarf nodded, and read:

> *In the darkest hour*
> *Of their darkest day*
> *The unicorns must face*
> *Their own darkness.*

"The darkest hour of their darkest day," repeated the Queen. "It would seem that, with Beloved preparing to invade, that day, that hour, are almost upon us, Moonheart. If this is a prophecy, certainly its time has come. Grimwold, there was another name in what you read, one I did not recognize. Who is the Whisperer?"

"That I do not know. I have searched the older Chronicles for any other mention of the name, but —"

The dwarf paused, looking uneasy.

"And . . . ?" prompted the Queen.

"I believe I found it in two places."

"*Believe* you found it?" snorted Moonheart. "What does that mean, Grimwold? Either you found it, or you didn't."

The Queen shot her brother a glance. He lowered his horn, acknowledging that it was her right to do the questioning.

Grimwold said, "In one of the oldest records, I found a passage that had been blotted out."

At these words an uneasy murmur rippled through the glory of unicorns. Cara could tell that some of them were horrified, some frightened, some angry.

"The Chronicles are sacred," Lightfoot told her, mind-to-mind. "Nothing should be blotted from them. Ever."

Grimwold waited for the disturbance to die down, then said, "The words of this page have been covered over with ink, something I have never seen before. I examined the page carefully, shining light upon it, then holding it up to a candle to let light shine through it from behind. Though I still could not read it, I could make out small parts — enough to make me believe that the name 'the Whisperer' is written there several times."

"You said you found it in two places," said the Queen.

"Not actually found it," said Grimwold. "However, while searching through another of the ancient books, I discovered that several pages had been torn out! Like the blotting, this is something I have never seen before."

Again, an uneasy murmur rippled through the unicorns.

"From what story were the pages taken?" asked the Queen.

"It was a story about the delvers, from the time they first appeared in Luster, or at least the time they began to be a problem for the unicorns."

Raising her voice, the Queen called, "Have any of you heard of this before? Does anyone among us know of this Whisperer?"

After a moment of silence, a dry, husky voice said, "I do."

CHAPTER IV

GNURFLAX

The musicians of Delvharken were trying their hardest. The drummers had worked themselves into a frenzy pounding on the carefully hollowed stones arranged in half-circles around them. The delver playing the skerzil bones had composed a new tune specifically for the King. The strange twang of the lizard-gut harps tied the music together.

None of it distracted King Gnurflax; after a time he waved his hand to dismiss them. Ignoring the worried looks of his queen and Namza, his court wizard, Gnurflax left the great cavern and headed toward his private caves. But he did not enter those caves. Instead, he walked past them to another cave, a cave forbidden to all but himself.

It was dark there, but delvers can deal with darkness.

It was silent, but silence in the underground world of Delvharken is not unusual.

He waited for something to break the silence, waited until it seemed every nerve in his body was strung as tightly as the lizard-gut harps. Finally he whispered, "Where are you, friend?"

He turned in a slow circle, peering into the dark corners of the cave, disgusted with himself as he did so. The search was foolish; in all the times the mysterious voice had spoken to him he had never seen a thing. Still, he had hope of doing so.

He had come to long for the voice's presence, and to feel uneasy when it was silent for too long. No surprise there! Had not the voice whispered to him secrets he needed to know to help bring down the unicorns?

With a sigh, he gave up and went to his own quarters.

There was a stone there he wanted to speak to.

Stone cannot think, of course. However, if you imprison a delver in a piece of stone, merge his body with the rock itself, it becomes a very different kind of thing. This was the fate of Gamzil, who had disappointed King Gnurflax by stealing one of the "Queen's Five," the amulets that allowed passage between Earth and Luster, then losing it before he could deliver it to the caverns of Delvharken. It was why he was locked in a boulder, his flesh intertwined with the stone.

To be entombed in stone was not the worst possible punishment for a delver. Gnurflax had far more frightening and painful ways to make someone suffer. But Gamzil was a nephew of Namza, and the old wizard had pleaded mercy for him. Despite his rage — Gnurflax's temper had been growing worse in recent years — he knew there was no wisdom in vexing a wizard. So he had given in to the request. Which was why Gamzil was now imprisoned in a large stone in the King's private chamber, rather than locked in a dungeon with something that would enjoy nibbling on his toes.

Having been imprisoned this way himself for two years when he was young, as punishment for offending his father's pride, Gnurflax knew well the fear and frustration that came from being locked in stone, unable to move, unable to speak, but still able to think — and to hear. Which was one reason he enjoyed coming to talk to Gamzil. He knew from experience that whatever curses and insults he heaped upon the boulder holding the little *skwarmint* would be heard.

Leaning close to that boulder now, he hissed, "The amulet would be in my hand this very moment, had you not lost it, you pebble-brained fool!"

It pleased him that Gamzil could not make his bleating excuses about how the Dimblethum — curse the shambling creature! — had stolen back the amulet after he, Gamzil, had ripped it from the girl's neck. Gnurflax hated excuses;

they were dirt beneath a delver's feet — crumbly, soft, and stupid, not hard and true like stone.

But, if Gnurflax was honest with himself, there was something else that pleased him about having Gamzil locked in stone this way, beyond the simple chance to vent his anger on a daily basis. It also meant he had someone to whom he could tell his secret plans without danger of them being whispered anywhere else.

"That woman from Earth, that Beloved, has an amulet now. So she thinks she doesn't need me. But she never knew my real plan. Oh, I didn't mind helping her and her Hunters break through. Let them and the unicorns fight it out. When they're done, Delvharken, above and below, will belong to the delvers, as it was meant to ever since the Maker carved it from the piece of fallen star and started it growing.

"But that's not all. That's not where it stops. I still intend to have one of those amulets myself. I've got five coves out looking for the girl even now. They'll find her. They'll do what you failed to do. And when I get it, I intend to travel the other way . . . back to Earth."

Gamzil, of course, said nothing.

CHAPTER
V

THE STORY SEEKERS

Cara watched as a cloaked, hooded figure stepped from between two unicorns in the second row of the gathering. The figure was stooped, and moved slowly. With its features hidden by the hood, Cara could not tell if it was a man or a woman.

Actually, she thought, *this being Luster, I suppose I can't even tell if it's a human.*

Even so, the figure looked oddly familiar. Cara realized she had seen the same cloak the day the unicorns gathered to say farewell to the Old Queen. She had been too lost in her own grief that day to wonder about strangers. Now she returned her hand to Lightfoot's shoulder and asked silently, "Who is that?"

"Alma Leonetti. She is the oldest human in Luster. There are nearly as many stories told about her as about your grandmother."

The woman stopped in front of the Queen and bowed her head. The Queen murmured a greeting that Cara could not hear from where she stood.

When the woman raised her head again, Grimwold and M'Gama both made slight bows of respect.

Lifting a pair of withered hands, Alma Leonetti drew back her hood. Her hair, white as the Queen's mane, was bound in a knot at the top of her head. Cara wished the old woman would turn around so she could see her face, but Alma Leonetti was speaking directly to the Queen.

"I do not know much about this," she said, her voice surprisingly strong for one so old. "And what I do know is only hearsay. But here it is: The Whisperer is your oldest and dearest enemy. Its roots — I say *its* for I do not know if the Whisperer is male or female, or beyond such things altogether — its roots are tangled with your own."

"Why have I not heard of this . . . this *being* before now?" asked the Queen.

"What we do not wish to remember we sometimes hide. That which we hide long enough is sometimes forgotten altogether, even if it never forgets itself."

The Queen nodded, then said, "Where did you first hear this . . . 'Whisperer' spoken of?"

"Forgive me, My Queen, but as you know, I have lived for many centuries. The memory of the name comes from hundreds of years ago, rising almost as from a mist. I will think, cudgel my brain, try to call up more — though I cannot guarantee success. In the meantime, may I make a suggestion?"

"Please do."

"You might do well to send someone to speak to the Chiron."

A murmur of uneasiness rippled through the assembled glory. It was little more than the sound a breeze might make passing over a meadow, yet so real that Cara felt a chill, and almost glanced up to see if the sun had gone behind a cloud.

"The Chiron?" Cara thought to Lightfoot.

"That is what the centaurs call their ruler."

"I didn't know there were centaurs in Luster!"

"We've got a little of everything here," the Prince replied, not sounding entirely happy.

"You don't seem to like the idea. Nor does anyone else, from the sound of it."

"They aren't exactly friendly with us. Things have always been a little uneasy between the unicorns and the centaurs because — Wait! The Queen is talking."

"You present me with a problem, Madame Leonetti," said Amalia Flickerfoot. "Given the danger that faces us, I can hardly spare any hooves to leave on such a quest. Yet it seems I must. Well, I will discuss this with the council. In the meantime, I thank you deeply for the information."

The old woman bowed, turned, and [...] among the unicorns. Gazing out across [...] Queen said, "Have any others among you [...] Whisperer?"

No one replied.

"All right, thank you all for gathering. Those of you who are members of the council please join me at the Council Grove. There is much for us to discuss. The rest of you may leave now. However, please do not travel far from Autumngrove. Even more important, until this threat is over, do not travel alone. No matter where you go, no matter how safe it may seem, there should always be at least two of you."

"Why two?" asked Cara, speaking privately to Lightfoot.

"It's a strategy. If there actually is an attack by a Hunter — or many Hunters — one of the two unicorns will try to draw them off. That way the other one can bring word back to court that the Hunt has begun."

"But the one who draws them off . . ."

Lightfoot finished the thought for her. "That one will almost certainly die."

Cara shuddered.

"The decision as to who tries to lure the Hunters and who will return to court must be made before they set out," continued the Prince, "since there will be no time to work it out once an attack occurs. One reason the Queen wants us to start this now is to get us used to the idea, so that we'll be in the habit by the time the Hunt does begin."

Most of the unicorns had drifted away, leaving the gathering as quietly as leaves on the wind. Cara, watching the last of them go, felt something behind her. It was Finder, who lowered his head over her shoulder. His silky cheek touching hers, he said softly, "I'll see you afterward."

Cara turned to embrace him. Then she and Lightfoot — they were both part of the Queen's Council, though Cara hardly felt up to the task — started down the slope. As they did, they passed Belle, who tossed her head and said tartly, "Nice of you to show up, Lightfoot."

"I always do, sooner or later."

"Usually later," replied Belle, with a shake of her head. Then she turned and trotted up the hillside.

"That's not a very nice way for her to talk to a prince," said Cara, offended on Lightfoot's behalf.

"As if Belle cares that I'm a prince! As if I care, for that matter. I'd rather not be, as you well know."

Cara was aware of Lightfoot's feelings, and was even starting to understand them. When she was little, she had thought it would be wonderful to be a princess. Now that it had turned out she actually was one, the feeling of responsibility was overwhelming.

Of course, she was only sort of a princess, since neither she nor anyone else seemed to know *exactly* what her status was in that regard. Though her grandmother was indeed Queen of the unicorns, she herself was human — or, at least, mostly so.

Sometimes the situation was so confusing Cara feared her head would burst if she thought about it too much. She turned her thoughts back to Lightfoot. She had a deep suspicion that the Prince was secretly in love with Belle. But the few times she had tried to tease him about it, he had gotten so cranky she didn't bring it up anymore. Still, it was easier — and more fun — to think about that than to try to figure out her own position in the unicorn world.

She was very glad that when she and the Prince were speaking mind-to-mind he couldn't actually *read* her mind. That would be too embarrassing! Fortunately, he could only receive the thoughts she *chose* to send him.

Cara's musings were interrupted by Moonheart, who snapped impatiently, "Hurry, nephew! We've already wasted enough time waiting for you today."

Lightfoot sighed and quickened his pace.

Cara had to run beside him not to be left behind.

Strictly speaking, the Queen's Council consisted only of unicorns, an even dozen of them. In addition to Lightfoot and

Moonheart, there were three Guardians of Memory —
unicorns who had spent a quarter of a century on Earth
to help keep alive the memory of what had been lost
when the unicorns fled to Luster. Another three unicorns —
Silvertail, Fire-Eye, and Manda Seafoam — were cousins or
nephews of the Queen. Other members of the council were
friends or trusted advisors of the former queen who
Amalia Flickerfoot had asked to remain on the council to
advise her.

Four humans besides Cara had been asked to stay for
the discussion: M'Gama, Jacques, Thomas, and Alma
Leonetti. Grimwold was there, too, though Cara was not
quite sure if he was considered human or not.

As the conversation began, Cara found herself wondering what her role would be in the coming struggle. Part of
her longed to be in the thick of things, fighting alongside
the unicorns. Another part was well aware that the middle
of a war was no place for a twelve-year-old girl.

But what can I do? she thought, half fearfully, half
rebelliously. *My family is too involved in this for me to turn
away now.*

Not surprisingly, Moonheart was first to speak. "I say
we simply ignore this fantasy of Grimwold's. While I agree
that the defacing of anything in the Chronicles is shocking,
it happened too long ago to mean anything now."

"By that logic, Beloved should be no problem either," said Fire-Eye. "After all, the tragedy that started her on her angry path also happened very long ago."

"They are not the same issues," said Moonheart sharply. "The threat of Beloved and her Hunters has been with us constantly. This other thing . . . this 'Whisperer' . . . is something we have never even heard of before."

"The shadow of the past is longer than any of us can imagine," said Alma Leonetti softly. "You cannot unweave the tapestry of time, Moonheart. Take any event, great or small, and you can trace the threads of cause back across century after century, threads that are woven from the smallest of happenings. In the same way, things that we do today, any one of them, may have implications and consequences a thousand years from now that we cannot yet begin to imagine."

Moonheart snorted, but said nothing more.

A mare standing beside him put her left foot forward, an indication that she was seeking permission to speak.

"That's Cloudmane," Lightfoot told Cara, mind-to-mind. "She was the first female to be a Guardian of Memory."

The Queen nodded to Cloudmane.

The mare — her thick, fine mane did indeed make Cara think of a cloud — took a step forward. "As usual, Madame

Leonetti speaks well and true. But there is another problem to consider. With the danger of attack so imminent, we can scarce afford to send anyone off in search of this legend. We will need all hooves and horns close by when the day of battle arrives."

"Yet what if in tracking down this Whisperer, we somehow find the very key to ending the Long Hunt?" asked Fire-Eye. "The passage Grimwold read spoke of our 'darkest hour.' As the Queen has said, it seems our darkest hour is nearly upon us."

"It's nonsense," snapped Moonheart. "Probably nothing more than the ramblings of some mystic muffinhead who stumbled into Luster from Earth and went mad as a result. In fact, I'd wager that's *why* the later references were scratched out — whichever of Grimwold's predecessors recorded them realized it had been a mistake. Would to goodness they had scratched out this first bit of nonsense as well."

Grimwold had been listening to this with increasing agitation. Finally, he was unable to contain himself. "There is no nonsense in the Chronicles!" he all but shouted.

Moonheart started to speak, then stopped himself, took a breath, and started again. "My apologies, Chronicle Keeper. My words were harsh. Even so, I do not believe it is impossible for there to be errors in those pages."

"We cannot know whether this is an error or not,"

said the Queen, her voice now gentle and soothing. "Therefore, the question remains: Should we seek to solve this riddle? I agree with Cloudmane that we can hardly afford to lessen our numbers at this time. Yet something within me says this may be important. Therefore, I have decided to send a small group to the Chiron to ask him about the Whisperer."

She paused, as if waiting for objections. Hearing none, she went on. "This group will consist of Lightfoot, Finder, and Belle for the unicorns. I want Cara and Grimwold to accompany them. Since M'Gama's home is on the way, they can also escort the Geomancer on her return trip."

Cara felt an immediate wave of confusion. Part of her was delighted to be chosen for this mission, especially since Lightfoot would be going as well. But another part of her wanted to stay at Autumngrove, where the danger was greatest. Not because she wanted to be in danger, of course. But she did want to be where she could help the unicorns most.

"Why the child?" asked Moonheart. "This is a dangerous journey, and the centaur king is hardly a friend of ours."

Though Cara had been wondering the same thing herself, for some reason it annoyed her to have Moonheart ask it.

Amalia Flickerfoot gazed at her brother for a moment, then said firmly — and in a tone that Cara recognized all too well — "A queen does not need to explain."

Moonheart looked startled, and Cara understood why. When her grandmother had first regained her true form and taken the position of queen, she had been confused and a bit reticent to use her power. Clearly that was no longer the case.

The Queen switched her tail, a way of softening her response, and said, "Though it is not required, Moonheart, I do not mind giving my reason, which is simply this: Cara's gift of tongues makes her particularly appropriate for going in quest of a story. I do not rejoice in sending her off like this; my granddaughter and I have all too recently been reunited, and I am well aware that there may be danger along the way. However, there is danger all around us right now, and — to my great pride — she has already proven herself a worthy traveler.

"As for the rest of my choices: Grimwold should hear and record this story — assuming there is indeed a story for the King of the centaurs to tell. We have no better guide than Finder, and no better guard than Belle, though I will miss having her at our side should the attack come while they are gone." She looked out at the group. "I hope you are all satisfied now?"

Her voice had become sharp and challenging.

"And Lightfoot?" asked Moonheart, his own voice just this side of a sneer.

"Our nephew is next in line to replace me. It is never a good strategy for the queen and her successor to be in the same place at time of war."

"I'm going to pay for that one," muttered Lightfoot. "My dear uncle will never let me forget it."

"Shhhh," whispered Cara. "He'll hear you." Her warning was too late. Moonheart had already turned to glare at his nephew. She found herself wishing, not for the first time, that she could find some way to make peace between them.

The Queen's voice rang out over the Council Grove. "Story Seekers, you will depart tomorrow morning. Travel safe, travel well. May those who have gone before be always with you." She paused, then added in a softer voice, "And may you return with a tale that will help us survive what is to come."

CHAPTER
VI

BELOVED

The castle was ancient. It stood on a mountainside, and at one time must have had rich lands to defend. Now it was in a place nearly forgotten, at the end of roads rarely traveled.

Gazing from the arched window of the topmost room of the tallest tower was a woman who was even older than the castle. However, no one looking at her would have suspected such a thing, for despite the fact that her long, curling hair was white as the moon, her face itself was smooth and unlined, its beauty marred only by the pupils of her eyes, which were a terrifying red, and the spasms of pain that continually twisted her features.

This was Beloved, ancient enemy of the unicorns, and as she gazed at the courtyard below she was swept with a feeling as close to contentment as anything she had known for several centuries.

In her hand she clutched an amulet, one of the Queen's Five. From her spies, she had gained enough of the amulet's history to know that it had once belonged to Thomas the Tinker, an old enemy. From Thomas it had somehow passed to the hand of the man named Jacques.

And now it was hers. Her fingers curled around it in delight. With its help, in only three weeks she would be opening a gate to Luster. Only three weeks and she would —

The thought was interrupted by a wave of pain — pain from the tip of the unicorn's horn that was buried in her heart. Beloved gasped and clutched at her chest, her eyes closed. After a moment, the spasm passed. But the underlying pain remained. That was always there. It ebbed and flowed, rose and fell, but was never gone altogether. Never, never gone.

As the centuries after her father's death had worn on, as science and medicine had advanced, Beloved had thought many times of having the piece of horn removed. But she knew that to do so would be fatal, for it was the horn's magic that had kept her alive all these centuries, not merely healing her as it wounded, but filling her with steady, unquenchable life. That was why she did not, could not, have it taken out.

It's not that I am afraid to die, she often reassured herself. *No, death would be a relief and a release. It's just that I cannot allow myself to die yet. I must hold on until I have fin-ished my sacred task and all the unicorns are dead.*

If she had had any doubts about that — and she had, especially in her early years — her secret friend had con-vinced her otherwise.

Where is he now? she wondered. Though she had long since given up the hope of actually seeing him, she found she yearned more and more for his invisible presence, for the reassuring words he whispered in her ear.

Even as she wondered about him, she felt the slightest disturbance in the room and knew at once that he had returned.

She closed her eyes and tipped back her head.

"All is approaching readiness," came the familiar whis-per, so soft, warm, and inviting. "The pieces are being assembled. Soon you can begin."

"Can it be true?" she murmured. "After all this time, is it really possible?"

"Have I not promised it would be so?"

Beloved took a deep breath, then winced at a new flash of pain. When she could breathe again, she opened her eyes to gaze down once more on her gathering Hunters. Soon they would all be here: five hundred superbly trained men, each a direct descendant, each ready to move at her command. All were men who could track and trail across the most diffi-cult conditions. All were men who had sworn loyalty to her.

At that last thought she frowned, for there was one of her children who, despite his oath of loyalty, had broken from her. Betrayed her. Beloved clenched her fingers, hoping the five Hunters she had sent to capture Ian would return with the traitor in time for her to administer proper punishment before the night of the invasion.

She flinched. Another wave of pain — a double pain, actually; pain from the horn, and the pain she felt over Ian's defection — washed over her. When the worst of it had passed she returned her attention to the men below.

Was it possible any others might turn away from her?

No, they would be faithful. No others had the strange family connections that had undermined Ian's loyalty. Perhaps it had been foolish of her to recruit him to begin with, though she had not known, when she did, how truly complex were the links that would end up dividing his heart between her and the unicorns.

She wondered, for a moment, if it had also been a mistake to place his wife in the Rainbow Prison. She brushed the thought aside. Martha Hunter had not been harmed by this placement. And she had become little more than an annoyance while she was still here on Earth.

But that girl, that daughter of theirs, that Cara Diana Hunter.

What was to be done about her?

CHAPTER
VII

AN AUDIENCE WITH THE QUEEN

Cara stepped around the trunk of a quilpum tree. Her grand-mother, the Queen of the unicorns, stood in the center of the clearing, waiting for her.

Amalia Flickerfoot lifted her head at her granddaughter's approach. A passing breeze made the branches shiver, and several silvery leaves — the blue trees of Luster turned silver in the fall — drifted down around her.

"It's time we talked, child," said the Queen. "Past time, actually."

"I've been waiting," said Cara, trying not to sound bit-ter. She had been both dreading this conversation and longing for it.

"I'm sorry I was not able to spend more time with you when we first returned to Luster, dearest. But Arabella knew she would be fading soon, and there was so much, so very much, I needed to know about being queen."

She sighed. "I'm afraid I am still ill-prepared for it, despite the coaching she gave me in those last days. Still, I hope I can do a better job at this than I did at being your grandmother."

Cara wanted to say that she had been a wonderful grandmother, but stopped herself. There was too much in the way, too much unfinished as yet.

The Queen closed her eyes and said softly, "Oh, that I still had arms and could hug you to me as I used to."

Cara felt a rise of anger, something she had promised herself she would try to avoid. "At least you regained your memory with your true shape. At least you know what you are!"

"And you would like to know what you are as well, wouldn't you, granddaughter?"

Cara nodded, trying not to look sullen.

"I wish I could answer that," said the Queen. "But the truth is, I don't know. There's never been anyone like you. Except, of course, your mother . . ."

Her voice trailed off, and Cara could hear the pain in it. But she had her own pain, and a question that had been burning inside her ever since her father had first told her the truth about her separation from her parents. She had meant to lead up to it, but couldn't hold it inside. "Why didn't you ever tell me?" she demanded.

"Tell you what?"

"Don't pretend! You know what I mean, Gramma! Why did you let me believe that my parents had abandoned me?"

She was crying now, though she didn't want to, for the wound of losing her mother and father when she was three had never entirely healed.

The Queen sighed and shook her head. "The simple, humiliating answer is just this: I didn't know how. At first you were too young. Then, as you got older, I kept thinking, 'Next year. I'll tell her the truth next year, on her birthday.' But I never found the courage. And then — well, and then all this happened, and it was too late." She paused, then said softly, "In the end, I guess it was just cowardice. I was too afraid of how you would react."

For a moment, neither of them spoke. Then her grandmother bowed her head and said humbly, "Forgive me, Cara. Those were difficult times. And I fear I was not very good at being human."

Cara wanted to stay angry, she truly did. Yet she felt something in her own heart begin to melt. The years on Earth had been difficult for her grandmother, too, of course — all the times they had moved without warning as she tried to stay ahead of the Hunters, without ever knowing entirely why they were after her.

Wiping at her eyes Cara said, "Why *did* you steal —" She saw her grandmother flinch and started again. "Why did you take me to begin with?"

"I was in a blind panic. I didn't know why the Hunters were so determined to catch me, only that the thought of it terrified me. It had been nearly twenty years since I had felt their presence. Perhaps that had made me too comfortable, so that the fear was even greater when they returned. And it was my fault they were back, I know that now."

"Why was it your fault?"

"When you were little, you became quite ill. I was so afraid you might not recover that I summoned Moonheart from Luster to heal you."

"He never said!" though Cara knew a unicorn had come to heal her, she was astonished to realize it had been the irascible Moonheart.

"He is not much for talking about what he has done — especially if what he has done is against the rules of Luster, which traveling to Earth at my request certainly was. But the Guardian of Memory was far away, and I needed help sooner than he could reach me. So Moonheart came to me, as he always did when I needed him. But things ripple outward, Cara. The magic I used to summon my brother, and the presence, however brief, of a second unicorn on Earth, these things must have roused Beloved, for suddenly the Hunt was on again."

Her grandmother pawed at the ground with one of her silvery hooves, then said softly, "It might have been all right if I had been alone when I sensed the first Hunters; I could simply have fled. But your parents had asked if you could stay with me for a couple of days while they went to a conference — this was a month or so after you had been ill, and we were all confident that you were healthy again. I was glad to have you, of course, having no idea that the Hunt was about to begin again.

"Shortly after midnight of the first night you were with me, I sensed them. I carried you to the basement, where I had prepared a secret hiding place — I never lived in any home where I could not do that — and we went into it. You roused when I closed the door behind us, but I shushed you, and you, good girl that you were, obeyed. We waited in silence, in the darkness."

Cara remembered the night she and her grandmother — still a human at that point — had hidden in the sanctuary of St. Christopher's. With that in mind, the terror was easy enough to understand.

"I heard the Hunters searching the basement," continued Amalia. "And then I heard something worse, something that filled my heart with new fear. One of them said, 'We want the grandmother. But if it comes down to one or the other, Beloved wants the child even more.'"

"Blind panic seized me. It was torment to stay in that cramped, dark space, waiting for them to leave, but I managed. Then, as soon as they were gone, I took you, and I fled." She sighed. "It was something I'd had a lot of practice at doing."

Cara was silent, trying to imagine the scene in the basement, her grandmother's fear, the nearness of the Hunters. More than simply imagine, she was trying to forgive her grandmother for doing what, she now understood, had seemed the only possible choice.

Amalia shook her head. "If I ever do see your mother again, it is going to be a painful meeting."

That "if" frightened Cara. "Do you think Daddy will be able to find her?" she asked in a small voice.

"Your father is far more resourceful than I guessed when I first met him, child, so yes, I think the odds are good." She lifted her head a bit. "I see you still wear that ring of M'Gama's, the one that helped us escape the green shaft of the Rainbow Prison."

"I had offered it to Ebillan when I was bargaining with him to be allowed to use his cave," said Cara. "I'm glad he didn't accept, or I never would have been able to fetch you back to your body." She paused, then said, "Will I need something to offer the Chiron, in return for the story?"

Amalia was silent for a moment. When she spoke, it was not really an answer. "I met him once, you know."

"I'm not surprised," said Cara, smiling for the first time since their conversation had started. "It seems you covered most of Luster when you were known as 'the Wanderer.'"

"I was restless. Anyway, I would like to think — I hope — the Chiron will give you this story simply as a favor to me. However, if he will not, I suspect the amulet you wear may hold the key."

"I'll have to give him the amulet?" cried Cara, her hand moving protectively to where it hung on her chest.

"No, dear, not give it to him. Simply use it. He is old and would like to see Earth again. That may be enough. If it is not, I do not know what else he may ask. The centaurs prefer art to mere treasure, and we are not artists." She curled up one side of her soft mouth. "Need hands for that! Be prepared for anything, dear one; the Chiron is old, and bitter, and likely to be more dangerous to your heart than to your body."

Cara felt suddenly young and small. And frightened.

CHAPTER VIII

THE BARGAIN

Ian Hunter spread his hands — a useless gesture, he immediately realized, when talking to someone who was blind — and said, "I am not a poor man. Indeed, I brought some jewels with me with which I hoped to pay for this knowledge. But which of these might be worth the jewel of sight, I cannot say."

"A diplomatic answer, Mr. Hunter. But I would ask you to think. The key is in your own words."

As Ian's mind ran back through the last few seconds it caught and recoiled at one phrase: "The jewel of sight."

Surely this man could not be asking him to give up his eyesight in return for the key to entering the Rainbow Prison!

"You are silent, Mr. Hunter. Have I failed to make my meaning clear?"

"I fear I understand you. However, I am not sure this is a price that I can pay. Not that I would not give my sight to accomplish the task I have set my mind to. But the very paying of that price would make the rest of my task impossible."

"Ah, you think me harsher than I am. I do not wish to make you blind. I ask only to have the *use* of your sight. On occasion. When I have need of it."

"The *use* of my sight?" asked Ian, puzzled and beginning to feel a touch of fear. His informant had told him the Blind Man was both powerful and strange, but this was beyond anything he had been expecting.

"Let's say a month's worth of vision, to be used as I have need of it — five minutes here, ten minutes there. Nothing excessive, never more than an hour or two at a time. I'll be kind and make it a short month, only thirty days. And, of course, you would be seeing only when you are awake. Let's say sixteen hours a day, though I suspect you are probably awake a bit more than that, and sleep less than the customary eight hours a night. Still, we'll call it sixteen hours. Multiply that times thirty and you get four hundred and eighty hours, to be spaced out over the next three years. Not such a bad price, is it really? Not even half an hour a day."

"And how am I to pay this price?"

"Ah, do not worry about *that*, Mr. Hunter. When I need use of your sight, I will take it."

"What if I am driving, or crossing a busy street?"

"Life, alas, is not without its risks. However, I will give you this assurance: Whenever I take over your eyes, I will first see what you are seeing, and I promise to do my best not to put you in danger. After all, if you should perish, I would lose the use of your sight as well, which would be a pity in my view." He chuckled at his own pun. "Still, I must be honest. While I am a kindly man, I am also self-protective. If it comes down to my life or yours, I fear I will have to side with myself." He sighed. "Ah, well. No trade is without its risks. So. Do we have an agreement?"

"Not yet," said Ian firmly. "The terms are still not clear enough. First, I need to know exactly what you are offering me in return for the use of my sight. Is it merely some vague clue about the Rainbow Prison? Or are you going to give me solid knowledge, a way in and out? Second — and I will admit to great curiosity about this — how, exactly, are we going to make this trade?"

"Reasonable questions. As to the Rainbow Prison, I have information that should make it possible for you to enter. That does not mean it will be easy, and I do not offer that promise. Making your way in will, to some extent, depend on your own abilities, and whether you can reach the proper location to make the transition. Leaving the prison will be even more difficult. But, then, it is a prison; leaving is not supposed to be easy. If it's any consolation, it does become easier; the first time in — and out — is always the hardest.

"As to your second question, the most important part is simply your agreement. Once you have accepted our bargain — and it must be true acceptance, absolute and complete — I will be able to take over your sight with very little trouble. In fact, I must insist on attempting it at least once before we close our deal, as it would be most distasteful to me to give you this information and then discover you were not willing to uphold your part of the bargain. I should warn you that once truly given this permission cannot be revoked, so do not think to cheat me in this. I will have access to your sight until the allotted price is paid."

"If I do give this permission, what guarantee do I have that you will keep your part of the bargain?"

"Unfortunately for you, there is not much I can offer save my good word. But since you want what I have more than I want what you have, I fear that will have to do. Now, come, Mr. Hunter; we've dallied long enough. Do we have a bargain? A month's use of your vision, to be paid in installments as I deem fit, in return for my telling you what you wish to know about the Rainbow Prison? If so, let us go forward. If not, you should leave, so you waste no more of my time."

A heavy silence hung in the darkness. Finally Ian said, "We have a bargain."

The man chuckled. "Good. Then let's try things out, shall we?"

The lights went on, causing Ian to blink. He was in a sparsely furnished room. Seated on a bench opposite him, about ten feet away, was an enormously fat man. He wore a white robe, but even beneath it Ian could see the rolls of flesh.

Between them stood a low table, holding a white teapot and a vase of yellow flowers.

"Ready?" asked the man.

"Ready."

Nothing happened.

"Come, come, Mr. Hunter. If you want to make this bargain you must agree to it *completely*. Let's try again. And this time, let go of your reservations — your reservations, and your sight."

"Letting go has never been my specialty."

"As that may be — if you want to make this bargain, you had better try again."

Ian took several deep breaths, trying to calm himself. In his mind he saw his hand as a fist, holding tight to his sight. One by one he opened those mental fingers. "I think I'm ready," he said at last — and instantly was plunged into a darkness deeper and more profound than anything he had ever experienced.

"Ah, you have excellent vision, Mr. Hunter! I appreciate

that. And, truly, you must admit that I am not as fierce a bargainer as you might have been thinking, or I would have asked you about that before we closed our deal." He sighed contentedly. "It will be a privilege to make use of your eyes from time to time. Are you ready to see again?"

"Yes, please," said Ian, trying not to let the strain sound in his voice. Before he could take another breath, his vision returned.

"How did you do that?" he asked, gasping and blinking.

"Oh, come, Mr. Hunter. That is not the information you bargained for. I trust you do not truly want me to answer that question, as it would also carry a price, a heavy one indeed. Instead, why don't we talk about the Rainbow Prison? Why do you wish to enter it?"

"Does that really matter?"

The Blind Man chuckled. "Point taken. Forgive me my idle curiosity. Let's start again. The nearest entry to the Rainbow Prison, as I suspect you are aware, is what those who know about these things call the Ruby Portal. The key to entering is contained in its very name. There are seven rubies that will unlock that door. Unless you have one of those, your task is pointless, and I will not hold you to your bargain."

"I do have one, as I suspect you already know."

"Do not be snide, Mr. Hunter. It does not become you. I guessed at this, true, but I was not certain. Now, let me tell you the location of the portal. It is not easily reached, but I suspect you are a man not easily deterred. Even so, I must tell you that finding the portal will be the least of your problems. It is *leaving* the prison that will truly test your skill."

It was dark when Ian stepped through the beautifully carved door of the Blind Man's home, back into the little courtyard at the end of the alley. The perfume of the brilliant flowers hung thick and heavy in the air.

Crossing the courtyard, he started up the alley, back to the bustle of the Chandni Chowk. His mind was as jumbled as the streets around him, filled with wonder and fear at what he had experienced, but concentrating on the long and difficult journey that lay ahead before he could reach the Ruby Portal. It was deep in the Himalayas, across several hundred miles of difficult terrain and beyond a well-guarded border. The best and fastest way to get there would be by plane, but of course no commercial jets flew to such a place.

Perhaps his focus on this problem was the reason his usually keen instincts failed to alert him to the person following him.

Lights still gleamed in a few store windows, but passersby were scarce now. Ian was near the edge of the Chowk when he heard the girl. She was in an alley to his right, weeping softly. He tried to harden his heart to the sound. The beggar children of India were legion, after all, and more than a few of them worked for adults who claimed most of their earnings. But he was too fresh from his last meeting with his own daughter, who had wandered so far and been helped so much by strangers, to ignore the tears of this child.

That impulse to kindness — a feeling which had nearly been drummed out of him by Beloved's training — was Ian's undoing. He had only to take a step into the alley for his dampened instincts to snap awake and scream that he had made a horrible mistake. It was too late. The attack was swift and fierce, and even as he spun to face his foes the first blow landed. He snapped out a fierce kick, then another, and another. At the same time he was trying to find the nearest wall so he could get it at his back. Before he could manage that, another blow struck him from behind. So, there were not two assailants, as he had thought, but three.

Ian fought fiercely and well; he was one of Beloved's trained Hunters after all, lean and taut, with a perfectly con-ditioned body. But his three opponents seemed to be equally well trained, and had the advantages both of surprise and numbers.

The girl had scrambled out of sight, and Ian felt an instant of relief. At least he didn't have to worry about . . .

he realized the truth, and felt a fool. The girl had never been in danger. She was simply bait!

With that thought came the certainty that his attackers must be fellow Hunters. Just like a unicorn, he had let the need of a girl in distress draw him into danger.

Furious at himself for being so easily tricked, and at his brothers — for all Hunters were considered the children of Beloved, and therefore thought of themselves as brothers — he fought back with renewed fury.

For a moment it seemed as if he might prevail despite their numbers. But as he dodged one blow while at the same time lunging toward another of the men, he went blind.

"No!" screamed Ian. *"Not now!"*

They were the last words he uttered before one of his "brothers" landed a blow that knocked him nearly senseless. Staggering, breathless with rage, lost in darkness, Ian fell against a wall. Swiftly he turned and pressed his back to it. Now at least no attack could come from behind. He would let the wall support him while he fought till the last second. He managed to fend off one blow by sheer luck, but a second later a fierce kick struck him in the side of the head.

Even as he began to slump he heard a challenging shout, followed by cries of anger and surprise. Clearly, someone else had entered the fray. *Who?* he wondered, just before another blow caused his knees to buckle.

His last conscious thought as he sagged to the pavement was fear for what would happen to his wife and daughter if he were to die in this alley.

Then he fell into a darkness even deeper than that of his blindness.

CHAPTER
IX

JOURNEY BEGINS

"Aren't you making this more complicated than it needs to be?" asked Lightfoot.

The Prince was standing at the edge of the small clearing where Cara had been sleeping since they came to Autumngrove, watching her try to pack. The process seemed to amuse him more than Cara would have liked.

"I mean," he continued, "it's not as if there's that much you *need* to bring."

"It's not as if there's much I *could* bring, even if I wanted to!"

This was true. She had jumped into Luster with nothing but the clothes on her back, and had little more than that now, though her wardrobe had been supplemented by gifts from M'Gama. The thought of those clothes — she was wearing some of them now — brought back fond memories of her first visit to the Geomancer's home. She was looking forward to returning, and to seeing Flensa, the gruff dwarf who was M'Gama's faithful guard and helper.

Maybe she'd even get to take another hot bath!

What made packing hard now was not that she had to choose what to bring. It was simply that doing so brought up unpleasant memories of all the times she and her grandmother had moved back on Earth — starting with that first time, when she was so young and thought that her parents had abandoned her.

She picked up the sphere that the gryphon, Medafil, had given her. Immediately, it began to glow. In Luster, where there were no light bulbs or flashlights, no batteries or electricity, this unfailing source of light had been a great gift indeed. She could adjust its size by twisting it between her hands, making it small as a cherry or large as . . . well, she didn't actually know how large she could make it. She had twisted it out till it was so big that its glow hurt her eyes, but even then it seemed as if it could get bigger. She debated a moment, trying to decide whether to put it in her pack or carry it in her pocket.

"Pocket," she said, speaking out loud. "Easier to get at. Besides, packs can get lost."

Twisting the sphere until it was no bigger than a marble, she tucked it into the pocket of the breeches M'Gama had given her.

"A penny for your thoughts."

Cara looked up, startled. The words had come from Thomas the Tinker. He and Jacques had arrived while she was absorbed in her packing . . . and her memories.

"Speak for yourself, Thomas," said Jacques, his tones as gloomy as usual. "I don't have a penny. Not that there's much use for them here in Luster. Still, I'd also like to know what you're thinking about, little one."

"My mother," she said softly.

Jacques nodded, but didn't say anything. Cara knew that Jacques suspected — hoped — that Cara's mother might be his daughter. Which would make the old acrobat her grandfather.

The moment of awkward silence was broken by Thomas, who said cheerfully, "We came to tell you safe journey, Cara." With a sigh he added, "I wish we were going with you."

"So do I!" said Cara fervently.

Thomas stepped closer and pulled something from one of his many pockets. "Here," he said, placing it in her hand. "This is for you."

Cara examined it. It looked like an ordinary pocket watch. However, she knew from past experience that Thomas's "watches" had many functions. "What does it do?" she asked.

"It keeps track of days, not hours. I watched you notch that calendar stick on our last journey, and I thought this might be a more, um, *elegant* way for you to keep track of the passing days."

"Thank you."

"Also, if you twist the top and fling it against a hard surface, it will explode, which can be useful. Of course, after that it's not much good for telling time with."

She raised an eyebrow at him.

"I'm serious!" he cried, sounding offended. Then he smiled, that broad smile of his, and she knew two things: first, that he was not at all offended and second, that the watch would indeed explode if needed.

"Thank you," she said again.

"Well, if I can't go with you, I thought it was the least I could do." He held out his arms, and she stepped into his warm embrace.

"Travel safe, travel well, my young friend," he murmured. "I hope our paths will cross again before too long. Now I must be off, for the Queen has given me an assignment of my own."

He patted Jacques on the shoulder, nodded to Lightfoot, then disappeared among the trees.

Jacques gestured to the ground beside her. "May I?" he asked, in his gloomy voice.

Cara smiled. "Pull up a seat."

Crossing his feet, Jacques lowered himself to a sitting position with a grace and ease that would have seemed impossible if you judged him by the lines in his face. "I also wish I were coming with you, my maybe-granddaughter."

"Why is it still *maybe*?" asked Cara impatiently. "Why don't you just ask the Queen if you're my grandfather?"

Jacques sighed and turned his head away. "There is still a barrier between your grandmother and me," he said at last. "And, truth to tell, I am so embarrassed about the loss of that amulet that I fear to speak to her of other things! Not to mention that she has a great deal on her mind right now, like the coming invasion of Beloved and the Hunters."

"It wasn't your fault Beloved got the amulet," said Cara firmly.

"Even so, I was the one who lost it to her."

"Why aren't you coming with us?" she asked, partly to change the subject, but even more because she had really hoped that he would. His presence had been deeply comforting to her on her journey to find the Wanderer.

Jacques shrugged. "As with Thomas, the Queen has other tasks for me. I should be flattered, I suppose. It means she still has some trust in me. I came now simply to wish you good journey. Alas, I have no gift but my love."

Putting a hand on his arm, Cara said firmly, "I hope you *are* my grandfather."

Jacques smiled, which did strange things to his normally gloomy face. She leaned against him. He put his arm around her shoulder and whispered, "Travel safe, travel well, my little wanderer. May those who have gone before be always with you."

Shortly after dawn Cara met the others in a clearing at the edge of Autumngrove. The first rays of the rising sun caught in the manes and tails of the three unicorns, tinting the long, milk-white hairs with shades of rose.

Cara was dressed for journeying, wearing her brown leather boots, a pair of sturdy breeches that were loose enough to walk in comfortably, a dark green tunic, a broad-brimmed hat, and her travel cloak. Like the clothing she had worn the day before, all were gifts from M'Gama — as was the sword strapped around her waist, which in many ways she considered to be the most important thing she had on. She had braided her long red hair to keep it from tangling or collecting too many bits of leaf and twig as they traveled through the forest.

Though the grass was still wet with dew, M'Gama was kneeling in the center of the clearing, working a spell with stones and feathers. She chanted over it in low tones, then gestured to Finder, who knelt and touched it with his horn.

"It's a casting for safe travel," explained Lightfoot silently, when Cara put a questioning hand on his shoulder.

Belle snorted. She started to say something but was interrupted by Grimwold, who stumbled into the clearing, grumping about uncivilized hours of the day.

Cara's mind flashed back to the last time she had begun a journey with a group of unicorns. For that trip there had been a great ceremony. She felt a little disappointed that the unicorns did not have a similar gathering now.

Stop thinking like a spoiled brat, she told herself sharply. *We were planning on going all the way back to Earth that time. Of course they made a big deal out of it.*

Still, she couldn't help but wonder if another reason there was no ceremony to launch this journey was that her grandmother was still not fully aware of all the ways and customs the queen of the unicorns should observe. That worried her. She wanted her grandmother to be a good queen.

It did ease her heart when another small group of unicorns — including, to her surprise, Moonheart — arrived to bid them farewell. Moonheart took Lightfoot aside for a moment. When the Prince came back, Cara put her hand on his side and asked silently, "What did he say?"

"He wished me luck," replied Lightfoot, sounding slightly amazed. "Well, he also told me not to do anything stupid, though I got the feeling he didn't think that advice would do much good."

"Are we going to travel this morning?" asked Belle sharply. "Or shall we just talk until it's time for lunch?"

Lightfoot rolled his eye at Cara. "We travel," he said aloud.

And so they set out, three unicorns and three humans, in quest of an ancient story that might hold the key to the doom that was stalking Luster.

Cara looked around for the Squijum, but he was nowhere in sight. That didn't mean he wasn't going to come along; the creature tended to disappear and then show up again on a regular basis. And he was at once so annoying and so adorable that she was never quite sure which she preferred — having him along, or having him gone.

She shook her head and laughed at herself. *Who am I trying to fool? Of course I want him with us.*

She glanced back, hoping he would show up soon.

Finder led the way, with M'Gama walking close beside him. Cara, Lightfoot, and Grimwold came next, walking side-by-side or single file, depending on the terrain. Belle insisted on bringing up the rear, since she said she was the only one who would pay proper attention to the possibility of an attack from behind.

"An attack this close to Autumngrove doesn't seem likely," said Lightfoot, when she first made this claim.

"All the more reason to be on guard," replied Belle, in a tone that made it clear what she thought of his reasoning.

When they stopped for dinner that evening, M'Gama said, "In my home I have a map that will show the best route to reach the Valley of the Centaurs. The path is not as arduous as the one you took to visit Ebillan, but it does lead through some dangerous territory."

"Centaurs," muttered Belle in disgust. "What a stupid idea: half horse, half human. As if humans weren't bad enough without —"

"Belle," said Finder gently.

"What?" she snapped.

"It doesn't do well to speak ill of the other residents of Luster."

"Wasn't this world opened for *us?*" she demanded. "What are the others — dragons, mermaids, gryphons, centaurs, and the Queen-alone-knows what else — but free riders?"

"I prefer to think of them as neighbors," said Lightfoot.

Belle snorted. "*You* would! You're friends with that Dimblethum thing, too."

"I have an idea," said M'Gama. "Why don't you two quarrel as we travel? We have at least an hour of light before we need to look for a place to spend the night. If we're going to reach my home in the four days we've planned, we should use it."

About an hour after they set out the next morning, the Squijum dropped to Cara's shoulder from the branches of a quilpum tree, shrieking, "Hotcha gotcha, sneaky runaway girl!"

"Don't *do* that!" cried Cara. Despite her sharp reaction, she was delighted to have the little creature back. She couldn't imagine having to make a journey without him.

The first few days of the trip passed uneventfully. They traveled mostly through deep wood, and Cara was fascinated to see that the blue leaves were turning silver with the onset of autumn. Now and then, the little band of travelers would cross a grassy meadow. Once, they skirted the edge of a small, still lake. Halfway around it, Cara saw a rowboat that had been pulled up on a pebbly beach. With so few humans in Luster, every sign of their presence was of interest to Cara, and she spent the next few hours wondering who it belonged to.

If not for her worries about Beloved's coming attack and her father's quest to free her mother from the Rainbow Prison, Cara would have enjoyed the journey immensely. Certainly she loved traveling through Luster — loved the mysterious countryside with its strange-but-familiar looking trees, so much like trees on Earth, yet made so different by their blue leaves and silvery bark; loved the way the forest was filled with bird song and the chittering of animals, thick with life that was unseen yet insistent on announcing itself; most of all loved the evenings when, after they had found a place to rest, Grimwold would make a fire while Cara and M'Gama gathered things to roast for that night's dinner.

The Geomancer was patient with Cara as they foraged, and showed her how to spot the areas where, by moving a pile of leaves, you would be most likely to find the dense, nut-flavored fungus known as *zillbun*. Though Cara had been skeptical the first time they uncovered one of the fist-sized things and she saw its knobby brown skin, a single taste had changed her mind.

Not at all like that horrible blue fungus Grimwold tried to feed me when we were journeying through his caverns, she thought.

The Squijum was actually helpful with this work, digging up the roots called *tarka*. Each time he found one he would jealously guard it for a few moments, then sigh and scamper over to present it to Cara, crying, "Look! Look! Much hotcha good!"

The nights were clear and cool, the air crisp and sweet, and the sky, once it darkened, spattered with stars in a profusion Cara had never seen back on Earth, where the lights of the cities masked the glory of the heavens. The moon was waning, a little thinner each night, a constant reminder of the passing time. Soon — too soon — it would be gone, only to begin growing again, moving inexorably toward the night of the Blood Moon. She felt the days like weights upon her shoulders.

Each evening after they finished their meal, Grimwold would tell them a tale from the Unicorn Chronicles.

Cara loved these stories, and once again found herself longing to explore the vast collection of books and scrolls she had seen the first time she visited the old dwarf in his caves. She felt she could spend the rest of her life studying the strange and wonderful things that had happened in Luster.

On the night before they would reach the Geomancer's home, Grimwold said, "You should choose the tale this evening, M'Gama, as it will be the last I tell before we leave you."

The Geomancer steepled her elegant ebony fingers in front of her face, causing firelight to flash from the rings and jewels on her left hand. After a moment, she said, "Perhaps a story about Alma Leonetti?"

"I'd like that," said Cara eagerly. "I've been wondering about her. She's so old she must have many stories."

"Many stories indeed," said Finder. "But I suspect M'Gama is suggesting the first of them, which tells how

Madame Leonetti came here, and of the burden she placed upon us when she did."

"Burden?" asked Cara. "What burden?"

"You'll see," said Lightfoot.

Plucking a twig from the ground, Grimwold said, "Give me a moment to recollect the details." He stared at the twig, twisting it between his stubby brown fingers as if the story were somehow to be found within its leaves. Just when Cara thought she would go mad with waiting, he began to speak.

CHAPTER X

FALLON

He wasn't dead, though the pain in Ian's head when he opened his eyes again almost made him wish he were. He blinked, and realized that his sight was back. How long had the Blind Man kept it? Had he seen Ian's danger and returned it at once? Or — a new and disturbing idea — was he actually in league with the Hunters? Was it possible he had taken Ian's sight to *help* them in their attack?

The thought made him groan.

"Ah, good," said a familiar voice. "I was sure you were alive, sahib!"

"Rajiv!" Ian tried to shift to see the boy, then groaned again as the movement sent a flash of searing pain through his head.

"Who else would it be?" asked the boy, moving into view.

Even in the dim light of the alley, Ian could see that he was grinning widely. "I told you it is never bad to have a friend when you are in a new place. You should have listened to me, sahib! If I had been scouting for you it might have saved you a bad headache."

Ian couldn't decide whether to scowl at the boy or thank him. He half suspected Rajiv himself had tipped off the men who attacked him. He closed his eyes for a moment. *Not "the men,"* he thought bitterly. *My "brother" Hunters.*

He groaned again, though this time not from the pain.

"Are you badly hurt?" asked another voice. This one came from the shadows to his left, and even in his distress Ian was struck by its beauty. Trying to lift his head, but failing, he said, "Who are you?"

The speaker stepped closer, and Ian caught his breath in astonishment. The man was huge, seven feet tall at the least. He was dressed simply, in close-fitting black shirt and trousers that made it clear he was powerfully muscled. Despite the very masculine body, his lean, brown face was soft — not quite feminine, but strangely smooth — with a high, wide brow and perfectly formed features, all framed by a flow of thick hair that tumbled past his shoulders and gleamed, even in the dim light of the alley, with the look of polished gold.

He was the most beautiful creature Ian had ever seen.

"Who are you?" he asked again.

The man squatted beside him, moving gracefully for all his size. "You may call me Fallon."

Ian was struck again by the beauty of the stranger's voice, which was equal to that of his face. The mellow tones held a note of sorrow so deep that simply hearing them almost brought tears to his eyes.

"It was you who drove off my enemies?"

Fallon nodded gravely.

"My thanks."

"Save that for later. First let's see how you are. Any broken bones?"

Ian closed his eyes, felt his body fully and deeply. "No," he said at last. "Some bad bruising, and my head is wounded. But no broken bones."

"Good." Fallon paused, then added, "This is not the way I would have chosen to meet. But there is much we must speak of."

Ian looked at the tall man sharply. Fallon stared back, then said something so startling that Ian tried again to sit up, though the lance of pain he felt quickly made him think better of it. The unexpected words were simple: "I understand that, like me, you seek to enter the Rainbow Prison."

"How do you know what I'm seeking?" gasped Ian. And then, more urgently, "And what do you know about the Rainbow Prison?"

"I have been trying to find my way into it for a long time now. Many things have prevented me — duty, the needs of others, things . . . required of me. And, of course, the fact that I did not have a key."

Rajiv crouched nearby, eyes wide, listening intently.

"Why do you want to find your way into this place? Do you know how hard it will be to leave?"

A shadow passed over Fallon's face. "I know. However, I am seeking a friend who has long been lost to me, and I have reason to believe this is one way to reach him." He paused, and Ian observed the tiniest twitch beneath his eye as he finished softly, "More than that, I do not wish to say."

"Do you have any idea of what I paid to gain the knowledge you are asking me to share?" Ian asked, scarcely able to mask the bitterness in his voice.

"No, I do not. On the other hand, you might consider the fact that I just saved your life advance payment of a sort."

Ian closed his eyes. "Forgive me. That was not very gracious of me. And —" He hesitated, not happy with what he was about to say, then decided to say it anyway. "And I have been trained to mistrust."

A pained expression flickered over Fallon's beautiful features, appearing and vanishing so rapidly Ian wasn't entirely sure it had even been there. "I will not claim you should trust me, for I know myself to be weak and fallible. Even so, as long as we share a common goal, we may do each other good."

Ian nodded. Then, partly to give himself time to think, he turned to Rajiv and said, "How did you know to follow me?"

"I thought you might need me," said the boy, spreading his hands as if the answer were obvious.

"And where did you pick up this character?"

Rajiv shrugged. "This character found me. This character asked to join me." The boy smiled. "This character is even harder to say no to than I am."

"Yes, I can see that," muttered Ian. He tried again to force himself to a sitting position. Succeeding, he put his fingers to the back of his head, where he found a mass of wet stickiness that made his stomach lurch.

"We'll need to tend that wound," said Fallon. "Heaven alone knows what kind of infections you might pick up from this alley. I have a place not far from here." He held out a hand to help Ian to his feet. "Come on, let's get you cleaned up."

Ian stared at the outstretched hand for a moment, then accepted the assistance. The size of Fallon's hand was startling and added to Ian's uneasiness at being helped, which was something he was not used to. That discomfort only increased once he was on his feet; not a short man himself, he found it disconcerting to be standing next to someone more than a head taller than he was.

"How do I know this isn't another trap?" he asked, once his feet were steady beneath him.

Fallon's smile was dazzling. "You don't. You'll just have to trust me."

"You told me not to."

"Sometimes you have to do things you shouldn't," replied the tall stranger with a shrug. "If not for the fact that you have something I need, I would be perfectly happy to leave you here in the street if you wanted. Fortunately, I also have something you need. So it's a match, and we may be able to do each other much good."

"What do you have that I need?"

"Would a small airplane, capable of flying beneath radar, suffice?"

Ian's eyes widened. With a smile he said, "Yes, it would do quite nicely."

"Let me come, too!" said Rajiv eagerly.

Ian shook his head, a gesture he immediately regretted, since it sent a bolt of pain shooting through his skull. "Where *you* are going is back to your home."

"I have no home."

"All right, you'll go back to your parents."

"No parents, either."

"Where do you sleep?"

"Here and there."

Ian longed to tell the urchin, "Well then, go back to 'here and there.'" But again the thought of his daughter — lost in another world, wandering, helped by the kindness of strangers — rose up and softened his response. How could he do less for this child than so many others had done for Cara during these last months?

He reached for his wallet.

"I don't want your money!" said Rajiv, and in his voice Ian heard both fear and anger. "I want to come with you."

Ian closed his eyes. The wound on the back of his head was throbbing. Even worse, he was still reeling from what he had just been through: the strange interview with the Blind Man, the attack in the alley, and most of all the way his sight had been snatched from him. Despite the fact that he had agreed to it, the experience had left him feeling as if his body were a house with no locks in a dangerous neighborhood, at risk of being robbed at any moment. He decided to do something he had not done in as long as he could remember: let someone else deal with the problem. Opening his eyes, he turned to Fallon and said, "You talk to him."

Fallon nodded. Kneeling in front of the boy, he said, "Why do you want to come with us?"

Rajiv dropped his voice to a whisper. "There is a man in the streets who wants to kill me."

Fallon shook his head and said sternly, "Do not lie to me."

"No, no, it is true! I have offended him, and he is out for my blood. You must believe me. If you leave me here I will be killed."

The boy's voice was desperate now, pleading.

Fallon laughed. "That was very good. But you are lying, Rajiv, and I will not bring you with us if you lie to me."

The boy looked amazed, and a bit crestfallen. "How did you know? I am a very good liar. People never know when I am lying."

Fallon's face grew serious. "I have met far greater liars than you, Rajiv, and suffered for believing them. I know a great deal about liars. Now, tell me the truth, or forget about joining us."

Rajiv started to speak, paused, started again, stopped himself, and finally said, "I think it will be fun. I think if I come with you that you will feed me and watch out for me. I think you are both good men, and I would like to help you." He paused, then grinned and added, "Besides, I want to have an adventure."

Fallon nodded. "All good reasons. Very well, you may come with us. But if you lie to me again, I will discard you without a second thought. Is that clear?" The man's voice had changed, the warmth and gentleness replaced by an edge so sharp Ian almost expected Rajiv to start bleeding.

"I will not lie," said the boy firmly.

There was no way to know if he was lying when he said it, of course. Even so, Fallon smiled and, with his voice once more filled with its normal warmth, said solemnly, "Welcome to our adventure."

Ian was aghast. When he had turned the problem of Rajiv over to Fallon, he had assumed the big man would find a way to get rid of the boy, not agree to bring him along.

"Fallon," he said urgently.

"What?"

"We can't bring him along!"

Fallon's face darkened, and he said quietly, "Rajiv, please go to the end of the alley. Keep watch there for us. We will join you in a minute."

The boy nodded and trotted away. Once he was out of earshot, Fallon said firmly, "You and I are about to become comrades in what is likely to be a dangerous trip. Before our journey is over, we may even become friends. As we travel, I will be glad to consult with you when we need to make decisions. However, if you ask me to deal with something and impose no conditions, I must be able to trust that you are turning the matter over to me to handle in my own way.

If that is not to be the case, we will not be able to continue together."

"But to bring the boy into such danger —"

"There are many dangers in these streets. Let me repeat: You gave the matter over to me, and I dealt with it as I saw fit. Now, will we be able to continue together or not?"

Ian thought of the plane, and the press of time, and his wife's imprisoned spirit, and said simply, "Let us continue."

CHAPTER
XI

THE TALE OF ALMA LEONETTI

Grimwold looked up from his twig. He seemed to be speaking directly to Cara when he said, "In the long ago and sweet of the world, when things were slower but hearts were no less fierce, there came a time when the unicorns had to leave Earth.

"This leaving was not done easily, nor was it done without grief, for Earth was their home, and they were part of it, horn and mane, hoof and hock. But to stay was to die, for the hunting of unicorns had become all too successful.

"So when a friend came to them and offered Luster as a place of refuge, they took his offer, with both gratitude and sorrow."

He paused, and when he continued his voice grew more solemn.

"Alas, creating the passage to Luster was not easy, and more than one unicorn gave its life in the making of that first gate. And even when the gate was ready, it took time for all the unicorns to find their way to Luster, for they were spread far and wide across the lands of Earth.

"When the exodus was finally over, and the very last unicorn had departed the world of his birth, it was as if Earth itself sighed with loss.

"For what kind of world is it that has no unicorns?

"That sense of loss grew within the hearts of the humans who had been left behind, left to live without unicorns. Even the ones who had never seen a unicorn, never heard of a unicorn, felt the passing of something sweet and wonderful. It was as if the air had surrendered a bit of its spice, the water a bit of its sparkle, the night a bit of its mystery.

"But only a very few knew why.

"Not all felt the loss in equal measure, naturally. The coarse and the crude were but vaguely aware of something making them uneasy in their quiet moments. Most people simply felt a little sadder, a little wearier, a little . . . smaller. But for those whose hearts were open to the beauty of the world, with all its joys and sorrows, there was an ache that grew greater by the day, until it seemed that grief would overwhelm them.

"Artists painted nothing but scenes of despair; singers and players made only mournful music; storytellers told naught but tales that made their audiences weep long into the night, and offered no happy endings for relief.

"As gloom enfolded the world, a young woman — a girl, really, for she was well shy of her twentieth year — decided something had to be done.

"She was the daughter of a storyteller, and seemed likely to become a storyteller herself. Her name was Alma Leonetti, and she had a heart of steel and fire. What follows is her story, as she herself told it to the Chronicle Keeper of her time."

Cara wondered how many Chronicle Keepers there had been, how far back the line could be drawn. While she was thinking about this, Grimwold closed his eyes, as if looking deep into his memory. When he began to speak again, Cara found herself being pulled more deeply into the web of his story, until it was almost as if the girl Alma was herself telling the tale.

I don't know when I first realized something had gone so wrong; the feeling crept over me slowly. But the time came when I could no longer deny it. So I went to my brother, Balan, and said, "Something is wrong, and I am going to find out what it is. Will you travel with me, brother?"

Balan, who was more given to doing than to thinking, to fighting than to feeling, had not felt this, and did not understand what was bothering me. Even so, he willingly agreed to join me, both for the sake of the adventure, and because he did not want me to travel alone. I gathered some food and a few coins, which I carried in a pack on my back, and several of my father's best stories, which I carried in my heart, and we set out. I went on foot, and Balan walked beside me, one hand always on his sword.

We needed that sword, for the road was perilous. It had always been dangerous, of course, even in the best of times. But with the passing of the unicorns, hearts had become hungry. In some, that hunger had turned to viciousness.

For three years Balan and I traveled the Earth, seeking, seeking. Many times his sword saved us from disaster, and many other times my stories gained us food and shelter, and sometimes even a clue.

And all those clues pointed toward an old magician named Bellenmore.

Finally, weak and weary, wandering through a deep forest, we made our way to his home. It was set in the side of a hill, and magic hung thick about it. The moment we approached the door, it began to sing, calling, "Bellenmore, Bellenmore! Wanderers two outside your door!"

At once a wall — or something like a wall, for we could not see it, only feel it — rose in front of us, and we could go no farther until the old man appeared. He looked just as a magician ought, with long white hair and a beard that fell nearly to his waist. He wore a robe of deepest blue, and in its fabrics were woven signs that shifted and moved, though you could never catch them in the process.

"What do you want?" he asked, in a voice that creaked with age. "If you're looking for Aaron, he's long gone. Great things doing. Great things. Probably couldn't help you anyway. Getting too big for his britches."

"We want to know what's gone wrong with the world," I said, my voice gentle, coaxing. "For three years now, things have been flat and stale. Stories don't sing to me the way they used to. The leaves are not as bright, the air not so sweet, and my heart weighs more than it used to."

Bellenmore closed his eyes, then released a sigh so heavy it seemed to flow not from his body but from someplace in the earth itself. "I was afraid of this."

"Of what?" asked Balan, struggling to raise his sword, which had somehow become frozen at his side.

"Of exactly what this girl — your sister, I assume, from the look of her — has just described. The unicorns have gone, and when they left they took with them something that is essential to the human heart."

"Where have they gone?" I asked anxiously. "And why? How did they get there? How can I follow them?"

"Hold, hold!" cried the old magician, raising his hands. "One question at a time."

He studied us for a moment, then made a small gesture — no more than a twitch of the little finger of his right hand, really. Instantly, the invisible wall disappeared. At the same time, Balan gained control of his sword.

"You may come in," said Bellenmore.

Balan glanced at me. "Do you think it's safe?"

"Nothing is safe," I said softly.

Then I stepped forward and followed the old man through the door into the hill.

The inside of Bellenmore's house was warm, cozy, and slightly strange. A green fire crackled on the hearth. On the mantel above the fireplace stood a row of earthenware mugs with hideous faces. One of them winked at me; another leered and rolled its eyes; a third stuck out its tongue and made a rude noise. Then they began to sing a bawdy song, until Bellenmore waved a hand to silence them.

The tables and chairs were made of dark wood, and ornately carved — some with odd designs, others with scenes of dragons and unicorns. At one side of the room stood a tall oaken stand, a thick book resting open upon it. The longest table held a glass box with no top. Inside the box was a lizard. It was resting its front legs on the upper edge of the cage and staring at us with a curious expression.

"Oh, good," it said, flicking out its long tongue. "I love visitors!"

I blinked, but forced myself not to seem too surprised at its comment — or the fact that it was speaking at all.

"Sit," said Bellenmore, gesturing toward one of the chairs.

I sat. Balan stood behind me, partly because he had not been invited to sit, and partly because he would not have sat even had he been asked. His hand rested on the hilt of his sword.

Bellenmore did sit, his robe shifting and whispering around him as if it were alive. "Alas, the unicorns," he said sadly.

"What happened to them?" I asked.

"They were driven away. There is a family which holds an ancient grudge against them, and the hunting had become so fierce that it seemed they all might perish. Finally the unicorn queen came to me and asked if I might open a gate for them, as I had for the dragons."

"The dragons?" asked Balan, confused.

"They were cousins," said the lizard wistfully. "I kind of miss them."

The magician rolled his eyes at the lizard, then said, "It was much the same with the dragons. The world is changing, boy, and wildness and magic are in retreat before the rise of men. Better — much better — it would be for science and magic, order and wildness, natural and supernatural to live together. But that cannot be, at least not for now. So the dragons have gone, and the unicorns had to leave as well. I helped them open a gate to a place that they have named Luster. It is a good place for them.

But they did take a piece of our hearts with them when they went."

"Send me through the gate," I said.

The old man looked startled. "That's not possible."

"Why not?"

Bellenmore blew a puff of air through his shaggy white mustache, then looked down at his knobby hands. Finally he said, "The Queen wouldn't like it."

"I don't like what's happened here," I replied firmly. "I must speak to them."

"They are not tame beasts, you know."

"I am not a tame girl."

Bellenmore stared at me, and I got the feeling he was weighing something deep inside my heart, something I hadn't even known was there.

"Wait here," he said at last.

He stood and went to a door at the far side of the room. When he opened it and stepped through, he seemed to disappear into a kind of shadowy gloom. Balan started forward, but I touched his arm, and he resumed his stance behind my chair.

When Bellenmore returned he was holding a golden chain, from which dangled a crystal amulet. Inside the crystal was coiled a long strand of white hair that seemed to glow with a light all its own. Lifting it so that it hung between us, he said, "This amulet was a gift of the unicorn queen. There are only five such in all the world. It will allow you to pass into the land of the unicorns."

I took the chain from him, and lowered the amulet into the palm of my right hand. It felt strangely warm.

Leaning forward, the magician whispered to me how to use it. My eyes grew wide, and I suspect that a hint of fear showed in them, but I nodded to indicate that I understood.

"And what do I do when I get there?" I asked when he was finished.

Bellenmore shook his head and said softly, "That, my girl, is entirely up to you."

"Come with me," I said.

The old man looked at me in surprise. He started to answer, paused, then shook his head. "This is for you to do alone."

Balan placed his hand on my shoulder and said softly, "Alma, this is not wise."

"Wise or not, I must do it. You go home, Balan, and tell Father where I have gone."

And so it was that I came alone into Luster.

It should be no surprise, I suppose, that I had adventures strange and wondrous. The most harrowing came when I was captured by delvers and held prisoner underground for three long years. In my escape, I saved the life of a young princeling named Windfoot, who was much beloved of his mother, the Queen. When the two of us made it back to the court together, the grateful Queen offered me a boon.

I thought for a long time. Finally, gathering both my breath and my courage, I said, "Come home."

I heard a murmur of horror ripple through the unicorns.

"Come home," I said again, and this time tears were coursing down my cheeks. "Come home, because something good is dying without you."

I stepped toward the Queen. No one stopped me. No one moved.

Pressing my cheek to the Queen's, burying my face in her mane, which felt like spun cloud and smelled of the sea and the forest and something more, something that cannot be named, I whispered, "Hearts grow hard and weary. Pain spreads, and joy diminishes. Those who hated you hate you still, but those who loved you, or would have loved you, or wanted to love you but never had the chance, are being scraped hollow by a loss they don't understand. Come home. Please come home. We are withering without you."

"Your world is not kind to us, child," whispered the Queen.

"It is even unkinder without you," I replied fiercely.

Then, with my face pressed close to the Queen's ear, I began to sing, as my father had taught me. I sang of all that the unicorns had left behind, the good and the bad, the oceans and the forest. I sang of all I had seen in three long years of wandering to find the unicorns. Through my song flowed the sorrow I had felt with their passing, and beneath that throbbed the love we all have of things unseen and mysteries unsolved — of untouched joy waiting just around the bend of the next moment — things that had vanished with the passing of the unicorns.

The Queen told me later that as I sang she remembered all the humans she had known over the years, humans who had fought for the unicorns, and died for them, and had loved them with open hearts. And she remembered the world that had given them birth, no more beautiful than Luster, but no less so, either. And she thought of her son, who I had saved from the delvers, and finally she said, "Peace, girl. Be silent. Here is what I will grant. From this time forth, there shall always be one unicorn, one and one alone, living in the world of our birth. That unicorn will have to be enough, enough to remind you of what was, and what can be. He will live alone, in the high places. He will not be seen often, or by many. But his presence should be enough to keep something alive in you. He will guard the memory of what has passed from Earth to this world, and the sight of him will help keep that memory alive. Those who know such things will know, and those who understand such things will *understand, and it will be, if not enough, then something. Something."*

Turning to Windfoot, she said, "Will you be the first, my son?"

Grimwold paused, and Cara found herself coming out of the trance of the story, which had become like a waking dream for her. The fire snapped. She shook herself and looked around, half expecting to see young Alma and Windfoot standing nearby.

"And so it was, and so it will be," said Grimwold. "The Prince returned to Earth for five and twenty years. When his time was up, a glory of unicorns gathered to choose a new Guardian, who went to take his place. And again it was done, and again, and yet again, for these many centuries, though not all the Guardians of Memory survive their full five and twenty years. For the Hunt still goes on, and the world is full of danger. But that is why there is — almost always — one unicorn still on Earth. Because the humans need the unicorns, and the unicorns, for ancient love and friendship, are willing to risk what must be risked to keep the dream of magic alive."

CHAPTER
XII

NEDZIK

Nedzik the delver trotted unhappily at the rear of the cove he had been assigned to travel with. The creature was a little over three feet tall, with a bulging head over which scraggled a few strands of hair. His eyes, made for seeing in the dark, were enormous. In contrast, his nose was a thin, upthrust thing that displayed two large, gaping nostrils. His arms and legs were lean, but corded with muscle. He wore a green tunic and a gray, hooded cloak.

In these things, he looked like every other delver in the cove. Where he differed was in his feelings. While they were all confident in their task, Nedzik was swamped with confusion — something delvers rarely experienced. The fact that the cove was moving so rapidly toward its destination only made things worse, since he could not decide what he should do when they reached it. Even worse, his time for thinking was running out.

Of one thing he was certain: The attack they were planning was wrong. No, more than simply wrong. If they obtained what they were after, it would allow King Gnurflax to help the Hunters enter Luster, and that was a thought that filled him with terror.

The problem was, he didn't know why he felt that way. And, not knowing, couldn't possibly explain to the others why his gut kept screaming to him that this was a hideous mistake.

Couldn't explain? He didn't dare even mention it! In the last few months the delver king, never gentle of judgment, had become increasingly irascible. Now the slightest questioning of his will was enough to send him into a boiling rage. Nedzik had puzzled much over what had wrought this change in the King, but it remained a mystery.

It wouldn't be so bad if he were traveling with his cousins, as was the proper delver way. But a few days earlier King Gnurflax had become enraged at one of those cousins and had sundered their family's cove like a hammer smashing a rock. At least, that was how it had felt to Nedzik. He could only guess that his cousins felt the same, since he had not been allowed to speak with any of them since that day.

What made things worse for Nedzik was that he was painfully aware that his cousin's "crime" had been committed because of things he, Nedzik, had been saying — things about how he feared the King was mad. So he was carrying a heavy guilt for their sundering. Traveling with this new cove made him feel alone and insecure. He was not really part of the group, just something that had been attached to it but didn't truly belong.

Like a wart, thought Nedzik ruefully.

The delver had been so lost in thought he hadn't realized that they were nearing the edge of the forest. It was only the discomfort caused by an increase in light as the trees began to thin that made him aware of it.

The cove leader, Farzkak, called a halt. Looking ahead, Nedzik could see that soon they would be traveling over rock. In some ways this was much to be preferred; rock was a natural surface on which to walk, after all, not like the strangely soft floor of the forest. However, the King had ordered them to travel both day and night — something that Nedzik took to be yet another sign that Gnurflax was going mad. They had the strength and stamina to travel that way, of course. It's just that it was . . . unnatural. During the daytime hours the open terrain would be flooded with harsh sunlight, vastly brighter than the shady forest. They would have to raise their hoods to protect their eyes from the cursed light. Even then the traveling would be painful. Not to mention the fact that they would be easily visible to their enemies.

But by moonlight, glorious moonlight, the going would be swift and easy, and it would be hard for any but the sharpest eyes to spot them.

Nedzik found himself longing for sunset. Alas, it was a long way off.

Farzkak gave the order. Lifting their hoods, they trotted out of the forest's comforting shadows and into the blazing day.

The cove reached its destination two nights later. It was a large house, built of stone and tucked into the side of a hill. Nedzik felt, more strongly than ever, the surge of uneasiness. This place might almost be a delver home, so lovingly were the rock and stone crafted — though, of course, building above ground was a clear sign of insanity.

The delvers settled under their cloaks to wait. Nedzik knew the others were enjoying the rest and the growing dark. He felt none of that enjoyment, only a steadily increasing panic. When at last the thin sliver of a moon slid below the horizon, so that only starlight remained, the cove rose as one. Farzkak gave the signal and they rushed forward, moving without sound until they were almost at the door. Then they shattered the silence with the weird, piercing battle cry that often froze their foes in terror.

Nedzik, however, did not accompany them. Turning away, trembling with terror at his decision, which he could not begin to understand, he ran in the opposite direction, disappearing into the night.

CHAPTER
XIII

UNEASY HOMECOMING

Cara, leaning against Lightfoot, had been so caught up in the story of Alma Leonetti she had not noticed when both Finder and Belle raised their heads to glance about nervously.

"Shhhh," said Belle after a moment. "I need to listen."

Instantly Grimwold fell silent.

Cara strained to hear whatever Belle was listening for. The world itself was not silent — their fire crackled, night birds cried in the distance, scaly creatures made a hissing song in the nearby swamp. But she could hear nothing unusual, nothing frightening.

After a moment Belle relaxed and said quietly, "Whatever it was, it's gone."

Finder shook his head and whispered, "Not gone."

"I hear nothing!" Belle sounded insulted.

"Nothing to hear," said Finder. "But something to smell." He flared his wide nostrils, then whispered, "Delvers. No. Delver."

Cara felt cold at the very mention of the word.

"Steady," thought Lightfoot, speaking mind-to-mind. "No need to fear. At least, not yet."

"Just one?" asked Belle.

"Yes, just one. Which is strange. They don't usually travel alone." Finder waited a moment, then sniffed again. "Good. He's moving away from us. I don't think he even knew we were here."

Cara let out a heavy sigh. After a time, M'Gama said, "We should sleep now, so we can get an early start tomorrow."

Though Cara thought it was a good idea, she found sleep was impossible. Finally she gave up tossing and turning and went to stand beside Finder, who was keeping the first watch. He nodded in greeting and, when she leaned her head against his high shoulder, said gently, "No need to worry, Cara. The delver is long gone."

"I know. It's just that I love Luster so much I sometimes forget how dangerous it can be. Then I remember, and — well, it makes it hard to relax."

She looked around. Here and there pale shafts of silver moonlight pierced the forest canopy. Tinted with blue from the leaves, they looked like the columns of some ancient temple. A pair of night birds called back and forth in the distance. The bark of the tree beside them had a sharp, sweet smell.

Sighing, she whispered, "Finder, why does such a beautiful world have to have things like delvers in it?"

The big unicorn shrugged. "Why does it have unicorns? Or humans? Why are any of us here? That's one of the great mysteries, isn't it? And who knows — maybe Chiron will help us solve the part about the delvers."

"I thought it was *the* Chiron."

"Actually, it's both. Thousands of years ago Chiron was the first king of the centaurs. He was a great and wise leader. Ever since, each new king has taken 'Chiron' as both his name and his title. The current Chiron has reigned for an unusually long time, ever since they came to Luster as a matter of fact."

"How do you know so much about them?"

"I have been to their valley before," said Finder quietly.

Cara looked at the big, gentle unicorn and smiled. Not long ago she would have been surprised to find that he had wandered through strange and difficult territory. But she had learned that, quiet and shy as Finder seemed, he had a taste for exploring that could not be quenched.

Comforted by his gentle voice and calm strength, she

stayed at his side until Belle rose and sauntered to where
they stood.

"I'll watch now," she said quietly.

"Thank you," said Finder. Moving closer to the others,
he folded his long legs and lowered himself to the ground.

Cara returned to her own place and slept.

The travelers were nervous all the next day, on high alert for
any sign of delvers. Even the Squijum seemed subdued, staying close to Cara and being unusually quiet.

Around midday Belle stopped and muttered, "They
camped here."

"They?" asked Lightfoot. "I thought there was only one
of them."

"I can't speak for the one who passed us last night, but
this was definitely a group."

"How do you know they were here?" asked Cara.

Belle swung her horn toward a scattering of brush. "See
those branches?"

Cara studied the pile of wood for a moment, then said,
"I don't understand. It's just a lot of fallen limbs."

"It's more than that," said Lightfoot. "It's the remains of
a delverden. They hate bright light, so they prefer to travel
by night and sleep by day. But they need darkness to sleep

well, so they usually gather branches to make a covering for themselves."

"They don't mind weather," said Belle. "Wind, rain, cold — that doesn't make much difference to them. But they really do not like light. When night falls and they are ready to travel again, they break up the shelter they had made and scatter the wood. If you know the signs, you can always recognize a place where delvers have camped."

"Do you think they're still nearby?" asked Cara nervously.

"Long gone," said Finder, who had crossed to examine the branches more closely.

"Let's press on," said M'Gama. "We have our own tasks to accomplish."

She sounded uneasy.

Evening was falling when they came to the rocky foothills where M'Gama made her home. Cara smiled when she spotted the stone turrets that rose from the top of the Geomancer's four-story house, the first sign that they had almost reached their destination. The turrets had baffled her the first time she saw them; now she understood that each was used to gather information that M'Gama needed to work her earth magic.

Before long they could see the house itself, its four levels so beautifully designed and built they seemed to have grown directly out of the hillside.

"Something is wrong," said M'Gama, her voice flat and grim.

"How do you know?" asked Lightfoot.

"Flensa should have greeted us by now. She is always aware when anyone has drawn this close to the house."

"I hope she's all right," said Cara.

"There is only one way to find out," replied M'Gama. She strode forward, long legs moving at such a pace that Cara had to run to keep up. They had not gone far when M'Gama stopped so abruptly Cara nearly bumped into her.

The Geomancer pointed to a scrap of coarse fabric that had caught on a sharp rock. Cara would never have noticed it, especially in the gathering darkness. But she knew what it meant, even before M'Gama whispered, "Delvers have been here."

"Are they still here?" Belle had come up beside them so silently Cara hadn't realized she was there until she spoke.

"I cannot tell," replied M'Gama, gazing toward her home with troubled eyes.

"What about Flensa?" asked Cara.

M'Gama shook her head. "I do not know."

Cara heard fear in that powerful voice; the sound of it made her shudder.

"I'll go forward to scout," said Belle.

"Don't be silly," said Lightfoot, who, with Finder at his side, had also joined them. "I should go."

"Don't be absurdly male," retorted Belle. "The Queen sent you along to keep you out of trouble, not steer you directly into it. Of the three of us, I'm the one who is a member of the Queen's Guard. Of course I should go."

Cara put a hand on Lightfoot's shoulder. He looked at her, then in the direction she was pointing. Belle and Finder turned to look as well. While they had been arguing, M'Gama had started toward the house, striding across the stony ground with swift, silent determination.

"Should we go after her?" asked Cara.

Belle shook her head. "She has made her choice. If she calls, we will come. If she is attacked, we will rush to her aid. But there is no sense in all of us walking into a trap."

M'Gama slowed as she approached the entrance to her home.

Cara heard no challenge, no sound of delvers preparing for attack.

The Geomancer pushed forward, through the front door.

A moment later, a wail of despair echoed down the slope.

CHAPTER
XIV

ESCAPE ROUTE

The rancid smell of old cooking oil assaulted Ian's nostrils as they climbed the creaking stairs of a building not far from the Chandni Chowk. Yet as soon as they entered Fallon's third-floor rooms, the odor was replaced by the light, pleasant fragrance of sandalwood. Ian wondered how the tall man had managed to do that.

The apartment was sparsely furnished, with nothing save a small wooden table and two chairs in the space that served as living room, dining room, and kitchen combined. A piece of brightly patterned cloth hanging next to the small refrigerator covered a doorway; Ian assumed it led to the sleeping area.

The furniture seemed too small for the big man.

Actually, the whole place seems too small for him, thought Ian, wondering again just who this stranger was and where he had come from.

After a quick glance at the room, Rajiv settled himself cross-legged on the floor in a corner near the only window, leaving the chairs for the two men.

"First things first," said Fallon. "Let's take care of those wounds." Using a bottle of water he took from the counter, he washed the cut at the back of Ian's head. After examining it more closely, he said, "Hmm. I fear some stitches may be in order."

"I don't have time to go to a hospital!"

"No need for that. I can handle it right here."

Having received plenty of instruction in field medicine during his training to become a Hunter, Ian had no objection to this.

"First thing we need to do is disinfect it," said Fallon, as he fetched a small pot of ointment from a cupboard above the tiny sink. He dipped a finger into the pot, then daubed the ointment liberally over the wound.

Ian made a cry of surprise. The salve stung like a thousand bees! To his relief, the sting quickly faded. Even better, it seemed to take with it the dull ache he had felt ever since he regained consciousness.

Rajiv watched with interest as Fallon sterilized a needle over a flame, then stood behind Ian and carefully stitched his scalp together. For his part, Ian made it a point not to cry out again, or even flinch.

"Well, that should hold it for now," said Fallon, tying

off the last stitch. Nurse work done, he went to the ancient refrigerator and pulled out two bottles of beer. Glancing at Rajiv, he reached to the back of the refrigerator and extracted a bottle of brilliantly colored fruit juice. Returning to the table, he set one of the beers in front of Ian, then tossed the fruit drink to Rajiv, who caught it handily.

"All right, let's talk," said Fallon, brushing a lock of golden hair back from his high, brown forehead. "Normally we would need to fuss for a while about who goes first. But if you will let my saving your life count as a point of privilege, we can move along more quickly. I would prefer you to start."

Ian, who had been trained by Beloved to be subtle and secretive, was taken aback by this blunt approach. On the other hand, if he was going to share what he knew with Fallon, there was no point in being slow about it. And time was important.

"You might begin by telling me your name," prompted Fallon, smiling slightly.

Ian smiled back, a rare event for him. "I am called Ian Hunter," he said — leaving it open to question whether that was actually his name, or simply what people called him.

Fallon nodded. "And what did you learn when you visited the Blind Man today, Mr. Hunter?"

Ian closed his eyes for a moment, as if recreating the occasional blindness he had paid in return for the knowledge. "Since you know of the Blind Man, should I assume you know why I sought him out?"

"Well, that's more of a question than an answer, but in the interest of moving forward, I'll say that I assume it has to do with the Rainbow Prison."

"So how do you know about this place?" asked Ian.

Fallon shook his head and smiled. "I think we agreed that you would go first, Mr. Hunter?"

"Ah. Yes, we did. All right, what I learned is what I had hoped for — that in the Himalayas there is a place where, if you have the right key, and know the right words, it is possible to enter the prison."

"The Ruby Portal," said Fallon, nodding. "And do you have such a key?"

"I do. And I have learned the words as well."

Fallon sighed and Ian could sense him relax, as if this was the information the big man had been hoping for. He was suddenly glad he had left the scarlet jewel in the safe at his hotel. Though Fallon *seemed* trustworthy, that was no guarantee.

Ian's thoughts were interrupted by Rajiv. No longer able to contain himself, the boy cried, "What is this Rainbow Prison, sahibs?"

Both men turned toward him. After a long silence, Fallon said, "It is a place between worlds," even as Ian said, "It is a world made of light."

They paused, glanced at each other. It was Fallon who continued. "In truth, it is both, Rajiv. There is a light that flows between the worlds. It is in this light that the Rainbow Prison is found."

"What worlds?"

Ian noted that, having been raised in a land rife with mystic beliefs, the boy had no trouble at all with the idea of other worlds.

"How many worlds there are, or where they all came from, I cannot say," Fallon replied. "In this case, the other world I am speaking of is a place called Luster."

Ian looked at the big man sharply, then told himself that if the Rainbow Prison was located in the light between the two worlds, then someone who knew about it would almost certainly know about Luster as well.

"Have you been to this world, this Luster?" asked Rajiv eagerly.

When Fallon shook his head, Ian let the answer stand for both of them; not quite a lie, just a silence. He was not sure how far to trust either of these new acquaintances yet, and felt no need to let them know he had indeed spent time in Luster.

"But what is this prison?" persisted Rajiv. "Who is held there?"

"The prison itself is a perversion of a great beauty," replied Fallon. "The light between the worlds, which reflects both worlds, should be a thing of wonder. But long ago an angry power realized it was possible to trap people — people you wished to have out of the way, but not dead — within that light. There are seven shafts in the prison, just as there are seven colors in the rainbow. How many souls are held in those shafts I cannot say." He turned to Ian. "Anything to add, Mr. Hunter?"

Ian paused, then said, "It takes considerable power, not to mention skill and secret knowledge, to imprison someone there. Or to enter it on your own. For someone seeking to enter who is not a master of this power, it is necessary to go to one of the places where the border between our world and the light is weakest. Just as there are seven shafts, there are seven portals, one for each shaft. All are well hidden and difficult to reach. And even at these portals it is not possible to enter without some sort of key."

"What is the key?" asked Rajiv.

Ian smiled and shook his head.

Rajiv, unoffended, simply changed the topic. "All right, once in, how do you get back out?"

"The best way is to have a connection to someone who is outside the prison," said Ian.

"And do you have such a connection?" asked Rajiv.

"I am hoping to find one when we get there."

"Not many people wish to break into a prison without having a way to get back out, sahib."

Fallon laughed. "Desperate men do desperate things, Rajiv. You may leave now if you wish. Neither of us will think the worse of you for it."

"Why would I leave?" asked the boy.

"Suit yourself," said Fallon.

Again, Ian found himself regretting the fact that he had given the matter of the boy over to his new companion so easily. Deciding to change the subject, he said, "My daughter once sang her way out of the prison."

Fallon looked at him in surprise. "This daughter of yours must be a remarkable child."

"She is a miracle."

Fallon shrugged. "Each of us is a miracle. Alas, it is a fact we too often forget." Catching Ian's dark glance, he added quickly, "Still, it is clear your daughter is an extraordinary person. Where is she now?"

Ian hesitated. Then, deciding that Cara was quite beyond reach, said simply, "She is in Luster."

For a moment the big man actually looked hungry. Making an obvious attempt to control his voice, he said, "How did she get there?"

"Family connections. It's not a method most people can use."

Fallon sighed.

Ian looked at him more closely. "Exactly what is it you're interested in, Mr. Fallon? The Rainbow Prison, or Luster?"

"It's just Fallon, please. And since you ask, I do indeed wish to go to Luster. At the moment, the Rainbow Prison seems my best route for getting there."

"Why do you want to go to Luster?" asked Rajiv, saving Ian from seeming too curious himself.

"I seek a friend who I believe to be living there." He turned to Ian. "Well, now you know what I am after. May we know why *you* seek to enter the prison?"

Ian paused, then said simply, "My wife is there."

Fallon's eyes widened.

Partly to divert the next question, Ian turned to Rajiv and said, "If we can find her, I am hoping that she will be able to help us leave the prison."

"Hoping?" asked Rajiv.

"There are no guarantees on this," said Ian.

After a moment of uncomfortable silence, Fallon said, "So, you have a key. And you know there is a place in the Himalayas where you can enter the Rainbow Prison. Do you know where this entry point is?"

"I learned the general location, and how to use the key I possess, from the Blind Man."

"Good. Now I will tell you what I have to offer. I know the *exact* location, and in fact have been there. Alas, not having a key, I was unable to enter. But I can lead you directly to the Ruby Portal. And, as I told you, I have a small plane in which we can travel. Will you consider these things, which should speed your journey, sufficient contribution, Mr. Hunter?"

Ian smiled. Extending his hand he said, "Make it Ian. And the sooner we start, the better."

CHAPTER
XV

FLENSA

Without a word, Cara and the others raced toward M'Gama's house. The unicorns took the lead, of course, with Cara coming after them as quickly as she could. The Squijum clung to her shoulder, muttering nervously. Grimwold, moving with a speed that belied both his age and his size, kept pace with her.

Cara was panting when they reached the entrance to the Geomancer's home. Even so, she found the breath to cry out in dismay when she passed through the door.

The massive stone table that took up much of the first room had been overturned. A jagged crack ran across its center. Even worse, the tools and tokens of M'Gama's magic, which normally covered that table, had been scattered across the floor, then stomped on as if by some malicious child.

"Delvers," muttered Belle in disgust.

M'Gama, who was still standing just inside the door when Cara entered, looked stunned. Suddenly, as if snapping out of a trance, she lifted her head and cried, "Flensa! Flensa, are you here?"

No answer.

M'Gama bolted forward.

"Wait!" commanded Belle sharply.

The Geomancer turned back, eyes blazing. "Wait for *what*?"

"We should stay together until we're sure the delvers are gone," said Belle, her voice firm.

"The scent of them is still strong here," agreed Finder.

Their words sent a jolt of fear through Cara, who had assumed the little monsters had left after ransacking the place. *I have to train myself to be more careful,* she thought, glancing around nervously.

The Geomancer drew a deep breath, then nodded. "You are correct, Belle. But if that's what you want, keep up with me, for I will not move slowly."

Cara knew that no matter how quickly they moved, it would take a long time to search M'Gama's home, since it had not only four levels above ground, but also many other levels and chambers carved deep into the hillside. Even knowing the search would take time, she had not expected how painful it would be, how each door through which they passed would offer fresh evidence of the damage the delvers had wrought.

M'Gama appeared to ignore the destruction, all her energy focused on finding her servant. Because Flensa was so small, and because she might be unconscious, the search was painstaking, and — it quickly became clear — best performed by those who could lift covers and open closet doors; in short, those with hands.

After finishing the rooms on the first floor, they mounted cautiously to the second level. Belle insisted on taking the lead as they climbed, in case of an attack.

The steps, carved directly into the side of the hill, led outside, bringing them to a wide terrace at the front of the house. A quick search was all it took to know Flensa was not there. But as they came back inside, they heard a low moan.

Pushing past Belle, M'Gama hurried toward it.

The sound came from a sleeping room, one Cara had not seen on her first visit to the Geomancer's home. She gasped when she stepped through the door. The bed in the center of the room had been overturned, its mattress sliced open. Now, with the feathers scattered everywhere, it looked as if there had been an indoor snowfall.

Again, they heard the moan.

M'Gama raced to the far side of the overturned bed, then dropped to her knees. Cara, who was close behind her, cried out in horror. Flensa was lying in a pool of her own blood, her small body marked by terrible wounds. The Squijum, still clinging to Cara's shoulder, whimpered and buried his face against her neck.

Tenderly, M'Gama lifted Flensa's head into her lap. "Poor faithful one," she murmured, stroking the dwarf's brow. "What have they done to you?"

Fighting down the lurching of her stomach, Cara whispered urgently, "Lightfoot! Lightfoot, heal her!"

The Prince had come around the bed. Now he, too, knelt so that he could be closer to Flensa. But after a moment he sighed and shook his head. Cara felt a new twist in her heart as she understood that the little woman was beyond even a unicorn's power to heal.

M'Gama nodded grimly to Lightfoot, telling him she understood.

Flensa's eyes flickered open. In a gravelly voice so faint that Cara had to lean forward to hear it, the dwarf whispered, "I am sorry, My Lady. I was not able to protect our home as well as I should have."

Cara could tell from Flensa's tone that her failure to do this pained her even more than her wounds.

M'Gama replied with a tenderness Cara had not suspected her capable of. Caressing the dwarf's brow, she whispered, "What happened, Flensa? Who did this to you?"

"Delvers," said Flensa, making the word sound like a curse. She tried to spit, but the bloody saliva clung to her lips. Then she coughed, her body tightening as a wave of pain swept over her.

Lightfoot sighed. "This much I *can* help," he said softly. He lowered his horn so that it rested across Flensa's chest. The little woman shuddered and twitched, then lay still, her breathing easier. Lightfoot lifted his head, murmuring, "Well, that's something, at least." Then his eyes rolled back, and he collapsed onto his side.

Before Cara could cry out, she heard a fierce whisper in her ear. "He's all right, simply drained. He took too much of her pain into himself."

It was Belle, who had come up behind Cara so silently that Cara had not known she was there.

Flensa's face relaxed, and it was clear that the pain had eased. Even so, her voice was still halting when she said, "They came last night."

M'Gama sighed. "You did not try to hide?"

Even with her eyes closed, even with her face so battered as to be hardly recognizable, Flensa managed to show her contempt for this thought. "They were trying to steal from you. I had to stop them." She coughed. More blood appeared on her lips.

M'Gama leaned closer. "Was it random, Flensa, or were they after . . . ?"

Though the Geomancer let her voice trail off, Flensa clearly knew what she meant, and nodded unhappily.

M'Gama closed her eyes, and the hint of fear that passed over her face sent a chill down Cara's spine. At last she whispered, "Did they find it?"

Flensa shook her head. "I do not know. I tried to fight them, but . . ." Another spasm of coughing shook her small frame. When it subsided, she said, "I was not so foolish as to attack the enemy face on. I came from behind, taking them one at a time, quietly, stealthily. I got some, but could not get them all. Once they realized they were not alone, they quickly caught me. I . . . lost the fight. I do not know if they found what they were seeking after that." She closed her eyes. "Forgive me, My Lady."

M'Gama wrapped her fingers around the dwarf's stubby hand. "There is nothing to forgive. You did your all, to the last measure."

The tiniest of smiles touched the corners of Flensa's mouth. She twitched and shuddered. A moment later her labored breathing ceased.

M'Gama stared at the lifeless body for a moment, then threw her head back and loosed a long wail of grief. The quivering ululation seemed to shudder its way down Cara's spine, carrying such deep hurt and hate that she felt as if she were spying on the Geomancer's heart just to hear it.

What happened next astonished Cara. Though she had expected the Geomancer to stay wrapped in her hurt, the woman carefully lifted Flensa's head from her lap, lowered it to the floor, then rose to her feet and said sharply, "There will be time to mourn later. Right now I must look for something."

"What is it?" asked Belle. "What have they taken?"

"I don't *know* that they've taken anything. I'm about to find out. If you will gather in the main room, I will join you soon."

"I don't think Lightfoot can move yet," said Cara.

"Then leave him," said M'Gama harshly. "You can tell him later what we have discussed."

Straightening her shoulders, she strode past Cara and Lightfoot, past Belle, past Finder and Grimwold, who had remained in the hallway outside the room. Something in her stance warned them against daring to offer sympathy right now.

Belle glanced down at Cara. "Come along," she said, her voice more gentle than Cara had ever heard it. "Lightfoot will recover on his own. Nothing you can do will speed the process."

Cara rose to her feet. Casting one look at Flensa's lifeless body, she shuddered, then followed Belle into the hall.

* * *

They waited for M'Gama in the large room Cara remembered so well from her first visit to the Geomancer's. It pained her now to see how the once-tidy place had been ransacked, the tables overturned, the shelves swept bare, the carefully wrought stone bowls scattered across the floor. Needing to do *something*, Cara began to gather the bowls. Some were cracked, some broken right in half. When she finished that task, she and Grimwold tried to right one of the stone tables. It was too heavy for them.

Cara was trying, pointlessly, to fit together one of the broken bowls when Lightfoot wobbled into the room. Dropping the stone fragments, she rushed to his side.

"Are you all right?"

"I'm fine."

"You don't sound fine!"

"I'm just a little . . . tired." The Prince gazed around the room, taking in the destruction, and sighed. Leaning against her so they could speak mind-to-mind, he said softly, "I hate not being able to heal someone."

She nodded, but said nothing, partly because there seemed to be nothing to say, partly because she feared that if she tried to speak she would start to cry and not be able to stop.

They stood together quietly until M'Gama returned.

Cara needed only one look at her face to know that the news was bad.

CHAPTER
XVI

THE CAPTIVE

It took the delvers three days to catch Nedzik. When they did he was not really surprised. He had not thought he could escape forever. What did surprise him was that they had sent only half the cove to do the job. Splitting a cove was unusual; yet another sign that the old ways were changing. When the other delvers had surrounded him — he didn't bother to run, since he knew in the end they would take him — Farzkak looked at him in angry puzzlement and snarled, "Are you a traitor, or just a coward?"

Nedzik could only shake his head.

Farzkak slapped him, then turned to the others and said, "Bind the fool. We will take him to the King."

They made a pole from a quilpum sapling and tied Nedzik to it, letting him dangle from it by his hands and feet as if he were freshly killed game. They took turns carrying the pole, not because it was tiring — delvers have great endurance — but in order that they might be able to take turns mocking him.

In another half day they went underground. Once there, travel was swifter, as the delver tunnels were smooth and straight. Three times they used transit points to speed the journey.

When they reached the delvercourt he was left, trussed and tied, while Farzkak reported to King Gnurflax. Even from where he lay, Nedzik could hear the royal bellow of rage, and cringed at what would come next.

Eventually two members of Farzkak's cove came to untie him. "The King wants to see you now," said one of them — Magtree, if Nedzik remembered correctly.

"I wouldn't want to be in your loincloth," said the other, who was a cousin of Magtree, of course. He sounded grimly satisfied, and his huge eyes seemed to glow with anticipation of Nedzik's punishment.

They hauled him to his feet, but he collapsed, for the binding had cut off the flow of blood to his legs and they could not hold him.

"Up!" snarled Magtree.

"The King said *now*," muttered his cousin. "Not next moonrise."

Grabbing Nedzik by the arms, they hauled him to his feet and dragged him down the tunnel.

CHAPTER
XVII

THE ANCHOR

Cara thought she would go mad waiting for M'Gama to speak. But finally the Geomancer drew a deep breath and said, "The delvers have stolen something very important. This is bad enough in itself. Even worse is the fact that they *knew* to steal it."

"Why is that?" asked Lightfoot.

"Because it makes me think that they are somehow being guided, probably by Beloved."

"And what makes you say *that*?" demanded Belle.

The Geomancer sighed. "Despite the destruction the delvers wrought, there is only one thing missing — a ball, woven from seven kinds of wire. To look at it, you would think it merely a trinket. It's attractive, but nothing of much value when compared to many of the other things in my collection." She paused, then said grimly, "Not much value, unless you know its true nature."

"Which is . . . ?" prompted Finder.

"This item could be used by someone who understood its true properties to ground an opening from Earth into Luster."

"I still don't understand," complained Belle.

M'Gama stood in silence for a moment, as if trying to decide how to explain. At last she said, "We assume that Beloved will soon be trying to open a door into Luster. The only good news we had in that regard was that in doing so she would face the same problem Cara encountered when she wanted to return to Earth to fetch the Wanderer: Where will the door open? It might be hundreds of miles from where she wants to enter. And since she cannot bring motors into Luster —"

This statement was so startling that Cara interrupted the Geomancer, something she would not normally have done. "What do you mean, she can't bring motors here?"

"Well, she could," said M'Gama with a weary smile. "But it wouldn't do her any good. Luster is hostile to that sort of thing; any motors they brought in would simply sit still and lifeless. So if Beloved were to open a door at, oh, the easternmost point in Luster, she and her Hunters would have to walk the whole distance to Autumngrove. And that's assuming they would even know where they needed to go."

The Geomancer drew a deep breath. "But with the right magic — which I have little doubt that she could have discovered, for she has had centuries to learn these things — Beloved could use this seemingly insignificant arrangement of wires as an anchor for her gate."

Finder looked at her, puzzled. "What do you mean by 'an anchor'?"

"If Beloved had someone in Luster to help her, she could link this item — this anchor — to the stolen amulet. That accomplished, she could use the link to open her new gate *wherever the anchor is placed*."

"Why would you have made such an object?" asked Belle angrily.

M'Gama sighed. "I did not. It was made by my teacher. And not for this purpose. Its magic is powerful and useful for many other things."

"It should have been destroyed," muttered Belle.

"There would not be much left if every useful thing that could be turned to bad ends were destroyed," replied M'Gama sharply. "Still, it is impossible to believe that the delvers would have taken that worthless looking gewgaw — and only that — at random. Therefore I must assume stealing it was the point of their attack. Which is why I am also convinced they are working in league with Beloved."

"But how would she have known about the anchor to begin with?" asked Lightfoot.

M'Gama shook her head. "I don't know. Magic has a habit of announcing itself to those who are sensitive to it, so there are a number of ways this might have come to her attention. But almost all of them would require that there be someone here in Luster — someone most likely not a delver — who is helping her."

Lightfoot shook his head anxiously. "For someone in Luster to help Beloved would be an incredible act of treachery!"

"Absolutely. But you must remember, not everyone who lives here is a friend of the unicorns."

"We have to go after those delvers at once!" cried Belle.

M'Gama raised a cautioning hand. "No. What you must do *first* is make some decisions. The Queen has given you a task, and it is not for you to abandon it so lightly."

"She sent us after a *story*," sputtered Belle. "Recovering that . . . that anchor of yours from the delvers is far more urgent!"

"Is that for you to judge?"

"But the power of the thing —"

"May be nowhere near as great as the power of the story we are after," said Grimwold.

"Precisely," said M'Gama. "Fortunately, I can offer some help in this regard."

"How?" snapped Belle, barely able to contain her fury.

"Like Grimwold, I have a scrying pool through which we can contact the Queen. I'd suggest we do so now."

Grimwold shook his head. "I don't think that's a good

idea, M'Gama. The last time I tried to use my scrying pool with Cara present, Beloved was able to break into the sending."

Cara shivered at the memory. M'Gama, however, merely shook her head and said, "That sort of magic is not your specialty, Chronicle Keeper. The pool here is much more secure." Pushing herself away from the table, she said, "Follow me."

They went underground, following passages lit by the glowing bowls of green light Cara remembered so well from her first visit to the Geomancer's home. The bowls sat in niches carved directly into the stone walls, and their cool light had a soothing quality.

For the first few minutes, M'Gama followed paths familiar to Cara. Then she led them into a side tunnel that made a steep descent for about a hundred feet before it leveled off and went straight into the rock.

At the bottom of the slope Cara pulled her cloak more tightly about her; this far below the surface of Luster the air was cool and damp. Another hundred paces led them to an arch that opened into a cave nearly twice the size of Cara's bedroom in the last house she had shared with her grandmother on Earth.

The cave was lit by three small cauldrons. Each cauldron was suspended from a tripod about six feet tall and filled with something that glowed a soft orange. Unlike the scrying room in Grimwold's caverns, the walls here were smooth, though on one side a trickle of water ran from ceiling to floor.

The tripods were spaced evenly apart, forming a triangle about nine feet on each side. At the center of the triangle rested a large stone basin filled with dark water.

M'Gama gestured to Lightfoot. "I can make the connection on my own, but it will be faster if you clear the water first."

Though she spoke softly, her voice echoed eerily from the stone walls.

Lightfoot dipped his horn into the basin. At once a thread of silver darted across the water, branching and spreading until it covered the entire surface of the basin. When that was done, M'Gama passed her hands above the basin and chanted in a low voice, "Ah lak minna mandos. Ah lak minna mandos!"

Slowly, so slowly it was hard to say when it started, the water began to glow. Leaning close, Cara saw an image forming. Soon she recognized it as Autumngrove. Turning to M'Gama, she said, "How do we talk to the Queen? I don't think she has a basin like this at Autumngrove."

"Wait," whispered the Geomancer.

The face of a unicorn appeared in the water. Cara recognized her as Laughing Stream, one of the Queen's messengers. In a light, bubbling voice the unicorn asked, "Who wishes to — oh, it's you, M'Gama! Is anything wrong?"

"We need to speak to the Queen at once. Tell her it is urgent."

"I will take the message," said Laughing Stream, and promptly vanished from sight.

M'Gama turned to Cara. "You were right — the Queen does not have a basin like this at Autumngrove. Nor does she need one, since she can designate *any* pool in Luster to receive messages from the scrying pools that Grimwold and I, and a few others, have been given. Sometimes when the court is traveling, it is difficult to reach the Queen, though usually a pool is chosen if they stop for a few days. But when they are at Springdell, Summerhaven, Autumngrove, or Winterkeep, there is always a receiving pool, and it is watched at all hours."

"I didn't know about this."

"Nor did your grandmother, until I told her. Alas, there is a great deal about being Queen of the unicorns that Amalia Flickerfoot did not have time to learn before the job was thrust upon her. She should have been in training all those years that she was lost on Earth. Perhaps —"

She stopped. The Queen's face had appeared in the basin.

"Greetings, M'Gama. Ah, and greetings to you, granddaughter."

"Hello, Gramma."

The Queen returned her gaze to M'Gama. "What news?"

When M'Gama told Amalia Flickerfoot all that had happened, the Queen's response was quick and decisive. "Belle and Finder, you will go after the delvers. Trail them cautiously. Come upon them from behind. Pick them off one at a time if you are able, and do everything you can to retrieve that anchor."

Belle looked angry. "Attacking from behind is not the way of a warrior!"

"I am not asking you to be heroic, Belle. While I regret the blow to your pride, this is not about being noble. It is about survival. And not just your survival. It's about survival for all of us."

Belle lowered her horn. "As you say, My Queen."

Though her words were appropriate, Cara could hear the resentment that lingered in her voice.

"Excuse me," said Finder. "What are we to do with this anchor if —"

"*When,*" interrupted Belle fiercely.

Finder nodded. "*When* we retrieve it? Do you want us to try to carry it back?" Whisking his tail, he added, "It won't be easy, given that we have no hands!"

"M'Gama," said the Queen, "can this thing be destroyed?"

The Geomancer closed her eyes for a moment, as if the thought pained her, then nodded and murmured, "Yes. Simply stomping on it will do the trick."

"Then that is what I want you to do, Finder. As for the rest of you, I want you to continue your journey to the Valley of the Centaurs."

"But —"

The Queen cut Lightfoot off. "I do not like dividing the group any more than you do, nephew. But we *must* have that story. It, as much as M'Gama's anchor, may hold the key to our survival. I need to know what happened in the past. Ignoring our history is a recipe for disaster."

"As you say, My Queen."

Amalia Flickerfoot sighed. When she spoke again, her voice was heavy. "I do not like any of this, either, nephew. I did not ask to become queen, and certainly not at the moment of our greatest danger. But someone has to make the decisions and that someone has turned out to be me. So while I am sorry to place such burdens on you, the fact is these are not easy times for any of us. We do what must be done."

Though her words were spoken gently, Cara felt their sting and was glad they had not been addressed to her. She wondered if unicorns could blush; if so, was Lightfoot blushing now, his red cheeks hidden by his milk-white coat? She moved closer and put a hand on his shoulder, not to read his thoughts, but just to comfort him.

The Queen paused for a moment, then said, "M'Gama, I am deeply sorry for the loss of your faithful servant. I know that Flensa was close to your heart."

The Geomancer replied in a voice of steel. "I will accompany Belle and Finder. I have a score to settle with those delvers. They *will* pay for what they have done."

"M'Gama, you are not one of my subjects, and I cannot command you. But as a friend, I ask you to reconsider. The task you agreed to undertake was to discover where the Hunters are most likely to enter Luster. Given what has happened, that is now more urgent than ever." Amalia paused, as if considering this, then asked, "Is such discovery still possible? Or does this change the situation?"

M'Gama was silent for several moments. Finally she said, "It will be more difficult now — in fact, I cannot guarantee that I can manage it. But, yes, it is *possible* I might be able to work this out."

"Then please do not turn away from the task for the sake of vengeance."

M'Gama's face looked as if it had been carved from

black stone, but at last she whispered, "I will do what must be done, Amalia. And if I cannot determine where the gate will open in advance, I guarantee that I will know the moment it does happen, and will be able to tell you then."

"Thank you. Now, let us make haste! The Blood Moon is coming. The tide is moving swiftly, and we must move with it. Travel safe, travel well. May those who have gone before be always with you." The Queen paused, then added softly, "Granddaughter, I am sorry to have drawn you into so much danger."

Cara, who stood with her hand on Lightfoot's shoulder, said simply, "There is no place in the world — in any world — that I would rather be."

Amalia Flickerfoot smiled and nodded. "You are everything I could have hoped for."

The pool swirled and went blank.

CHAPTER
XVIII

THE PUNISHMENT

The "Great Hall" of Gnurflax, King of the Delvers, was actually an enormous cavern. Huge stalactites thrust down from the stony ceiling like mighty spears. Beneath them stalagmites rose as if in response. Jutting twenty feet high and more, they looked like giant fangs in a crushing jaw.

Pots of glowing moss — an enormous number of them — cast a dim light over the entire space. Two rows of these "potlamps" lined the main path to the throne. Other groups of potlamps sat along the walls, or hung from tripods, or were mounted on stalagmites that had been cleanly sliced off halfway up to create stone pedestals.

The light was appropriately dim, the cavern pleasantly dank and cold. Yet Nedzik felt nothing save hot fear. Rows of fierce looking delvers, most of them clutching spears, lined the walls. He scanned their faces, looking for a hint of sympathy, of understanding.

He found nothing but anger and contempt. Even the face of his teacher was cold and stony. But that was to be expected. He could not show any hint of connection now. It would not be safe. Still, Nedzik yearned for a smile or a nod from that direction. He did not receive it.

In a voice that sounded like stone grinding against stone, the King cried, "Nedzik! Is it true that you deserted your cove while they were on duty?"

Nedzik felt, for a moment, as if a small, cold fish had gotten wedged in his throat. Fighting down his fear, he managed to push himself to his feet. He was still wobbly, and a hot wave of prickles had attacked his legs. Willing himself to stay standing, he looked his ruler straight in the eye and said, "King Gnurflax, wise and glorious, I know that I have failed you. I do not know how to explain, but I have been most uneasy for some time now. I feel we are on a road that will lead to great danger for us, for all of Delvharken, and I —"

Gnurflax's rage was awesome to behold as he screeched, "Are you now king? Is it now Nedzik who is to decide what is dangerous for the delvers and what is not?"

Nedzik wrung his huge hands in misery. He was certain the King would be driven to even greater rage by what he truly wanted to say. But if he did not speak, who would? Though he knew Gnurflax was as likely to be convinced by his words as a wall lizard was to pick up a spear and start marching, Nedzik felt he had to say what was inside him.

"My King, I am loyal to you, and to all delverkind. It is only because I am loyal that I have the courage to tell you this: I believe that if we help the Hunters enter this world, it will bring danger to all of us — not just to the unicorns, but to the delvers as well."

"You doubt my wisdom?" shouted Gnurflax, leaping to his feet.

An angry mutter came from the delvers who lined the walls.

"No, no!" cried Nedzik, holding out his hands imploringly. "I only meant that there are more things —"

"Silence!" roared the King.

At that moment Gruzzik, who had known Nedzik since they were but delverlings, stepped forward. Looking uncomfortable, he said, "King Gnurflax, duty compels me to tell you what else is rumored of my old friend, Nedzik."

"There's more?" snarled the King, his eyes widening.

Gruzzik glanced back at Nedzik. Looking uneasy, as if speaking of a great scandal, he whispered, "It is said that he has spoken with unicorns."

The muttering from the sidelines turned to a gasp of shock.

"Is this true?" bellowed Gnurflax, staring at Nedzik as if the trembling delver were some new and horrible kind of slug.

Nedzik simply lowered his head.

"His own silence convicts him!" Gnurflax held out his hand. "Give me a stone."

One of the nearby delvers did as he requested.

The King held the stone up so that all could see, then cried, "I name this stone Nedzik!" He glanced once at the miserable delver, then spat on the stone. "See this! Feel what it means, you traitorous fool!" Raising his arm, he smashed the stone to the floor with such force that it shattered in a spray of little pieces.

Nedzik felt his heart shatter with it.

"Now you have no name!" snarled the King.

Gasps rose from all around them. The taking of a name was the ultimate punishment among the delvers, one that had not been used in more years than most could remember.

"From this moment on, your bond to us is severed, you nameless thing," said Gnurflax. Sinking back into his throne, he waved a hand in disgust. "Take *it* away."

Two guards grabbed the nameless delver by the arms and hauled him from the throne room.

He did not resist.

The guards dragged him centerward, ever deeper into Delvharken, following a complex system of tunnels that were dimly lit by glowing orange lines that ran shoulder high along the walls.

At last they came to the dungeon. Throwing their prisoner into the cell, they slammed the door behind him. He heard the faint sound of the key turning in the lock, then the slap of bare delver feet against stone as his jailers walked away, then nothing but the slow plink of water dripping somewhere in the distant darkness.

Sinking to the floor, the now nameless delver dropped his head into his hands and thought miserably, *What is the matter with me? Why can't I stop thinking so much and simply do as I am told?*

CHAPTER
XIX

FUNERAL RITES

Belle and Finder were the first to leave M'Gama's, as they had no time to let the delver trail go cold.

The parting was rushed, and more painful than ever, since each of the travelers felt keenly the possibility they might not see the others again. M'Gama's and Grimwold's farewells to the two unicorns were formal, but heartfelt. When Lightfoot stood beside Finder, the big unicorn said, "We will meet again, friend."

"And when we do, we will share a gallop over the widest plain we can find," pledged Lightfoot.

The Prince's farewell moment with Belle was more subdued. "Until we meet again, Lightfoot," was all she said.

"Until we meet again," he repeated.

Watching this, Cara had the sense that Lightfoot wanted to say more to Belle than was possible. But she had no time to think about that, because suddenly it was her turn.

Putting her arms around Finder's neck, she hugged him close, wrapping her fingers into his silken mane and trying not to cry. "Travel safe, travel well," she whispered to the big unicorn. "May those who have gone before be always with you."

"And with you, little wanderer."

Cara turned to Belle. She did not hug the fierce unicorn, but after speaking the ritual farewell, added respectfully — and truthfully — "I am sorry we are parting."

"As am I," said Belle. "But we do as we must." Then she nudged Finder and the two of them turned and moved into the gathering darkness.

"I don't like them going off on their own," muttered Lightfoot.

"You mean you don't like Belle going off with another guy," sniffed Cara, wiping at a stray tear.

"Oh, hush! We have real problems to worry about."

Cara didn't say anything more. But she took Lightfoot's irritation to mean that her suspicions about his feelings for Belle were correct. She leaned against him, and they watched until Belle and Finder had vanished from sight.

When they finally reentered the house, M'Gama said, "I will need your help for yet one more farewell, Cara." When Cara looked at her in puzzlement, the Geomancer said, "We must prepare Flensa's body for its final resting place."

Cara gulped and tried not to show the horror she felt.

"I can help," offered Grimwold.

M'Gama shook her head and said firmly, "This is women's work, Chronicle Keeper." Then she motioned to Cara. Feeling both proud and a little frightened to be considered ready for "women's work," Cara followed the Geomancer up the stairs to the room where Flensa's body lay.

"First we must right the bed," said M'Gama.

This was easily enough done. The next task was harder; it was to lift the corpse onto the bed. Cara hesitated, fearful of touching the cold, dead flesh. But as M'Gama showed no qualms, Cara felt that she must not either. Trying to suppress her shudder, she grasped the dwarf's ankles.

"It is nothing," said M'Gama dismissively, reading the look on Cara's face. "Flensa is gone. This is merely the shell that held her. It served her well, and she loved living in it. But now — it is nothing. Lift!"

The corpse was heavier than Cara expected.

Once they had placed Flensa on the torn mattress, M'Gama sent Cara to fetch a basin of water. Using strips of fabric torn from the already damaged sheets, they washed the dwarf's many wounds.

When the cleaning of the body was finished, M'Gama said, "I will be back in a moment."

Left alone with the small corpse, Cara decided she should try to honor Flensa by remembering good things about her. What came first to her mind was the time Flensa had led her to the bathing pool in the caves beneath M'Gama's home and watched as M'Gama combed out the tangles that had snarled her long red hair.

The memory brought fresh tears to her eyes.

Afraid, yet somehow feeling it was the right thing to do, she placed her hand on the dwarf's cold brow and whispered, "I am sorry you are gone." She knew Flensa could not hear her. Even so, she felt better for having said it.

M'Gama returned shortly after, carrying a clean cloak. Cara helped her ease Flensa's body into it, silently thankful that the wounded flesh would now be covered. They lifted the cloak-wrapped body and carried it to the first level of the house, where they paused so that Grimwold and Lightfoot could bow their heads in respectful farewell.

Grimwold opened a door for them, and they started underground, descending, first by stair, then by tunnel, their path lit by the cool, steady light of the glowing bowls.

Deeper they went, and deeper, until Cara's arms grew so weary she feared she would have to beg for rest. She forced herself to go on without complaining, but was relieved when M'Gama finally turned through an opening on their right and said, "I will take the body now." The Geomancer pulled Flensa to her, cradling the body as if it were that of a child. "Go back out into the tunnel and fetch me one of the lights."

When Cara returned with the bowl she saw by its green

glow that the cave they had entered was long and narrow, and had deep niches carved into both walls. M'Gama placed Flensa's body in one of these niches, then arranged the cloak with tender care. When she was satisfied, she passed her hands over the body from head to toe, chanting softly as she did.

Cara cried out in astonishment as Flensa's skin turned a cool gray. The dwarf's lifeless features coarsened. Cracks split the skin. Unable to resist, Cara put out a hand to touch Flensa's face.

Stone. Unmistakably stone.

M'Gama placed a gentle hand on Cara's shoulder. "Come. Flensa has returned to that from which she came. So must we now return to the others, and the life above. Come."

Despite her words, the Geomancer paused as they were leaving the cave, and stared back into it for a long time.

CHAPTER
XX

INTO THE MOUNTAINS

Not ten hours after he met Fallon, Ian Hunter found himself staring out the window of a small plane, watching the first ramparts of the Himalayas pass below them.

"We'll be crossing into Nepal soon," said Fallon, who was piloting the plane with an ease that Ian envied.

Rajiv was in the seat behind him, gazing down with wide eyes. The boy had vomited twice since they had taken to the air, and the foul odor of his sickness filled the plane's tiny cockpit. Glancing over his shoulder, Ian noted that Rajiv still looked queasy. Yet despite his nausea, the boy could not tear his eyes from the world below.

Ian understood. The peaks they were passing over — merely the beginnings of the great range, but already higher than much of what were considered mountains in other parts of the world — were starkly beautiful. It must have been stunning for Rajiv, who had never before been in a plane, to look down at the verdant, rumpled earth.

"Is it much farther?" asked the boy with a moan. Then he moaned again, more loudly, to make sure he could be heard above the drone of the engines, which were so loud that they made shouting the only possible way to converse.

Ian was glad the boy had asked the question, as he had been wondering the same thing himself. Though he was well used to air travel, Fallon's small plane — buffeted by unpredictable updrafts and flows of mountain wind, and filled with the smell of Rajiv's vomit — was more nausea-inducing than a small raft on a stormy sea.

Fallon, who was staring through the window with an intent look on his sculpted face, simply laughed and said, "We will be there in good time, Rajiv. Don't forget, you asked to come!"

"That was before I knew we would be traveling in a machine invented by devils!"

"I'd prefer we not speak of devils," Fallon said, turning to scowl at the boy.

"Bad experience with them?" asked Ian, trying his hand at a joke — something he had nearly lost the knack of during his years with Beloved.

Fallon's nut-brown hands tightened on the steering gear. "To speak of something is to bring it closer to you. Better, then, to speak of good things, such as luck, or success."

"Or the Ruby Portal," said Ian.

"Or the Ruby Portal," agreed Fallon with a nod. "Ah! There's the spot we're looking for!"

He banked the plane to the right, so that Ian and Rajiv could see what he meant. The boy groaned at the motion.

Less than a thousand feet beneath them — to avoid radar, they had been flying very low — lay a small village. At one end was something that might have been taken for a landing strip, if you happened to be extremely optimistic.

Fallon, clearly an optimist, smiled and headed for it.

The landing was smoother than Ian would have hoped for, given the ride so far. Nevertheless, when they climbed out of the plane, Rajiv flung himself to the ground and kissed it fervently.

"I promised the gods I would do that if I lived through this," he explained when he was standing again.

"You stink," was all Fallon said. "We'll have to find a way to clean you up."

They tethered the plane as well as was possible, though Ian couldn't help but wonder if they would ever come this way again.

By the time they were done securing the aircraft, a small crowd of villagers had gathered, watching them curiously.

Fallon had explained that the reason there was a landing

strip here was that the village provided a launching place for a small number of hardy trekkers and mountain climbers who preferred routes rarely traveled. Which meant that the village actually had a place where they could spend the night and get some provisions.

With luck, thought Ian, *we might even be able to get the smell of airsickness off Rajiv.*

The next morning, refreshed and somewhat less odorous, the trio found themselves jouncing along something that was no more than a hint of a road, in a battered jeep driven by a smiling villager who was convinced Fallon was an American basketball player. "What team you play for?" he kept asking, in an accent so thick it had taken three times before Ian understood what he was saying.

The villager deposited them at the head of a steep trail, insisted one more time that Fallon send him an autographed photo of his team, then drove away, singing "Stairway to Paradise" at the top of his lungs.

Looking at the trail rising above them and the mountains that soared beyond, Rajiv said, "I knew many crazy people back in Delhi. I think you two may be crazier than any of them."

"If we were truly crazy, we wouldn't have taken the time to buy you boots and warm clothing," said Fallon jovially.

Then he shouldered his pack, which was laden with food and supplies, and started climbing.

Ian followed close behind.

"Doing something sensible every now and then doesn't mean a person isn't still crazy," muttered Rajiv, looking down at the clothes they had purchased for him before leaving Delhi. Then he started after the two men.

The trek was arduous, but all three of them were in good shape. Still below the treeline, they passed through forests of bamboo, groves of rhododendron, stretches of hemlock. Birds called around them, and in the distance they saw the occasional goat and, once, a large black bear.

The snowcapped peaks towering in the distance brought an early sunset. It grew cooler then — not freezing, for spring was advancing and they were not that high in the mountains — but decidedly chill.

They found a broad space to pitch their tent, ate some food from cans, then talked softly as stars began to appear in the deepening black of the sky.

After a while Rajiv glanced up, then leaped to his feet, crying, "Where did they come from?"

Ian looked at the boy in puzzlement. "Where did what come from?"

"The stars! *The stars!* Sahibs, there are so many of them!"

Fallon laughed. "They were always there, Rajiv. It's just that the lights of the city make it impossible to see them."

Rajiv spread his arms, then turned in a circle, staring up in wonder. Gazing up himself, Ian couldn't blame the boy for his excitement. The Himalayan night was unlike anything any city-dweller had ever seen.

Later that night, after Rajiv was asleep, Ian took the key to the Ruby Portal from his pack. It was an enormous scarlet gem his daughter had given him, perfectly cut and the size of a duck egg. He stared into it, as he had so many times before, hoping, longing, for a glimpse of his wife, for even a hint of the kind of connection that Cara had told him she once made through the gem. But though he sat gazing intently into the stone for more than an hour, nothing happened.

With a sigh, Ian slipped the jewel into his pocket, then crawled into the tent. Rajiv and Fallon were already in their bags, Rajiv making a small high snore, Fallon lost in soundless slumber.

Ian wasn't sure how long he had been asleep when he was woken by warm breath against his ear. "Sahib," whispered Rajiv. "We are not alone. Someone is outside the tent!"

Ian listened carefully. At first he could hear nothing but silence. Then he caught it — the faint sound of someone breathing. Not from inside the tent, but from the other side of the nylon wall.

As Ian was trying to decide what to do he felt a touch on his shoulder. It was Fallon — something he realized just in time to keep himself from crying out in alarm.

"I heard," whispered the big man, his mouth as close to Ian's ear as Rajiv's had been on the other side.

The three waited in the darkness, listening intently. Questions surged through Ian's mind. Was there only one man out there, or more? Was it a man at all? Tales of the yeti, the "Abominable Snowman" of the Himalayas, flashed through Ian's memory. Though the idea was usually dismissed as nonsense, by now Ian had seen enough of the world to know how much he didn't know, and so considered even that a possibility.

With its walls sealed to the floor, the tent was an enclosed world, making Ian feel as if they were trapped in a nylon balloon. Then he heard the slightest rustle. Their stalker was trying to cut his way in. The silver glint of a blade appeared near the peak. To Ian's surprise, once it had opened a slit, it withdrew.

What was going on?

He understood an instant later when a twisting shape appeared at the opening.

With a lurch of fear, Ian realized whoever was outside the tent wasn't trying to cut his way in. All he had wanted was that small opening.

Just large enough to drop in a snake.

CHAPTER
XXI

ATTACK

When Cara and M'Gama returned to the main room, they found Grimwold sitting with a board across his lap, writing. Glancing up, the old dwarf said, "I have been preparing a chronicle of what happened here."

Cara wondered if M'Gama would be vexed that he was writing, rather than working to straighten up the mess the delvers had left. But the Geomancer simply nodded and said, "Good. Flensa will be remembered — as will the treachery of the delvers." Turning to Cara, she said, "I am going to get a map that will be of use to you. I'll be back in a moment. See if you can set up a place where I can spread it out for you."

She strode out of the room, leaving Cara to figure out how to come up with a suitable surface.

"I'd be glad to help," said Lightfoot, who was standing

nearby. "Except . . . well, this is the kind of thing that calls for, you know . . . *hands.*"

For the first time Cara wondered if her friend actually envied her for having hands. She decided not to ask.

In the end, she was able to use two chairs and some broken shelf boards to create a makeshift table. She was absurdly pleased when M'Gama reentered the room, glanced at what she had come up with, and said, "Good work."

The Geomancer was holding a large sheet of cream-colored parchment. Unrolling it on the surface Cara had created, she said, "This is the best map of Luster that I have."

The world it showed was roughly diamond-shaped, its borders irregular and, in some cases, blurry. She remembered Finder saying something about "unfinished places" when they had last been at M'Gama's, and how quickly he had tried to change the subject when she asked him to explain what he meant.

"Is Luster a continent?" she asked M'Gama now. "Is that a sea surrounding it? Are there other continents?"

M'Gama shrugged. "We are indeed bordered on all sides by water. Whether any lands lie beyond those waters, I cannot say. What you see here is what I know."

Cara spotted a key in the bottom left corner of the map. Studying it, then looking at the map again, she came to the conclusion that Luster stretched about five hundred miles from top to bottom, and about the same from east to west.

She leaned closer. In the center of the northern portion she found a marking for Summerhaven, where she had first met the old queen, Arabella Skydancer. About three hundred miles due south of Summerhaven lay Winterkeep. In the eastern portion of the continent she spotted Springdale. Following the logic of it, she traced a line directly to the west. It didn't take her long to find Autumngrove. She smiled. The four gathering spots formed a diamond within the greater diamond of Luster.

As Cara continued to study the map, she located markings for the seven dragon territories, including those of Firethroat, where she had been given the gift of tongues, and Ebillan, where she had journeyed to make the crossing back to her grandmother's house on Earth. Then, on the northeast coast, halfway between Springdale and Summerhaven, she found a place labeled "Valley of the Centaurs." She put her finger on the spot. M'Gama nodded and said, "Yes, that is your destination. The journey from here should take about three days. Grimwold, why don't you copy as much of this as you need, and make notes on some of the landmarks that will help you."

"What's this?" asked Cara, pointing to a spot at the exact center of the map. "'Axis Mundi.' What does that mean?"

"Literally, it would be 'Axis of the World.' Some call such a place the 'Omphalos,' which means 'Navel of the World' but I prefer Axis Mundi, as you see here. It is not merely the center of Luster, it is also its heart."

"Your friend the Dimblethum lives quite close to it," said Grimwold. Scowling, he added, "The main entrance to the delver world is also nearby."

"Light attracts dark," said M'Gama, her own voice taking on a darker tone. She closed her eyes, as if shaking away the thought, then said reverently, "At the center of the center stands the biggest tree in the world."

"How big?" asked Cara eagerly.

"Its trunk would fill this room. I doubt that twenty men linking hands could make a circle around it."

"And how tall?"

"It touches the sky. It is both sacred, and awesome." M'Gama shook her head, as if coming out of a trance. "Now, come along; we need to get you on the road while there is still daylight."

Two hours later, her pack now containing some new clothes from M'Gama's stock, as well as a considerable amount of cheese, dried fruit, and waybread, Cara stood with Grimwold and Lightfoot at the Geomancer's front door.

"If you succeed in learning the story, come straight back

here," said M'Gama, adjusting Cara's cloak. "We have only sixteen days until the Blood Moon. If you come here, we can use the scrying pool to let the Queen know what you have found; it will save several days."

After that the farewells were brief — all of them knew there was nothing to be gained by lingering — but heartfelt. M'Gama slipped a bit of biscuit to the Squijum, then turned and disappeared back into her home. With sun at their backs, the little group started across the rocky ground.

Two hours of walking led them back into the forest, where Cara really preferred to be. Though it was cool in those shady blue depths, she was wearing a new cloak and vest M'Gama had given her; both garments were lined with something fleecy, and she was feeling quite prepared for a trek through the autumn wild.

Grimwold stopped a few times to consult his notes and look for landmarks, but at no time did he seem to be actually worried about finding the way.

The first of the fallen leaves, their blue turned mostly to silver, rustled gently about their feet. The air was crisp and sweet. Yet despite the beauty of the forest and her happiness at being with Lightfoot and Grimwold, Cara found she could take no pleasure in the journey. She was burdened with sorrow over the death of Flensa, heavy with worry over the friends who had left on a perilous mission of their own, and ever mindful that other delvers might still be on the prowl. As if to confirm her concerns, she noticed that even the Squijum seemed subdued.

Occasionally Grimwold would tell a story as they walked, which did help to take Cara's mind off their current cares and dangers.

"How many stories do you know, anyway?" she asked, late in the afternoon of their second day.

"How many trees are there in Luster?" said Lightfoot with a laugh.

"Tut," said Grimwold. "That is a gross exaggeration, Lightfoot. It would be several hundred, at most, though in truth, I've never bothered to count. The thing is, I spend my days with stories — except when I get caught up in one of them, as seems to have happened now. I assure you, Cara, this is *not* my preferred way of doing things. I would much rather be recording someone else's adventures than having one of my own!"

That night they made camp in the shelter of an overhanging rockface. They had pushed extra hard during the day, trying to make up some lost time, and Cara was exhausted from the journey. Feeling safe knowing that Lightfoot was on watch, she fell quickly into a deep sleep, and a series of dreams about her father and mother.

She was jarred from those dreams by a bugled cry of

warning. Heart jolting with fear, she grabbed her sword and sprang to her feet, all grogginess erased by the sense of immediate danger. It was the dark of the moon, so there was no light save that which came from the stars and the faded glow of their campfire. So she could not see, at first, the cove of delvers that came pouring out of the woods. She heard them, though, as they announced their attack with a savage burst of screaming. Standing with her back to the rock wall, sword at the ready, Cara saw Lightfoot — his silver coat glowing in the dim light of the dying campfire — rear and slash about him. His shining hoofs moved so fast they were nothing but a blur.

As her eyes adjusted to the darkness, she saw the Squijum leap onto a delver's back and sink his teeth into the creature's neck. Grimwold had drawn his sword and was wielding it with surprising vigor.

Cara had no time to see more than that, for the delvers were upon her. She slashed about her with her own sword, grateful again for Thomas's lessons. The delvers leaped back, nimbly staying just out of her reach. There were too many of them! Suddenly the creatures began to chant, repeating over and over the same words she had heard the last time they were attacked by delvers: "Get her! Get her! Get her!"

The cry sent cold fear sluicing through her. She was their target. The other delvers, the ones not after her, were simply trying to keep her friends from protecting her. In her terror she thought, briefly, of using the amulet to escape to Earth. But she didn't dare draw attention to it; if she put her hand to it they might snatch it from her before she could use it.

On the other hand, what difference did it make now that Beloved already had one of the amulets? Would having two of them allow her to open her gate more quickly? Or did the delvers want it for some other reason altogether?

Cara's mind raced as she tried to think this through and at the same time battle her attackers.

The delvers surrounding her had no such problem: They were single-minded in their desire to get her. And there were too many for her to fight. Even as she drove back three of the wiry little monsters, two more leaped on her from behind, knocking her to the ground. The impact drove the breath from her lungs. At the same time her sword was snatched from her grasp. Then she herself was lifted by several sets of delver hands.

Terror clawing her heart she screamed, "Lightfoot! *Lightfoot, help me!*"

His bugled response gave her courage, and she writhed in a wild attempt to see him. But she could not break the hold of her captors, who turned and ran with her into the dark and obscuring forest.

Twisting her head, Cara caught one last glimpse of her friends. They were still fighting. Grimwold, his back to a tree, was slashing out with his sword. The Squijum leaped from one delver to another, biting and screeching. Lightfoot bucked and reared in an attempt to shake off the delvers clinging to his legs.

"Lightfoot!" she screamed, one last, desperate time.

He reared, trumpeting wildly, then plunged in her direction.

More delvers grabbed his legs, tangling him, twisting him.

Cara cried out in horror as she saw him crash to the ground.

"Lightfoot! *Lightfoot!*"

"Cara!" he bellowed again, as he struggled to rise.

Then he was lost to her sight, as her captors carried her into the darkness.

CHAPTER
XXII

HUNTERS

Ian's heart raced as he felt the snake crawl up his sleeping bag. It was fairly small. It was also almost certainly poisonous. His muscles were tense, rigid. But he dared not move, for fear of tempting the snake to strike.

He wondered why the thing wasn't sluggish from the cold, then realized the assassin had probably carried it close enough to his skin to keep it warm. Dropped into the tent, it would quickly seek the warmth of another living body.

Normally, of course, a snake would not care where the warmth came from; it might as easily have gone for Rajiv or Fallon. But this would not be a normal snake. Coming from Beloved — he was certain that must be the case — it would have been ensorcelled to focus on him and him alone.

It was on his chest now.

Ian felt a desperate urge to thrust up with his hands and send the snake flying. But it might land on Rajiv or Fallon. Frightened, it would strike instantly.

The thing hissed. Before Ian could move he felt something brush against him. With a start he realized Fallon had plucked the snake from his sleeping bag. He heard an unpleasant squishing sound in the darkness, then the dull smack of lifeless flesh being flung against the side of the tent.

After that, things happened very fast. Fallon was on his knees, rending open the tent where the knife had slit it. Cries of surprise from outside, then Fallon through the opening, Ian hard at his heels, Rajiv close behind both of them.

In the dim starlight they could see five men. Ian assumed that three of them were the same ones who had attacked him in Delhi, though this time the stalkers were at least as surprised as he was. He braced himself for their attack. To his surprise — especially given their numerical advantage — rather than attack, one of the men stepped forward and said, "It is only you we are after, Ian. Surrender, and we will let your companions go in peace."

Though it was too dark to see the man's face, Ian recognized the voice. It was Kieran, one of the group who had trained him when he first joined the Hunters. He was still considering his response when Fallon stepped forward and said, "We have chosen to travel together. One does not lightly surrender a companion."

"Then one may die," replied Kieran matter-of-factly.

Fallon shrugged his massive shoulders. "Indeed, one may. Then again, one may not. I can think of worse things than death. Betraying a friend would be one of them."

"Betrayal is exactly the crime of the man beside you!" snapped Kieran.

"He has not betrayed *me*. Now, I think it would be better for all concerned if you were to turn away and leave us in peace."

Ian expected Kieran to laugh at this request, but the man actually seemed to be considering it. After a long moment, he shook his head and said, almost regretfully, "Alas, that is not possible. To do so would mean we had betrayed our own mission."

"I understand," said Fallon sadly. Then he launched himself at Kieran, striking a single blow that sent the man crumpling to the ground.

With cries of outrage, the other four attacked. Two flung themselves at Fallon, who actually laughed as he swooped one of them into his arms and swung him about, causing his feet to strike the other in the head. That was all Ian saw before he found himself grappling with his own opponent. The man was strong and wiry, and soon they were rolling on the ground. Ian had just managed to get on top, and had his fist raised for a blow to his opponent's jaw, when a voice bellowed, "I've got the boy!"

Ian's heart sank. Even as he had been fighting, he had been worried about Rajiv. Now a quick glance told him all he needed to know. The remaining Hunter, one arm wrapped around Rajiv's throat, barked, "Give up now, both of you, or I'll break the boy's neck."

Ian would have surrendered at once. But before he could utter a word, Rajiv turned into a flurry of action. He began by bending back his captor's little finger. The man didn't let go, but loosened his grip just enough for Rajiv to pull his head in, slide down, and sink his teeth into the tender spot at the base of the thumbnail. Howling, the man pulled his hand away — which gave Rajiv the freedom to duck down and thrust back with his elbow. It struck hard against his captor's groin.

The Hunter gasped and staggered back, then collapsed in pain.

Rajiv dove into the tent, reappearing an instant later with a knife in his hand.

He didn't have time to use it. Ian landed a fierce, open-handed upthrust on his opponent's chin that instantly knocked him unconscious. Without hesitating, he launched himself from the fallen man and onto the one who had been holding Rajiv. The man, just struggling to his feet, fell back beneath Ian's attack. In an instant Ian had the man's arm twisted behind his back, pulled up tight, so he couldn't move.

Ian glanced toward Fallon in time to see him fling away one of his attackers. The man landed with a thud and lay still. The other was already crumpled at the big man's feet.

Quickly Fallon crossed to where Ian held the single assailant who was still conscious. Taking the captive's head in both hands — hands so big they made it seem like the head of a child — Fallon stared directly into his eyes and said, "Who sent you?"

The man struggled wildly, trying to break free. Ian half expected him to spit in Fallon's face. But as it became clear that he could not break Fallon's grip, he abruptly ceased his efforts.

"Who sent you?" asked Fallon again.

"Grandmother Beloved."

"What does she want?"

"We were to capture Ian."

"You mean kill, don't you?" snapped Fallon.

The man shook his head. "The snake would not have killed him. Its venom would only have made him *seem* dead. We would have taken his body to her to be revived. She wants to deal with him herself. She does not take betrayal lightly."

Fallon scowled. "How could you know the serpent would bite Ian and not the boy or myself?"

"The snake was imprinted to Ian's scent. It had been prepared and trained to attack him and him alone."

"You can't train a snake that way."

"Beloved can," said the man with calm assurance. "It would not have come near you or the boy."

Fallon glanced over his shoulder to make sure the other men were still down. Following his gaze, Ian saw Rajiv standing nearby, still holding a knife. Fallon noticed the boy, too, and said quietly, "Rajiv, please fetch the drawstring from my sleeping bag."

Rajiv grinned. "Right away, sahib!" He slid into the wreckage of the tent and reappeared a moment later, cord in hand. Fallon took the cord and passed it to Ian, who used it to bind the man's hands behind his back.

"Why does Grandmother Beloved want me back so badly?" he asked, as he pulled the knots tight. When the man did not answer, he wrenched the cord tighter, causing it to bite into the man's flesh.

"She desires to give you a chance to redeem yourself by telling her what you know about the unicorns." The man's voice held a note of acid he had not used when addressing Fallon; he clearly considered Ian a traitor beneath his contempt.

Fallon sighed. "Put him on the ground, Ian. Face down. Keep holding him."

When the captive resisted, Ian thrust a foot into the back of his knees. They buckled, and Ian quickly bore him to the ground. At once, Fallon sat on the back of the man's thighs, facing his feet. Grabbing his legs just below the knees, he pulled them toward him and snapped, "Rajiv! Undo his boots!"

With deft fingers, the boy unlaced the man's boots. At a nod from Fallon he pulled them off.

"Hand me one of the laces."

Rajiv removed the lace from one of the boots and handed it to Fallon, who wrapped it around their captive's ankles, binding them tightly. Standing up, he said, "All right, let's do the others."

Moving quickly, the trio took off each man's boots, then used the laces to bind them, hands and feet.

The Hunters were beginning to rouse from the blows that had felled them. One, realizing what their quarry had done, said, "You can't leave us here like this!"

"Shut up!" snapped Kieran.

Fallon began patting down the last man he had bound, searching for hidden weapons. Removing a blade that had been strapped to the underside of the man's right arm, he said, "Ian, Rajiv, check the others."

Ian found himself torn between gratitude to Fallon for saving him from the Hunters, and resentment for the way the big man had taken charge of things and was ordering them around. Nonetheless, he did as Fallon requested, relieving the man at his feet of a long blade strapped to his leg.

"I do not understand," said Rajiv, who had found a similar weapon. "Why did they not use these on us?"

"They were not expecting resistance," said Fallon.

"We are not killers," said Kieran, at the same time.

"Except when it comes to unicorns," replied Ian.

Kieran ignored him.

"Fortunately for you, we are not killers, either," said Fallon. "You will be able to free yourselves soon enough — as I am sure you well know. I would prefer that you not follow us. We could take your boots to pretty much make certain of that but, alas, it is unlikely you would make it back to the village without them. Still, I am not willing to count on your goodwill in this regard. Rajiv, gather their boots."

The boy did as Fallon directed, bringing the boots and dropping them in front of the big man.

"A deep ravine runs about a hundred paces to our right," said Fallon, speaking to the Hunters. "Rajiv is going to fling your boots over its edge. You will be able to retrieve them, but it will take you some time."

One of the Hunters cursed. "Quiet!" snapped Kieran.

"Ian, would you keep watch while Rajiv and I dispose of the boots?" asked Fallon.

"Gladly," said Ian, appreciating the fact that Fallon had phrased it as a question, rather than an order.

Dawn was breaking as Ian and Fallon examined the captured Hunters one last time, making sure their bonds were tight — but not, Fallon insisted, so tight they couldn't free themselves with a few hours of struggle.

"Hard to say how long it will actually take them to get loose," said the tall man, once he and his companions had traveled out of earshot of the Hunters. "They may find a sharp rock and have those laces cut in less than an hour. But getting their boots out of that ravine should keep them occupied for a good stretch of time."

"Do you think they will follow us once they are free again?" asked Rajiv.

"Without question," replied Ian. "Hunters in pursuit are not easily turned back. And they have a great deal of stamina — they can track for sixteen hours a day, if need be. How far is the portal, Fallon?"

"We have at least a three-day journey ahead of us." He frowned. "I did not realize your . . . cousins . . . could be so obsessive."

"That's because you haven't met Beloved."

"Who is this Beloved?" asked Rajiv.

Ian hesitated, then said, "She is the head of our family."

"You have an unusual family, sahib."

Ian laughed. "You don't know the half of it, Rajiv."

He expected more questions, but the boy seemed satisfied. And when he glanced sideways at Fallon he saw that the big man was looking straight ahead, as if he had already moved past the conversation.

He's not as curious as most people I've met, thought Ian. And then another thought: *Or maybe it's that if he asks questions about my past, he knows he'll be expected to answer questions about his own.*

Once again, and not for the last time, Ian Hunter found himself wondering just who he had taken up with.

CHAPTER
XXIII

UNDERGROUND

The delvers had to struggle to keep their grip on Cara, for she twisted and squirmed like a captured cat as they carried her into the forest. Their muttered curses merged with the shouts and shrieks of the battle they were leaving behind.

As the sounds of that battle faded, Cara's fear increased. The feel of the delvers' cold hands, the open-grave smell of their fetid breath, filled her with a creeping horror.

Suddenly she stopped fighting and let herself go limp, as if she had fainted. The delvers grunted with satisfaction and, after a time, slowed to a walk. As they tramped along, her body drooping between them, Cara counted slowly to one hundred in her mind. Battling her own panic, forcing herself to stay loose, she made the count again, and yet again.

When she finally thought enough time had gone by, she counted to three and began to thrash insanely.

The delvers were caught unaware. Two lost their grip, so that she had one arm and one leg free. Thrashing harder than ever she screamed for Lightfoot again. At the same time she landed a ferocious kick on a delver who was lunging at her. He howled and rolled away. Wrenching loose from the last hand that held her, she leaped to her feet and began fumbling in her shirt for the amulet, not caring where on Earth it might land her, simply wanting to get away. But before she could grasp it, wiry hands grabbed her from behind, wrenching her arms back and pinning them tight.

Her cry of frustration was cut off as the delvers tumbled her face-first to the ground. One held her feet, two more her arms. A fourth sat down hard on her back, driving the breath out of her. The fifth grabbed her braid and lifted her head. Leaning close to her face he whispered, "Like it or not, you're coming with us. One more trick like that and we will break your legs, then truss you to a pole and carry you. That way we won't have to worry about you trying to run away."

"What's the point in talking to her, Brank?" said the delver on her back. "She can't understand!"

"Oh yes she can, Dworkin. Haven't you heard? She has the gift of tongues from Firethroat. So she knows good and well what I'm saying — don't you, girl?"

Cara nodded, but did not speak aloud. During her struggle, she had been propelled by a mixture of fear and rage.

Now the rage was draining, leaving only the fear in its place — a fear rapidly blossoming into pure terror.

You will not cry, she ordered herself. *You will not cry!*

Brank, the delver who had spoken to her, glanced around then muttered, "All right, we're far enough away from her friends to take the time to do this properly. Dworkin, hand me your rope."

The delver sitting on her back removed a coil of rope from his side and handed it to the speaker, who quickly tied Cara's hands behind her back. Next he ripped a piece of cloth from the bottom of his filthy tunic and stuffed it into her mouth.

"Not a sound," he hissed, his mouth close to her ear. "Not if you want to keep your tongue in your head." He smiled evilly, showing stony teeth. "Would you like that? Do you *want* to keep your tongue?"

Eyes wide, heart pounding, Cara nodded.

"Then come along nice and peaceful and silentlike." They hauled her to her feet, then positioned themselves so that there were two in front of her, one at each side, and one behind her. As they continued into the forest, Dworkin, the delver in back, prodded her with his spear whenever she faltered or slowed.

Terrified as she was, Cara was also wracked with worry over her friends. How had their battle turned out? Had the delvers abandoned the fight once they had her? Or had it

gone on to a fatal conclusion? Though she refused to give
voice to her sorrow, tears streamed down her cheeks at the
memory of her last sight of Lightfoot.

How long they walked, Cara couldn't have said. It was
long enough that she was exhausted when they stopped —
though given the fight and her capture, she had been close
to exhaustion before they even started.

They had descended into a rocky hollow ringed by
tall trees with drooping branches. The hollow itself was
shaped like an irregular cup, about fifty feet across and perhaps twenty feet deep. The delvers scrambled and slid down
the smooth sides, two of them holding Cara so that she
didn't fall.

The bottom of the hollow being too dark even for delver
eyes, one of the creatures took a flint from a pouch at its
side and lit a small fire, something he managed with expert
efficiency. The fact that the tinder and twigs were already in
place told Cara the delvers had been planning on returning
to this spot.

They bound her feet together and pushed her to a kneeling position. Brank pulled the gag from her mouth. "You
can scream now if you want. It won't make any difference."

She refused to give them the pleasure, simply stared at
them in stony silence. The delvers stared back, their huge
eyes luminous in the near-dark. The flickering shadows from
the small fire made their bulging heads and gaping nostrils

look even stranger and more eerie than usual. All wore the same simple clothing: brown boots and hooded, dark green tunics that were belted at the waist. The tunics were stained, and torn from the fight. Each delver also clutched a spear. Cara noticed that their hands seemed too big for their bodies. Their arms and legs, through scrawny, were corded with lean muscle.

Finally Brank said, "King Gnurflax wants the amulet."

The words sent a chill through Cara. Fighting to hide her reaction, she said, "What amulet?"

"Don't play games with us," snarled another of the delvers.

"No, really. I have no idea what you're talking about."

"Just take it, Brank," said a third delver. "You're not afraid of her, are you?"

"Shut yer gob, Gragga! The King forbid me to do exactly that. If this amulet isn't taken properly, it could weaken the magic. Orders are, if she won't cooperate we bring her back to court and let the King's wizard handle her. Old Namza will be more than happy to do it. He likes that sort of stuff." Turning to Cara, he leered evilly and said, "How would you like to take a trip to Delvharken?"

"I don't think —"

"Shut up!" Brank stepped closer. Though she was kneeling, her head came almost to his chin. He extended his right hand and slipped a finger inside her collar.

His skin was cool and dry. Even so, Cara shuddered at his touch.

"Ah," he said, as he caught the edge of the chain from which the amulet was suspended. "Just as I thought." He pulled on the chain, drawing the amulet out of her shirt. "What amulet?" he asked in a mocking, mincing voice. The words sounded doubly weird coming from his hideous face. "*This* amulet, you lying vixen!"

He let the chain slide back under her shirt.

Though Cara forced herself to keep from showing any reaction, her stomach was tight with horror. What did the delver king want with the amulet? The Hunters already had one. She couldn't let another fall into the hands of their enemies.

"Come on, you lot," snarled Brank. "As long as we have her, we should head straight back to the King. The others are probably already on their way."

Quickly they put out the fire, scattering the ashes so thoroughly it was as if it had never been there. Then two of the delvers grabbed her arms and pulled her to her feet. Another undid the rope that bound her at the ankles. A fourth prodded her back with the tip of his spear, propelling her forward.

Unwilling to reward them with any cry of terror or pain, Cara stumbled silently into the darkness. After only a few steps, they came to a mound of soil with a hole in the center, something like a large rabbit's burrow. One of the delvers scooted into it, disappearing quickly and quietly.

A second followed.

"Your turn, girl," growled Brank. "Untie her, Dworkin."

The delver undid the ropes that bound her hands, then prodded her in the back with his spear again. Having her hands free made her itch to use the amulet, but she didn't dare try with Dworkin right behind her. He would probably grab her arms the moment she reached for it. Even worse, such a move might make them decide that the danger of her using the amulet to escape to Earth was worse than the danger of angering the King's wizard by taking it from her themselves.

She had to wait for a better moment.

"Help her move!" snapped Brank.

Dworkin prodded her with his spear again.

Reluctantly, Cara dropped to her knees and crawled into the hole. Made for delvers, it was barely large enough for her to enter, and she had to push and squirm to get in. After three or four feet the tunnel became so narrow she couldn't have pulled her hands back to grab the amulet if she wanted to. Her chest grew tense with the terror of being trapped in this tight, dark place.

"Move it, move it!" growled Dworkin, poking the back of her leg. It was not hard enough to cut her, but enough to make her lurch forward.

Arms stretched straight ahead, Cara dug her fingers into the loose soil and pulled herself along. Dirt caked beneath her fingernails. The ends of roots brushed her face, some cool, moist, and threadlike, others thick as a thumb and digging into her skin. The damp, earthy smell and the complete darkness made her feel as if she were being buried. When something with many legs began to crawl over her arm it was more than Cara could bear. With a scream and a shudder, she pulled herself violently forward.

Suddenly she felt nothing beneath her hands. She was jolted by an instant of fear, but the tunnel held her in its grip, so while her head and arms flopped downward, she did not fall. Stretching out her fingers, she was relieved to find that the drop was only about two feet. With a final lunge, she pulled herself free of the tunnel, landing with a thud on the hard-packed earthen floor.

The delvers that had come in ahead of her were talking to each other. She could hear the delvers that had been behind her scrambling forward. This was her chance! Reaching for the amulet, she rasped in a breath. Not knowing *where* on earth the magic would take her, not caring, wanting only to escape, she whispered, "Earth, take me back!"

She waited eagerly for the gust of magic that would sweep her away from the delvers.

Nothing happened.

CHAPTER
XXIV

ON THE TRAIL

"Those delvers must be in a flaming hurry to get that anchor back to their king," muttered Finder toward the end of their first day on the track. "They're not usually this careless."

"Well, at least it makes it easy to follow them," said Belle.

In truth, so far she had let Finder take the lead in actually tracking their quarry. Not only was he skilled at the task, it left her free to focus her attention on guarding against attack.

It was unclear how much of a start the delvers had on them, and both unicorns knew their enemies could travel for long periods of time without resting. Fortunately, they could do the same, and move faster than delvers while they were at it. Still, even a unicorn cannot go endlessly without rest, and later that night Belle and Finder decided to stop for a while. They drank from a clear stream, nipped the buds from some late blooming *tamtims*, then settled beneath a quilpum tree.

"I'll take the first watch," said Belle, touching her cheek to Finder's so they could speak mind-to-mind. Finder would have been glad to stand the watch himself, but he knew better than to argue with her. He considered for a moment whether to sleep standing up or lying down. If he remained standing he could move into action more quickly, but lying down would provide a deeper rest. Deciding that with Belle on watch he would have plenty of warning if there was trouble, he settled gracefully onto his side.

While Finder prepared to rest, Belle stared into the darkness, listening for any sound of danger. It seemed unlikely the delvers would come back this way. Even so, she was willing to take no chances.

Against her wishes, she found her mind straying to the others. Had they left M'Gama's yet? If so, how far had they traveled?

Her thoughts were interrupted by Finder softly calling her name.

"You're supposed to be sleeping!" she replied, her voice fierce even though she was whispering. "I want you alert when it's your turn to watch!"

"I'll sleep soon. I just wanted to ask you something about Lightfoot."

"What about him?" she snapped, her voice no louder than before, yet somehow even more fierce.

"Do you really dislike him?"

Belle was silent for a time, her mind struggling with an answer. Finally she said, "It makes me angry that he has not been more faithful to his duties."

"But do you dislike him?"

"No," she said at last, her voice even softer than before. "No, I don't dislike him, Finder."

"Ah."

After that, he was silent.

Belle tried to focus her thoughts on the watch again, to think only of what she was listening for. But Finder's question left her wondering, and a little uneasy. Had her companion guessed at her feelings for the Prince? For that matter, what *were* her feelings for Lightfoot? How could she find him so infuriating and so attractive, all at the same time?

She shook her head. *Focus, Belle,* she ordered herself. *There's no point in thinking about Lightfoot now. You have other matters to attend to.*

But when Finder nudged her gently a few hours later and said, "My turn. You rest for a while," she found that her thoughts were still on Lightfoot.

With a sigh, she closed her eyes.

But she did not sleep.

*   *   *

The next morning they came to a shallow river. They crossed it with no trouble, but it took them a while to pick up the trail on the other side.

"They went downstream much farther than necessary for just crossing," said Belle. "I wonder if they know they're being followed."

"Hard to say," replied Finder, his voice tense. "Could be they were simply heading downstream anyway."

"Could be," said Belle. But she didn't sound as if she believed it.

It was evening when they finally caught sight of their quarry.

"I expected there would be more of them," whispered Finder. "Delvers usually travel in larger groups."

"I'd like to think some died along the way," said Belle fiercely. "Only I suppose we would have seen their bodies."

Finder glanced at her and shuddered. They followed the group in silence for a while, staying far enough behind that they were unlikely to be noticed.

"The Queen asked us to pick off any stragglers," said Finder at last. "But they don't straggle. They stick very close together."

"They have better discipline than unicorns," said Belle, with grudging admiration. "We'll follow for a while longer.

If no one lags back, we'll have to attack the next time they rest."

"But there are only two of us!"

"What difference does that make? The point is not to survive. The point is to keep those delvers from getting that anchor back to their king. If we turn back, we fail. If we simply follow them, we fail. If we attack, we *may* fail — but we may succeed. Even if we don't live through it, we may be able to destroy the thing. Unless you have a better idea, I say we attack."

"I have no better idea," said Finder, trying to ignore the way his stomach clenched at the thought of attacking the delvers. He would have found it hard to explain to Belle that it wasn't dying he feared.

It was killing.

As it turned out, Finder didn't need to worry about either dying or killing any time soon, since the delvers continued to travel for several hours without stopping. The night grew cold. Eventually a light frost began to form, coating the blue vegetation with a dusting of silver.

"Don't those delvers *ever* stop to rest?" Finder muttered as the sky began to edge from ebony back toward gray.

"They prefer the dark for travel," Belle reminded him softly. "I suspect they'll stop before full morning comes. I just hope they don't reach one of their burrows first. If they go underground, we'll lose them for good."

Her prediction about morning proved true. When the first of the sun's rays poked through the silver and blue leaves the delvers quickly huddled together, drawing branches and leaves over them to shield themselves from the coming daylight. They did it so artfully that, had the unicorns not been watching, they might well have thought the delver resting place nothing more than a pile of brush and scrub, blown together by insistent winds, or perhaps gathered by some woodland creature.

Moving close enough to Belle that they could touch, Finder asked silently, "What now?"

"We wait, then attack."

Though her words came without hesitation, Finder could sense her uneasiness.

"What's the matter?"

"I don't like the idea of attacking a sleeping group. It seems like something . . . well, like something delvers would do."

Finder was pleased to think that Belle's fierceness had some check on it. Not tenderness of heart, perhaps, but at least some warrior code. Speaking to her directly, he said, "You are fierce, Belle, but I am practical. The thing we seek was stolen. Flensa paid in blood to protect it. All of Luster will pay in blood if we do not regain it. The question is simply this: What is the best way for us to take them on?"

CHAPTER
XXV

WHEN MAGIC FAILS

Cara lay as if stunned, more shaken by the failure of the amulet's magic than by anything that had happened so far.

She had always thought of the amulet as a life preserver, a last-chance escape route that would be there for her no matter what. Now that security had been snatched from her. Why wasn't she back on Earth? Was something wrong with the amulet? Was it possible it didn't work underground? Was some delver counter-magic interfering with it? She felt a sudden, desperate wish that she had asked M'Gama more about how the amulet worked, instead of just assuming it would always take her home.

Struggling to keep from bursting into tears, Cara pushed herself to her knees and tried to regain her breath. She found herself longing for her father, for his strength and protection.

All five delvers were in the cave now. They began to chant, a grating sound that made her cover her ears. After a moment or two of this, a glowing orange stripe appeared on the side of the tunnel. The width of a man's hand, the stripe stretched ahead as far as Cara could see. Meant for the enormous eyes of the delvers, its light was too weak for her to get any detailed sense of the tunnel. But after the pitch blackness that had surrounded her, even this dim bit of illumination was a relief.

Two of the delvers hauled her to her feet. Unfortunately, the tunnel, like the light, was designed for delvers, not humans — which meant it was so low Cara banged her head when she tried to stand.

"Move!" growled Brank. Another delver — Dworkin, she assumed — poked her with his spear.

She started to walk, but was forced to hunch over so far by the low ceiling that she began to wonder if it might be easier to crawl. Except she didn't want to do that in front of the delvers.

Slowly, very slowly, her eyes grew accustomed to the dim light. As they did, she saw that the floor of the tunnel — which was about three feet wide — was smooth and hard packed. The walls, too, were smooth, making the tunnel like a hallway carved through the earth. Cara was surprised; she had not expected such craftsmanship from the savage creatures.

After several minutes, the tunnel came to a T with a much larger tunnel, one that was high enough for Cara to stand easily. The relief she felt at this was lost in her growing fear at how far they were traveling into the delver world.

Like the first tunnel, this one had a glowing orange stripe along one side, this time already lit when they entered. Though it stretched into the distance, they hadn't gone far before her captors turned again. They started on a downward slope. They had gone about a hundred feet when Brank stopped and said, "Blindfold her, Dworkin."

"Why?" asked Cara.

"None of your business, girl!" snapped Dworkin, who was wrapping a piece of dirty cloth around her eyes.

When he had the cloth secure, they began moving again, though their progress was necessarily slower now. She wasn't sure how long they continued before Brank ordered another stop. A moment later she heard him begin to chant something, but despite her gift of tongues, the words were too low for her to make out. A moment later Dworkin poked her again and said, "Get going!"

She stepped forward, then cried out as a sudden burst of energy skittered over her skin. She felt as if she were stepping through a curtain of rain and electricity. The feeling didn't hurt, exactly, but it was so startling that it made her shout in surprise.

"What was that?" she cried.

"Nothing you need to concern yourself with," growled Brank. Then, almost grudgingly, he said to Dworkin, "You can take off the blindfold now."

Cara looked around. As far as she could see, nothing had changed. They were still in a stone tunnel lit by an orange stripe. Yet she had the definite feeling that something was different.

They began to walk again, following tunnels that continued to split and branch. Twice, a tunnel they were in opened up, so that instead of walking through a kind of tube they were suddenly following a narrow ledge with a solid wall on one side and a yawning abyss on the other. At least, it seemed as if it must be a yawning abyss. In truth, the orange light was so dim Cara could barely see the edge of the path, which in some spots was barely a foot wide. Though she found these places terrifying, the delvers seemed barely to notice them.

Try as she might, Cara could see no markings to distinguish one tunnel from another. Yet her captors never hesitated or seemed uncertain of their route. Sometimes they would enter a chamber from which four or five tunnels led out; even in these places they did not pause.

And every turn they made, every new tunnel they entered, continued downward, taking them deeper into the realm of the delvers.

At first, Cara hoped that by keeping track of the turns she might be able to find her way back to the surface if she could manage to escape. But all too soon she realized she was hopelessly lost, and there was no way she could retrace their route. Simply heading upward would not be enough. There were too many tunnels.

As her fear and despair grew, fresh tears trickled down her cheeks. Still, she refused to cry out loud — refused to let her captors know how badly they had frightened her.

Sometimes the delvers chanted as they walked. Once in a while, they did this to turn on another of the glowing orange stripes. More often, though, the chants were simply marching rhythms, half sung, half growled in their guttural voices:

> *Deeper and deeper*
> *Into the earth*
> *Into our mother*
> *Place of our birth*
> *Dig dig dig dig dig dig DIG!*

Down they went, and farther down, and deeper still, until Cara lost all hope of ever seeing the surface again. Twice they met other delvers — first a lone traveler, who sneered with delight when they told him who they had captured; then a small group, who were carrying tools and were on their way to make a new tunnel.

At last they came to a cave where, much to Cara's relief, Brank called a halt.

"Drink, if you want," he said, pointing to a pool of dark water.

Cara knelt and lifted a handful to her lips. It was bitter and tasted strongly of minerals, but her thirst was such that she forced it down anyway.

Longing for Lightfoot to come and rescue her, she huddled into herself and stared at her captors with sullen eyes.

"You'll rest now, if you're smart," growled Brank.

She scowled at him, but let her exhaustion convince her she should indeed lie down. After that, they paid little attention to her, scarcely bothering to guard her.

Why should they? she thought wearily. *If I tried to run, they would catch me before I got very far. Even if I did get away, where would I go? I'd probably end up lost in these tunnels forever!*

With slow horror, she realized that being lost in the tunnels might be better than being taken to the delver king. It would definitely be better than having him use the amulet to open a door that would let the Hunters enter Luster.

Could the amulet still open a door? Or had the magic left it altogether for some reason?

A coldness gripped her as she realized she couldn't take that chance. If there was the slightest possibility the delvers could use the amulet, then she *should* run off — even if it meant wandering endlessly in the dark.

CHAPTER
XXVI

WOUNDED HEARTS

Belle and Finder waited for the delvers they had been tracking to settle more deeply into sleep. Moving so that her
shoulder was touching Finder's, Belle thought to him, "As I
see it, we have two problems."

"And they are?" asked Finder silently.

"Problem one: Is there a delver acting as a guard? I don't
see one, but that doesn't mean they don't have one."

Finder pondered this, then replied, "They have no reason to think they're being followed. And they're well hidden.
So I suspect they're doing without a guard. What's the second problem?"

"Which delver has the anchor? We won't gain anything by attacking if one of them manages to escape with
the dratted thing. But I don't see any other alternative."
She paused to think for a moment, then added, "All right,
here's what we'll do. If one of them breaks from the group,

I want you to go after him. He'll be the one with the anchor."

"I can't leave you to fight the rest of them, Belle!"

"Our job — our *only* job — is to get that anchor from the delvers and destroy it. What happens to you or me doesn't make much difference, Finder — won't make any difference at all, if those monsters manage to get that thing back to their king."

"All right. But let's do it the other way around. If one of them bolts, you go after him."

"Don't be foolish. I'm the one who's trained to fight. You're the one who finds things. Let's just each do what we do best."

Finder sighed. "I suppose you're right."

"Of course I'm right! Now, we'll wait a while longer, to make sure they're really asleep. Then we attack. The idea is to knock them senseless, not kill them — though we'll do that if we have to. They may think we're attacking on general principles, but if they even suspect we're after the anchor, they'll take moves to protect it. Watch for that. Even if none of them bolt, we may get a clue as to which one of the little beasts is carrying it. You go in from that side, around that small tree. I'll take them from this side."

Finder nudged her with his shoulder. "Why, Belle. That's the longest speech I ever heard you make."

"This is no time for foolery!" she snapped.

He cringed back, then leaned against her again, trying to pretend the words hadn't stung. She gestured with her horn to a nearby shadow. Using a method of marking time that was common among unicorns, she said, "When that shadow has moved far enough to touch that big root, we attack."

Finder nodded but said nothing more. Despite his earlier attempt to sound lighthearted, he was terrified that he would not be able to do his part in the battle. Fighting did not come naturally to him, and it felt even less natural to attack a sleeping foe.

Unicorns do not usually worry about time, and are content to let it pass as it will. But now, for Finder, the moments dragged like hours. He tried not to watch the shadow, to instead quietly muster his strength and resolve. But his eyes kept creeping back to the marker they had chosen.

Why didn't it move?

Around them, the day was growing brighter. Autumn sunlight, filtering through the silver and blue leaves, dappled on Belle's hide, masking her fierceness, making her more beautiful than ever. Bird song, high and melodic, sounded from a tree just to the left. He could sense small creatures scuttling through the branches above him.

And still the shadow seemed stuck in place.

Will it ever touch that root? he wondered. And then, knowing the answer, knowing that the moment would indeed come, he asked himself the harder question. *What will I do when it does? Can I play my part with honor?*

Suddenly he felt her shoulder touch his, and in his mind heard, "It's almost time."

He glanced at the shadow; it was nearly touching the root.

"When the moment comes," continued Belle, "we move as quietly as we can to each side of their hideaway. Watch me. When I nod, we race forward. At the edge of that tangle of brush where they're sleeping, we bugle our attack. We need to wake them fast, scare them into mindless action."

"Good luck, Belle."

"I don't believe in luck. I believe in being ready and fighting fiercely. This is about blood, Finder. Ours, or theirs. I know you don't like to fight, but a small skirmish now may save a big war later. You can't be timid here. It's all right to be afraid —"

"Are *you* afraid?"

"Of course I'm afraid! Only a fool feels no fear before a battle. It's all right to be afraid. What's *not* all right is holding back. Lives depend on what we do now — not just our lives, the lives of all the others."

"I understand."

And he did, though his understanding only made the fear worse.

And then the tip of the shadow touched the branch.

"Now!" she thought, the word moving straight from her mind to his.

On silver hooves that struck the ground with less sound than the whisper of a spring breeze, the two unicorns separated, then took their positions on either side of the delver hideaway.

Belle raised her head, caught Finder's eye. When he nodded to indicate he was ready, she bugled her challenge. Finder joined her, their voices loosing a defiant cry of anger that carried with it the memory of Flensa's death.

The delvers erupted from their nest, confused and instantly light-dazzled. Even so, each of them was clutching a spear. Belle and Finder's punishing hooves — flashing in the morning sunlight — rained down silvery blows, causing the delvers to shriek with pain and anger. They jabbed and jabbed with their spears, blinded by the sun, but so close to the unicorns that they could not miss. Time after time the lacerating points dug into Belle and Finder's chests. Silver and crimson blood spurted from a dozen wounds.

Then came the moment Belle had been waiting for. One of the delvers bolted from the pack and ran into the forest.

"Catch him!" she cried. *"Finder, catch him!"*

He turned and started toward the fleeing delver. The big unicorn was swift and strong, but before he had made his first leap, two of the delvers grabbed his legs. He tried to shake them off, but they clung like leeches, slowing him, making him stumble.

Trumpeting in rage, Belle started toward him. Two more of the creatures leaped forward and grabbed her, one latching onto her left front leg, the other to her back right. Their goal was clear; it was no longer to fight the unicorns, but simply to slow them enough so their comrade could escape.

Belle reared back, pawing the air. The delver clinging to her front leg swung wildly but managed to hang on. She came down hard, catching the delver's leg beneath her foot, and heard a satisfying *crack!* as one of his bones broke. He howled in pain and fell away. At the same instant she bucked, flinging her hindquarters up so that the delver who had been clutching her back leg went flying. She didn't stop to see what had happened to him, but bolted toward Finder.

It was too late. One of the delvers had thrust his spear straight into Finder's chest. The great unicorn was lying on his side, gasping for breath.

To Belle's surprise, the delvers had withdrawn, forming a half circle around him. One of them stood, staring at his hands, which were empty.

The other delvers backed farther away.

Belle knew she should try to chase the delver who had fled, the one who had the anchor. But he was well out of sight, and could have gone in any direction.

So instead she knelt by Finder's side.

Silvery-red blood was pulsing along the shaft of the spear. Belle grabbed that shaft with her teeth, close to the point where it entered Finder's flesh. She pulled gently at first, trying to extract it without causing more pain. But the blade was barbed, and would not come out easily. Releasing the wood, she said, "Brace yourself, Finder."

He nodded without speaking.

Belle gripped the spear again. Using the powerful muscles of her neck, she wrenched it free from Finder's massive chest. A spurt of hot blood arced out, striking her leg. Then the bleeding slowed to a mere ooze, pulsing a bit less with each beat of Finder's heart, slowing, slowing, slowing.

He gazed up at her, his golden eye dim, fading. "We failed," he whispered.

"We tried," was all she could answer. "Now hold still, so I can heal you."

"It's too late for healing. You know that, Belle."

She did know, but refused to believe it. She pressed her horn to his chest, expecting to feel a jolt of pain, a flow of energy, knowing it would drain her and leave her so weak and vulnerable that the delvers could kill her as well, and not caring. But she felt nothing — nothing save a cold dread. If the healing magic refused to flow, it could only mean one thing: It was indeed too late, and Finder was going to die.

She looked up, wondering why the delvers hadn't attacked. To her surprise, there were none left, save the empty-handed one, the one whose spear she had pulled from Finder's chest.

She was even more surprised to see that he was weeping.

"Go!" she bellowed. "Go, before I kill you!"

He didn't move. She didn't care. She returned her attention to Finder.

"Belle," he said softly, "I always thought you were beautiful."

"Don't . . ."

"I never said it, because I know that's not where your pride is. And I thought you might love Lightfoot. But now, I have to tell you, tell you before . . ." His voice faltered. "I just wanted to say it once."

"Finder!"

"Don't," he whispered. "Don't say anything. Just stay beside me a little longer."

She did as he asked, leaning her head against his neck, so that they could be close even if she could not heal him.

She stayed that way until the last breath whispered through his silken nostrils. Then she reared back and trumpeted a call of loss and sorrow, a cry she knew would be taken up across Luster as the unicorns felt the death of one of their own.

She knelt again and brushed her muzzle against his silver cheek.

"I wish I had been kinder," she whispered.

Then she stood and walked into the forest.

CHAPTER XXVII

OVER THE EDGE

Cara cried out in pain as a sudden sense of loss, sharp and horrible, stabbed her heart. She knew — without knowing how she knew — that something dreadful had just happened.

What was that? she thought frantically.

But nothing else came to her.

Restless, frightened, overwhelmed with a sorrow that came from something beyond her own captivity, she stared into the darkness, aching for someone to come and take her away from this.

But she was alone, and she knew it.

She steeled herself for what she must do next — then realized that if she did succeed in escaping into the caves, she wouldn't actually wander endlessly. It would be only a matter of days before lack of food did her in. And that was assuming something else, something worse, didn't get her first.

She shuddered at the thought of what terrors might lurk in the dark passages that spread their way through the secret heart of Luster.

Stop it! she told herself firmly. *This isn't the time to try escaping anyway. Not while the delvers are all around me. Later, when they sleep — if they sleep — will be the time to run.*

Then she had another thought. If she didn't know when — or if — she could escape, maybe she should take the amulet off now and just leave it in the dark. That way the delvers couldn't use it to create a gate for the Hunters.

But it would also mean she could never use it to get home.

Cara stumbled on the word. Home. Where was home anyway? Back on Earth, or here in Luster? Was it with her grandmother, or with her mother and father?

She didn't even know where her mother and father were now.

Would she ever see any of them again?

She forced the thoughts away, ordering herself to focus on the problem at hand. Simply leaving the amulet in this cave wasn't good enough; the delvers might still find it. She needed to put it someplace where they could never find it at all.

But to do that, she would have to be ready.

Hunching forward, turning slightly away from the delvers yet keeping her eyes in their direction, Cara hooked her fingers into the chain that held the amulet. At once she realized that the back of it was trapped under her braid.

I should have had M'Gama cut my hair right off, she thought bitterly.

She counted to a hundred, then rolled over once more, this time so that she was facing the delvers. Though she could scarcely see them in the dim light, she knew that she couldn't count on them being equally blind. Snail slow, moving by inches and half inches, sometimes even less, she worked her braid — which now seemed miles long — under the chain. Never once did she take her eyes from the delvers. Several times she stopped completely, snorting or wiping her hand across her face as if something had disturbed her. More than once this was no act; she really was brushing away some many-legged thing that had begun to crawl across her cheek.

When Cara finally had the chain over her head, she rolled onto her other side again, fearing that when she pulled the amulet from her shirt it might be too easily seen by the delvers.

Inch by agonizing inch she drew it out until at last she had the amulet clutched in her hand. *Let's give it one more try,* she thought. Pressing it to her heart, hoping against hope, she whispered, "Earth, take me back."

Nothing.

She sighed. All right, what to do with it now that she had it? The best bet, she decided, would be to drop it into a deep crevice somewhere. They had already passed a few. Maybe they would come to another.

What if she jumped into the crevice herself while she was holding the amulet? Jumped and whispered, "Earth, take me back," as she did. Would the magic work then, as it had that first time when she jumped from the tower of St. Christopher's? Or would she simply dash herself to oblivion on the rocks below? Or maybe — and this thought was truly terrifying — maybe she would just keep falling forever. She wasn't sure Luster was actually a planet like Earth.

For a moment she thought even such an endless fall — though it wouldn't be endless for her, of course, since she would eventually starve to death — might be preferable to being a captive of the delvers. Then she remembered that Grandmother Morris had always said if you were alive, you had a chance, and as faint as the hope seemed, she pushed the idea of jumping aside. Better just to toss the amulet. Then it would be safe from the delvers. As for herself — well, she *was* alive. Therefore, she had a chance.

Though what would happen when the delver king discovered she no longer had the amulet — well, that was something she didn't want to think about.

They started out again, Cara now carrying the amulet in her vest pocket. She slipped her hand into the pocket every thirty seconds or so, both to make sure it was still there, and to be ready to pull it out and toss it should the opportunity arise.

Her chance arrived about an hour after they had begun walking. They had come to another of those places where there was a solid wall on one side and nothing but a yawning emptiness — barely visible in the glow of the orange stripe — on the other. Cara wrapped her fingers around the amulet. At the same time a coldness wrapped around her heart.

Can I really do this? she asked herself.

I have to!

But what if the drop wasn't deep enough? In the dark she had no way to tell whether it was a few inches, or a few thousand feet. She began brushing the path ahead of her with her foot, hoping to find a loose pebble or stone which, if knocked over the edge, might give her a sense of the depth of the opening.

Finally she found one. Kicking it to the left, she began a slow count. She reached seven before she heard a distant *plunk*. Perfect! The pebble had fallen into water.

"What was that?" cried Brank.

"I knocked a rock over the edge."

"Well, be careful!"

"Sorry."

Fearing that if she hesitated the opportunity would be lost — and feeling as if it were her own heart she were discarding — Cara pulled her hand from her pocket and flung the amulet into the abyss.

She counted again, trying to think of what she would tell Brank this time.

There was no need.

This time, there was no sound at all.

Her puzzlement was buried in the aching sense of loss that overwhelmed her.

Cara had no idea of how long they traveled — it seemed like an eternity — before they were stopped by a solid stone wall. At first she wondered if the delvers had made a wrong turn somewhere. But they began to chant again. A moment later a grinding sound filled the air.

She caught her breath. The wall was splitting apart.

On the other side of the opening stood a dozen delvers. Beyond them, Cara could see, dimly, a vast space.

Four of the new delvers, standing shoulder to shoulder, held up spears. "Halt!" ordered the leader of this group. "Who seeks to enter the Great Hall of Gnurflax, King of Delvharken?"

"I am Brank, leader of the Seventh Cove. My cousins and I return with the human girl that the King has been seeking."

The already huge eyes of the delver guards widened. "Oh, the King will be pleased with this news," said their leader with a gravelly chuckle.

They stepped aside.

Cara's captors moved forward, dragging her into the hall of the delver king.

CHAPTER
XXVIII

THE RUBY PORTAL

The vegetation grew more sparse as Ian, Rajiv, and Fallon climbed higher on the mountain's slope. By late afternoon of the next day they were walking through scrub pine, and the air had become so thin they took deep, gasping breaths as they walked. It was colder, too, and they had been forced to add more protective clothing. And ever ahead of them loomed the Himalayan peaks, vast, skyscraping, and awesome.

Fallon was leading, of course, as he was the one who knew the location. Ian walked at the rear, keeping watch for renewed pursuit. He could not help keeping an eye on the clouds as well, for they were growing thick and heavy, and he feared a storm was on the way.

As the group neared the top of a stony ridge, Ian turned back for another look from the improved vantage point. Suddenly the world went black. He uttered a low curse, then froze where he was, calling to the others to wait for him.

Rajiv hurried to his side. "What is it, sahib? Are you all right?"

"I am blind, Rajiv. It will pass."

"Blind?" cried the boy, clutching at his hand.

Ian heard Fallon's footsteps as he came back to join them.

"Did you say 'blind'?" asked the tall man, sounding confused.

Ian sighed. He had not informed his companions of the price he had paid to learn about the Rainbow Prison. At first this was simply because things were moving so rapidly. As time went on, he had held back because he felt a kind of shame that he had given up something so intimate as his sight.

Now, reluctantly, he told them the full story of his meeting with the Blind Man.

"That was a desperate bargain," said Fallon.

Was that a hint of disapproval in his voice? Ian wondered. *Or am I just imagining it?* Either way, he felt stung, and replied sharply, "Without that 'bargain' we would not be able to enter the Rainbow Prison."

In that moment, his sight returned. He shook his head and blinked against the brightness.

"You can see again, sahib?" whispered Rajiv in awe.

"Yes. Let's move on."

He lost his sight twice more before the sun set, once for only a moment, once for nearly an hour. He wondered what the Blind Man was up to, that he needed to take his vision three times in such a short period. Then, a more chilling question hit him: Was the man spying on them, checking their progress, reporting it to someone? The idea lodged itself like a parasite in the back of Ian's brain, and nothing he could do would remove it. The most frustrating thing about his suspicion was that there was no way to find out if it was true. And, he realized, nothing he could do about it if it were.

No, that was not true. If worse came to worst, there was *one* way he could prevent the Blind Man from using his eyes. But it was a way so desperate that his mind recoiled in horror at the thought.

Around noon of the third day after they had left the Hunters, Rajiv took Ian's arm and whispered, "Look, sahib!"

Ian turned. It took him a moment to find what the boy was pointing at. Then he spotted them — five figures cresting a distant ridge. Quickly he tried to calculate how long it had been since they had crossed that ridge themselves. Four hours, maybe.

Fallon, turning to see what had caught their attention, muttered a low curse, then said, "We'll have to pick up our pace. It's not that far now. We may be able to get to the portal before they catch up with us."

If I don't lose my sight along the way, thought Ian bitterly.

An hour later they decided to drop their packs so that they could move faster.

"I hope they have food inside this Rainbow Prison of yours, sahibs," muttered Rajiv, gazing wistfully at what they were leaving behind.

Neither Fallon nor Ian replied.

The way became steeper. The faint trail they had been following — little more than a goat path, really — dwindled, then vanished. Fallon had to stop more often to get his bearings, sometimes taking a sighting against a distant mountain peak, sometimes searching for some oddly shaped rock. The thin mountain air made it hard to catch their breath. The clouds grew thicker and darker, and lightning flickered in the distance.

And always, they were aware of their pursuers. Since the Hunters had no goal other than the three travelers, they needed no landmarks and did not have to keep stopping to make sure of their way.

Which meant they continued to close the gap between them.

Late that afternoon the storm broke. Ian's group was crawling up a steep rock face at the time, so exposed that they could easily be seen, he was sure, by their pursuers. Fallon was leading, followed by Rajiv, then Ian. They were about halfway to the top when, with a sudden hiss of lightning, the sky opened and cold rain began to slash down. In seconds their clothes were plastered to their bodies, the stone instantly so slick that their hands slipped perilously as they fought for each new grip. A fierce wind howled around them, clutching at them as if it wanted to tear them from the mountainside.

Bellowing to be heard above the wind and rain, Ian cried, "Fallon! How much farther?"

"We are close! An hour, perhaps two."

The big man seemed tireless. Ian — working to match his pace — was glad of the intense training he had received when he became a Hunter. But the thin mountain air was a strain even for his superbly conditioned body. He looked at Rajiv, barely visible through the blinding rain though he was only a few feet above him, and wondered how the boy was doing.

The way grew steeper still, and they were in constant danger of falling. Yet Fallon was moving without hesitation now, seeming completely certain of their direction.

Suddenly Rajiv gave a cry of terror and began sliding backward. Ian had only a second to brace himself before the boy rammed into him. Both of them clutching desperately at the slick rock, they slid down about ninety feet before Ian's foot struck a rock outcrop. He braced himself against it, then nearly lost an arm holding Rajiv from falling past him.

Gasping for breath, Ian clung to the slippery stone, willing his aching fingers not to lose their grip.

"Thank you, sahib," panted the boy.

"Start climbing," was all Ian could reply.

Another hour of steep slopes, made bearable by the occasional level spot where they could catch their breath, brought them to a narrow ledge. As they stood there, a stroke of lightning revealed that they were facing a sheer cliff, unscalable without the kind of equipment they had abandoned when they dropped their packs.

"Now what?" moaned Rajiv.

"Wait," said Ian, who knew, from what the Blind Man had told him, that here they would find a cave. "Watch Fallon."

The big man was moving sideways along the ledge, pressing himself against the cliff lest he be blown off. Soon he called, "Here!"

Moving faster than was really safe, Ian and Rajiv quickly joined him.

"It's nice to be out of the storm," said Rajiv as they hurried into the cave. "But we'll be trapped here when your crazy family catches us, sahib."

"No," said Ian. "This is where we will finally escape them." He didn't add the rest of what he was thinking, *If I can just open the portal fast enough.*

The cave stretched deep into the side of the mountain. They turned a corner, and the darkness was complete.

Fallon muttered some low words.

To Ian's amazement, the man's hands began to glow, offering just enough light for them to move forward. Rajiv muttered some low words, too. Ian took them to be a prayer.

In the light from Fallon's hands they ran, slid, and scrambled their way into the mountain, until they were stopped by another rock wall, this one so smooth it looked as if it had been polished.

"Not again!"

"Quiet, Rajiv!" ordered Fallon, his voice soft but fierce.

Ian pulled the jewel from his pocket and began searching for the "keyhole," the place he would have to insert it. There! He had spotted it! But before he could move his hand to insert the great gem, his sight was taken. In the shock, his fingers trembled — and he dropped the stone.

"I've lost it!" he cried, falling to his knees. He began running his fingertips over the stone floor, frantically searching for the gem. He felt Rajiv on the floor next to him, also searching.

"I saw it bounce," said the boy. "It went this way. Sahib Fallon, can you make your hands any brighter?"

Though Ian could not see it, Rajiv's grunt of satisfaction told him Fallon had done exactly that. He continued to sweep his own hands over the floor, frustration and fear boiling within him.

They heard a shout from behind.

"They're in the cave!" hissed Rajiv. "Your cousins are in the cave!"

"Quiet," warned Fallon. Then, "I see it!"

In the same moment, Ian's sight returned. His relief was tempered by a groan of frustration from Fallon. "What is it now?" asked Ian.

"The gem fell into an opening in the floor. It's too narrow for me to get my arm in."

"Let me try," said Rajiv.

Another shout from behind, closer now.

The three of them gathered around the gap in the stone floor. Rajiv pressed his face to the opening, then said, "Sahib Fallon, put your hand in so I can see!"

Fallon thrust his right hand, still glowing, into the miniature crevice.

"Ah! There it is!" Rajiv stretched his arm down. "But I cannot reach it!" He turned on his side and strained in farther. "Sahib Hunter, press on my shoulder. Push me down, push me down!"

Ian pressed, desperate to retrieve the jewel but fearing to hurt the boy.

"Ian Hunter!" roared a voice, not nearly far enough away. The words echoed around them.

"Harder!" sobbed Rajiv. "Push harder, sahib! Ah! Almost. Almost! Got it!"

Ian let go. Rajiv withdrew his arm from the crevice. The gem, clutched in his fingertips, sparkled in the light from Fallon's hands.

"Good work!" said Ian. He took the jewel and returned to the wall. Pressing one hand to the rock ahead of him, he groped for the socket he had spotted just before his sight vanished. His questing fingertips found it. Hardly daring to breathe, he lifted the scarlet stone and set it in place, then leaned close to the wall and whispered the secret words the Blind Man had given him.

He gasped and felt a sudden clutch of terror. The gem — so crucial to leaving the prison once he had found Martha — had been pulled from his fingers, almost as if it were being sucked into the rock.

A sudden burst of warmth surrounded them. The rock wall vanished. In front of them — below them — swirled a pool of ruby red light. It reminded Ian of the emerald light he had jumped into the night he leaped from the tower of St. Christopher's to follow Cara into Luster.

"Stop!" roared Kieran, his voice appallingly close.

Fallon started forward.

"Wait!" cried Ian. "The opening is only good for *one* passage. We have to go together."

For a terrible moment he feared Fallon was going to betray him and go through the portal on his own. But the big man scooped an arm around Ian's waist, even as Rajiv, who was standing to his right, took his hand.

"Now!" roared Fallon. "*Jump!*"

Together, they leaped into the swirling light.

CHAPTER
XXIX

DUNGEON

Some twenty delver guards stood in place, gripping their spears. Cara didn't notice them at first — partly because the light was so dim, but also because, standing still as stone and pressed against a wall or a stalagmite, each guard seemed almost part of the cavern. As she began to realize how many there were, she wondered what their purpose was. What danger could the delver king face here, so far underground?

Brank and Dworkin, gripping her arms, led her forward. Glancing over her shoulder, Cara saw the other three delvers who had been traveling with them lying face down, their hands stretched toward the King.

Gnurflax's throne was on a raised platform. In the low light it took Cara a moment to discern that platform and throne were actually a single piece of stone, carved directly from the cavern's floor.

The King was larger than most delvers, his pale face seamed with deep lines that looked as if they had been chiseled there by some stonecutter. On his brow rested a crown of reddish-brown stone. He wore a gray tunic — coarsely woven, though of much better quality than she had seen on any other delver — and a short brown robe. He stared at her with burning eyes. And in his hand . . . Cara gasped. In his hand was a ball, woven from wire, glowing softly of its own accord. M'Gama's anchor. It had to be!

Which meant that Belle and Finder had failed.

Cara's heart clenched and her knees wobbled. But Brank and Dworkin were holding her so tightly she could not sink to the floor.

Her desperate thoughts were interrupted by Gnurflax, who spoke in a voice that sounded like breaking stones. "Human child, friend of unicorns and therefore enemy of the delvers, do not even try to pretend you cannot understand me. Word of your 'gift of tongues' has reached us even in these caverns. Therefore, I will say this only once: Give me the amulet."

"I do not have it," said Cara, trying not to let her voice tremble.

"Do not toy with me! I want the amulet, and I will have it, one way or another. Now where is it?"

"I don't know. I lost it along the way." Now she felt free

to let the tears she had been hiding creep into her voice, hoping they would help make her story seem more real.

"She lies, Mighty Gnurflax!" cried Brank. "I saw the amulet myself!"

"Search her!" ordered the King.

The rough hands of Brank and Dworkin made Cara shudder, as the feel of them pulled up the horrible memory of the delver who had attacked her so soon after she first arrived in Luster. She clamped down on her scream, held it in, forcing herself to behave with a dignity she hoped would be appropriate for the granddaughter of the Queen of the unicorns.

The delvers felt around her neck, but of course the amulet was not there. Next they checked her pockets, where they found only the watch that Thomas had given her, and Medafil's sphere, which she had wound down until it was no bigger than a cherry. Since neither item was what they were looking for, and the sphere did not light in their grasp, they dropped both to the floor. The watch bounced once, but stayed shut. The sphere, however, rolled away. Cara watched in horror as it headed toward the throne, stopping only when it was caught by some flaw in the cavern's floor.

Meanwhile Brank and Dworkin had begun patting all over her body, checking for any feel of the amulet.

The King sighed. "Take off her boots, you fools. She may have hidden it there."

Dworkin pulled her arms behind her. Brank lifted one of her feet, pulled off the boot, shook it out.

Nothing, of course.

He repeated the process with her other foot.

"Her clothes!" shrieked the king. "Take off her clothes!"

They stripped her of her tunic, then her shirt. Cara yelped in anger, but refused to let this indignity make her cry in front of them.

Let them see me, she told herself fiercely. *It doesn't matter. They're only delvers, so it doesn't matter!*

But still, it hurt, and she felt herself blushing hotly, a condition that grew worse when they pulled off her breeches.

"There is nothing," said Brank at last, sounding astonished. He flung himself to the floor, face down. "I swear, Your Majesty, she had it when we took her!"

Gnurflax trembled with fury. "Then you, Brank, are a miserable failure. You had the amulet in your grasp and lost it. You are relieved of your command!"

Brank's voice trembled. "But, Your Majesty . . ."

"Be grateful I do not feed you to the skwartz!" Turning to a pair of delvers close to the throne, Gnurflax snapped, "Take her to the dungeon! Lock her away until she sees fit to tell me where she has hidden the amulet." He paused, then turned and spoke directly to Cara. "You will find that it does not pay to thwart me, human child. My dungeon is cold, and it is dank, and there are creatures in it that are better not spoken of. Spend a little time in one of my 'guest rooms,' and you may find yourself ready to tell me the truth after all." Shifting his gaze to the guards, he snarled, "Take her away."

Cara knelt to scoop up her clothes. Taking advantage of the moment, she scrambled across the floor and retrieved Medafil's sphere as well.

"Hurry up, hurry up!" snarled the King.

Clutching her clothes to her chest, she let the guards hustle her from the cavern.

Behind her echoed the grating sound of delver laughter.

Her new escorts led her through a maze of tunnels. She wanted to put on her clothes again, but though she asked the delvers twice to let her stop and dress, they refused both times, their voices as cold as the smooth, stone floor beneath her bare feet. Her arms grew tired, but she didn't dare shift her grip, for fear that if she dropped anything they wouldn't let her stop to pick it up. Despite the increasing pain, she held everything tight against her, both to keep it safe, and because it felt like a kind of shield.

She tried to keep track of where they were going, but it was impossible to remember all the twists and turns, and she was soon more hopelessly lost than ever. She knew only that every tunnel sloped down, so that they traveled ever deeper into Delvharken.

After a while they entered tunnels where the glowing orange lines were so dim she could scarcely see the floor in front of her. This did not seem to bother the delvers, but Cara stumbled a number of times. Finally they stopped so abruptly that she bumped into the delver just ahead of her.

"Watch it!" he snapped. Then he stepped away. She heard him take something from the wall. A moment later the sound of metal clinking against metal made her realize it was most likely a key. She waited to hear the sound of a door creaking open. It did not come, so she was surprised when the second delver thrust her abruptly forward. She staggered, then fell.

The floor was cold and damp against her face.

Though she did not hear the creak of a hinge, she did hear the door slam shut, then — barely — the turn of the key in the lock, followed by another metallic clink as one of the delvers returned the key to the wall.

"Enjoy your stay," sneered the first of the guards.

She wanted to answer, to be rude and defiant, but feared her voice would tremble and betray the true depth of her despair. So she remained silent. The guards turned to leave. She focused all her attention on the sound of their footsteps, as a way of holding her fear at bay. It wasn't until the last echo faded that she finally felt free to let her tears begin to flow.

She dressed as she wept, fumbling in the darkness yet feeling that the clothing would protect her, not just from the cold and the damp, but from something even more uncomfortable.

At least I know I was right to throw away the amulet, she told herself as she pulled on her boots. *Whatever the King wants it for, it can't be good for the unicorns.*

But though she told herself this, she couldn't deny the way her heart longed for it. Even if it wouldn't work here in the realm of the delvers, simply holding it would give her a dim feeling of hope, something that had vanished from her heart altogether. The thought brought forth a final spasm of tears.

When she finally stopped crying, when her breathing slowed and her mind began to clear, she heard something — something that the departing footsteps of the guards, and then the sound of her own weeping, had covered before.

In the darkness behind her, someone — or some*thing* — was breathing.

CHAPTER
XXX

LIGHTFOOT ALONE

When Lightfoot opened his eyes it was still dark. The Prince shook his head, then staggered to his feet, groggy and unsteady. What was he doing alone in this forest?

Suddenly memories of the delver attack came rushing back. He trembled as his mind yielded up the terrible image of Cara being carried away by a throng of delvers. He had fought desperately to reach her, but there had been too many of the little monsters. They had swarmed over him, borne him to the ground.

But how had it ended? Where had they gone with Cara?

Frantic, he called out for Cara and Grimwold, but got no answer. Ignoring the pain from his wounds, he began to search the area where they had been encamped. If his friends were still here, wounded but alive, he could heal them. Beyond that, the Prince wasn't sure what he feared most:

finding their lifeless bodies, or discovering that they were delver-taken.

Why was he not dead himself? Maybe the delvers had simply wanted him out of the way while they captured Cara. But even if she was all they had been after, the ones who dragged him down could easily have killed him before they rejoined their band. *Why hadn't they?*

As Lightfoot considered it, he realized he couldn't recall *any* time delvers had actually killed a unicorn. It was a surprising thought, since the two groups were sworn enemies.

They killed Flensa! he argued to himself, but then had to admit that though the dwarf woman had died of wounds she received while fighting the delvers, they had not moved in to finish the job. Instead, they had simply left her . . . just as they had left him. Though his mind resisted the thought, he began to wonder if delvers were slightly less murderous than he had believed.

Murderous or not, the little monsters had Cara, and if he was going to save her, he had better get started.

He looked at himself, trying to assess how badly he was injured. His flanks were coated with blood — his own, mostly, but the silver and crimson were mixed with streaks of muddy-green delver blood. The sight made him feel unclean and a shudder rippled along his sides. He would have to bathe as soon as possible. Though the pain was intense, with his wounds hidden beneath the drying blood it was hard to tell how bad they actually were. For a moment he wished he had another unicorn with him, one who could help heal the wounds.

They'll heal fast enough on their own, he told himself firmly. Which was true; unicorns did not suffer long from wounds that were not fatal. What was of more concern to him was that he was lame in his left rear leg. Pain he could ignore, but lameness was going to slow him at a time when he wanted speed above all.

Lame or not, it didn't take long to ascertain that neither Cara nor Grimwold, whether alive or dead, was anywhere nearby. Nor was the Squijum, for that matter. Had the delvers taken them, too? Though he was concerned for the old dwarf and the chattering creature, it was the thought of Cara in the clutches of the little beasts that drove him nearly mad with worry.

I've got to find their trail!

He continued to cast around their camping place in widening half-circles and after several desperate minutes found something that gave him both hope and despair: a stain of blood, not muddy green like that of the delvers or silvery like his own. This was the rusty red of human blood after it has dried. He wondered for a moment what color blood a dwarf like Grimwold had, then spotted a strand of long red hair that had been caught on a branch. It was definite: The delvers had brought Cara this way.

Dawn was creeping into the forest. By its dim light the unicorn prince began to pick out the path the kidnappers had taken. When they were being slow and careful, delvers could move through the woods without leaving much sign of their passing. But when they were racing off while trying to hold a struggling, squirming girl, they could not help but leave traces. Still, they were only traces, and Lightfoot boiled with frustration at not having a clear trail so he could gallop after them at full speed — even though another part of him knew that he was so weakened by his own loss of blood that a full gallop was impossible, even were he not already limping.

Ignoring the pain and the weakness, he hobbled along as fast as he could.

Late in the morning, he reached the rocky hollow that marked the end of the delvers' aboveground journey. He didn't realize that, at first, and looked for the trail to continue on the other side. When he could find no sign of it he doubled back and searched more carefully.

It took several minutes for him to find the hole through which the delvers had departed the surface world. When he did locate it, he stared in horror. The opening was little more than a foot in diameter — easily big enough for a delver to pass through. Large enough, even, the Prince realized bitterly, for a girl the size of Cara. But it was far, far too small for a unicorn. He could no more squeeze through that narrow gap than a dragon could pass through the eye of a needle. The hard truth hit him. Cara was underground, and there was no way he could help her.

The unease, the near panic that he had been holding at bay vanished in a wave of black despair as he tipped back his head and trumpeted, "Cara!"

His cry was swallowed by the forest.

There was no response. Why would there be? There was no one to hear, no one to help him rescue Cara.

Now what? He could go back to Autumngrove to get help, but that trip would take days — days in both directions — and there would be no telling where the delvers might have taken Cara by then. And who was there that could help anyway? No unicorn could enter the delver realm through that hole, nor could any of the humans he knew.

Think, Lightfoot, he ordered himself. *Think!*

He wished he could contact the court and ask the Queen for advice. But without a scrying pool that was out of the question.

All right, if I could *reach Amalia, what would she tell me?*

He knew the answer at once, but disliked it so much that he pushed it away and asked himself a new question.

What would Cara say to do?

He came to the same answer — and disliked it just as much.

All right, let's try the hard one. What would my father have said?

But no matter how he framed the question, he got the same answer: The girl is beyond your reach, and there is nothing more you can do to help her. You have a task, and it is important — more important than a single life. It may mean survival for all the unicorns. *You know what you must do! Go to the Valley of the Centaurs. Finish the mission.*

Though he knew it was the right thing to do, it still wrenched something inside Lightfoot when he turned from the delver burrow to make his way — alone, limping, filled with helpless rage — to the Valley of the Centaurs.

An hour later he uttered a cry of deep despair, then turned from his path.

Cara had been taken by the delvers.

The Dimblethum lived near the main entrance to the delver caverns.

With a single glance over his shoulder, with a heart torn between duty and duty, with no sense of what good it might do but the clear feeling he could do no else, the Prince turned and headed for the center of the world.

CHAPTER
XXXI

THE NAMELESS ONE

The ragged breathing coming from the darkness filled Cara with terror. What kind of monster had the delvers locked her up with? Silently she groped in her pockets until she found Medafil's sphere. Clutching it tightly, not ready to release its light, she whispered, "Who's there?"

For a moment, there was no response. Then a raspy voice — clearly that of a delver — exclaimed, "I've met you before!"

Now Cara did twist the sphere between her hands, expanding it until it was nearly three inches wide and glowing like a small moon. For her dark-accustomed eyes the sudden light was almost painful. Clearly it was even worse for her cellmate, who hid his face and shrieked, "Too much light! Too much light!"

Twisting the sphere back to a smaller size, Cara cupped it between her hands to shield him from its glow.

"Better?"

"Yes."

The answer was almost a whimper.

By the light, which was made rosy by shining through her fingers, Cara could see a delver cowering against the far wall. He looked terrible. Well, all delvers looked terrible, of course, but this one was worse than usual. His clothes were torn, his face and arms bruised, his huge eyes sunk deep into his ugly face. To her surprise, she felt a twinge of pity for him.

"Who are you?"

He hesitated, then said, "I have no name."

"What do you mean?" she asked, startled by the depth of pain in his voice.

"My name was taken from me as punishment for my crimes. But you've met me. I came upon you when you were traveling with the unicorn prince and some other creatures. I helped you avoid the pursuit of a band of delvers that day."

Cara remembered the incident well. It was not long after she had first jumped into Luster. Lightfoot, the Dimblethum, and the Squijum were taking her to Arabella Skydancer, who was then Queen of the unicorns. Lightfoot had been thoroughly startled when a group of delvers approached and their leader told them he thought the delver king was wrong in his plan to help the Hunters enter Luster — and even more startled when that same delver had helped them escape other delvers who were pursuing them.

She wracked her brain for a moment, searching for his name, then cried, "I remember! You're Nedzik!"

The delver screamed and covered his ears. "Don't say that! Don't say that! That name has been taken from me!"

"What do you mean?"

"I am being punished for treason. And if you believe that loyalty to the King is more important than concern for the safety of Delvharken, I suppose I truly am a traitor." He sighed, and said, "The problem is, I can't make myself feel like one."

"So you're here because of that time when you helped us in the woods?" asked Cara. She felt vaguely guilty, even though it had been his idea to speak to them, and she herself had not said a word during the conversation. Indeed, that had been before Firethroat had given her the gift of tongues, and she had only understood what was happening because she had kept her hand on Lightfoot's flank the whole time.

The delver shuddered. "It is my good fortune that the King does not know of *that* moment. If he did, I would not be in such a safe and comfortable place as this cell. More likely my hands would be caught beneath a boulder somewhere near the den of one of those scaly creatures that gnaw on you so slowly it takes days for it to finish eating you. No, it was a more recent crime that put me here."

"What did you do?" asked Cara, after a period of silence.

He hesitated, then said, "I refused to join an attack that I thought ill-advised."

"An attack where?" asked Cara, terrified there had been some new crime against the unicorns she had not yet heard about.

"A group of us were sent to ransack the home of the Geomancer. We were supposed to recover a certain magical object —"

"Do you know what happened there?" screamed Cara, furious at this reminder of Flensa's death, and how the delvers had caused it.

"How could I?" he asked, clearly startled by her reaction. "I told you, I turned away."

Cara forced herself to be calm, trying to separate this delver from the ones who had killed Flensa. "I'm sorry," she said, after a moment. "I was there *after* the others had done their work. It was ugly, and there was death." She paused, then added, "I'm glad you turned away."

"I am, too. Even so, I suppose the King is right when he says that to do so was the act of a traitor." He paused, then began to slap at his head, crying, "I do not understand *what* is right anymore! I DO NOT UNDERSTAND!"

"Stop!" cried Cara. "Just stop!" She wanted to grab his hands and force him to stop, but she would have had to drop the sphere to do so, and she knew she could never catch those flailing hands in the darkness. "Just stop," she said again. "Please?"

The delver sagged against the wall, breathing hard. Finally he said, "I'm sorry. I'm just so confused. To go against the wishes of the King is treason. But by his very wishes I fear he is bringing doom upon us all."

"What do you mean?"

"I told you the last time we met, King Gnurflax wants to open Luster to invasion by the Hunters."

"But isn't that what all delvers want?"

Her question was greeted with a gravelly sigh. "Just because the unicorns are our enemies, it does not follow that we need to invite in others who may become enemies as well. There is no guarantee the Hunters will be our friends once they have gained what they want. Who is to say that if they rid Luster of the unicorns they will not then take it over themselves? Though we hate the unicorns, they are not a danger to us. But the woman Beloved is mad. Who knows what she would do if she came here? Besides, my teacher thinks that the opening of another gate between Earth and Delvharken would be dangerous."

"Your teacher?"

"Every delver has a teacher. I love and honor mine." He paused, then said, "I will not name him. It is not safe."

Cara had a sudden sense that life in the delver world was more complicated than she had guessed. She took a few minutes to frame her next question, finally asking, "How do you know about Beloved and the Hunters?"

"I was there the night Beloved first contacted the King." He shuddered at the memory. "To hear that voice, coming from another world . . . it was stranger than anything I could have imagined. But it was exactly what Gnurflax had been trying for."

"How did he do that?"

He paused, and she could tell that her questions were starting to make him nervous. At last he said, "I would not know. I'm not even certain if it was Gnurflax or Beloved who made the first attempt. I do know that she has a great deal of magic. Of course, eventually we were all aware of her. Stories get out. Creatures talk. And we gloried to know that we delvers were not the only enemies of the unicorns."

This raised a question that had been much on Cara's mind. "Why *are* the delvers and the unicorns enemies?"

"The unicorns did us a great wrong," was the quick reply.

"What was it?"

The nameless delver hesitated. When he finally spoke, he sounded embarrassed. "To be truthful, I don't know. But the Whisperer —"

"*The Whisperer?*" cried Cara, astonished to hear him mention so casually the very name that she and the others had been sent to learn about. "What do you know of the Whisperer?"

"Very little. It is not given to us common delvers to know him. But the King speaks to him often enough."

"Gnurflax speaks to him? Who is he? *What* is he?"

"A voice. What else he might be I do not know. He speaks to the King in private, and the King tells us what he has said. I suspect it was the Whisperer who put the King and Beloved in contact with each other." He paused, then added, "Actually, I suspect it is the Whisperer who has driven the King mad. But that, too, is probably a treasonous thought."

Cara sighed in frustration. "The reason I started on this journey was to find out about the Whisperer. There is an old prophecy about the Whisperer, the delvers, and the unicorns. We need to make sense of it."

"This is very strange," said the delver uneasily. "Even so, I would be glad to help in that particular task. We would all do well to know more of these things. Alas, neither of us is going anywhere right now."

"Is there no way out of this cell?"

"Would I still be here if there was?" he replied with a bitter laugh. "Delvers do not build dungeons to be escaped from."

Cara thought for a moment. "The guards bring food and water, don't they?"

"If they remember."

She felt her heart sink. She was about to speak again when the delver whispered, *What was that?*

"What?" asked Cara, dropping her voice to match his whisper.

"*Shhhh!* Someone is out there. It might be a spy for the King. If that is the case, I am doomed." He paused, then added, "Let us hope that is *only* a spy."

"What do you mean?"

"There are worse ways to die in these caverns than even Gnurflax can devise."

Cara felt a chill shiver down her spine. Quickly she twisted down the sphere until it was no bigger than a hazel nut, then dropped it into her pocket, plunging them back into total darkness. No need to help whatever was out there by letting it see them.

They sat in silence, waiting.

She could hear the sound now, too, soft but clear — the sound of claws scrabbling against stone.

It was drawing closer.

CHAPTER
XXXII

MARRED IN THE MAKING

The Dimblethum had gathered some wood and was crouched in his cave, attempting to craft a smaller version of the large, moss-padded chair where he usually sat. It was something he hoped to have ready in case Cara ever came to visit. But he was finding it hard to make his paws, so large and clumsy, do what he told them to, and his temper was rising.

His muzzle clenched as he tried to force a branch into the shape he wanted. He almost had it when the branch snapped and split — as had the previous two. Growling in frustration, he flung the splintered piece aside and reached for another. As he did, a too-familiar voice whispered, "I know what you want."

The words seemed to come from somewhere above him. Or maybe — and this was much worse — from behind him, from the secret part of the cave.

Closing his eyes, the Dimblethum dropped the branch and clamped his paws over his ears, trying to shut out the voice. But just as those paws had failed him in shaping the wood, they failed to block out the whispering, which sounded not merely inside his head, but reverberated in the very core of his being.

"I know what you want," repeated the voice again and again, its tone sweetly seductive.

"GO AWAY!" roared the Dimblethum.

To his surprise, the voice fell silent. The Dimblethum waited, expecting it to return.

The silence continued.

When he was satisfied that he was alone, the creature shook his head and forced his attention back to the recalcitrant wood. But his paws were trembling too hard for him to work. Finally, he snapped the branch and threw it aside.

Why was it so hard to make things?

And why did he always mar them in the making?

CHAPTER XXXIII

DARKNESS AND LIGHT

Fear had eased the natural suspicion that would have kept Cara and the delver apart. Sitting so close to him, Cara became aware of his scent, which wasn't nearly as unpleasant as she would have expected. It reminded her of stones just after a rainfall.

Another sound from outside the cell twisted her fear to a new height. She slipped her hand into her pocket to retrieve the sphere. It lit the moment she touched it, of course, but by cupping her hand around it she was able to contain the glow completely. She wasn't sure whether to use it yet. Though its light would let them see what was outside, it would also let whatever was out there see them.

Of course, the bars on our cell door would keep it out, she thought, almost happy, for the moment, to be imprisoned this way. *Or will they?* With a twist of nerves, she wondered how effective the bars really were. What if the thing in the tunnel was some kind of serpent, or some horrible creature with grasping tentacles?

She clutched the sphere more tightly. Maybe with a sudden twist she could blind whatever it was out there long enough to . . . well, to get some kind of advantage.

As Cara debated with herself, she heard a scuttling sound. The creature was inside the cell! Pulling her hand from her pocket, she closed her eyes and twisted the sphere, creating a burst of light.

The nameless delver shrieked, though whether it was from the sudden brightness or from fear of the intruder Cara could not tell. At the same moment a high, squeaky voice cried, "Ow, ow, owieee! Too much light! OWIEEE!"

Quickly twisting the sphere back down, she opened her eyes. On the floor in front of her, little paws clasped over his face, the Squijum was flopping around, crying, "Girl hurt Squijum! Stinky girl hurt Squijum eyes!"

Flooded with guilt, Cara jammed the sphere back into her pocket. In the darkness she crawled across the floor to where she had last seen the Squijum. She moved her hands carefully until she felt her fingers brush against his fur, then gently scooped him up, murmuring, "I'm sorry, Squijum! I didn't know it was you."

"Mean owiee girl," he whimpered.

"It will be all right in a minute," she promised. "And

you could have let me know it was you coming through the bars. You nearly scared me to death!"

"Squijum find stinky girl long gone! Hotcha good finder Squijum!"

Cuddling him close, loving the feel of his thick fur beneath her fingers, she felt a wave of relief at his silly presence, despite the scare he had just given her. "Hotcha good finder Squijum," she agreed.

From somewhere behind her the nameless delver said, "What *is* that thing?"

"He's a friend of mine. I'll explain more later. And, um, sorry about the light. I didn't have time to warn you." Returning her attention to the Squijum, she said, "How did you get here, anyway?"

"Squijum follow stinky delvers!"

Squirming out of her grasp he climbed to her shoulder, which pretty much let her know that whatever discomfort he had suffered from the burst of light was over. She wondered if it had been as bad as she first thought, or if he had simply been pushing for sympathy.

"Squijum follow delvers underground so Squijum not lose stinky girl." He made a sound of disgust. "Too much underground. Too much dark. Phooey!"

Reaching into her pocket, Cara returned her hand to the sphere. It lit instantly. She realized that the fabric of her breeches softened the light, almost like a lamp shade.

"Is that too much?" she asked the delver.

"It's bearable," he muttered.

Looking back, she saw that though he had his hands clasped over his eyes, he had parted his fingers to peer between them.

"Yike!" squeaked the Squijum. "Delver!"

"Hush. He's a friend. Kind of."

"Squijum hotcha good best friend!" cried the creature, leaping from her shoulder back to the floor. "Good Squijum friend find shiny thing girl dropped. Girl careless. Squijum good finder. Hotcha!"

"You saved the amulet?" cried Cara, hardly able to believe this news. "Squijum, did you really?"

"Girl wait. Delver wait." The Squijum went bounding away. He returned moments later, clutching the amulet in his little paws. "Squijum catch when girl drop. Squijum good?"

"So *that's* why I never heard it land!" exclaimed Cara, her heart almost bursting with relief. "Yes, Squijum hotcha good!"

He squeaked with delight and bounded back to her shoulder.

"Squijum," she asked in a thoughtful voice. "Do you know what a key is?"

"Sure sure! Squijum hotcha-gotcha much smart. Squijum know key."

"Well, there's a key on the wall somewhere outside our door. It will be on a metal ring. Can you get it for me?"

"Hotcha yes! Squijum get key!"

He bounded away again. Cara heard him scrabbling around outside and realized he was climbing the wall. She was wondering how well he could see in the dark of the tunnel when his little voice exclaimed, "Hotcha Gotcha! Squijum got you, you bad key!"

"Shhhh!" hissed Cara, fearful some delver might be close enough to hear. "Be quiet, Squijum!"

"Squijum good," he muttered defensively. "Squijum got key!"

A moment later he reentered the cell, dragging with him the metal ring that held the key.

"Squijum *very* good," Cara assured him warmly as she took the ring. Holding the sphere in one hand so that it continued to shine, she went to the cell door. The opening between the bars was barely wide enough for her to push her arm through, and she had to twist awkwardly to get the key into the lock. Even when she finally managed to align it properly she couldn't get the leverage to turn the key, and had to let go of the sphere so she could use her other hand to brace against. She was cursing softly to herself when the delver said, "Let me try."

Feeling foolish, she extracted her arm from the door — a painful process in itself — and passed him the key.

"A little light — *just* a little — might be useful now," he said.

She slipped her hand into her pocket and grasped the sphere.

The delver thrust his arm through the bars and pressed himself to the frame. He groaned with the effort, then let out a sob, then cried triumphantly, "There!"

He pulled his arm back, then gave the door a push.

It swung open without a sound. Cara had noticed the same silence when the guards had first flung her in here, and said so.

"We make things carefully," replied the nameless delver. He sounded almost insulted, as if the idea that they would do anything less was foreign to him.

Cara stepped out of the cell, the Squijum on her shoulder, her delver companion following close behind.

Now what? she thought. *We've gained our freedom, but what kind of freedom is it when we're still trapped in these wretched tunnels? Where do we go next?* Turning to the delver, she said, "Do you know your way back?"

"I can figure it out. But what would be the point? We cannot return to the heart of Delvharken. If we tried, we would simply end up right back here again." He paused, then added softly, "Or somewhere worse."

"Do you know another way to the surface? One that doesn't go by well-traveled tunnels?"

Before he could answer, the Squijum scrambled up her side. Perching on her shoulder he chittered, "No, no! Not go up top. Follow Squijum! Follow Squijum!"

Without pausing to see if she was indeed going to follow, he leaped to the floor and scampered down the tunnel.

CHAPTER XXXIV

BARNABAS

It was like falling through all the red in the world.

The color swirled around them, in more shades and tones than Ian had ever imagined to exist. He saw the crisp reds of ripe apples, the blazing reds of sunsets, the mellow reds of roses. He was wrapped in cinnabar and scarlet, vermilion and burgundy, and a thousand other reds besides. The colors grew sharper, more intense, until finally it seemed the world must be made of nothing but blood and fire. He was vaguely aware of Rajiv and Fallon, falling somewhere close to him.

Then he saw something else in all that redness, another flash of red, but separate and clear: the scarlet jewel with which he had opened the way into the prison — and which would be necessary to their leaving it.

He stretched for the gem, but could not reach it. He

strained until he feared he would pull his arm from its socket, but got no closer. The jewel fell beside him, gleaming, tantalizingly close, but completely untouchable.

Suddenly their fall ended.

Though Ian had expected to land with a jolt that would knock the breath out of him, they simply stopped — which was almost as stunning.

The gem! Where was the gem?

He rolled over and found he was lying on scarlet grass. He began to scramble through it, looking for a flash of red among the red stems. Finally it was touch, not sight, that came to his aid, as he felt a polished hardness beneath his thumb. With a gasp of relief he plucked up the jewel and slipped it into the pocket where he had carried it throughout their trek.

"Sahib! Are you all right?"

Turning, he saw Rajiv and Fallon just a few feet away, sitting on a swath of scarlet grass that sloped down to a shimmering pool, its water the color of ripe raspberries. A crimson sky stretched overhead. Halfway between the horizon and zenith blazed a garnet sun.

"I did not believe you, sahibs," murmured Rajiv, pushing himself to his knees and staring about in awe. "I said I did, but I was not ready for . . ." He waved his hand, as if to let sight fill in where words failed him.

Fallon rose smoothly to his feet, also looking about in wonder. "It's as if all the other colors have been stolen, and only red was left behind."

"That's pretty much the way of it," said a voice from behind them.

The three spun about. Beneath a nearby tree — a tree whose wine-red leaves and carmine bark made it look almost as if it were on fire — stood an old man. He was dressed in a tuxedo, which was odd enough; the fact that he was barefoot made it even odder. He was also the only thing in sight, besides themselves, not made in shades of red, though the red reflecting from all around cast a scarlet tint over him — as it did over each of them.

The old man stepped toward them, staring curiously. Suddenly his eyes widened. "You have bodies!"

"Of course we have bodies," said Rajiv, sounding indignant.

The man made a wheezing sound that it took Ian a moment to recognize as a laugh. "No 'of course' about it, boy. It's certainly not true for *most* people who come here."

"What do you mean?" asked Rajiv.

The old man stepped toward them and held out his hand as if offering it to shake. Rajiv reached out to take it — and gasped as his own hand closed on nothing. "You're a ghost!" cried the boy, backing away in alarm.

"Unfortunately, I'm very much alive." The man wrinkled his brow. "At least, I think I'm alive. I'm not sure what would happen if my body actually died while I'm a prisoner here. Maybe I *would* just linger on as a ghost, not even realizing it. Well, I don't like that idea much! If you just came here to scare me, you can leave right now."

Ian glanced at Fallon, who rolled his eyes, clearly sharing the same thought: This man might have useful information, but it wasn't going to be easy getting it out of him.

"Where is your real body now?" asked Ian.

The man sat down and began counting his toes. "Hard to say. Somewhere on Earth, I know that much. But it could have been moved many times since I was first thrust into the Rainbow Prison. I would have no way of knowing."

"Who put you here?" asked Fallon.

The man's eyes shifted, and he began to back away from them, scooting across the scarlet sward without standing up. "I'd rather not say," he whispered, fear thickening his voice. "No point in attracting his attention."

His, thought Ian, noting the pronoun. *So Beloved is not the only person who knows how to send someone to this place.* Aloud, he said, "How many souls are imprisoned here?"

The old man shrugged. "I don't think anyone's ever done a census. I run across other prisoners on occasion, but everyone is pretty suspicious. No one much likes to take up with others because, well, you know —" And here he dropped his voice to an urgent whisper, "*They might be after your toes!*"

"Why would they want our toes?" asked Rajiv.

The old man curled his fingers protectively over the end of his feet and cried, "Don't try to take mine!"

"Do you know of a woman?" asked Ian, desperately hoping to get some useful information. "Quite beautiful, with red hair —"

"*Everything* is red here!"

Struggling to keep his temper, Ian nodded acknowledgement of the fact. "She is quite beautiful," he continued. "Her name is —"

"Stop!" Tucking his feet underneath him, the old man said, "No one speaks their true name in this place. I tell you this as a friend, and you can take it as proof that you can trust me."

"Why does no one tell their name?" asked Fallon.

Their informant glanced about, as if half expecting someone to be spying on them even now, then said softly, "Many of the prisoners of the scarlet shaft are magic workers themselves. That's why you have to watch out for your toes, of course."

"If they are magic workers, how is it that they are here?" asked Ian, deciding to avoid the topic of toes altogether.

The man shrugged. "Each somehow made an enemy out of another magic worker whose power was even greater.

Perhaps they stole a secret. Or a woman. Maybe they simply looked to be on a path to power that would be threatening. A few are actually here at the judgment of the Council of Nine, who felt they had become dangerous and must be locked away."

Ian wrinkled his brow. "The Council of Nine?"

The old man looked nervous. "I shouldn't have mentioned them! Suffice it to say that they are powerful magicians who guard Earth from darker forces. My point is simply that being in this place does not strip a magic worker of *all* his power. For ones such as that, a name is a tool that can be used to work mischief. Wiser not to offer it."

Ian nodded. "For this warning, our thanks. But I have to ask — if no one tells his name, how do you speak to one another?"

"We use false names, of course. You may call me Barnabas. But that is my name only for now. If you meet me again, I will not answer to it. And don't call me Toby. Ever!"

"Thank you . . . Barnabas. I return to my first question. Do you know of a woman who is held here?"

"I have met a few women on the scarlet paths. None was young and beautiful though. And they all had their shoes on." He paused, as if thinking, then said, "Oh! I have heard a rumor of someone beautiful . . . 'The Woman in the Tree,' they call her."

Ian felt a lift in his heart. When Cara had told him of the vision she had while gazing into the same scarlet jewel he had just used to bring them through the Ruby Portal, she said she had seen her mother sitting in the hollow of a great tree.

"What do you know of this woman?" he asked, working to sound calm and not let this "Barnabas" know how eager he truly was.

"They speak of her as a mystery. She sits in the tree trunk and does not speak, does not come out, does not move. I'm not sure if she's wearing shoes or not. You would never know she was there, had not someone heard her shout once and gone to look inside."

"What did she shout?" asked Ian.

Barnabas wrinkled his brow and rolled his eyes up, as if searching the contents of his brain. Finally he said, "According to the rumor, it was 'Cara? Cara, is that you?'" He glanced at Ian slyly. "Of course, this is just gossip — something safe to talk about if you happen across someone else while you are wandering. Who knows if there's any truth to it?"

Truth enough to start me on my search, thought Ian. Speaking aloud, he said, "Where is this tree?"

"I said I'd heard of it. I didn't say I'd seen it."

Ian sighed and looked around. A big world — who could tell how big — and no clue to where his wife might be hidden, other than that she was in a tree. He straightened his shoulders. Well, he was a Hunter, was he not? He had been trained for exactly this kind of task. It was time to go to work. Somehow, some way, he would find Martha. Turning back to Barnabas, he said, "For your help, I thank you."

"Am I being dismissed?"

"You can stay right where you are," replied Ian, a little tartly. "However, we are about to be on our way."

"Which direction will you go?"

"Why do you care?"

Barnabas shrugged again. "I just want to watch."

Ian turned to Fallon. "You choose. If something might be in any direction, it doesn't matter which way we head first."

Fallon nodded. But instead of choosing a direction, he turned back to Barnabas and said, "Do you have any other advice for us before we go?"

The old man smiled. "I wondered if any of you would ask." Squeezing his toes, he said, "I know a secret!"

CHAPTER XXXV

"ROCKY"

"Squijum, wait!" cried Cara.

It was too late; the little creature was already out of sight.

She sighed in exasperation. "We'd better follow him," she said, surprised to find herself apologizing to a delver. "At least *I'd* better." She hesitated, then — wondering at herself even as she did it — she asked, "Do you want to come with me?"

The delver shrugged. "I have nowhere else to go. And I am curious about this story you speak of."

Cara took the sphere from her pocket, cupping it in her hand so as not to hurt her companion's eyes. Soon the two of them were trotting along the tunnel's twists and turns, Cara watching carefully for any side tunnels into which the Squijum might have darted. "Squijum!" she called softly. "Squijum, wait for us!"

She wasn't sure how long they had been running when they rounded a corner and found her furry friend sitting on a rock and looking smug.

Sitting next to him was Grimwold.

"How did you get here?" cried Cara, barely able to contain her delight.

"Squijum bringum," chattered the Squijum, hugging his tail with glee. "Squijum hotcha good finder follower."

"That's pretty much true," said Grimwold. "I would not have been able to keep up with you without our furry friend here. When we were fighting in the forest and I saw the delvers carry you off, I peeled away to follow. I knew —"

"What about Lightfoot?" interrupted Cara. "Is he all right?"

Grimwold closed his eyes. "I do not know. He was still battling the delvers when I headed after you." The old dwarf shook his head. "It was very painful to leave a comrade in battle. But there was no choice, Cara. Someone had to trail you and I was the one who could get away. Lightfoot may well be all right. He's strong, and a good fighter." He paused, then said glumly, "Still, there were an awful lot of the little monsters."

Cara closed her eyes for a moment. *Let him be all right!* she prayed. *Let Lightfoot be all right!*

"Squijum came trailing, too!" squeaked the creature, leaping to her shoulder.

Grimwold nodded. "And a good thing you did. I was able to follow the delvers to the point where they took you underground, Cara, but after that it was the Squijum who kept track of you. I'm used to traveling through tunnels, and I don't need a lot of light, but I'm not as fast as I used to be. Fortunately, your furry friend there is fast enough that he was able to follow you and also keep scooting back to help me stay on your track. And we almost lost you at those spots where they just went through the walls." He shuddered at the memory. "When you were taken to the delver court I had to drop farther back to avoid being spotted — there was a lot of traffic in those tunnels. Fortunately, the Squijum, annoying as he is, was able to wait and watch unseen until you were brought out again."

"Clever Squijum hold tight to roof! Silly delvers never look up! Hotcha clever Squijum!"

"Thank you," said Cara. "Both of you." She felt a sudden wash of gratitude for the risks the two of them had taken to free her, even as she wanted to chastise them for not staying to help Lightfoot fight the delvers. Then she realized an odd thing: Because she was a girl and Lightfoot was an adult male, if they were both in danger, she was *always* the one who would be protected first. She realized it, but couldn't decide how she felt about it. Pushing the thought away, she asked, "What now?"

"Well, I think the first thing we should do is have you explain who that is standing behind you."

"She cannot explain," said the delver. "I have no name."

Cara stared at the delver in astonishment. "You can understand him?"

The delver nodded. "Yes. His speech is strange, and I can't make out all the words. But, yes, I understood."

"I can understand him as well," said Grimwold, "though the way he mangles and distorts the true language is painful to my ears. But what does he mean when he says he has no name?"

"The delver king took it from him, as punishment for disobedience. He was in the dungeon with me and, well, he's sort of on our side."

Grimwold looked incredulous. Turning toward the delver, she could see that he was regarding Grimwold with as much suspicion as the old dwarf felt toward him. Their mutual distrust made her uncomfortable. The fact that she could understand why each of them felt that way only made her discomfort worse.

Glancing from one to the other, she saw that they were about the same height. But where Grimwold was plump, and dressed in a full robe, the delver was lean — scrawny, almost — and dressed in only a loincloth. For all that he was cranky, Grimwold's face had a pleasant feel to it, like that of some old great-uncle who scares you when you first meet him but then turns out to be one of your favorite relatives. The delver, with his bulging bald head, enormous eyes, and pushed-up nose, was simply grotesque.

Even so, Cara felt she could trust him. Speaking quickly, she explained who Grimwold was. "But I need to tell him who you are. Can't you just give me your name?"

He began to quake, as if the very question had filled him with fear. "I told you, I have no name! It has been taken from me."

"Well, I have to have something to call you when I talk to you!"

He looked at her with interest.

"I'm going to give you a new name," she said firmly.

His interest turned to terror. Covering his head with his hands, he flung himself to the floor of the tunnel, quaking with fear. "No," he whimpered. "No! A name is sacred. Mine has been taken. I cannot have a new one!"

Cara stared at the quivering delver, vexed that he was not willing to ignore what seemed to her mere superstition, and at the same time feeling that she had to come up with a solution, since she needed something to call him. With a sudden burst of inspiration she said, "All right, if I can't use your real name, I'm going to give you a nickname!"

The delver looked up at her. "What is a *nick*name?"

"It's NOT a real name," she said, sensing his resistance. "It's something your friends or family call you *in place of* your name. It's a friendly kind of thing." As she said this a sudden memory sprang up, piercing her with both happiness and deep loss. "My father used to call me 'Pookie.' It was his special name for me, but *not* my real name."

The delver nodded slowly. "I think I understand. So you're going to call me Pookie?"

Cara laughed out loud. "No, I don't think that would fit you! Let me think for a second." She recalled the delvers who had captured her. Two of them were named Brank and Dworkin. *So, they use* k *a lot*, she thought. *Well, "Pookie" has a* k *in it, but it still won't work.* She studied the delver for another minute, thinking about what he looked like, and the world he came from, and finally the answer came to her. "I'm going to call you Rocky!"

He didn't respond right away, other than by twitching his grotesque nose, almost as if he were tasting the name. He smiled, showing his pebbly teeth. Then he astonished her by dropping to his knees, placing his forehead against her foot, and crying, "Thank you!"

"Stand up!" she said urgently, embarrassed by this display.

The delver pushed himself to a kneeling position. "Put your hand on my head!"

She looked at him in astonishment.

"Please!"

Reluctantly, trying not to show her aversion, she did as he asked. To her surprise, the flesh of his skull was cool and smooth, and not at all unpleasant to touch.

"Now say my . . . my *nick*name again. Say that you *give* it to me!"

Looking at him, she understood his need, and his urgency. Like a queen dubbing a knight, she said grandly, "I give you the nickname Rocky, to be yours for as long as you care to hold it."

"Rocky" climbed to his feet. Looking happier than she had imagined possible for a delver, he said, "I will never forget this."

"That was well done," said Grimwold from behind her. "The King's punishment was cruel. This 'Rocky' of yours will always long for his real name, of course, and feel its absence like a hole in his heart. But you have given him something to hold on to."

She felt unexpected pleasure in Grimwold's approval. Pushing the thought away, she asked again, "What do we do now?"

"The Queen has given us a task," said Grimwold simply. "As long as we are able, we must try to fulfill it."

"I think Rocky should come with us."

Grimwold looked astonished. "You want a delver to accompany us?"

"Well, for one thing, he's more likely to know the way out of here. Besides, the story is about delvers, too."

"How do we know he wasn't simply put in the dungeon to make friends with you?" asked Grimwold. "It's an old trick — throw someone into a cell with someone else who seems to be a prisoner. Let him gain her confidence, convince her he's her friend . . ."

"No," said Cara. "I don't think that's true." Speaking quickly she told Grimwold about how the delver now known as Rocky had been imprisoned for refusing to join the attack on M'Gama's home. "Besides, it's not just that. I've already met him. He's the one who came to us in the forest, shortly after I first arrived in Luster."

Grimwold studied Rocky, who glared back at him.

"Even if he was a spy, what's he going to learn that will do him any good?" asked Cara, hardly able to believe that she was arguing on behalf of a delver.

After a long period of muttering and grumbling, Grimwold said, "All right, tell him where we want to go. Maybe he can help us find the way."

"She doesn't need to tell me anything," said Rocky. "I can understand you, despite the vile way you speak." He looked away, then said, "We do have a tunnel that opens

close to the Valley of the Centaurs. I can guide us there."
He paused, then added, "It will take several days. Do you
think you can eat the things we delvers do, the food that
comes from underground?"

Cara looked at him nervously. "What kind of food?"

He shrugged. "Food. Mushrooms and fungus. Little animals. Blind fish, sometimes. They're very tasty."

Cara sighed. "I'll do what I have to." She paused, then
asked, "You don't mind leading us?"

This earned her another shrug. "Where else do I have to
go? And I want to know this story. Maybe it will help me
make sense of . . . myself."

So they set out, the girl, the old dwarf, the renegade
delver, and the Squijum. With Cara's sphere to light the
way — kept dim enough not to hurt the delver's eyes but
bright enough that the others could see to walk without trip-
ping — they were able to move more swiftly than they
would have otherwise.

"That light of yours is a good thing," commented Rocky
after a while. "It means we don't have to summon the travel
lines."

"Travel lines?" asked Cara.

"Those orange lights that run along the sides of most of
the tunnels. Without that strange small moon of yours, I
would have to light the lines for us to travel. But that might

alert other delvers that someone was using a tunnel who ought not be. So it's better not to."

Cara was more glad of Medafil's gift than ever.

Her biggest challenge as they journeyed was to keep the Squijum quiet. No matter how aware the little creature was of the danger, he could not help chattering now and then.

Cara had no idea how many hours they had been walking when Rocky stopped and said. "Ah, here we go!"

Then he began to beat his head against the wall.

CHAPTER
XXXVI

AXIS MUNDI

When the last of her visitors departed, the Geomancer stood for a time on one of her home's many terraces, watching their figures dwindle into the distance — a bit of sentiment she would not have wanted them to be aware of.

The moment they were out of sight she flung herself into action, passing with long, sure strides through the surface levels of her dwelling to the place that was her truest home, the tunnels and caves that lay below.

They had sixteen days until the Blood Moon, when it seemed most likely that Beloved would make her attempt on Luster. Sixteen days for her to find the most likely location for that breach between the worlds to open. Sixteen days for the unicorns to prepare a defense. But even if she could determine the most likely place, how could the unicorns reach it in time to make any difference?

In a cave lit only by glowing bowls, M'Gama unrolled several ancient scrolls. To keep the scrolls flat, she held the corners down with stones which she pulled from the pockets of her robe. Once the parchments were secure, she began to study them intently.

Though she knew Beloved's attack might come anywhere, eleven places seemed most likely to her, depending on both the state of the world, and the state of Beloved's magic.

First, and most likely, was one of the seven gates that already existed between Luster and Earth. Though their locations were deeply guarded secrets, if Beloved could link to any one of them, she might be able to use that link to make the transit.

The remaining possibilities were the four great resting places: Springdell, Summerhaven, Autumngrove, and Winterkeep. These places had not been chosen merely because they were well suited to the seasons; they also possessed deep reserves of natural power and magic. Of course, right now the most useful of those four spots for Beloved's purposes would be Autumngrove itself.

M'Gama shuddered at the thought. If the Hunters managed to come through right where the unicorns were gathered, the carnage would be awful. But could Beloved possibly know that was where most of the unicorns were at this time?

It depends, I guess, not only on her magic, but on how good her spies are. It was a worrisome thought.

She set to work, neglecting meals and staying up late into every night. After a week of stretching her magic to its limits, and sending her spirit to walk lines of power from which she risked never returning, she uncovered the answer, which was so startling it snapped her back into her body, gasping in dismay.

When she could breathe again, she returned to the main table, studied once more the maps, the lines of power, all she had noted about the movement of magic, and the enchantments she knew were being woven. Over and over she checked what she had learned, willing the answer to come out differently. But it was the same every time. Her shoulders slumped as dreadful certainty took hold. Beloved's opening would not appear at any of the places she had anticipated. Instead, the attack would occur at the most powerful and sacred place in all of Luster.

Beloved was going to try to breach the Axis Mundi.

I must contact the Queen, thought M'Gama.

Fortunately, that was a magic swiftly managed.

At least, it should have been. But to her astonishment — and horror — just as the face of a unicorn appeared in the scrying pool, the connection was severed.

Disturbed, M'Gama recast her spell.

The same thing happened — as it did the next three times she tried. Finally she gave up, frightened and angry. Who — or what — had the power to interfere with her magic like this?

As happened several times a day, she found herself turning to speak to Flensa, old habit triumphing over painful new reality. She caught herself, but spoke the questions out loud anyway, though she had only herself for an audience. "All right, now what? Either I head back to Autumngrove to give the Queen the news, or try to reach the Axis Mundi myself, to see if there's anything I can do to prevent this."

She made some quick calculations. It was almost two hundred miles to Autumngrove, a trip that — pressing as hard as she could — would take five days at a minimum. Maybe more, given how exhausted she was from a week of grueling work and little sleep. Another half day, at least, would be lost in passing the information to the Queen and her council and then waiting for them to decide what to do — if they could decide at all. M'Gama shook her head; fond as she was of the unicorns, their fecklessness sometimes infuriated her. They needed more — more edge, more fire, more fierceness — if they were to face down this challenge.

She returned to calculating her options. If the unicorns

did actually decide they wanted to be at the Axis Mundi to challenge the Hunters, it would mean another journey of at least three days.

And there it was. The numbers were undeniable. There was simply no way she could take her warning to the Queen in time for the Queen to get a glory to the Axis Mundi before the rise of the Blood Moon.

M'Gama paced back and forth in front of the maps. Even if she could somehow manage it, having the unicorns at the spot the Hunters entered might not be good strategy. Far better if she could somehow block Beloved's magic before they entered at all. She sighed and accepted the fact that she had no choice. She would have to go to the Axis Mundi herself, with the desperate hope that somehow she could prevent the looming catastrophe.

She stretched her ebony hands before her and studied her long, slender fingers. Both hands were deft at shaping power. But could she possibly summon enough magic to thwart Beloved's attempt to create a new opening into Luster?

She curled her open hands into fists. Possible or not, she had to make the attempt.

Moving swiftly now that her mind was made up, the Geomancer gathered the items she thought would be most useful to her: a set of plain-looking stones into which she had slowly, patiently been channeling power for more years than she could remember; four pieces of polished rootwood, one from each of the ancient trees that stood at the center of the four great resting places; a cloth bag filled with soil from the Axis Mundi itself; and a half dozen other oddments tied to the power and magic of Luster. Once these necessities were packed, she changed into traveling clothes, discarding the flowing, brilliantly colored robes she preferred for a set of sturdy trousers, a linen shirt, and a miraculous brown cloak that would not only shield her from wind and rain, but also — at a gesture — puff itself up to make a comfortable pad in which to wrap herself at night. She was more than capable of finding food along the way, but that would take time — time she didn't have to waste. So she added traveler's fare: some dried fruit and a packet of dense biscuits that were sustaining if not particularly tasty. M'Gama felt a twinge in her heart as she wrapped the food and placed it in her pack; it had been prepared for her by Flensa.

Gear assembled, the Geomancer stepped outside, kissed her door with a promise to return, then strode swiftly and purposefully across the stony shelf on which her house was built.

She had no need of maps. She had spent decades linking herself to Luster, learning its lines of power, connecting them to her heart. Aside from the unfinished places, she could no more get lost in its vast and untracked forests than she could in her own home.

In truth, all of Luster was her home, and no place more so than the Axis Mundi.

Which was why she had to protect it.

No matter what it might cost her.

CHAPTER
XXXVII

STUCK

"Stop it!" cried Cara. "Rocky, stop it! What's the matter?"

The delver flung himself to the floor. "If I wasn't a traitor before, I am now. This is a great delver secret."

Cara looked at him in bafflement. "What is?"

"Don't you see?" asked the delver, sounding equally surprised. He sighed, then covered his eyes and said, "Give yourself some more light."

She twisted the sphere slightly. In its expanded glow, she saw what she had missed before: the outline of an arch carved in the wall to their right. Etched into the stone beside it was a series of jagged symbols. "I don't understand. What good will this do us?"

"It's what we call a 'transit point,'" said Rocky. He turned away and pressed his forehead against the wall again. Cara and Grimwold stood silently as he muttered to himself for what seemed like several minutes. Finally he sighed and faced them once more. "What I do now is perhaps my greatest act of treachery. Ah, well. The King can only kill me once — though he can choose ever more painful ways to do it. Be silent, and watch."

He took a deep breath, then began tracing the symbols carved along the side of the arch with his fingertip. He murmured to himself as he did. It took Cara a moment to realize that he was chanting something. Even then, his voice was so low she could not make out what he was saying. But the light of the sphere revealed something she had not expected: The symbols were words — and she could read them!

When Rocky had finished tracing and chanting the last symbol, the space within the arch began to glow. "Follow me," he said.

Then he stepped through the wall and disappeared.

Cara looked at Grimwold, who made an "after you" gesture. She stepped up to the arch, the Squijum cowering on her shoulder, then pressed her way into it. The sensation was familiar, a thousand tingles skittering over her skin, as if she were walking through a mist made of electricity.

So, these were what we were going through every time Brank blindfolded me, she thought.

"I'm still not sure I understand the point of these," said Grimwold, who had come through the arch just behind her.

"The point is that we just saved three days of travel," said Rocky, as if he were speaking to a somewhat slow child. "That transit spot links two tunnels that are many, many miles apart."

Understanding dawned on Grimwold's face. "So that's how you delvers manage to move around so quickly," he said, sounding impressed. "It certainly explains some things you've managed to do over the years."

"There is more to we delvers than you think," said Rocky sharply. "Shall we continue our journey?"

Grimwold bowed. "By all means."

Without sunrise or sunset, day or night, it was hard to keep track of time. Cara would have lost all sense of how many days they had left if not for Thomas's calendar watch, which she checked every time they stopped to rest.

"We have only eight days before the Blood Moon," she said nervously during one such stop. "I don't see how we can possibly get the story and get it back to Autumngrove before then."

"I share your concern," said Grimwold. "But there's no point in buying trouble. Since we don't know how far we have left to go, all we can do is keep moving."

They did indeed find food and water along the way, as

Rocky had promised, but it didn't take long for her to grow tired of fungus and raw fish — one meal, to be precise.

Some of the water they came across was cold and clear and tasted good. Other times it was stale and stagnant, which always made her yearn for Lightfoot, who could cleanse it so easily with his horn. But it wasn't merely that she wanted him to clear the water. It was more that once she started thinking about him, she would be flooded with worry. Had he survived the delver attack? If so, where was he now?

The caves were cool, but that did not seem to bother Rocky or Grimwold. Cara's cloak, filthy though it now was, kept her warm enough. At night — or whenever it was that they slept — the Squijum would snuggle beside her. His small body didn't really provide much heat. Even so, she somehow felt warmer with him there.

Sometimes the little creature would scamper away from them and vanish into the darkness. It always frightened Cara when he did this. What if he was not able to find his way back? Or, even worse, what if he came across some awful creature that would consider him nothing more than a tasty morsel?

Once when he reappeared after what seemed like hours, she said sharply, "Don't do that again, Squijum. Stay with us!"

"Stinky girl not nice to hotcha good Squijum!" he pouted.

She was too weary to answer. Nor did she have time to, for Rocky hissed, "Put out the light! Hide it, darken it, quickly!"

Cara twisted the sphere until it was no bigger than a cherry and dropped it into her pocket. At once they were immersed in complete darkness. She put out her hand until she touched the delver's arm. Sliding closer to him she whispered, "What is it?"

"I'm not sure. I heard something ahead of us. It may have come from a cross tunnel — could be a cove heading out on a mission. He paused, then added, "If we're lucky, that's all it is."

"What else *could* it be?"

"Not even the delvers know all the things that lurk in these tunnels," he answered grimly.

The Squijum bounded to her shoulder, silent for a change. Grimwold, who had been trailing behind, hurried forward to join them. The unlikely quartet huddled in the darkness, listening intently for whatever was ahead of them. Just as the silence itself seemed it might become unbearable, a mournful wail echoed down the tunnel.

Cara gasped. "I know that voice!"

The wail came again, seeming to be made of equal parts fear and sorrow.

She started toward it.

"What are you doing?" hissed Grimwold.

"Don't worry," she said, not even looking back. "It will be all right!"

"Hotcha crazy girl," muttered the Squijum, who was still clinging to her shoulder. Cara ignored him. A few more paces brought her to the cross tunnel the wail had issued from. Enlarging the sphere allowed her to see that the tunnel, which stretched to both the right and the left, was narrower than the one through which they had been traveling.

Which direction had the cry of distress come from?

Another pitiful yowl answered the question. Cara darted into the tunnel at her left and hurried along it, twisting the sphere as she did so that it grew larger and shed more light. A moment later she rounded a corner and came to the source of the sound, a strange creature whose bulk blocked the tunnel. Its head was that of an eagle, save that it was adorned with tufted ears unlike any eagle had ever worn. Cara could not see its wings, which were folded against its sides and hidden by the tunnel, but she knew they were also those of an eagle, even if vastly larger. Nor did she need to see the creature's hindquarters to know that its lower body changed form to become that of a great, tawny lion.

She stepped closer. "You poor thing. How did —"

"Gaaaah!" cried the creature, striking forward with its sharp beak.

"Yike!" squeaked the Squijum. Leaping off her shoulder, he scampered into the darkness.

"Medafil!" screamed Cara. "Stop!"

CHAPTER XXXVIII

A LESSON IN SHIMMERING

"Are you willing to share your secret?" asked Fallon.

The old man, who was counting his toes again, look up blankly. "What secret?"

"We asked if you had any advice for us, and you said you knew a secret," said Ian, struggling to keep from snapping at the old man.

"Oh, *that* secret!" Barnabas frowned. "I'm not sure I should tell you. If I do, it won't be a secret anymore."

"You could tell *me*," said Rajiv, settling in to sit next to the old man. "I am a great keeper of secrets."

Barnabas glanced at the boy warily, then at the two men. "Would you tell them?"

"I would have to," said Rajiv, nodding sagely. "That is my job. But that way *you* will not have told them. And you can trust *me* not to tell anyone else."

"Actually, I don't suppose it matters," said Barnabas with a shrug. "Everyone here figures it out sooner or later." He scowled. "Of course, sometimes it is much, *much* later."

"Ah, but I might be too old by then," said Rajiv conspiratorially. "Perhaps you had better tell me now, before it is too late."

"That is an excellent point!" Barnabas glanced around, then whispered, "All right, here it is: Traveling in the Rainbow Prison is easier than you might think. In fact, that's all you have to do: Think. That's rather nice . . . don't you think?"

"Sahib!" said Rajiv chidingly. "It is not nice to make fun of a poor boy!"

"I'm not making fun," said Barnabas. He closed his eyes and began to vibrate, then blurred into a red streak and disapppeared.

"I swear, sahibs, I did not mean to drive him off!"

"I'm over here!"

They turned. Standing on a rise about a hundred feet to their left was Barnabas.

Ian started toward him.

"No need to rush," said Barnabas, shimmering out of sight again. "It's easier this way."

Ian turned and saw the old man standing in the very place he had been sitting moments earlier.

"How did you do that?"

Barnabas shrugged. "We call it 'shimmering.' It's one of the few good things about the Rainbow Prison. Almost makes up for the way you have to watch out for your toes. If you have a clear vision of where you want to go, you can just think yourself there. After all, there's nothing to this place, really. It's just light." He paused, and looked slightly alarmed. "Hmmm. On second thought, I'm not sure moving this way will work for the three of you, since you have *real* bodies. Well, I don't suppose it will hurt you to try. You probably won't explode or anything."

"How is this done?" asked Fallon.

"Can I touch your toes?"

"You can't touch anything," said Fallon reasonably. "You have no body."

Barnabas sighed. "I nearly forgot. All right, I'll tell you anyway. You start by forming an image in your mind of the place you want to be. Once you have that good and clear, just let go! Your mind will take you there. Of course, it's very hard to go someplace you haven't already seen. What that means for you three — at least at first — is that you won't be able to travel farther than you can see. Even so, it's a lot faster than walking! Easier on your toes, too! Go ahead, try. See if you can take yourselves to where I was just standing."

Ian looked toward where the old man had gone. The

constant red was starting to hurt his eyes. Ignoring the discomfort, he set the image in his mind: a low knoll with four trees — three clumped together, and a fourth off to their right. Once he was sure he had it, he closed his eyes and tried to "let go" . . . whatever that meant.

After a moment, he opened his eyes.

To his frustration, he was standing right where he had been. Even more frustrating was the fact that Fallon and Rajiv were standing on the ridge, looking back at him!

"Come on, sahib!" cried Rajiv, waving a hand. "It's fun!"

Ian closed his eyes and tried again. When he opened them, he was still standing in the same place. Before he could shout to the others, they blurred, then reappeared beside him.

"How did you do that?" he asked, trying not to let his frustration overwhelm him.

"Just do what Barnabas told us, sahib. It's easy."

Barnabas chuckled. "Probably easier for a child than an adult. It takes a while to get the mind to really let go. And even then your toes can hold you back. They tend to be set in their ways."

"He has a point," said Fallon.

"About the toes?" asked Rajiv, astonished.

"No. I just mean that to do this you don't have to let go simply of where you are standing. You have to let go of some of your deepest ideas of how the world actually functions."

"All right, that explains why Rajiv can do it," said Ian. "How about you?"

The big man shrugged. "I suspect I am less attached to a fixed view of how the world is arranged than you, my friend." He smiled. "It has to do with my upbringing."

Ian muttered something under his breath. Barnabas cackled, a gleeful sound that made Ian want to throttle him.

"See the place clearly," said Fallon. He was speaking softly now, close to Ian's ear. His low, rich voice had a soothing effect, and Ian felt his anger begin to ebb. "Once you have a strong image of the spot, imagine yourself in it. Let your mind put you there. And relax as you do it, Ia —" Fallon stopped, glanced at Barnabas, who was watching them eagerly, and quickly rephrased, leaving out Ian's name. "Relax as you do it. This takes as much *not* trying as it does trying."

"Yes, you must try not to try!" cried Rajiv, clearly amused at himself.

Ian nodded. Closing his eyes, he worked to see the knoll as clearly as if his eyes were still open. He strained to fill in the details, making the vision as specific as his imagination was able.

Once that was done, he envisioned himself standing beside one of the trees.

"Relax," whispered Fallon.

Holding on to the image, Ian tried to let the tension drain from his shoulders. He felt a vibration, and gasped. But when he opened his eyes, he was still standing with the others.

"That was strange, sahib. You sort of . . . *smeared* for a minute. I thought you were gone, but you weren't. It was very interesting."

"More letting go is all you need," said Fallon. "Try again."

Ian closed his eyes, retrieved his vision of the knoll, then mentally planted himself there, making himself part of the scene. He slowed his breath, trying to let go, let go . . .

Suddenly he felt a slight tremor, then an instant of cold, as if something icy had rushed through him.

"Almost," said Fallon.

It took another three tries before he opened his eyes and found himself on the knoll.

"Well done, sahib!" cried Rajiv, shimmering into place beside him. An instant later Fallon was there as well.

Ian glanced back toward where they had been standing. The old man, Barnabas-for-the-moment, cried, "Watch out for your toes!"

Then he vanished.

"That was interesting," said Fallon. "Do you suppose our 'Barnabas' truly just happened upon us? Or was he waiting for us?"

"What do you mean, sahib?"

Fallon swung his arm to indicate the crimson world around them. "This place is not what you would call densely populated, Rajiv. Yet 'Barnabas' — or whoever he really is — found us virtually the moment we arrived. I suppose it could have been coincidence . . ."

"That seems unlikely," said Ian. "Hmmm. If the Ruby Portal *always* opens to that spot, it's possible he has been keeping an eye on it."

"For what purpose?" asked Rajiv.

Ian shrugged. "Could be nothing more than boredom. I suspect not a lot happens here. Or maybe, as Fallon said, he's waiting for someone specific."

"Or maybe," added Fallon darkly, "he's been *assigned* to watch the spot and is reporting back to someone." Then he smiled and said, "Of course, he was rather more helpful than you might expect if that were the case."

Ian nodded. "I agree. All right, let's start searching." With a twinge of anxiety, he suddenly remembered that Fallon's quest was not his own. The thought made him unexpectedly sad. "Or will you be heading off on your own now?"

"What? Sahib Fallon, why would you leave us?"

"Ian and I do have different goals, Rajiv."

"But . . . but which of you . . ."

"No need to worry about that right now. Since neither Ian nor I has a clue where to begin, we may as well continue to follow the same path. We have the whole of the Rainbow Prison to cover after all, and I'm as likely to find the way into Luster while searching for his wife as I am looking for it on my own."

Ian smiled, pleased to know that Fallon, who was the closest thing he had had to a friend in as long as he could remember, would be staying with them for the time being. He looked around for a moment, then said, "I think the thing to do is keep moving about until we find someone else. The best clues, for both of us, will probably come from other people. And now that we can . . . *shimmer* . . . we'll be able to cover a fair amount of territory pretty quickly."

Fallon's reply was interrupted by a terrified shout from Rajiv. "Sahibs! *Sahibs!*"

Ian spun, and saw the boy standing beside a tree about thirty yards away. He could not see anything that looked as if it endangered Rajiv. Even so, the boy's face was twisted in panic.

"What is it, Rajiv?" called Fallon. "What's wrong?"

"We have a big problem, sahibs. *Very* big!"

CHAPTER
XXXIX

FLIGHT

The gryphon halted its strike just before it would have sliced open her arm. Its eyes widened in astonishment. "Cara? *Cara?* What are *you* doing here?"

"I asked you first! At least, I tried to, before you almost took my arm off!"

"Dadgimbled girl, always did ask too many questions. All right, if you must know, I'm lost. Stuck, too, which is just as bad. Worse, maybe."

"Stuck?" she asked in horror. "You mean you can't move at all?"

"Jammed in like a cork in a bottle. You'd better go. I expect something horrible to come along and eat me at any moment."

"I am *not* going to desert you, Medafil," said Cara firmly. "But what are you doing down here?"

The gryphon heaved another enormous sigh. "After I nearly broke my back flying that blat-forgled Dimblethum out of Ebillan's cave and across the Northern Waste, I decided to head for the coast to get some sea air. Needed a bit of a vacation, you know. Well, while I was there I got talking to a mermaid who told me she'd heard about a golden frippery that was hidden in a certain cave. I believed her, fool that I am. Sog-fuddled water people can't tell a straight story to save their lives! Anyway, I started into the cave she told me about, and found a tunnel at the back of it. That tunnel led to another tunnel, and that led to another tunnel, and one thing led to another, and next thing you know, here I am, stuck in the dark, waiting for the flit-borgled delvers to find me and eat me." The gryphon sighed heavily. "I'm sorry I almost bit you. I was frightened. And I certainly didn't expect to find a friend down here!" He paused, then added. "Besides, I had my eyes closed. There, I've answered. Now it's your turn. What are *you* doing here?"

"It's a long story."

"Well, do you have a pressing engagement anywhere else? I certainly don't."

"As a matter of fact, I do. We're heading for the Valley of the Centaurs."

"Gaah! Why would you go *there*? Those frak-waddled

creatures are not very friendly. They might even be dangerous. And who is 'we'? And how in the world do you know
your way around down here?"

Cara laughed. "Weren't you the one complaining about
too many questions? What order do you want me to answer
you in?"

"Start with how you know your way around."

"Well, I don't. But we've got a delver —"

"Gaaahhh! Don't tell me you're traveling with one of
those treek-bingled creatures! Have you lost your mind?"

"No, and I haven't lost my way, either — which is more
than I can say for you. Let me get the others, then I'll
explain what's happening."

"Don't leave me! What if the delvers come?"

"I'll be right back." She kissed him on the beak. "I
promise."

He sighed. "Oh, all right. I'd ask you to leave that light
I gave you, except I know the blig-dorted thing won't stay lit
once you let go. Never could see the use of it, so I'm glad it's
doing *you* some good. Well, never mind me. I'll just stay
here in the dark."

"I won't be gone long. And you were in the dark
already."

"Yes, but I didn't like it!"

Cara turned to fetch the others, but found that Grimwold
had already come up behind her. Somewhat to her surprise,

the Squijum was perched on the old dwarf's shoulder, something Grimwold would never normally allow.

Rocky, standing a little way behind them and looking both confused and fearful, said, "What *is* that thing?"

"He's a gryphon," replied Cara. "And a friend. His name is Medafil."

"What in heaven's name are you *doing* down here?" asked Grimwold, staring at Medafil in astonishment.

"Gaaaahhh! I've already answered that question. Once is enough for one day. Or night. Or whatever this is. Let's talk about how we're going to get out instead." He paused, then added, "Well, maybe you'll have to go on without me. I'm stuck."

"What do you mean?" asked Grimwold.

"I'm stuck! *Stuck!* Isn't that clear enough? I was wriggling down this furt-wangled tunnel and it got too tight for me. I can't back up because I keep catching my wings. I'm afraid I'll tear them right off! And I can't move forward because the tunnel is too narrow for my hips. I'm going to die here!"

Cara was tempted to tease Medafil about needing to lose weight, but decided sympathy would be wiser. "You poor thing!" she said gently. "Here, let me try to squeeze past you. Maybe I can help."

She removed her cloak, then slipped in next to the gryphon. He shifted to the right to make a little room for her.

The warmth of his furry body felt good after the coolness of the tunnels, and there was something comforting about his catlike odor. Lifting her hand, she could feel the sleek feathers of his enormous wing. She knew that some of them were as long as her arm.

"Can you suck in your sides a bit?"

Medafil grumbled, but did as she requested. She got another foot or so, then found that the tunnel was simply too narrow for her to go any farther. Struggling her way back out she called, "Squijum! See if *you* can make it past Medafil to look at where he's stuck."

"Hotcha stinky wingbeast catcritter," muttered the Squijum. Then, instead of trying to squeeze past Medafil's side he scooted over the gryphon's tawny back.

"Gaaaah! That tickles!"

"Be quiet!" ordered Cara. "You don't want to attract delvers, do you?"

"Well, the skittery-bumpused thing is tickling me!" Medafil managed to say this in something like a whisper. Suddenly his eyes widened. Letting out a terrible squawk, he lurched forward.

"What's wrong?" cried Cara.

"The little beast bit me!"

"Squijum!" called Cara. "What are you doing?" But even as she did, she noticed something. "Medafil, try crawling toward me."

"Don't be ridicu . . . gaaahhhh! *I can move!*"

"Good Squijum bite big wingcritter on butt!" chittered the Squijum, darting out from beside Medafil. "Good Squijum get catbutt birdhead unstuck!"

"Is it true?" asked Cara eagerly. "Are you free, Medafil?"

"I would have preferred a more dignified way of making it happen," sniffed the gryphon. "But, yes, I seem to have moved past the point that was holding me. Back up and let me see if I can keep going. The tunnel ahead looks wider than the spot I just got through. Though what good that will do, I don't know, since I still can't turn around."

Cara, Grimwold, and Rocky backed down the tunnel. Medafil crawled toward them. After a little while they came to the place where the two tunnels crossed, which was a bit roomier, with a ceiling high enough that the gryphon could finally stand. He stretched and sighed with relief, then leaned close to Cara and whispered, "You have no idea how terrified I was!"

"I can imagine," she said, stroking his silky ears and thinking of her own experience of being dragged into the delver tunnels. Turning to Rocky, she said, "I would like my friend to come with us to the Valley of the Centaurs. Will he be able to fit through the tunnels we still have to travel?"

Rocky studied the gryphon carefully. Finally he said,

"It's hard to tell. It will be a tight squeeze in some places. Even so, I *think* he can make it."

Cara translated this for Medafil, then said, "Do you want to try?"

"It's not like I could find any other way out. And if I'm going to die down here, which seems likely, I'd rather do it with friends than lost and alone. Don't worry: If I get stuck again you can just abandon me."

"Don't be silly!" said Cara — though in fact she was already wondering just what would happen if they did come to a spot the gryphon could not pass.

Water, at least, was not a problem, since it seemed never to be far away. They crossed numerous underground streams, came through places where the tunnel walls were slick with wetness, and twice even walked along the shores of an enormous underground lake, always with the light from Cara's sphere to show them the way. Once something quite large jumped out of the water. Though it was far from shore, the unexpected smack and splash of its return startled Cara so violently that she almost dropped the sphere.

Food, however, did become an issue. While it was easy for Rocky to find things he considered edible (though in many cases Cara thought that his idea of "edible" was really stretching the term), it was nearly impossible for Medafil. The gryphon complained frequently enough of his hunger that Cara began to worry for the Squijum's safety — especially when the little creature annoyed him, which was fairly often.

They slept when they were tired, taking shifts so that one of them was always awake to listen for the approach of any delvers that might be passing their way.

Cara fretted constantly, her worry list shifting so that sometimes it was topped by concern for Lightfoot, while other times that spot was replaced by fear for all the unicorns, and still other times a deep wondering about her father and his quest to find her mother. And always there was her concern about time, and whether they had a chance of learning the story of the Whisperer and getting it to the Queen before the Blood Moon. Every time they stopped to rest, she checked the calendar watch.

Despite her exhaustion, she rarely slept well.

Most times when they stopped to rest, Grimwold would tell a story, or sing some of the old songs of Luster. Cara's favorite — aside from "Song of the Wanderer," of course — was one called "Hoof and Horn," and after a while she had learned it well enough to sing it to herself while she walked.

They passed through three more transit points. Cara

watched carefully each time Rocky worked the necessary spell to open the gateway, and by the third time she thought perhaps she could do it herself. *At least, I can do it if the magic will respond to a human hand, and doesn't require a delver's touch to work. All he's doing is chanting the symbols carved beside the doorway as he traces the carvings with his fingertip.*

Since the gift of tongues allowed her to read the symbols, too, she knew she could manage that. She was tempted to ask Rocky to let her try, but decided that might not be a good idea, given how guilty he felt over having shown them the secret to begin with.

Medafil seemed to want to travel beside her most of the time. Once, when they reached a cavern so big that it extended farther than the reach of the light from her sphere, he said, "I need to stretch my wings."

"You can't fly in the darkness," replied Cara reasonably. "You might bump into something."

"Grubdum fussy girl," grumbled Medafil. After a pause he said slyly, "Do you want to fly with me? You could light the way!"

"No."

"Please? I'll be a much better traveling companion once I stretch my wings. Flig-spiddled things are starting to ache from lack of use!"

"Well, all right," said Cara, who had actually been eager to take up his offer the minute he made it. "But just a quick flight, Medafil. We need to keep moving."

He crouched, and she climbed onto his back. "Watch out for the light, Rocky," she called.

As the delver turned away, she twisted the sphere until it was nearly two feet wide. Then she locked her knees against the gryphon's tawny sides and cried, "Ready!"

Instantly, Medafil sprang upward. Stretching his great wings, then pumping them to catch the cool air, he rose into the empty space above them. It was vast, and even with the light her sphere was casting, Cara could not see its edges.

She looked down. Forests of stalagmites stretched below them, upthrust spears of smooth rock that glistened with deep, rich colors. Cara found them unexpectedly beautiful, and felt oddly pleased to think she was the only human who had ever seen them, that the light she was now shedding on them was likely the only light ever to have shone in this place. Turning her gaze upward, she gasped. Thousands of stalactites thrust down toward them like shimmering fangs.

She was about to look down again when she saw a dark form peel from the side of one of the stalactites. With a piercing shriek, it spread jagged wings and circled out. It was joined by another, then another, and then a sudden rush as thousands of the creatures descended from the cavern ceiling.

"Down!" cried Cara, shrieking to be heard above the deafening flutter of tens of thousands of wings. "Go down, Medafil!"

The gryphon was already diving, plunging toward the cavern floor so rapidly that Cara had to redouble the grip of her legs against his sides to keep from falling off. She was trying to wind down the sphere at the same time, but didn't dare twist it too fast for fear of slipping off Medafil's back.

The batlike creatures starting shrieking, a high, piercing sound that was like needles jabbing into her ears. It took everything Cara had not to drop the sphere so that she could clap her hands to the sides of her head. Medafil howled, a sound lost among the squeals and squeaks of the dark flock.

Cara suddenly realized that the creatures were staying at a steady distance, wheeling around them as if they were both attracted by the light she carried, and yet afraid to approach it too closely. She reversed her twisting of the sphere, making it larger again. They squealed in agitation, and moved a little farther away.

She and Medafil continued downward, caught in the center of a living globe of winged fury. As they neared the cavern floor, Medafil veered away from their friends. When they were about ten feet from the stony path, the lowest flying of the creatures swirled to the sides to avoid slamming against the rocks. Medafil landed in a catlike crouch.

Instantly some of the dark things began rushing in, eyes blazing, fangs bared, getting closer each time they came. Cara's heart was beating as rapidly as the wings surrounding them.

"What will we do?"

Though Medafil roared his question, the words were barely audible above the thunder of their tormentors' wings.

Without answering, Cara started winding down the sphere.

"What are you doing?" cried the gryphon as the creatures began closing in toward them.

"I have to get something from my pocket!" she bellowed.

When the sphere was small enough that she could hold it securely against her with one hand, she dug the other hand into her vest until she found the watch Thomas had given her. Remembering his words — "Twist the top, then fling it against a hard surface" — she managed to tuck the watch against the glowing sphere. Holding it in place with her left hand, she twisted the top with her right.

"Brace yourself!" she cried to Medafil.

Then she dashed the watch to the floor about a dozen feet ahead of them.

The thunderous explosion silenced the shrieking creatures. They raced away in panic.

Instantly Cara wound her sphere down to the size of an apricot and jammed it into her pocket, plunging them into darkness.

They listened as the flutter of wings grew more distant.

Finally Cara drew a deep breath of relief. "I think they're gone," she whispered.

"I hope so," muttered Medafil.

Rocky, Grimwold, and the Squijum soon joined them.

"Did you enjoy your flight?" asked Grimwold dryly.

"Ding-borgled dwarf," muttered Medafil. "Let's just get moving before they decide to come back."

Cara started to reply, but was interrupted by a low growl that rumbled from the darkness behind them.

"Now what?" she whispered.

Before anyone could answer, a blue glow arced through the air.

"Run!" cried Rocky, his voice shrill with panic. "*RUN!*"

CHAPTER
X L

"YOUR HEART'S DESIRE"

The voice returned each morning, just as the Dimblethum was waking.

"Do you know your heart's desire? I do. I know how to . . ."

For the first several days, the Dimblethum would clamp his paws to his ears and shake his head, though it never made any difference, never blocked out the words. "I know what you want . . ." They came, over and over again, as if the Whisperer had somehow burrowed into his heart.

Not fair! thought the Dimblethum furiously. *Not fair!*

In truth, the shambling creature had long ago turned from expecting life to be fair. Even so, for more years than he could remember his cave had been his one true refuge, the single place he felt safe, and free from memories. Not that he could ever actually get at his memories, hidden as they were behind a wall of fog that seemed to block his past.

Sometimes he thought he had a memory of having memories . . . the unpleasant sense that there had once been more to his life than he knew, but that it had somehow been lost to him.

It was in his cave that he felt most free of that nagging sensation, sheltered from things that might stir his awareness of the blank in his mind. To have that sanctuary violated by this invisible intruder made him feel small and vulnerable — an odd sensation for the huge creature.

As the days passed, the voice began to come not just in the morning, but at all hours, whispering promises the Dimblethum did not want to hear, but could not help listening to — promises laden with hooks that sank deep into his heart, catching on snags he hadn't even known were there.

Far at the back of his mind a warning memory stirred in response. He could tell it was there, like an itch he could not reach. But it was too well hidden behind that curtain of fog for him to find it.

CHAPTER
XLI

THE SKWARTZ

As another burst of blue light arced through the air behind them Cara cried, "What is it, Rocky? What's doing that?"

"Run now, talk later!" screamed the delver, who was already several feet ahead of her.

She ran, the Squijum clinging to her neck. She was slowed by having to hold the sphere, which kept her from letting her arms swing free. But if she pocketed it, they would be running in the dark, or, more likely, stumbling and falling in the dark. Fear and frustration tore at her stomach. What was behind them that had so terrified Rocky?

Grimwold padded along beside her, surprisingly fast given his age. Medafil stayed at the rear. Cara knew the gryphon was doing so in order to be ready to defend them if necessary.

They ran until they had no more breath, then paused, gasping, then walked, then ran again, continually urged on by Rocky, who was caught in a kind of terror Cara had never seen before.

The next time they stopped she listened carefully, though it was hard to hear above the sound of her own gasps. "Everyone hold your breath," she finally ordered in a low voice. "Medafil, you have the best ears. Can you hear anything?"

The gryphon paused for a moment, then shook his head. "Not a grib-fizzled thing."

Cara sighed in relief. "Then we've lost it."

"No, no!" said Rocky, his face twisted in panic. "We haven't lost it. Trust me on this."

"What did he say?" asked Medafil.

Cara translated for the gryphon, and continued to do so through the rest of the conversation, which continued with Grimwold demanding, "Just what do you think that was?"

"Not think. *Know.* All that noise you made has woken a skwartz. I thought there was only one of the monsters, but there must have been another down here."

In the light of the sphere, Cara could see that the delver's normally pale face had grown even paler, his large eyes made even larger by his fright. "What is it?" she asked.

Rocky shuddered. "A skwartz is something like a worm, something like a lizard, and twice as long as all of us laid end to end — longer, maybe. And that's not counting its tail. Two things make it especially dangerous."

"What are they?" asked Grimwold. Cara could hear the fright in the old dwarf's voice, which only sharpened her own terror.

"The first thing is that blue glow you saw. It's a liquid that the skwartz spits. The glow lets it find its way in the dark. It also helps it spot its prey."

"Well, we have light, too," said Cara, cradling the sphere like a shield.

"That's not the worst of it! If that blue liquid touches you, it burns like fire. The skwartz uses it to bring down its prey. If you get a face full of it, it will peel your skin right off. If it strikes you in the back, it will eat through the skin and fuse your spine."

Cara's stomach clenched with fear.

"Those things certainly make it dangerous," admitted Grimwold. "But as bad as that sounds, we've escaped now, right?"

Rocky shook his head. "I was only counting the light and the acid as a single thing."

"Then what's the second thing?" asked Cara, trying not to let her voice tremble.

"Once it's on your trail, a skwartz doesn't stop. *Ever.* It's slow, much slower than us. But it doesn't sleep, it doesn't rest, it doesn't tire. It's been moving toward us all the time we've been standing here. We'll get far ahead of it, but we'll have to stop sometime, have to sleep sometime. It won't. It will keep coming, and coming, and coming, slithering toward us through the dark. Everything is a race between us and the skwartz now. We've got to get out of these tunnels before it catches us, because if it does, there is no way we can fight it."

"Yike," muttered the Squijum, tightening his grip on Cara's neck.

"How much farther do we have to go?" asked Grimwold.

Rocky glanced around. "I'm not sure. It's not as if I've traveled this route before. Probably we'll need to sleep twice before we reach the Valley of the Centaurs."

"Is there any other way out before that?" asked Cara.

"Not that I know of. If we find a transit point, we can use it to get away from the skwartz. It will probably take us somewhere we don't want to be, but even so . . ." He glanced behind them and shuddered.

"I see what you mean," said Cara. "All right, let's get moving."

Travel became a nightmare of apprehension. Until they aroused the skwartz there had been the vague dread of Beloved's threatened invasion. Now, after Rocky's explanation of what was trailing them, they lived from moment to moment, in terror of the nightmare that was slowly, relentlessly drawing nearer and nearer. Twice Cara tried to use the amulet, hoping it could draw them away from this living nightmare. Each time it failed. So they walked and ran and walked and ran again until they had worn themselves to exhaustion. But that exhaustion did not guarantee rest when they stopped.

How do you sleep when you know that every minute you're not moving that . . . that thing . . . *is getting closer?* thought Cara as she lay on her back, staring into the darkness. But if sleep was impossible just then, so was moving on; her legs had been trembling, and she was barely able to stand when they finally called a halt.

Medafil took the first watch.

"Couldn't sleep anyway," he muttered to Cara. "Not knowing that gum-dobbled creature is back there." He paused, then added, "Besides, this is my fault."

Cara wanted to tell him not to be silly, but they both knew that if they hadn't taken that flight in the cavern they might not have stirred the skwartz into action. "My fault, too," she murmured. "If I hadn't agreed to fly with you . . ." Her words trailed off in a surge of regret.

Medafil nudged her with his beak. "You were only doing me a favor. Sleep now. I'll watch."

Wrapping herself in her cloak, she finally did drift into sleep. But it was a sleep marred by endless dreams of being chased through the darkness, dreams made worse because in them she had the horrifying sensation of not being able to move, while her pursuer drew ever closer. When Grimwold finally nudged her awake and said, "I've taken my turn. I need you to watch for a time," she felt as if the day had never ended, as if she had never stopped running.

Pulling herself to a sitting position, she wrapped her arms around her legs and whispered, "You sleep, I'll listen."

"Thank you," whispered Grimwold.

Only the sound of her friends' breathing kept the darkness from being totally terrifying. She longed to light the sphere, but feared that if she did, it would draw the skwartz on more quickly.

To her amazement, despite her fear, she had a hard time staying awake. The dark and the silence and her exhaustion conspired to lull her back to sleep, so that ever and again her head would drop forward. She would wake with a start, terrified that she had slept too long and the creature was almost upon them, then listen so hard she thought her head would split.

Then the drowsiness would creep over her again. . . .

Rousing with yet another start from another almost-nap that had tried to seize her, she heard it — the soft slither of a long, scaly belly being dragged over cold stone. Though it jolted her to full wakefulness, for a moment she was frozen with terror. She held her breath to listen more carefully. How far back was it?

Impossible to tell.

She scrambled to her feet, groping in her pocket for the sphere. She twisted it until it was the size of an apricot. Holding it cupped between her fingers so only the tiniest amount of light escaped, she found each of her companions and shook them awake with a whispered warning to silence. Soon they were on the move again, trotting through the dimly lit tunnel in a waking nightmare that seemed little more than an extension of the horrible dreams that had plagued her almost-sleep.

Behind them crawled their nemesis, slow and falling back for now, but never resting, never pausing, drawing nearer again every time their exhausted bodies forced them to stop.

CHAPTER
XLII

HUNGER AND THIRST

Fallon shimmered into place beside Rajiv, who was clearly frantic. Ian thought about trying to do the same thing, but decided it would be faster — and possibly less humiliating — to simply run back to where the two were standing.

When both men had reached him, Rajiv said, "Watch this, sahibs." With trembling hand, he stretched upward to pluck an applelike piece of fruit.

His red-tinged fingers passed through it as if it were nothing but air.

Rajiv turned back to the two men, fear blossoming anew in his face. "What does it mean, sahibs? *What does it mean?*"

"A world made of light," murmured Ian. "Why didn't I think about this before we came?" Then, his jaw tightening, he added, "And why didn't the Blind Man warn me?"

"I should have realized, too," said Fallon. He seemed to be talking more to himself than to the others.

"But how shall we eat while we are in this place?" cried Rajiv. Before either man could answer, he shimmered out of sight, only to reappear at the spot where they had first entered the Rainbow Prison.

"Rajiv!" shouted Ian. "What are you doing?"

The boy didn't answer. Instead he trotted to the pool that was near their entry place. He dipped his right hand into the water — or what appeared to be water. The hand came out dry. He tried again, first cupping both hands and trying to scoop some up, then, in desperation, thrusting his face right into it.

An instant later, he was standing beside Ian and Fallon again. "That water is not water, either, sahibs. I know I begged to come, but you did not tell me we were going someplace like this, someplace where nothing is real. How does that man Barnabas stay alive? How shall we?"

"He stays alive because his body is not here," said Fallon. "That's why he was so surprised to find that *we* had brought our bodies with us!"

Ian glanced down. "I wonder how it is that we do not plunge right through the ground?"

"Sahib! Where would we go if we did?"

Fallon shuddered. "That question does not bear thinking

on, Rajiv. Let us simply be glad there is something here to hold us."

"But we must be able to eat! Sahib Hunter, can you use that jewel of yours to take us back?"

"Where would we end up if we did go back?" asked Fallon. "If you'll remember, Rajiv, we jumped into an abyss in order to enter this place. If the stone returned us to where we left our world, we would still be falling."

The boy's face twisted in new fear. "What have we done?"

"What we set out to do," said Ian grimly. "Found our way into the Rainbow Prison. What I intend to do next is continue looking for my wife, just as I had planned. Remember, finding her is our best — perhaps our only — chance of leaving here."

"But without food, without water —"

"Martha is our way out," repeated Ian firmly. With a sigh, he added, "But I did think we would have more time to find her."

"Perhaps we should split up after all," said Fallon.

"Sahibs! I do not want to get lost!"

"Fallon has a point, Rajiv. Think about it: Since shimmering will let us travel so easily, we can cover three times as much territory if we split up. And since as long as you set a place in your mind you can shimmer back to it, each of us can get back to *this* spot instantly."

A light of understanding dawned in the boy's eyes. "And from here we can travel back in a single shimmer to the farthest place we have visited, and start again from there!"

Ian nodded. "We have to move fast, cover as much ground as possible. Doing so, we may meet other people. Perhaps one of them will know where Martha is. Let's get started. We truly have no time to waste."

"We must be sure to keep track of the jumps we make," said Fallon. "Though each of us could shimmer back here after a hundred leaps out, we wouldn't be able to lead the others straight to a new location. That will have to be done jump by jump."

"Right!" said Rajiv, following his line of thought. "Since you can only go as far as you can see, if I find the memsahib, I will have to lead you through each shimmer I took to get to her."

"Can you do that, Rajiv?" asked Ian. "Keep all the steps in your head?"

The boy laughed. "How do you suppose I find my way around the streets of Delhi? It is you two I should be worried about! If you think *you* can manage it, let us begin!"

"One more thing," said Ian. "We must plan to reconnect here on a regular basis, in case one of us learns something." He paused, then added, "You are seeking something, too, Fallon. Is there a way we can help you while we search?"

"I want only to move from this place into Luster. If you find any way — any hint of a way — I can do that, I will be grateful." He looked around for a moment, then pointed off to their right. "I'll go that way." Instantly he shimmered out of sight, reappearing on a ridge that was about as far away as either Ian or Rajiv could see.

"Travel safely," said Ian to the boy. "I'll check back here every half hour or so."

"I hope to see you soon, sahib," said Rajiv. Then he, too, shimmered into the distance.

Ian looked around, chose the place he wanted to move to, and let himself relax into it.

Instantly, he was there.

He did a quick scan, hoping he might see someone who could help him, but there was no one in sight. He shrugged, took a moment to set the location firmly in his mind, then looked ahead, picked his next target, and shimmered again.

Though it was exhilarating to be able to move so easily, the search itself was frustrating. By sunset none of them had found anyone who could help — or anyone at all, for that matter.

Under normal circumstances this wouldn't have bothered Ian; he was patient, and had been trained to the long, slow hunt. But now they had so little time — so little time to find his wife, so little time to live themselves if they could not escape from this red, red world — that it was all he could do to keep from screaming.

"I am perishing of thirst, sahibs," complained Rajiv when they decided to pause for the night. "Hunger, too. But the thirst is much worse."

Ian felt a new pang of guilt for having allowed the boy to come with them. *I should have pushed back when Fallon said it was all right,* he thought bitterly. *The boy should not be here.*

He felt, too, the first stabs of a growing panic. Not about dying. He did not fear death, or at least, not much. This was a deeper fear, one that had to do with letting people down.

The world grew dark around them, a darkness tinged with red, into which rose a red moon, surrounded by red stars. When Rajiv's breathing was still and steady, Ian whispered, "Fallon, are you still awake?"

"I'm here."

"Tell me about the friend you're looking for."

The silence that followed lasted so long that Ian wondered if Fallon had drifted into sleep after all. But finally he began to speak.

CHAPTER
XLIII

THE LIGHT AT THE END
OF THE TUNNEL

"I can't stop now, I can't stop now, I can't stop now," Cara murmured to herself over and over as they slogged wearily through the tunnels of Delvharken.

Her exhaustion was so deep and painful she began to wonder if it might be better to let the skwartz catch them. Except she could not forget Rocky's vivid description of the creature's acid saliva, and how painfully it would burn. Fear of that agony, even more than fear of death, drove her on.

Underneath those fears, and even more compelling, was the urgent sense that they still had a mission to fulfill — that the fate of the unicorns, of Luster itself, might depend on their retrieving the story of the Whisperer.

With the only light being that which came from her sphere, it was impossible to tell how long they had walked since their last rest. Even hunger was no guide, since they had not stopped to eat for so long that the gnawing in their bellies had become a constant, unvarying companion.

And now the skwartz was close enough that they dared not stop at all, since every time they did they would hear the ever-closer sound of the creature's great length dragging across the tunnel floor behind them.

"The way out isn't much farther," Rocky kept saying, though whether the delver spoke out of fear or hope or simply a desperate desire to keep them moving Cara could not tell. Life had become nothing but a race between themselves and the crawling horror that pursued them, a contest between their fading strength and their will to live.

They ran when they could, but those bursts of speed grew shorter and shorter as their reserves of energy dwindled. Even the Squijum seemed exhausted, and clung to her neck far more often than usual.

And still the creature came on, and on, and on.

A sudden flare of blue light behind them pierced Cara with new terror. They began to trot again, a plodding burst of almost-speed that she knew would taper off all too soon.

"Is it trying to hit us?" she asked Rocky.

"Not yet. That just means it's close enough to see us."

Suddenly Grimwold, who was a few feet behind her, gasped, "I can't go any farther."

"You have to!" cried Cara. She turned to him, then screamed, as a sapphire streak of flaming liquid landed with a sizzle not ten feet away. In that momentary flash of blue light, she saw, for the first time, the face of their nemesis. The image seared itself into her brain. The creature's face was lizardlike, but with eyes out of all proportion, eyes enormous even for its enormous head, eyes made for a world of darkness. Its shoulders nearly filled the tunnel. Worst of all was its tongue, which had been flicking out. Slate gray, forked like a snake's, but thick as her arm, that searching tongue had reached nearly as far as the searing blue spittle.

It took courage Cara hadn't known she possessed to go toward the beast so she could grab Grimwold and drag him away.

"Cara, I can't go on," he wheezed. "I have nothing left. I'm much too old for this. Besides, if I stop here it may slow that monster down enough for the rest of you to escape."

"Climb on my back," ordered Medafil.

"I don't think . . ."

"Don't think!" snapped the gryphon, more forcefully than Cara had ever heard him speak. "Just climb on my back so we can keep going!"

"Do it, Grimwold!" screamed Cara. *"Now!"*

Another burst of the blue acid landed not five feet behind them.

Medafil knelt beside Grimwold. The old dwarf climbed on, clutching the gryphon's fur.

Side by side, Medafil and Cara ran forward, stretching the distance between themselves and the skwartz again. But it was only a temporary reprieve. The skwartz was tireless. They were not.

The hours dragged by. The skwartz — slow, relentless, unstoppable — drew ever closer. They could hear it constantly now, even when they gathered the strength for a brief sprint. First it was the heavy drag of its body, never far enough away, never far enough. Then, all too soon, its eager hissing became a sound they could not escape.

The blue acid blazed more frequently. Before long they could hear that, too — hear the revolting cough the skwartz made just before it spat the searing stuff, then the hiss and sizzle it made when it struck the tunnel floor.

Cara was flagging and stumbling. Rocky walked beside her so he could help her to her feet when necessary, always urging her onward, onward. Suddenly he sprinted ahead. She feared, for a moment, that he had abandoned her. But he was running his fingers over some markings on the wall. "This is it!" he cried. "The tunnel I've been looking for! We can get out here!"

The wave of relief Cara felt sent new strength surging into her. But as she tried to sprint forward she tripped. The sphere fell from her hands, plunging the group into total darkness.

"Get up!" urged Grimwold from his position on Medafil's back. "Cara, get up!"

"I have to find the sphere!" she cried, scrabbling around on the tunnel floor, her fingers searching desperately.

"Forget the sphere!" shrieked Medafil. "The skwartz is almost here. Get up, *get up!*"

Cara knew he was right; she could hear the skwartz behind them, sliding nearer, nearer. But she had to find the sphere. Her hands slid across the cool stone of the tunnel floor, seeking, seeking.

When the too-familiar cough sounded again she actually welcomed it. An instant later, the blue light flared — revealing the sphere.

The Squijum reached it ahead of her, squeaking, "Got you, you bad sphere!" He snatched it up and rolled it back toward Cara. Though the blue light had faded and the sphere itself was dark, she managed to clap her hand over it.

"Got it!" she cried, even as it began to glow.

She leaped to her feet, then cried out again, this time in pain.

"What is it?" asked Medafil.

"I twisted my ankle when I fell. I . . . I don't know if I can walk."

"Lean on me," said Rocky. "Let's go!"

They started up the tunnel, slower than ever now, Cara limping, Medafil muttering nervously as the ceiling grew lower, the tunnel walls closer together.

The possibility of escape gave them new strength, and they increased their pace. Even Cara, hobbling beside Rocky, came close to running, running past the pain in her ankle, the pain in her muscles, the pain in her lungs, knowing that the current pain was nothing compared to what she would feel if the skwartz caught them.

And then, ahead of them came a cry of despair from Medafil that pierced her heart with new fear. "What is it?" she shouted.

"The tunnel is too narrow. I can't go on!"

"You have to!" screamed Cara. "The skwartz is almost on us!"

"I can't, I can't! I'll tear off my wings!"

"And you'll be eaten if you don't!"

An arc of blue acid landed not ten feet behind them. She and Rocky scurried ahead, then stopped. Medafil's bulk was blocking the passage, filling it completely. Grimwold, who had crawled off his back, was standing behind him, pushing.

And then a new sound, one they had not heard before. The skwartz bellowed, a huge rumble that echoed so powerfully in the tunnel Cara could actually feel it against her skin.

The sound — fierce, hungry, awe-inspiring — filled Cara with a deeper terror than ever. But with that terror came inspiration.

"I've got an idea! Grimwold, Rocky, come stand beside me."

The dwarf and the delver did as she asked, though it meant turning to face the skwartz.

"Take my cape," she said, shrugging herself out of it. "Hold it in front of me. Rocky, shield your eyes."

They did as she requested. Blue flame hissed through the air, landing almost at their feet. Moving swiftly, Cara twisted the sphere, unwinding it as far as her arms could stretch, until it was so large she was forced to turn her head sideways. Her cheek was pressed against its oddly cool surface, and she had to close her eyes to shield them from the brightness — which meant she would not be able to see whether her plan worked. When her arms could stretch no farther she cried, "Now drop the cape!"

Grimwold and Rocky did as she asked, Rocky flinging himself to the floor to shield his eyes.

The skwartz's agonized scream when the blinding light struck its eyes — eyes that had lived forever in a world of darkness — tore at her ears.

"The light is driving it off!" reported Grimwold. "But it can't turn around. The tunnel is too narrow. It's backing away!"

"I'll hold it off. You two go push on Medafil. See if you can get him past the place where he's stuck!"

Clutching the sphere as if it were a small sun, Cara limped *toward* the monster that had trailed them for all this time. The blazing light of the sphere was so intense she could not open her own eyes, so she had to walk forward blindly, praying that the light was continuing to force the beast backward.

She heard it scream again, a harrowing cry of anger and distress.

Smiling grimly, she took another step forward.

Behind her, she heard the delver and the dwarf shouting and grunting as they pushed on Medafil.

"Squijum!" she cried, bellowing to be heard above the screams of the skwartz. "Bite the catbutt birdhead again! Bite him as hard as you can! *Make* him move!"

Then she took another step forward.

She heard a scream of agony. Only this one didn't come from the Skwartz.

It came from Medafil.

The sound terrified her. The pain in his cry was worse — far worse — than would be caused by the bite of the Squijum.

"What is it?" cried Cara. "What happened?"

"Wind down the sphere!" shouted Grimwold. "We've got Medafil free. Hurry! *Hurry!*"

Cara twisted the sphere in reverse, shrinking it between her hands until it reached a manageable size. When it was only a couple of feet wide she risked opening her eyes just a slit. Beyond the brightness, she could see the skwartz was shaking its vast head from side to side, trying to evade the light. One of the enormous, bulging eyes was oozing a thick, black liquid. She realized the creature must have smashed it against the side of the tunnel in its panic, tearing it open.

Turning away, still twisting down the sphere, she hobbled up the tunnel, all exhaustion forgotten. She reached a place so narrow she couldn't imagine how Medafil had gotten past it. But almost immediately beyond that spot the tunnel widened, opening into a good sized cave. She felt a wave of relief knowing the skwartz could never pass that narrow point.

Her relief vanished when she entered the cave.

"Medafil!" she cried.

Then she burst into tears.

CHAPTER
XLIV

STORIES IN THE DARK

Fallon sighed as he began. "His name is Elihu, and the two of us were as brothers for . . . well, for as long as I can remember. It's odd, in a way. Though we looked a great deal alike, our dreams were very different. Yet our hearts were bound so tightly that . . ."

He paused, and Ian wasn't sure if the big man was embarrassed by what he was revealing, or simply searching for the right words. Finally he began again: "The strongest friendships in the world are between young men, for their hearts cleave to one another in a way that fades as adulthood makes them both more independent and more isolated. All men know this, though they don't think about it often. Yet for Elihu and myself, that somehow never happened. Our friendship was as fierce and powerful as if we were young men. Which we are not."

Ian felt the force of those words as they brought to mind his best friend from his own teenage years. They had been inseparable, closer than brothers. Yet it had been over a decade since they had spoken. Was that always the way of it? Was his loneliness when he entered the adult world one of the things that had made him vulnerable to Beloved when she came to recruit him for the Hunters?

"What happened?" he asked at last.

Fallon sighed. "We had a disagreement."

"All friends disagree on occasion."

"This disagreement was profound, and deep. In the end I did something, felt I *must* do something, that Elihu saw as a betrayal. We have not spoken since that day. Yet still my heart cleaves to him, this almost-brother of mine. I feel the time has come to heal the breach."

"And why do you think he is in Luster?"

Fallon paused, as if thinking. After a moment he said only, "That is something of which I would rather not speak."

Ian waited for the big man to say more, but Fallon remained silent, gazing into the sky. At last Ian returned, reluctantly, to the thing that lay most heavy on his own heart, the thing he couldn't bring himself to say in the daylight, but could not hold inside any longer. Gathering his courage, he whispered into the darkness, "Fallon, I'm afraid."

"That we will die here?"

"No, no. It is not death that I fear. It's letting down my wife and my daughter. I would die to protect them. But to die without being able to do that . . . to die while my wife is imprisoned and my daughter in danger — that is a heavy thought."

"A heavy thought indeed."

Again the men were silent. Fallon finally said, "We have not pried into each other's pasts, Ian. Nor do I want to do so now. Still, it is sometimes good to talk. If you care to tell how your family came to be so sundered, I will listen."

Ian did not answer right away. When he did speak, his voice was low.

"Long ago — a lifetime ago — I was a teacher."

"What did you teach?"

"First grade." A warmth crept into his voice. "It was considered an odd choice for a man, but I truly loved it. In my third year of teaching, the school got a new art teacher. She was beautiful, talented, and slightly mysterious, keeping to herself as if she carried some dark secret."

"Irresistible," murmured Fallon.

"Completely. Her name was Martha Morris, and I fell head over heels for her. We started dating. Within a year we were married. A year after that, Cara was born." Ian sighed. "She was the most joyful infant imaginable, with a laugh that seemed to rise from deep in her soul." He paused, caught by sharp memories of his daughter's infancy — of her dancing eyes; of the deep gurgle of her laugh, which seemed to contain some secret joy; of the way she would cup his cheeks in her chubby hands and stare into his eyes, a stare that also seemed to contain some secret.

"Clearly her father's darling," said Fallon softly.

"Beyond all reason or measure. But when she was three —" Ian felt his throat tighten at the painful memory. He had never talked about this before. Yet something about Fallon seemed to invite trust. And he had been carrying it for so long . . .

"When she was three, she was taken from us."

He heard Fallon shift beside him. But the big man remained silent, letting Ian decide whether to continue or not.

"She was taken by my wife's mother." Ian began to speak more quickly, the words tumbling out as the memories pressed at him. "I didn't know such grief was possible. It was as if a piece had been ripped out of my heart. It was even worse for my wife, since she had not only the loss of Cara but the betrayal of her mother to deal with." Ian paused for a while, then said, "The pain became like a wedge between us. A wedge, and then a wall. A wall I could not scale. I was sick with worry and sorrow and anger and hate. And then . . ."

"And then?"

"Beloved came."

"Beloved?"

Ian snorted softly. "It's an odd name for someone who is so filled with hate. But it comes from her childhood, when she was her own father's darling." Ian paused, wondering for the first time what the implacable Beloved must have been like before the tragedy that started her on her path of destruction.

Fallon waited in silence.

Ian turned on his side, wondering how his friend would react to the next part of this story. Finally he said, "It's clear that you know the world is bigger — and stranger — than most people think."

"Of course."

"All right. Beloved is an ancient woman who has a blood-anger against unicorns."

He waited for Fallon to react to his mention of unicorns — to laugh, or express scorn, or ask if he had lost his mind. When the big man remained silent Ian said, "Beloved has trained generation after generation of her offspring to hunt and kill them."

"That would seem to make for more Hunters than there are unicorns."

"You're right about there not being many unicorns — though I'm interested that you acknowledge they exist at all."

"As you said, I am aware that the world is bigger and stranger than most people think."

Ian wondered if Fallon knew that Luster, the world he was seeking to enter, was the very world to which the unicorns had fled when they left Earth. Such knowing seemed likely, but not certain. Should he tell his friend? Just how secret was the knowledge? And how trustworthy was Fallon? Clearly, there had been parts of his own story he was not willing to share. Finally Ian decided to simply continue where had had left off.

"Because of that scarcity of unicorns — there is now rarely more than one unicorn on Earth at a time — Beloved had almost given up the Hunt. Then — something happened."

Ian fell silent, staring up at the red stars. Again, Fallon waited.

"I did not know — nor did my wife — that her mother had a strange connection to the unicorns. Nor did we know that, when Cara fell seriously ill, Ivy — that was her mother's name, Ivy Morris — called on her connections to the unicorns to bring one to her."

"Why did she do that?"

"To make our daughter well again. The unicorns have great healing powers."

"Ah, of course."

"As I said, Martha and I did not know what Ivy had

344

done. All we knew was our joy at Cara's recovery, which the doctors called — quite properly — a miracle. But Ivy's summoning of that unicorn had consequences far beyond her intentions."

"And they were?"

Ian took a breath. "The magic she used in that summoning roused Beloved from her lethargy. She had been seeking Ivy for years, for . . . various reasons. Now that she had a lead again, she revived the Hunt. It didn't take long for Ivy to realize this had happened. When she did, she panicked. That was when she fled, taking Cara with her. We didn't know why she did this back then, of course. In fact, my wife still doesn't know what her mother's motives were, since I only learned them a little while ago myself. We knew only that our daughter was gone, taken by the one woman my wife should have been able to trust more than anyone in the world."

Ian paused, fighting to keep control as the pain of that loss stole around his heart once more. "Not long after the kidnapping, Beloved came and offered to train me to the Hunt, with the promise that she would help me find Cara."

"I imagine you could not resist such an offer."

"Who could? And in this, Beloved was true to her promise: Her training and the Hunt finally did lead me back to

Cara. But it took eight years, Fallon. *Eight years!* And when I finally did find Cara the reunion was . . ." He paused, forcing down the lump in his throat, and finally said, "It was not a happy one. It took one more meeting for me to shake off the spell of Beloved."

"Where was your wife while all this was going on?"

Ian shifted uncomfortably. "Joining the Hunt was not unlike enlisting in the military. I had to go off for my training. Martha knew where I was going, and she approved. But I was gone longer than either of us expected. When I returned I saw Martha briefly, then was immediately sent out on my first mission. And then another. Our contact grew less frequent, and I could sense Martha's resentment growing. I kept telling her I was trying to locate Cara, but she wanted to be part of it, and that was something Beloved would not tolerate. I was torn between them. Beloved seemed to offer the best chance of finding our daughter. But I could sense that I was losing my wife in the process."

"An unhappy choice. I presume, given the men who pursued us, that you stayed with Beloved, at least for a time."

"I reasoned that if I managed to find Cara, I could make everything right with Martha."

"How is it that your wife ended up in the Rainbow Prison?"

"That I do not know. I fear Beloved decided she had become too much trouble and put her here to get her out of the way."

"I don't want to sound bleak, but I suspect that if we do find your wife, you will have a great deal of explaining to do."

Ian laughed uncomfortably. "A great deal."

The men spoke no more. But Ian lay awake for a long time, listening to the steady breathing of his companions as he stared into the dark sky with its red moon and stars. When he finally did drift off, he dreamed all night of his daughter.

In his dreams she was calling for him, calling for his help.

But he couldn't reach her.

When he woke, he was trembling, and bathed in sweat.

CHAPTER
XLV

THE WING

Medafil's right wing had been nearly severed in his struggle to get past the narrow spot in the tunnel. The once
glorious appendage now dangled uselessly at his side.
Crimson blood pulsed from the wound, soaking the
feathers.

"Medafil!" cried Cara again. Ignoring the throb in her
ankle, blind with tears, she rushed toward him.

"Gad-fimbled thing," he moaned.

"What do we do?" she asked, turning to Grimwold.

"What can we do? If we had a unicorn with us, it might
be possible to save the wing. The best we can do now is try
to stop the bleeding."

"We need something to bind it with," she said. "If only
I hadn't left my cape in the tunnel!"

"You didn't," said Rocky softly. "Well, you did, but I
brought it out for you."

Turning, Cara saw the delver holding up the garment. Quickly she finished winding down the sphere. She slipped it into the pocket of her breeches, then took the cape from Rocky with a whispered word of thanks. Working by the dim light from the mouth of the cave, she tried to tear it into strips she could use to bind the wounded wing. She growled in frustration; the weaving was too finely done, and she could not get it started. Regretting again the loss of her sword, she suddenly realized where the sharpest edge was to be found.

"Medafil, can you extend your claws?"

Unable to answer with more than a moan, the gryphon did as she asked. It was as if he had unsheathed a row of curving ebony knives.

"Lift your foot just a bit," she said softly.

He complied, and she pressed the cape under the tip of one of his claws. It easily cut through the hem, which allowed her to tear off a strip the length of the garment. Within minutes she had several of these, which she then tied into a single, long bandage. When this was ready, she said, "Can you lie on your left side, Medafil?"

Slowly, painfully, the gryphon got himself to the floor.

"This is going to hurt," she warned.

"I know," he said softly. "Blat-fribble it."

With Grimwold's help, Cara manipulated the wounded wing back into place. Medafil's body shuddered with pain several times while they were doing this, but he remained uncharacteristically silent. Cara shuddered, too — at the blood, at having to work with the torn flesh, at the pain she knew he was feeling.

Once they had positioned the wing, she tried to bind it in place, but in the end it took all four of them — Cara, Grimwold, Rocky, and even the Squijum — to accomplish this. When it was done she whispered, "That's the best I can do."

"Thank you," rasped Medafil.

With a struggle — and the help of Cara and Grimwold pushing against his good shoulder — he got to his feet. She could see in his eyes that he was in excruciating pain. Even worse, she could see his aching sorrow that he had lost the sky.

"We'd better go," she said wearily. Then she noticed that the Squijum was crouched against one wall of the cave, clutching his tail and crooning mournfully to himself. Gathering him into her arms, she said gently, "It's not your fault, Squijum. He would have died if you hadn't got him to push through that spot. We *all* would have."

"Squijum still good?" he whimpered.

She hugged him. "Squijum hotcha good."

He climbed onto her shoulder and buried his face against

her neck. Though he was silent, she would have sworn she felt tiny tears dropping against her skin.

They emerged into twilight.

Rocky sighed in relief. When Cara shot him a questioning glance, he said, "I feared there would be too much light. Even covering my eyes, I nearly screamed when you made all that light back in the tunnel."

She nodded and glanced around. They stood on a hillside overlooking a long, narrow valley.

Is this it? she wondered. *Have we actually made it?* She gazed down the slope ahead of them, longing for some confirmation that they truly had achieved their destination after the hardships and horrors of the journey. The sun was setting behind the hills on the valley's far side. Though the deepest parts of it had already fallen into darkness, the last lingering rays still reached the spot where they stood, adding a rosy tint to the silvery blue bushes that surrounded them.

Cara reached out to touch the nearest leaf, thinking, *I didn't realize how much I had missed plants.* She drew in a deep breath of the cool air. She was tempted to shout with the delight of being in the open, but forced herself to hold in her excitement. Her caution was justified a moment later when the Squijum leaped to her shoulder squawking, "Big manhorses coming this way! There! There! *Look!*"

Cara turned, and gasped to see a band of centaurs galloping up the hill.

Even though she had known what to expect, she gazed at the creatures in wonder. Their lower bodies were those of horses, sleek and powerful, with coats that ranged from sorrel and chestnut to jet-black to palest gold. At the shoulders the horse's bodies merged into those of men, also sleek and powerful. Half were holding spears, the others clutched enormous bows. Quivers of arrows, their feathered tops just visible over their human shoulders, were held in place by leather straps that ran diagonally over their broad, muscular chests.

Noticing all these things, Cara noticed one more thing as well: They did not look happy.

Forgetting her injured ankle, she felt a momentary temptation to turn and run. But even ignoring the fact that there was no doubt these powerful creatures could outpace her, where would she go? And to what purpose? Their Chiron was exactly who she had come in search of.

The centaurs thundered to a halt about ten feet away, stopping when their leader raised his arm. They towered over Cara and her companions, taller even than Medafil.

The leader approached. His long hair and full beard, the same sorrel color as his coat, nearly hid the fact that he had a very handsome face — as did the angry glare he directed at them. "Can any of you speak our language?" he demanded.

"I can speak to you," said Cara.

The centaur looked surprised, but when he replied his voice was somewhat less angry than before. "Why do you disturb the peace of the centaurs? Do you not know that this valley is reserved to us?" Looking at them more closely, he narrowed his eyes. "And why do a human, a dwarf, a delver, a gryphon and a . . . a . . . *whatever* that little gray thing is, travel together?"

"We come in search of a story, which we believe may be known by your Chiron," replied Cara, glad again of the gift of tongues that let her speak to all creatures in Luster.

The centaur glared at her. "Why should the Chiron grant you audience, much less a story?"

"The request comes from the Queen of the unicorns."

"The Queen is no particular friend of ours."

"Are you sure of that? The old Queen has faded; a new Queen has taken her place."

The centaur looked startled. "Is this the truth?"

Cara spread her hands. "Why would I lie about such a thing?"

"That depends on what you are trying to do. Still, this is something I think the Chiron must hear for himself. Therefore, we will lead you to him."

"Thank you," said Cara, making a slight bow.

The centaur returned the gesture, bending from the place where his human form merged with his horse body. "My name is Arkon. I must warn you, I make no promise the Chiron will receive you. Whether he will actually share a story with you is more than I can imagine — though it is possible he will grant one in return for this information about the Queen. Follow me."

Clearly confident they would do as he ordered, Arkon turned and started down the hill. Cara was surprised to see a crest of hair running from the nape of his neck all the way along his spine. *Almost like a mane*, she thought.

"Nasty snooty horseman," muttered the Squijum.

"Shhhh!" cautioned Cara. "We don't want to offend him!"

"Stinky girl!" he chittered, giving her hair a tug.

Seconds later the rest of the band of centaurs closed around them. After that, the Squijum was silent.

The sloping path down which the centaurs led them wound through brush and scrub as high as Cara's shoulder — which meant neither Grimwold nor Rocky could see over it at all. Leaving behind the fading light that clung to the sides of the valley, they descended into darkness. They had been so long accustomed to traveling with little light that moving back into the gloom was almost a relief, even to Cara's eyes. But when it grew deep enough that it was hard to see the ground ahead, she brought out Medafil's sphere and twisted it until it cast enough light for her to move forward without stumbling — or at least, without stumbling more than was due to her exhaustion and her sore ankle. How long had it been since she had slept, anyway?

When she lit the sphere, the centaurs turned toward her in surprise; even Arkon looked back to see what had caused the light. But none of them said anything.

The air was cool, but drier than it had been in the delver tunnels. Its fresh smell was tinged with the earthy musk of the centaurs, an odd mixture of man-sweat and horse-sweat. The only sound was the steady thud of their hooves against the path; Cara found it sharp and heavy compared to the light tread of a unicorn.

The darkness grew deeper. Here and there across the valley floor they saw the flare of newly lit torches.

Cara heard Medafil groan. Though she was used to the gryphon's grumbling and complaining, he had been silent since the centaurs arrived, and she could tell the sound he made now was not to gain either attention or pity. It was simply something he could no longer contain. Dropping back to hobble beside him she asked softly, "Are you going to make it?"

"I'm not sure." His voice was soft, and edged with pain.

"I wish I could do something."

"Just stay beside me."

She put her hand on his side and promised, "I will."

The walk seemed endless, the more so because her ankle was throbbing with pain. She began to fear she might have to beg the centaurs for a rest herself, something her pride was resisting. She was on the verge of surrendering that pride when Arkon stopped. Turning to them, he said, "It is too late for you to see the Chiron tonight. Therefore, you will be left in a place that is safe, but which you will not be able to leave."

"You mean we'll be prisoners," said Cara.

The centaur shrugged his broad shoulders. "Call it that if you wish. But remember, you chose to come here. It was not at our invitation. So until we know we can trust you, you will not be allowed to roam free." He smiled, and added, "You might remember this as well: While under our guard you will be protected from anything roaming the valley that might wish to harm you. Trust me, such things are out there. For this protection, you might consider being grateful."

Cara decided not to argue.

Arkon led them to a cave. When they went in, she cried out in delight.

Standing not far from the entrance was Belle.

Cara ran to her. "How did you get here?" she asked eagerly. "And where's Finder?"

"Finder is gone," said Belle, her head drooping.

"Gone?" asked Cara, not wanting to believe what she feared Belle was telling her.

"He died trying to get the anchor from the delvers."

Until that moment Cara hadn't known you could actually feel words. But these struck her like a hammer in her chest. She had tried to stay brave through all that had happened, but the death of the big, gentle unicorn was more than she could stand. Sliding to the floor, she collapsed in sobs.

She wasn't sure how long she had been crying when she felt a hand patting her back, comforting her. To her surprise, it was Rocky.

"Rest," he whispered. "Rest now, little warrior. You saved us all today. Rest."

But I couldn't save Finder, she thought dismally, ignoring the fact that she hadn't been anywhere near him when he died.

She sobbed until her body was so drained that sleep was able to claim her at last.

CHAPTER
XLVI

NAMZA

Namza the wizard pressed himself to the stone wall and listened. That he should be reduced to spying on King Gnurflax was a sign of how bad things had become.

Once the King had trusted him with everything. That was before the Whisperer arrived.

It made Namza bitter that the only reason he knew about the Whisperer at all was because he had followed the King one night and eavesdropped on him.

The delver wizard took a bug from the pouch at his side and munched it nervously. He had served as court wizard since before Gnurflax took the Crown of Stone, and in those many years had always been able to steer the King from the worst of his follies. But that had changed; the Whisperer clearly had more sway with the King. And it was leading Gnurflax to actions that Namza feared would in turn lead all of Delvharken to disaster.

"Friend, where are you?" asked Gnurflax.

Namza checked to make sure the cloaking spell he had used was in full force, then slid closer to the cave door.

"Friend?"

It galled Namza to hear the longing, the desperation, in the King's voice. Where was Gnurflax's pride?

Suddenly he felt a change in the air, and knew — from the feeling of power that prickled over his skin — that the Whisperer had arrived. This was what he had come for — to see, at last, the King's mysterious visitor. Heart pounding, Namza dropped to the floor and crawled forward until he could peer around the door.

As always, Gnurflax appeared to be alone in the chamber, which was lit by a few pots of glowing moss. Yet out of the seemingly empty air, a voice purred, "I have been working on your behalf, as always, O Mighty King."

Namza pulled from his cloak pocket the piece of mica into which he had poured so much time and magic over the last three days. No thicker than an eyelash, it was nearly as clear as water, and the first enchantments had been simply to give it the strength to survive being picked up and carried. With those in place, he had used every spell of seeing he could think of. Now he lifted it to his eyes.

The wizard had hoped to put a shape, a face, to the power that came and whispered instructions to the King. But all he saw was a smudge of darkness, hovering in the air ahead of Gnurflax. Suddenly the darkness began drifting in his direction, almost as if it sensed him. Terrified, the old wizard willed his heart to stop its dreadful pounding, which seemed as if it must be louder than the court drums. Next he ceased his breathing, stilling himself until he was almost stone. It was dangerous, because there was always the chance that he might not be able to come back from this. But the gaze of the Whisperer felt even more dangerous to him.

His eyes dimmed by what he had done, Namza could no longer see the smudge of darkness when it turned from him to focus on the King. But he heard it whisper, "All is nearly ready, my friend. Are you ready as well?"

"The cairn has been built. The guard coves . . ."

Namza heard no more. His spell had overcome him.

When King Gnurflax left the cave a few moments later, he walked right past the new protrusion of rock attached to the wall just outside the door. It was half invisible, after all, and not doing anything as noticeable as breathing.

CHAPTER XLVII

THE ONE-EYED KING

Cara was woken by sunlight streaming in from the front of the cave. With a moan — she had slept restlessly — she blinked and turned away from the light. Finally opening her eyes, she cried out in fright at the sight of Belle lying unmoving on the floor.

"She's all right," said Medafil quickly. "Just tired."

Cara, who was not used to Belle being tired, did not want to admit to her first terrible thought, which was that there had been another death.

"Healing me took a lot out of her," added the gryphon.

At these words Cara noticed what had escaped her in her panic over Belle: Medafil's binding had been removed. "Your wing?" she cried happily. "Belle healed your wing?"

"Well, first we had to get her calmed down about the fact that we have a delver with us," said Medafil. He shuddered.

"What a dangfordled fuss that was! I thought there was going to be blood on the floor for a little while."

"I can't believe I slept through that!"

"We were trying not to wake you. I don't think I've ever been in an argument where emotions were so high and voices so soft. Anyway, once we convinced Belle that Rocky was all right, she did indeed do some healing work on me."

Medafil stretched out the wounded wing to prove it, but winced before it reached its full extent. "Well, not completely," he said, folding it back in place. "It still hurts like mad. But at least I'm not going to lose the drib-boodled thing." He sighed. "I'm going to owe Belle an awfully big favor."

"What is she doing here, anyway?"

Stepping into the conversation, Grimwold said softly, "She told me that after Finder died she tried to trail the delvers who had the anchor, but they soon went underground. After that, the only thing she could think to do was return to the original task and head for the Valley of the Centaurs. She hoped she would meet us along the way, or even find that we had already been here and gained the story. But if it turned out we had failed, or been delayed, she would try to get the story herself. As it happened, she got here just a day before we did. She said the centaurs were not particularly happy to see her." He grimaced. "I suspect she did not do much to improve the situation. Even if she could speak centaur, diplomacy is not Belle's specialty."

From the floor where she appeared to be sleeping, Belle made a rude noise.

Before Cara could ask more, a shadow fell over her. Looking up, she saw a centaur looming at the mouth of the cave. Because the light was at his back, it took her a moment to realize it was Arkon. Two more centaurs stood behind him, spears clutched in their hands.

Pointing to where Belle lay on the floor, Arkon scowled and said, "Is she all right?"

"She's recovering from a healing," said Cara, scrambling to her feet.

"Ah. I've heard that such work saps most of a unicorn's energy. Well, let her sleep. We've brought you some breakfast. Once you have eaten, the Chiron will grant you audience." Glancing at Cara he added, a bit more gently, "You might want to wash up a bit, too."

"How?" she asked, suddenly embarrassed to realize how filthy she must be.

Arkon pointed toward the rear of the cave, where she saw something she had missed in the exhaustion and despair of the previous night: a stone basin with water bubbling up in its center.

She was tempted to head for it immediately, but Arkon

stepped aside, and the two centaurs who had been behind him entered the cave. Each was bearing a silver tray. Each tray held mounds of food and had a large silver pitcher and a set of tumblers at its center.

Cara's mouth began to water as the enticing aroma of freshly baked bread reminded her that it had been far too long since she had eaten.

The centaurs walked to the side of the cave, where Cara saw something else she had missed the night before — a pair of beautifully crafted wooden tables. The centaurs set the trays on the tables, made slight bows to Cara and her companions, then turned and left the cave.

"We'll be back mid-morning," said Arkon. Then he, too, left.

Cara, Grimwold, and Rocky hurried to the trays. One was filled with several kinds of bread, still warm and deliciously fragrant, as well as a variety of fresh, succulent fruit. The other had strips of dried meat and something else she couldn't identify, until Grimwold told her it was smoked fish. One pitcher held fruit juice. The other — to the great delight of Grimwold and Rocky — was filled with dark beer.

The centaurs, it seemed, were good hosts, as there was something for everyone, from Rocky (who savored the smoked fish) to Medafil (who eagerly devoured the dried meat) to Belle, who staggered to her feet, then ate with surprising daintiness from a bowl of berries and blossoms. The Squijum was perched on the edge of one table, happily devouring fruit.

For Cara, it was the freshly baked rolls and the surprise of a carefully labeled pot of sunberry jam that filled her with delight. She found it blissful to eat something that was nether fungus nor raw fish — and to do so without the terror of knowing that something horrible was crawling toward them from behind. For a moment the sudden memory of what they had so narrowly escaped caused her to tremble, and she had to place her hands flat on the table to stop their shaking. The fear subsided, but in its place came a cold, hollow feeling as the loss of Finder overtook her once more.

She put down her roll and turned away. Grimwold touched her shoulder. She glanced at him. He nodded as if he understood, but said nothing.

Her appetite largely gone, she went to the basin to wash her face and hands. It felt wildly luxurious to clean away the grime that had accumulated during their underground journey, and she wished she could wash her clothing, too.

As she was shaking her hands dry, Cara realized that before seeing the Chiron she must check the amulet to see if it worked now that they were out of Delvharken. Lifting it from her shirt — hoping that if it did work it would not land her in the middle of busy traffic — she murmured, "Luster, let me go."

With a now familiar lurch she pulled from Luster and swirled across spaces she did not understand. In an instant that seemed eternal, yet shorter than a breath, she found herself on a hillside. One look at the green landscape was all it took to convince her she was indeed back on Earth. "Why couldn't you have done that while I was trapped in Delvharken?" she said chidingly to the amulet.

Then she returned herself to Luster. No sooner had she appeared in the cave that Arkon arrived and said, "The Chiron will grant you audience now."

Cara did not need to translate. Together, the companions followed the centaur out of the cave. The morning light was intensely bright. Cara, seeing Rocky wince in pain, passed him what was left of her cloak to shield his eyes. "Thank you," he murmured, draping it over his shoulders, then lifting it so that it actually covered his head.

Arkon led them along a stony path that curved up the hillside. Looking out, Cara saw what she had missed in the twilight of the previous evening: The Valley of the Centaurs was well cultivated, with orderly fields and vineyards, and extensive orchards.

Well, she thought, *that explains breakfast!*

They followed the path until they were a few hundred feet above the valley floor. At that point it leveled out, coming to an end at a broad, flat area where two centaurs flanked the mouth of a cave. Both were even larger and more ferocious looking than Arkon. Both held spears and elaborately painted shields.

"I have come with the prisoners, as the Chiron requested," said Arkon.

"The Chiron is resting," said the centaur on the right.

"Resting or not, he wishes to see the visitors," said a musical voice from within the cave. "As you well know, Danbos."

From the cave stepped a beautiful female centaur. She had wide hazel eyes and a magnificent flow of chestnut hair that matched the glossy hide of her lower quarters. That hair, thick and curly, tumbled nearly to her waist. Though a great deal of it fell over her chest, it did little to hide her full breasts. Cara felt herself blush at the sight.

The female centaur looked them over and smiled. "What an odd group of visitors you bring, Arkon."

Bowing slightly at the point where his human waist merged with his horse body, Arkon said, "Messengers from the unicorn queen, Princess Arianna."

"My great-grandfather awaits them: I'll take over from here, my friend."

Arkon bowed and backed away. Princess Arianna beckoned to Cara and her group and said simply, "Follow me."

So it was that, with the Squijum clinging to her shoulder, with Rocky and Grimwold walking beside her and Belle and Medafil just behind, Cara Diana Hunter entered at last the caves of the Chiron.

She gazed around in wonder. The first cave, clearly set up as a kind of living area, was lit by four glass bowls, suspended from the ceiling by brass chains. Inside each bowl burned a flame that seemed to have no fuel. Though the light they cast was cheery and inviting, it constantly flickered, making the shadows shift and change from moment to moment.

Even more surprising than the light was what it revealed. Set directly into the cave's walls were numerous shelves. Many of these were filled with beautiful pieces of art — carvings, mostly, but other things as well, including delicate pieces of glass and perfectly formed pots. Most startling of all for Cara was what occupied the rest of the shelves: rows of books.

Until that moment, she had not realized how much she had missed her own books. It was all she could do to keep herself from running to the closest shelf and plucking out a volume to examine.

"Are you surprised to find books here?" asked Princess Arianna, who had been watching her closely.

"A little."

"And why would that be? Have we not hands? Have we not eyes? Why, then, would we not have books? Do you think us stupid?"

Startled, blushing a little, Cara stammered, "Of course not! It's just that I have hardly seen any books since I came to Luster." This was true enough, even if not the whole truth, since she really had *not* expected centaurs to be readers. "What is in them?"

Arianna's eyes grew softer. "They are filled with ancient tales — which are the best kind, I believe." The Princess moved to the shelves and ran her hand lovingly across the spines of the books, murmuring almost to herself, "Dear friends, each and every one." She glanced at Cara and the others, and a shadow crossed her face. "You say you come seeking a story. I suspect my great-grandfather has a price in mind. I wonder if you will be willing to pay it."

Arianna led them deeper into the hillside. It soon became clear that while the first section of the cave was natural, this back area had been hewn out of the rock by hard work. Cara wondered aloud how long it had taken the centaurs to do it.

"Many tens of years," said the Princess. "Though much of the work was done by the delvers, of course."

Cara blinked in surprise. "The delvers?"

"They are masters at working with stone," said Arianna.

"Rocky," said Cara, "why didn't you tell me about this?"

"About what?" he asked, reminding her that he could not understand what Arianna was saying.

"That delvers had helped the centaurs carve out these caves?"

"I thought you knew. Why else would we have had a tunnel that came so close to their valley? It's well out of our normal territory."

"I . . . oh, never mind."

She was getting used to the fact that the more she learned about Luster, the more complicated and mysterious it became.

They passed through a series of rooms, some of which had other rooms opening off them. Arianna paused for a moment in a six-sided chamber, its walls as smooth and even as glass. In the center of each side was a deep niche. Five of these niches held beautifully carved statues of noble-looking centaurs, one statue per niche.

"My ancestors," said the Princess, gesturing. "As each King passed from life back on Earth, a carving was created in his memory. We brought them with us, of course." She paused, then added in a heavy voice, "The artist is working on my great-grandfather's statue now. It will be placed in its own niche when the time has come." She looked around, then added, "His successor will have to find someplace new for *his* statue."

"Won't you be the successor?" asked Cara.

Princess Arianna shook her head, causing her chestnut tresses to slide and shift. "I am hardly next in line. Besides, the Chiron is chosen by combat, not by lineage. And I am not a warrior."

She led them through two more caves, each filled with precious things. They came at last to a smaller cave. This one was lit with the same glass bowls, though they burned more dimly here. In that low, flickering light Cara saw something that pierced her heart with pity.

On a slightly raised platform lay an ancient centaur. Though the horse portion of his body rested on its side, he was twisted slightly at the place where he changed; the human part was propped up by numerous cushions made of brightly colored fabric.

A simple band of gold circled his brow. His hair and beard, both of which flowed to his waist, were of a tired looking gray. His arms were withered, his face creased and ravaged by time. He shifted toward them as they came in, and Cara saw that he wore a patch over one eye. Lifting a trembling hand, he wheezed, "Is that you, Arianna? Have you brought our guests?"

"Yes, great-grandfather, they are with me."

"Introduce yourselves, please," said the Chiron.

Stepping forward, Cara said, "My name is Cara Diana Hunter. I will speak for all of us."

"*Hunter?*" asked the Chiron, sounding astonished.

She bowed her head slightly. "Mine is a long story."

"And what is that thing perched on your shoulder?"

"He's called the Squijum, Your Majesty."

"*The* Squijum? Does that mean there is only one of his kind?"

"As far as I know."

"Who are your companions?"

She motioned to Grimwold, who stepped forward and said, "I am Grimwold, Keeper of the Unicorn Chronicles."

The Chiron nodded. "I have heard of you, dwarf, and of your good work. Welcome to the Valley of the Centaurs."

When Cara had translated this, Grimwold bowed and said, "Thank you."

He stepped back among the others and Cara motioned to Rocky, who came forward, bowed, then said in the grating delver language, "I am called Rocky."

"Surely that is not a delver name?" asked the Chiron.

Cara was surprised to hear him reply in perfect delvish, until she remembered about the delvers helping with the caverns.

"It is my new name — my *nick*name — given to me by the girl we travel with."

"And why does a delver who needed a name travel with an embassy from the unicorns to begin with?"

"As my young friend here told you, it is a long story, Your Majesty."

"Well, I have time for a story. Alas, I have time for a very long story indeed. But first let me meet the rest your group."

Cara motioned to Medafil, saying, "Come and introduce yourself. I'll translate."

The gryphon stepped forward. "I am Medafil," he said, bowing his head and spreading his wings to their full span, clearly a sign of respect. He winced as he did so, and though he managed not to cry out he turned his head toward Cara and made a face that clearly said, *"Ow!"*

"He says his name is Medafil, Your Majesty," said Cara.

"I am pleased to meet him," murmured the Chiron. "I used to number many gryphons among my friends."

Belle was the last to step forward, placing one foot before the other and lowering her head slightly. After Cara had introduced her, the Chiron said, "Is it this Belle, then, who will speak for the unicorns?"

Cara repeated his words to Belle, who replied, "Tell him that you are our representative."

Cara translated. The Chiron looked surprised. "So. The unicorns — who make fun of us for being half human, half horse — send a human to speak for them. Well, child, speak up. What does Arabella Skydancer want with the centaurs?"

"Arabella Skydancer asks for nothing, for she has faded, and is no longer with us. It is the new Queen, Amalia Flickerfoot, who seeks your help."

The Chiron's surprise turned to genuine astonishment. "Amalia Flickerfoot has been found?" He stroked his beard with a trembling hand and narrowed his single eye. "Exactly who are you, child? And how is it that you understand the speech of the centaurs?"

"There are none in Luster to whom I cannot speak, for I have been given the boon of tongues by the dragon Firethroat."

The Chiron sighed. "Clearly there have been great things happening while we stay here in our valley. All right, I ask again: Who are you, that you travel with dwarf and delver, gryphon and unicorn, and speak so easily of queens and dragons?"

"I am the Queen's granddaughter."

The Chiron burst out in a wheezing laugh, which turned into a wracking cough. When he had finally recovered, he said, "And how is it that the unicorn Queen has spawned a human child — much less one who bears the name of *Hunter*?"

"As I have said, Your Majesty, it is a long story."

She stated this so seriously that the Chiron stopped laughing. Fixing her with his single good eye, he said, "Then perhaps you should begin telling it."

"Are not stories better shared in comfort and friendship?"

The Chiron looked angry for a moment. Then his face relaxed and with a nod he said, "You are correct. We so rarely have guests — much less human guests — that I forget my manners." With just a hint of a smile he added, "Of course, your desire to sit so often is not something that makes sense to us."

The statement prompted Cara to ask something that she had long wondered about. "Do centaurs usually sleep standing up, as horses do?"

The minute the words left her mouth, she wished that she could pull them back. To her surprise, the Chiron merely laughed. Even more surprising was how comforting a sound it was. "Our divided nature does make such things a puzzle, does it not? Though our lower bodies are made for the standing rest, that does not suit our upper bodies. No, even those centaurs who are not as old and feeble as I lie down to sleep, child. You may make yourselves more comfortable."

Scattered about the chamber were a large number of cushions. "Gather them as you wish," said Princess Arianna, gesturing toward them. "The Chiron wishes you to be at your ease."

"All save you, child," said the Chiron. "I will ask you to stand as you tell me your story."

Cara watched with a touch of envy as Medafil settled against one wall, folding his good wing across his back, leaving the still-healing one slightly open. Rocky and Grimwold each took two or three cushions and piled them against opposite walls to make a place to sit. Cara noticed that they took care to leave a good distance between themselves. As for the Squijum, he remained clinging to Cara's shoulder.

When all were settled, Cara began the tale of her grandmother, Amalia Flickerfoot, who could not resist the call of Earth. She told how Amalia's grandmother, Arabella Skydancer, became so concerned by her granddaughter's dangerous journeys that she had an enchantment made for her, a spell that would transform Amalia into a human should a Hunter ever come too close to catching her — and how, indeed, that had finally happened.

Strange as the story was, the Chiron did not react until Cara said, "Her human name was Ivy Morris and —"

"*Ivy Morris?* The Wanderer was Amalia Flickerfoot in human form?"

"That is so, My Lord."

The Chiron sighed and bowed his head. "My apologies, young traveler. Had my warriors known Ivy Morris was your grandmother, our greeting would have been more gracious."

"Why is that, Your Majesty?"

"Ivy Morris once did the centaurs a great favor."

"From what I can tell, the Wanderer did many favors in her time," said Cara quietly. Then she continued her tale, telling all that had happened to her since she fell into Luster, right up to the point when the old queen had finally faded into nothingness, leaving behind only her horn, and how the Geomancer had broken that horn, unleashing its magic so that it could restore Ivy Morris to her true form as Amalia Flickerfoot.

The Chiron was staring at her with an expression that made her deeply uncomfortable. She wasn't sure, but he looked almost . . . hungry. "Child," he murmured, "that is the strangest tale I have ever heard. But you have not yet told me what brought you to our valley."

"We have come in search of another story," said Cara humbly.

The hungry look on the Chiron's face blossomed into something she could only describe as greed. "And what story would that be?" he asked.

"It is about someone called 'the Whisperer.'"

The Chiron nodded in satisfaction. "So," he murmured solemnly. "At last they think to ask. But I wonder, child, if you will be willing to pay the price I have in mind."

Cara, thinking he meant a return to Earth, nodded uneasily, wondering if his ancient body could stand the strain. She was distracted from her concern by an unexpected sound. Turning, she saw that it had come from Princess Arianna, who had put her face in her hands and begun to weep.

CHAPTER
XLVIII

NEARING THE CENTER

M'Gama's journey toward the Axis Mundi had been tiring, partly because she was already exhausted when she had begun, partly because she had driven herself to reach the center, resting as little as possible. *But I've almost made it,* she told herself triumphantly. *Another day, two at the most, and I'll be there.*

With that thought she stopped for a moment to luxuriate in a patch of late afternoon sunlight she had found — a shimmering bit of warmth and brightness in the cool, dark forest. She rubbed her hands over her arms, loving the way her ebony skin absorbed the heat.

Now that she was so close, she felt she could pause to enjoy this brief moment of sunlight before starting the final leg of her journey.

Yet she was eager to move on . . . eager and also apprehensive. The eagerness came because it had been years since she last visited this sacred place, and she was longing to see it again. For this she had many reasons, not the least of which was the fact that so much of her own power was centered in the tree and its roots.

The apprehension came because she was filled with dread at what she might find.

How, exactly, was Beloved planning to work the spell that would open the door between the worlds? Did she have someone here in Luster to help her? It seemed she must. But how could she have made such a connection? Who in Luster would be willing to do such a thing?

Well, the delvers, of course. But the question remained: How could she have made contact with them?

Unable to relax, even though she was so close, perhaps *because* she was so close, the Geomancer left her patch of sunshine and continued her journey toward the heart of Luster.

Two days, she told herself. *In two days I'll know.*

CHAPTER
XLIX

BLOOD BOTH ROYAL AND MAGICAL

"So you do know the story?" asked Cara, trying to mask her eagerness.

The Chiron nodded. "It has been in my keeping for centuries."

"How did this come to be?" asked Grimwold, when Cara had translated this exchange, as she was doing for all their conversation.

"The pages that tell this tale were brought to us long ago, by someone who saved them from destruction."

"Who brought them?" demanded the Chronicle Keeper.

"That I cannot answer. The pages were handed to one of my sentries in the darkness, given by a cloaked figure who quickly turned and fled. I know only this: Whoever it was told the sentry that the pages had been torn from the Chronicles, and he felt that they should not perish. Because we are storykeepers ourselves, I committed them to memory."

"Do you still have the pages?" asked Grimwold eagerly.

When Cara had translated, the Chiron shook his head. "They were stolen from us many, many years ago."

"Stolen?" cried Cara. "By whom?"

"If I knew that, we would have had them back by now." He turned to Princess Arianna; voice breaking, he said, "You understand, I intend to drive a hard bargain for this tale."

Arianna, who had stopped weeping now, closed her eyes and nodded. The look on her face frightened Cara. The girl glanced from the Princess to the Chiron, then back, then back again. Finally she was able to identify what she saw on both their faces, the raw emotion that underlaid everything else. Curiosity overcoming caution, she said, "Why are you so sad, Your Majesty?"

The Chiron looked at her in surprise. "Who are you to question my mood?"

"No one," said Cara, bowing her head. "I did not mean to seem rude. I was just curious. You are a king, after all. And it seems your people are faithful. So I wondered what could make you as unhappy as you appear to be."

His tones softer, almost pleading, the Chiron said, "Look at me, child. I am old and withered, and my delight in life has long since passed away. Even worse, I have lived my life — my very long life — without having come close to realizing my great dream."

"What dream is that?"

"To return to Earth!" he cried, his aged voice shaking with passion. "Where is my joy, while the green hills of home are denied to me? Where my delight in lands that are not our own? What am I king of, save a hidden-away valley, given us at the sufferance of the unicorn Queen?"

Uneasily, Cara moved her hand to where the amulet lay against her skin.

The Chiron closed his eye. "I am a king in exile, and my people are a people without a home. This world was made for the unicorns. What are *my* proud people but unwelcome guests? All the creatures of magic — unicorns, dragons, gryphons, centaurs, the merfolk, and others, too, ones you have likely never heard of — we are all exiles, all driven from old Earth, which was our home. But only for the unicorns was this world made. The rest of us came as beggars at the feast."

"Were you made to feel as beggars?" asked Cara gently.

"That is not the point! No matter how gracious the unicorns were, Luster always was and always will be the world that was made for them, not us. We, too, are a proud race. But pride does not come easily when you live your whole life — live for centuries — as a guest. It does not come

easily when your portion of the world is but a single valley given out of charity, and pity."

By the flickering light of the clear glass bowls, Cara
could see tears running from the Chiron's single eye into
the lines of his withered cheek. "Luster is not our home; it
is our prison. But we have nowhere else to go. Earth has
become the realm of man, who does not share with that
which he does not understand. It is lost to the creatures
of magic." His outstretched fingers curled, as if he were trying to grasp something just out of reach. "How I have
longed to feel the soil of the world that was our home
beneath my hooves just once before my death. How I have
longed to breathe the air of the world that will never be
ours again."

Cara, listening with rapt attention, had wiped away
a tear.

"Do not weep for me, child! Who are you to pity me?"

It was not until that moment that Cara realized she
was crying. Quickly she said, "I do not weep for you,
Mighty King, but for all that was lost when magic fled
from Earth."

A smile twitched at the Chiron's withered lips. "A
quick answer — and a wise one, even if not completely
honest."

"Do you truly miss Earth so deeply?"

"More than any of my people can understand."

Cara, who was ready now to produce the amulet and offer him a way back, wrinkled her brow. "Why would your people not miss Earth as well?"

"Because I am the only one of us who has seen it. I am the only one who has breathed that air, who has felt that soil beneath my hooves." He paused, then said softly, "We centaurs do not live as unicorns do, child, lives stretched out for century after century. None of us have lived that way, save me."

Cara heard a sound from beside her. Glancing to her right, she saw that Princess Arianna was shaking her head sadly, and tears were once more rolling down her cheeks. Turning back to the Chiron, feeling that the situation was twisting in a direction she didn't understand, but that somehow felt dangerous, Cara asked uneasily, "How is it that *you* have lived so long?"

"When it became clear that Earth was no longer safe for us, I realized we faced a mighty task. And though I knew that we must leave, I also dreamed we might one day return. For these two reasons — understanding that I must bring my people to safety, but also knowing I would ever long to see Earth again — I made a desperate bargain."

He fell silent for a moment. Cara waited, fighting the urge to ask what the bargain was. Finally the Chiron went on.

"I went to a woman who knows how to do these things, and had my life force placed into an egg. The price for this was dear . . ."

As he said this his hand moved toward the empty eye socket. Cara shuddered as she understood what he had traded for his immortality.

"As long as my vital essence is in that egg, which is stored in a miraculous wooden chest, I could not be killed, nor could I die. Even my aging was slowed. Slowed, but not stopped. As you can see all too clearly, age did creep over me as the centuries crawled by. But no matter how I aged, death could not take me. Only by breaking the egg could I be killed. But who was to break the egg? I could not do so myself; the very spell that placed my life force in that egg prevents it."

"Will none of your people do this for you?"

The Chiron shook his head, "It is part of the spell that the egg must be broken by one whose blood is both royal and magical. But none of my children, or their children, or their children's children can bring themselves to do this thing for me. That is why they are not here now. They will not stay near me, because they know I will beg them for release, and they cannot bring themselves to it. Only Arianna has stayed close by. But even her loving heart is hard to my pleas."

Cara felt a deep uneasiness creeping over her. "Why are you telling us this?"

Closing his single eye, the Chiron said softly, "Because, child, *your* blood is both royal and magical. And because that is the price of the story. If you want to hear it, you must promise to break the egg and end my life."

Cara stared at the Chiron in horror. "I can't do that! I can't . . . can't kill you."

"It is the price of the story."

Desperate, she pulled the amulet from around her neck and held it out. "I came prepared to pay! I offer this amulet. It is the answer to your dream! It can take you back to Earth."

A gasp escaped the Chiron's lips. He swallowed hard, then said, "Cruel. Cruel, child, to offer me now what I longed for for so long, to offer it now when I am . . . what you see." Spreading his withered arms, he bowed his head as if in supplication. "Cara Diana Hunter, daughter of humans, daughter of unicorns, know that I am old beyond measure and kept alive by an enchantment that never should have been. My hope of peace rests in your hands. To break that egg will be an act of deepest mercy."

"But —"

"*And* it is the price of the story you seek. This is an old tale, and a strange one, and it is indeed something the unicorns need to know." He paused, then looked at her so fiercely through his one good eye that she felt as if he were drilling a hole into her heart. "You cannot know how I long for this, child. But I . . . I can know how hard it will be for you. Part of you will feel like a murderer. You will carry this burden with you for the rest of your life. But though it is cruel of me to demand it, I have no other hope. In return for this story, you must become my angel of mercy."

Cara turned to Grimwold, desperately hoping he might take this on. But before she could speak, the Chiron said, "It must be you, child. As the granddaughter of Amalia Flickerfoot, you have blood both royal and magical running through your veins. I told you none of my kin will do this thing. Without you, I have no hope. Without you, I will live on and on, a withered husk kept alive by magic, a soul that should have been freed long, long ago. Knowing your own story, who and what you are, I would beg this of you, anyway. But I suspect you would not do it, no matter how I pleaded. You would think yourself merciful, when in truth you lacked mercy. But I have something you need. And so, cruelly, I put this choice before you. Take the tale and in return end my life, or leave this place now."

Cara stood in silence for a long time, feeling as if her own heart were an egg being crushed in the palm of destiny. She knew that death was natural, and must come to all things. But to be the agent of that death . . .

Yet it was what the Chiron longed for.

Would this be murder? Or would she simply be restoring the natural order?

"Please," murmured the Chiron.

She closed her eyes, trying to sort through this in her mind. She knew that if she did as the Chiron asked, it would weigh on her soul for all her days.

But if she did not . . .

She opened her eyes and looked at the Chiron again.

He stretched his hands toward her in supplication.

Feeling as if her heart had been encased in lead, she said softly, "Tell me the story, O Chiron. Then I shall do as you have asked."

CHAPTER
L

DARK WHISPERS

Desperate, the Dimblethum sought refuge in work, trying to block the voice by focusing on willow-weaving and berry-gathering. But these tasks were not sufficient distraction, and he could find no peace because ever and again the voice would return to whisper seductive offers of his deepest desire if only he would do one thing.

One evening he could take it no longer. "What do you want the Dimblethum to do?" he roared.

"Nothing much," came the whispered reply. "I simply want you to set a certain thing in a certain place."

"Why?"

"You do not need to know that."

"Go away!"

"Are you sure you want me to go? I can give you what you want. I know your heart's desire."

Silence. Then, uneasily, "What will this thing do?"

The voice did not answer for a long time. Just when the Dimblethum thought it was gone — an idea that filled him with both hope and fear — the voice whispered, "It will help the Hunters enter Luster."

The creature shook his head furiously. "The Dimblethum can't do that!"

"Why not?"

"It would hurt the unicorns."

"What have the unicorns ever done for you, except for . . . well, you know. Don't you?"

The Dimblethum was silent. Did he know? Not that he could remember. Finally, longingly, he said, "Lightfoot is the Dimblethum's friend."

"Your *only* friend among all those invaders! Who was here first? Not the unicorns. Whose world was this? Not theirs!"

The Dimblethum growled, but said nothing.

"Think of what I am offering. You know what you want, even if you can't say it. It's in your heart. I've seen it, even if you will not. *And I can make it happen!* You need only do this one small thing for me. And it will hurt no one but your enemies. Think of that. Weigh those things. What it will cost, and what you will gain. Such a simple task for such a wonderful result!"

The Dimblethum closed his eyes and shook his head, trying to forget everything. But the combination of whispered promises and his own anger at the unicorns was too powerful to ignore.

"Tell the Dimblethum more," he said at last. His voice was soft, subdued . . . beaten.

"It's a small thing, really," whispered the voice. "You won't need to fight. You won't need to hurt anyone."

The Dimblethum opened his eyes and said wearily, "That is no answer. What is this small thing?"

The voice sighed, a sigh of contentment. Then, in soft, caressing tones, it said, "I want you to make an arrangement of stones in a certain place not far from here. I will guide you to the spot, though you know it well. Once we are there, I will tell you how to arrange the stones. When that is done, you will place atop the stones a ball of wire you will find waiting for you. It is simplicity itself, an act so small it can hardly be called a betrayal. Yet it will mean so much to me — and I will give you so much in return. I will give you your heart's desire. Remember! Your heart's desire . . ."

"Leave me alone!"

"*Your heart's desire,*" whispered the voice one more time.

Then it was gone.

For a long time the Dimblethum remained sitting at the front of his cave, staring into the distance.

Finally he shambled back inside.

A short time later anyone standing outside the cave would have heard terrible noises — the sounds of carefully crafted wooden things, things that had been made with painstaking slowness — being torn asunder.

When that ended, there came another sound, even more terrible to hear.

It was the sound of a great heart breaking.

CHAPTER
LI

THE BIRTH OF THE WHISPERER

The Chiron drew a long, heavy breath. Then he began to speak.

"The unicorns are wondrous. But they wanted to be more than that. They wanted to be perfect, which is a dangerous and impractical wish. Still, nothing might have come of this desire, had not tragedy befallen."

He paused so that Cara could translate this for the others. She did, condensing his words just a bit.

"Of the story of the first unicorn to be killed, I will not speak long. His name was Whiteling, and his death came at the hand of a misguided Hunter, as all unicorns know. But here is what the unicorns do not know, because they have chosen to forget: In the confusion and sorrow and panic that followed Whiteling's death, they chose to try something desperate, something unheard of, something too filled with pride for any good to come of it."

393

Cara noticed that as the Chiron moved into the story his voice became richer, stronger, as if the story were somehow taking him over.

"What they decided to do," continued the Chiron, "was purge themselves of *all* taint or touch of wrong, drive out their own internal darkness, seek absolute purity. In short, they decided to make themselves what they had always wanted to be, and what others often thought they were. They decided to become perfect."

When Cara translated, something she continued to do throughout the story that followed, she could not help but notice the way Medafil and Rocky flinched when she described this decision. Belle turned her head away, as if she wanted to shut out what she was hearing.

The Chiron waited for Cara to finish, then began again:

"In the days and weeks that followed Whiteling's death, the unicorns were filled with fear and sorrow, anger, and even hate, which none of them had ever felt before. And their councils were filled with despair, for many of them thought — correctly, as it turned out — that the killing had just begun, and that if something were not done it would go on and on, without end.

"'It is the evil of the humans,' said some of the unicorns.

'They are wounded spirits, and we will never be able to live in peace with them.'

"'No, it is something within ourselves,' said others. 'We are not yet all that we might be. Good we are, and filled with magic. Blessings we bring, and much that is fine and lovely. Still, we have our own darkness within us, and darkness calls to darkness, and from that calling evil grows. If we could but rid ourselves of all our darkness, what glorious creatures might we be then?'

"Of course, even in this desire there was pride, which is a danger and a darkness in itself.

"The dispute went back and forth for many weeks until a unicorn named Goldenwords finally argued so convincingly for the effort that all agreed: The unicorns would try to purge themselves of anything that was dark within them.

"Only one rose to speak against the plan — not a unicorn, but one who was their friend. 'This idea is not wise,' he said. 'You will destroy your own balance.'

"But to this the unicorns would not listen.

"'This is pride, and pride is folly,' warned the friend, who knew what the Greeks knew, that the downfall of the wise and the mighty comes not from being strong or wise, but from thinking you are stronger and wiser than you truly are, than any being can truly be."

The Chiron smiled ruefully. "They had a word for it, those Greeks. It was called *hubris*, and it had infected the unicorns.

"Still, though the decision had been made, there was a great deal yet to be done to put it into action, and there was still a chance that the unicorns might turn back from this rash plan. Then another unicorn was killed, the second to die at the hands of man, and in the panic that followed, Goldenwords had his way; the unicorns *would* try to purge themselves of all darkness, all sin, any taint or tint of corruption. Alas, that decision was made not in calm reflection, as such things should be settled, but in the throes of fear and terror, which is the time when many bad actions come to pass.

"Of course, many still secretly doubted the wisdom of this plan. Unfortunately, they no longer dared to speak, to say this was a dangerous idea and filled with folly, that there is a balance in the world of good and bad, of light and dark, and that it is not to be tampered with thoughtlessly. To say such things now was to be called a traitor and be driven out.

"Unity was demanded, and unity was achieved.

"But there is a cost for silencing the voice of dissent, and the unicorns have paid that price, without ever knowing it."

*   *   *

Until this moment the others had listened in silence when Cara translated. But now Belle objected, demanding, "What price have we paid?"

"Wait," said the Chiron, "and you will hear."

Cara noticed that he turned his eye toward Rocky when he said this, and wondered what that might mean. Then the Chiron started to speak again, and she had to focus all her attention, not only so she could hear the story, but so that she could continue her translation.

"Now, even having been made, this decision was not easy to act upon. The moon waxed and waned many times while the unicorns struggled to create the ceremony that would accomplish their goal. In those months they consulted many magic workers, quickly learning to ask their questions in a guarded way, for they discovered early on that almost anyone who guessed what they were attempting would draw back, afraid to be a part of such a prideful quest.

"Even so, the night finally came when everything was ready. All the unicorns on Earth gathered for the rite of purification, some coming from thousands of miles to be part of it. This was the greatest glory ever assembled, a multitude of unicorns shining under the light of an enormous full moon.

"The man they had enlisted to help them, whose name was Elihu, guided the ceremony. As the moon rose he cried out words of high magic, and the unicorns willed that those words should pull from their hearts all that was dark, impure, angry, or hurtful. All that was envious, jealous, spiteful, and hateful. All that was less than perfect.

"They were not completely successful, of course. No living being can be purged of all that. It is part and parcel of being alive that there is good and evil in each of us. But much, much, much of it was pulled out, leaving the unicorns stronger in some ways, and weaker in others."

The Chiron paused. Cara, looking at Belle, saw that she was deeply uneasy.

"I do not like this story," said Belle, when she noticed Cara's glance.

"What does she say?" demanded Chiron.

"That she does not like the story."

"Tell her it is not for liking or disliking, approval or disapproval. It is simply what happened."

Scarcely giving Cara time to translate, he began again.

*   *   *

"When this drawing out of darkness was accomplished, the unicorns fell into a deep sleep.

"In their pride, neither the unicorns nor Elihu had realized that so much negative power and energy could not simply vanish. It hung in the air above the sleeping unicorns. And while they slumbered, a strange thing happened. The jealousy and petty envy and false pride of a thousand unicorns — very little in any one of them, for they were indeed marvelous good even before this ceremony, yet strong indeed when multiplied a thousandfold — those dark desires, those fears, those angers, those grudges, all of which were ripe with the magic and life of the creatures they came from, began to draw together. There in the moonlight, hovering above the unicorns, the things they had pulled from their own deepest selves coalesced into something new, something wicked, something devoid of anything positive, as it was born only of the negative. For dark feeds on dark, and grows at its own urging. And thus, in their prideful desire for perfection, the unicorns created what would, in time, become their own worst enemy.

"Those who know of the being formed that night — and they are few — call it 'the Whisperer.' It does not have a body, for it came from bodiless thoughts. But feelings it has, and they are dark and envious, strange and sneaky, filled with fear and jealousy, all the worst of what even a wise and loving creature may harbor. This Whisperer is devious and plotting. It wishes nothing but ill to others, and, in their actions, sees only intent to harm itself. It is filled with fear and anger, but it is also filled with pride and greed.

"And when it chooses its partner in treachery it begins to whisper — tempting, seductive whispers that few, if any, can resist.

"This is the Whisperer.

"And it is the unicorns' own creation."

CHAPTER LII

THE PRICE AND THE GIFT

A dreadful silence had fallen over the cave while the Chiron was telling his story.

"How do you know all this?" asked Cara at last.

The Chiron shrugged. "Most of it was in those pages given to us so long ago. But some of the details of the night of the spell . . . well, I was there."

This startled her. "Why were you there, if the ceremony was for unicorns?"

"I wanted to be part of it." The Chiron shook his head, and gave a wheezing laugh. "The unicorns refused me, of course — refused out of the very pride they claimed they wanted to rid themselves of. Yet it was that refusal, which filled me with bitterness at the time, that saved me from sharing the unicorns' fate."

"And what is their fate?" whispered Cara.

Fixing his eye directly on her, he said, "To have a

powerful, bitter, intimate, and eternal enemy who is always seeking their harm."

"What of the man Elihu who was helping them?" asked Grimwold.

"He disappeared. Whether he died in the making of the magic, or fled, or simply was of no more importance, I cannot say. The unicorns spent some time looking for him — as did I, for I had some questions. But he was never seen or heard from again."

After Cara had translated this exchange for the others, Rocky stepped forward and said, "The words that sent Cara here spoke of delvers, too. Yet I have heard nothing that would link us to this story."

Cara was startled to see something that looked like pity in the old centaur's eye. Answering in Rocky's own language, he said, "Here the story becomes even stranger. One of the first acts of the Whisperer was to attach itself to a tribe of dwarfs. It stayed with them for decades, tempting them, filling their hearts with all the dark emotions of which the unicorns had purged themselves. More than that, it put part of itself into them, congealed upon them in a way. The source of the delvers' great hatred for the unicorns is simply this: They were shaped and formed by the unicorns' own darkest feelings."

Grimwold stared at the Chiron in astonishment. Then

he turned his gaze on Rocky and shuddered, as if recognizing in the delver some distant, horrible relative.

Cara gasped. "Are you saying that's where delvers came from?"

The Chiron gazed down at her. "Of course. But it's often the case that our most intimate enemies are rooted in our own darkness. The delvers are dwarfs bent and shaped by the Whisperer. And the Whisperer is a living thing formed from the unicorns, pulled from their own hearts in that misbegotten ceremony. This is why delvers are drawn to unicorns at the same time that they despise them. They burn with hatred yet also with a deep desire to connect. They are wounded creatures who cannot name the wound, nor understand where it came from, and so remain locked with the unicorns in a web of fury and longing. It is why they followed the unicorns here to Luster. They are the unicorns' dark shadow."

"This is a bitter legacy," said Rocky, his voice tight and pained. "Is there any balm for this wound?"

The Chiron shook his head. "None that I know of. Now, you must understand that the Whisperer did not restrict itself to the delvers. In time, it found another who had a dark connection to the unicorns, someone who deeply desired their destruction."

"*Beloved!*" gasped Cara.

The Chiron nodded solemnly. "Of course. Because her hatred and her hurt were wrapped in that piece of unicorn horn lodged in her heart, she was like a beacon, calling to the Whisperer without even knowing it existed. But once it found her, it began to work on her, as it has done all these centuries, breathing on the spark of her pain to bring it to a raging fire. It is the Whisperer who has kept her desire for revenge burning at fever pitch, stoking that desire with its constant murmured reminders of how she was wounded, and what she lost, and what the unicorns had to do with it. Most of this was lies, of course, but lies woven with enough strands of truth and memory — which is the best way to make a lie seem real — that she could believe them. It is these lies that have kept the hate ablaze within her."

The Chiron looked straight at Cara. "So you see, it is the Whisperer who is the unicorns' greatest enemy — greater than the delvers, greater than the Hunters, greater even than Beloved. For it is the one who urges all the others on."

"And it came from the unicorns themselves," murmured Cara.

The old centaur nodded. "It is their darkest thoughts and fears made real." He paused for a long moment, then said, "And now, Arianna, if you will fetch the chest that contains that egg, it is time for our guest to make good on her part of the bargain."

Cara felt her heart clench with terror.

Without speaking, Princess Arianna went to an opening in the wall on the far side of the Chiron's bed. A moment later she returned, carrying a small chest made of polished red-brown wood. Its hinges gleamed in the flickering light.

Tears streaming down her noble face, she opened the casket.

Inside, on a velvety blue cushion, rested a golden egg.

Trembling, Cara stepped forward.

The Chiron closed his eye and sighed heavily. "Wait, child. I give you back your pledge. Despite my longing, I will not demand you fulfill your side of our bargain against your will."

Cara's own sigh was almost like a sob. She had been cold with dread at the thought of what she must do, and now she felt a warm rush of relief.

The Chiron raised his hand. "I am not done. Though I will not demand this thing, still will I ask it of you. But only if you can do it freely, with open heart, acting out of compassion, not demand. In your hands lies my fate, Cara Diana Hunter. Please free me from this body. But if you cannot, then go, and go quickly, for my heart cannot bear that I look upon you any longer."

Cara did not go quickly. Instead she stood looking at the Chiron for a long time. He gazed back at her, and though he spoke no more, with his single eye he told her much of age, and despair, and of a spirit — kept artificially alive — that had long since ceased to find joy in the world. At last she sighed and nodded. "I will do as you ask, Great Chiron. But first, may I offer a gift?"

He looked at her curiously.

She held out the amulet. "Let me take you back to Earth. Not for long, for time presses on me. But if you wish, you can breathe that air, see that sky, feel that soil beneath your hooves one last time. I must warn you, it is a risk. The world has changed, and I cannot guarantee where the amulet will take us, or that you will like what you see. But I can take you back."

A smile of wonder creased the Chiron's face. "I ask so much, and yet you turn and offer more." He bowed his head. "I accept this gift, and the risk that comes with it."

"Then let us not delay," said Cara. Stepping forward, she held out her hand. The Chiron's own hand, when he reached to take hers, was dry and wrinkled, but warm with life.

Clutching the amulet in her other hand, Cara whispered, "Earth, take me back."

They emerged on an isolated hillside, overlooking a lake.

It was near sunset, and the Earth — at least where they stood — was rolling, green, and beautiful. Something in her heart lifted at the sight. *I love Luster,* she thought. *But I love this, too.*

Now that she had lived in two worlds, would she ever again be completely at home in either of them? Or would part of her always long for the other, no matter where she was?

The Chiron, still clutching her hand, was silent for a moment. At last he said, in a trembling voice, "The air. The air!"

At first she was puzzled. Then she took a deeper breath and understood. The difference was subtle, but there was no doubt about it. The air was different. It was the air she had breathed all her life, and the scent and taste of it, which she had mostly ignored, made something well up in her heart, something that sang of home.

The Chiron let go of her hand and stepped forward. He spread his arms and turned in a slow circle, as if trying to pull in everything that surrounded them.

"It is not that it is more beautiful than Luster," he said, then stopped, as if he didn't know how to explain.

He didn't need to. "I understand," said Cara. And she did, in some place so deep inside that she could not understand *it,* but could not mistake what it was telling her.

They stood for a time, just looking, as the sun moved lower in the sky. At last the Chiron sighed and said,

"Oh, that I could die here, and let my bones rest upon these hills. But I must return to my people. I owe them that much."

He stretched his hand to Cara, and she took them back to Luster. The Chiron resumed his place, settling slowly, painfully onto the cushions where he had been when she first saw him.

Arianna came forward with the wooden chest, her hooves ringing softly against the stone floor. She paused in front of the Chiron, set the chest down, then knelt beside him. He took her hands in his. They stayed that way for a long time, not speaking, just staring into each other's faces, until finally he murmured, "Enough, granddaughter. I must go now."

The Princess nodded, and got to her feet again. She was calm now, but Cara could see the tears that trembled in her eyes.

Trembling herself, Cara walked forward and lifted the egg from its pillow in the wooden chest. It was lighter than she had expected, and sweetly warm to the touch.

Can I really do this? she wondered, awed and horrified at holding the Chiron's life between her hands this way. She wanted to turn and run, to flee this horrifying task. But though the Chiron had released her from her pledge, she could not forget that she had made it. Nor could she forget what she had seen in his desperately pleading eye.

He did not plead now. Instead he murmured something even harder to turn away from. "For this blessed rest, I thank you, child."

Swallowing hard, Cara closed her eyes, and then tightened her hand.

The egg didn't break. The shell, rather than being brittle as she had expected, was almost leathery.

Heart thudding, stomach churning, she tried again.

This time the egg collapsed beneath her fingers.

No liquid flowed from the shell. Instead she felt a warm rush of wind, followed by a deep sigh from the Chiron. Unable to stop herself, she opened her eyes.

The Chiron had slumped against the cushions.

His arms hung limp at his sides.

His single eye, still open, held no life.

His mouth, though loose, was curved by the slightest of smiles.

Arianna was sobbing.

Cara spun and fled the cave, running past the sentries, down the trail, until she had returned to the place where they had been held prisoner the night before. There she flung herself to the floor, and wept for a long time.

CHAPTER
LIII

THE MARK OF THE CHIRON

To Cara's surprise, it was Arianna who came to comfort her.

"I want to hate you, but I cannot," said the princess, her voice husky. "For you did what I could not, what had to be done, what I was too weak to do."

Unable to speak, Cara could only shake her head and stare at her hand, the hand that had killed a king, which she now held clenched shut, as if afraid to ever open it again. She felt as if another hand, cold and hard, had closed around her heart, and was squeezing it still, squeezing it as she had squeezed the egg.

"You are brave," continued the Princess. "Braver than I. But your work is not yet finished, Cara. You paid a terrible price for that story. Now you must not let what you have done go to waste. You must take the story to your grandmother as soon as possible."

Numbly, Cara nodded.

Arianna took Cara's clenched fist and held it between her hands. "It was my great-grandfather's right to demand a price for that story. You not only paid it, you offered him a gift greater than he could have hoped for. Yours is a generous heart, Cara Diana Hunter." As she spoke, she stroked Cara's hand. "Now relax, child. Let it go."

Slowly, Cara began to uncurl her fingers. She gasped. Emblazoned on the flesh of her palm, about an inch wide and vivid as a tattoo, was a golden hoofprint.

"Well," said Arianna softly. "I did not expect that. He has marked you."

"A mark of my crime," said Cara dismally.

As she spoke, a deep voice arced across the valley. "The Chiron is dead! The Chiron is dead! Weep, ye centaurs, weep, for the Chiron who guided us to safety when Earth shut its heart to us has finally left this world."

The words echoed from the valley sides. As they faded another sound arose, a wail of loss and sorrow.

"There will be watch fires tonight," said Arianna, a catch in her voice. "And sad songs. And then for the first time since we came to Luster, a trial by combat to choose our next chiron."

"Will I be an enemy of the centaurs?"

"No, young one, not an enemy. If anything, a hero. That

mark on your palm is a badge of honor that will be recognized by all centaurs."

"I don't feel like a hero."

"I suspect you do not. But to act with mercy can sometimes be the hardest thing of all."

They stood in silence, until a sound at the front of the cave made her aware that Belle and Grimwold had entered. She saw Medafil and Rocky standing not far beyond them. One look at their faces made it obvious that they were waiting to tell her something.

"What is it?" she asked, wiping a hand across her eyes.

"That was well done," said Grimwold, bowing his head.

Cara nodded, accepting the compliment, then said, "That isn't what you came to tell me."

Grimwold inclined his head. "No, it's not."

"Well, then, what?"

"Time is against us," said Belle.

"I know that," said Cara, though she had set aside that knowledge in her pain.

"We've spoken to Medafil," said Grimwold. "He thinks he is strong enough to fly you back to Autumngrove. The Blood Moon is only two nights away. He can have you back by then. It will be too late for the Queen to do anything to stop Beloved if she does make her attempt that night. Even so, better for her to have this information before that happens than after."

Cara started to protest, to say that they had to return together, just as they had started out. But she knew that was wrong. The main thing, the only thing, was to get the story of the Whisperer back to the Queen as quickly as possible. Returning on foot would take many days, even assuming they didn't face new dangers along the way. But that still didn't add up to *her* going back. "You should be the one to go, Grimwold. You're the Chronicle Keeper. Medafil can fly you as easily as me."

Grimwold shook his head. "You were the one who earned the story. And you heard it from the Chiron's lips. I can offer only a translation of a translation. It is yours to tell, Cara."

"I can't do that!" she cried, blushing at the very thought.

"Yes, you can. Simply tell the Queen what the Chiron told you. And do not be shy about doing it. It's the story that's important, not the teller."

"What about you and Belle and Rocky?"

Grimwold shrugged. "I should be able to make my way home without much trouble. I'm used to traveling through the wilderness, and I know my way around pretty well."

"You're going *home*?"

"I need to be among the Chronicles, in case the Queen needs to consult me. That is my true job, in case you have forgotten: tending the Chronicles, and being ready to pull information from them whenever it is called for. Such information may be crucial in whatever is to come. Even if not, I must be ready."

"As for me," said Belle. "I will make my way back to Autumngrove on my own."

Cara turned to Rocky.

The delver looked uncomfortable. "I am not sure what I will do next. This story the Chiron told is shocking and my people need to know it. But how can I tell them, when I do not even exist? What I do know, without question, is that King Gnurflax will not listen to me. If I go back to Delvharken he'll simply throw me into the dungeon again." Rocky paused, scrunched up his hideous face, then added, "Actually, since I have already escaped from there once, he'll likely come up with some worse punishment."

"You mean he'll have you killed?" asked Cara, horrified.

"It is unlikely he would be that merciful. As I told you, he keeps a skwartz. It is but one of the many ways he has to punish those who displease him."

"Then what will you do?"

"I do not know. I am confused. I must go to the stones to think."

"Good Squijum go with Cara!" cried the Squijum, leaping up to her shoulder. "Good Squijum ride beaknose wingcat back to queen!"

"If I go, you can come with me," said Cara, putting a comforting hand to the little creature.

"Why do you say 'if?'" snapped Grimwold. "Do you have a better idea?"

"No, it's just that . . . no, I don't. But I hate the thought of leaving you on your own."

"We are at war, Cara, or nearly so. Which means we do what must be done. That's simply the way it is."

Cara sighed. She knew that what Grimwold said was true. And she also knew what it meant right now. Though she longed to linger, to rest for a while, she said, "Since we have no time to waste, Medafil and I should be on our way as soon as possible." She turned to the gryphon. "Shall we go?"

"Gaaaah! I'll be glad to see the last of these gad-fimbled centaurs. Half horse, half man indeed. It's not natural!"

"Unlike someone who is, for example, equal parts eagle and lion?" asked Grimwold.

"I am ignoring you. In fact, I think you are a figment of my imagination. Climb on, Cara. But tell that bort-bongled squawkbox of yours that if he wants to come along he had better stay on your shoulder. I do *not* need him tickling me while I'm trying to fly!"

"Hotcha cranky nasty hornbeak," muttered the Squijum. But he said it very softly, so that only Cara could hear him.

Cara went to embrace Grimwold. Holding her more tightly than she had expected, the old dwarf whispered, "Travel safe, travel well, little wanderer. May those who have gone before be always with you. And remember: More may be riding on your mission than we yet understand."

"Travel safe, travel well, Chronicle Keeper. May those who have gone before be always with you."

She turned to Belle, and was surprised at the warmth and tenderness in the warrior's breath as they whispered the ritual farewell.

When she came to Rocky she hesitated, uncertain how to bid the delver farewell. He saved her the embarrassment of trying to figure out what to do by crossing his arms over his chest, bowing his head, and murmuring, "Earth and water, air and fire, may you find your heart's desire."

She repeated the gesture, and the words. Before she could decide whether to hug the delver, Medafil cleared his throat. Feeling a bit of relief — and at the same time feeling embarrassed by that relief — she hurried to the gryphon's side. Once mounted on his back, she gestured to the Squijum. He sprang to her shoulder, burrowed under her hair, and took a tight grip on her neck.

Being on Medafil's back, she found herself almost at a height with Arianna. The Princess took Cara's hand and turned it over. Tracing the hoofprint that was emblazoned there, she said softly, "You will always be a friend to the centaurs."

"Thank you," whispered Cara.

"Ready?" asked Medafil, flexing his wings.

"Ready!"

"All right, here we go!" He took a few running steps, carrying them out of the cave and across the ledge that fronted it. Without hesitation, he leaped into the air.

The land dropped steeply away below them, but that didn't bother Cara until she heard Medafil cry, "Ow! Did-fiddled wing!"

They wobbled sideways. For a terrifying moment Cara forgot the sorrow of the farewells as she wondered if they might crash back to the ground. But an instant later Medafil managed to catch the winds, and she felt her heart leap with the delight of once again soaring into the sky on the gryphon's back.

Medafil circled once, and she waved to Grimwold, Belle, Rocky, and Arianna as they shrank below her.

Medafil flew higher, and Cara found herself rejoicing in the beauty of the world that spread below them, its silvery-blue hills, its vast forests, its shimmering mountain peaks.

This is good, she thought, as they soared over a deep blue lake. *This is Luster, and it's worth fighting to protect.*

TWO DAYS LATER . . .

CHAPTER
LIV

FELICITY

Hunger and thirst were making it hard for Ian to focus. To add to his discomfort, the constant red was irritating his eyes.

No, not just my eyes. It's my soul. I feel as if some vital part of the world has been drained away.

He found himself longing, desperately, to see any color other than red. But late in the day, rather than seeing another color, he lost his sight altogether.

I had wondered if the Blind Man would be able to take my sight once we entered the Rainbow Prison, he thought ruefully. *Well, at least now I know the answer! And because he'll have seen through my eyes, he'll know I made it here.*

He shuddered, wondering what, if anything, the Blind Man would do with that information.

He waited impatiently for his sight to be restored, not wanting to make his next shimmer until it was.

When he could finally return to their meeting place, he found Rajiv sitting in silence. The boy, clearly exhausted and frightened, said, "We are not going to make it, are we, sahib?"

Ian wanted to lie, but could not bring himself to do so. "It's not over yet, Rajiv," was the best he could come up with.

Late on the third day — he had lost track of how many jumps he had made — he spotted an old woman sitting next to a stream of flowing red water. She was staring into the distance, and didn't notice when he shimmered into place behind her. Not wanting to startle her, he waited a moment then shimmered to the far side of the stream, reasoning that his sudden appearance wouldn't frighten her, since the rainbow prisoners must be used to seeing it happen.

Even then she did not notice him right away, for her focus was all on the water. Finally he cleared his throat to attract her attention. She jumped slightly, looked up, then broke into a broad smile. "Ah! I was wondering when you were going to show up, Mr. Hunter. I've been waiting for you!"

Ian looked at her in astonishment. Barely able to get the words past his parched throat and cracked lips, he croaked, "You have?"

She nodded.

Ian studied the woman more closely. With her wide eyes, high cheekbones, and delicate nose she had clearly been attractive in her day, and in fact still carried a kind of regal beauty. She was dressed in a simple shift that showed her to be both slender and surprisingly shapely. It was impossible to tell the shift's true color since, like everything else, it was tinted with red.

When she did not volunteer more information, Ian said, "Why were you waiting for me? Who told you I was coming? And why would you expect me to find you, since I have no idea where I'm going?"

The woman laughed. "I was told to look for you by a friend from the outside."

Ian wrinkled his brow until the obvious answer occurred to him. "The Blind Man!"

"Very good," the woman said, nodding in approval. "A little slow, but I'll make allowances for your condition. My name is Felicity." She winked at him. "At least, that's what you can call me for the time being."

"But how could he contact you? I thought the Rainbow Prison was cut off from all contact with the outside world."

Felicity shrugged. "It is, for most people. He is different from most people."

"Well, I'll grant you that! How do you happen to know him?"

"I used to be his wife." Felicity made a little pout. "I'm disappointed he didn't speak of me."

Ian swallowed several replies, finally settling on, "What are you doing in the Rainbow Prison?"

"My former husband sent me here." Seeing the look on Ian's face, she added quickly, "Oh, I didn't blame him! I did betray him, after all." She smiled, as if savoring a memory. "Quite badly, as a matter of fact. So it wasn't an unreasonable reaction on his part. In his shoes, I probably would have done the same."

"But you're still in contact with him?"

As if explaining something to a rather slow child, she said, "Just because I betrayed him and he imprisoned me doesn't mean we can't still be useful to each other. Actually, we're quite fond of each other, in an odd sort of way. It's only trust that is lacking."

"Why did he tell you to watch for me?"

"He said if you made it this far, I might give you a little assistance, if I felt like it. He'll be pleased. He figured your odds were no better than one in fifty, especially given who was after you, and he always likes to root for the underdog. Also, I think he likes the fact that you were not frightened by him. Most people are, and he finds it tiresome. That was one of the things he loved about me, of course. I was *never* afraid of him."

"What is the assistance that you can give me?" asked Ian, trying not to sound too eager.

"I can lead you to your wife."

"Thank you!"

"I said that I can. Not that I would."

"Why would you refuse me?" Ian asked, struggling not to let desperation color his voice.

"Because I can. Because it's interesting. Because I don't have many ways to amuse myself here, and it might be fun to let you try to convince me I should do this."

Ian fought down an urge to grab the woman and wring the information out of her. He would have been glad to do it, and would not have felt the slightest sense of guilt. But she was insubstantial, and he could no more put hands on her than he could grab and hold smoke.

Felicity smiled. "I'll tell you what. Why don't you beg me for the information?"

"What?" asked Ian, not quite able to believe she meant what she was saying.

"Beg me," she repeated, her voice suddenly steely. "On your knees."

Ian stared at her in shock.

"I'm quite serious. You seem like a proud man. I think it would be fun to watch you grovel. Of course, you could just go off and continue searching on your own. You might even find her, maybe in a day or two, maybe in a year. But you don't have a day or two, do you?"

"No, I don't," said Ian, his voice a dry croak.

"Then why not get down on your knees and see if you can convince me to take you to her?"

Ian's stomach twisted, and hot anger boiled in his chest. The woman was maddening. And as she had no physical presence, there was nothing he could do to her, no threat he could make. Worse, she could shimmer out of sight at any second, and he would have no idea where she had gone. But the idea of begging . . . something hard and fierce inside him resisted.

"I'm waiting," she said softly, her voice intolerably amused.

Ian felt as if he would explode with rage. But he held it in. Turning the fierceness of his resolve against himself, he thought, *What would I not do for my daughter?*

The answer was easy. There was no pain, no humiliation, no degradation he would not suffer in order to get back to Cara. He closed his eyes and chased the idea.

For my wife?

The answer to this was far more complicated. His love for his daughter was pure, simple, and clear as a mountain stream. His feelings for his wife were tangled with guilt and desire and sharp-edged memories of conflict and loss and obligation and anger. But despite the complications, the answer was the same: There was nothing he would not do.

"Ah, well, I had other things to deal with today anyway," said the woman lightly. "Perhaps our paths will cross again some other time."

"Wait!" cried Ian. Keeping his eyes closed, fighting something inside, he dropped to his knees in front of her.

"I'm begging you."

Felicity curled her lip in disdain. "Say it as if you mean it!"

"Be merciful, Felicity. I beg it of you."

She yawned. "I'm not really believing you. And look at me when you talk to me!"

Ian opened his eyes and swallowed hard. He gazed up at her face for a moment, then lowered his head and made as if to kiss her feet — though of course there was nothing solid there for him to kiss.

"Ah," murmured Felicity. "That was a nice touch. Just a little more. On your belly, I think."

Martha, thought Ian. *Cara.*

And he sank to his belly.

Felicity laughed, a sound that felt like broken glass grinding against his heart. "Now crawl," she said, backing away from him.

He crawled.

She continued backing away, laughing as she did. "Just a little farther, Mr. Hunter. No, no, not enough. Farther. Farther!"

He continued to crawl. "Please," he said. "I'm begging you."

"You really are, aren't you? Well, then, that's good enough. Stand up and let's go."

Ian was shaking when he got to his feet, torn by a welter of emotions as disgust, sorrow, shame, relief, and fury warred for first place in his heart. And beneath all those feelings was another one, hard and cold. It was the feeling that something had broken inside him, something that could never be fixed.

It's nothing! he told himself fiercely. *It's nothing! Let it go and move on.*

But even as Felicity began to lead him, shimmer by shimmer, to the place where his wife was imprisoned, Ian Hunter felt as if he were leaving a piece of his heart lying on the scarlet grass where he had knelt, and begged, and crawled.

CHAPTER
LV

HOMECOMING

Late on the second day after Cara, the Squijum, and Medafil left the Valley of the Centaurs, they spotted Autumngrove ahead of them. Cara gasped in awe. From the sky she could see what she had not realized before: Though Autumngrove was in the center of a vast forest, it was also clearly distinct — a great circle of tall trees that rose high above the surrounding woodland like a city rising from a plain.

From the center of those trees soared another tree, so tall it made the rest seem like saplings.

The leaves of all the trees shimmered silver-blue in a clear light that streamed in sideways, under a cloud-heavy sky.

As they had discussed the night before, Medafil came to ground outside the limits of Autumngrove, and they approached on foot. A unicorn sentry challenged them, then quickly said, "Ah, it's you, Cara. I'm glad you are back. The Queen has been greatly concerned about you for some days now." Glancing behind her, he said, "You've brought company."

Cara smiled. "This is Medafil; he's a very good friend." She paused, tempted to ask if the fact that Autumngrove was so well guarded meant anything, then decided it would be better to save the question for her grandmother. "May we enter?"

"Of course. You'll find the Queen in her clearing."

As Cara and Medafil walked toward her grandmother's private space near the center of Autumngrove, she got the sense that there were more unicorns present — many more — than had been here when she left some three weeks earlier. About halfway to their destination, they were joined by Cloudmane.

"I'm glad that you have returned," said the unicorn softly. "Did you succeed in your mission?"

"I have the story."

"Excellent. I'm eager to hear it."

A few minutes later they reached the Queen's private grove. Cara raced to the center and threw her arms around her grandmother's neck.

"Welcome back, granddaughter," said the Queen. And though her voice was filled with love and greeting, Cara found herself wishing that the unicorn who had once been

Ivy Morris still had arms and could hold her close, the way she had when she was human and Cara was little.

After a moment she drew away.

"You are well?" asked her grandmother.

"Well enough."

"And what of those who went with you?"

Cara closed her eyes. "I left Grimwold and Belle at the Valley of the Centaurs. We agreed that I should fly back with Medafil, in order to bring you the story more quickly."

"What of Finder?"

Cara swallowed heavily, then whispered, "Finder is dead."

The Queen flinched. "I knew we had lost one of our own, but I did not know it was Finder. His was a sweet and noble spirit. How did it happen?"

"He died trying to get the anchor the delvers stole from M'Gama."

"Did he succeed?"

"No. The delvers have it."

The Queen was silent for another moment, before asking, "And what of my nephew?"

"Lightfoot was separated from us many days ago, defending me when we were attacked by delvers. I do not know where he is now."

The Queen bowed her head, as if the words were simply too heavy, too awful to absorb. Finally, as if looking for something, anything, on which to pin a hope, she said, "And the story you were sent in search of?"

"I have found the story." Cara hesitated, then decided not to tell her grandmother, at least right now, what she had done in return for that gift. Instead she said, softly, "I don't think you're going to like it."

"We don't have time to worry about whether it will be to my taste or not. Let me gather the council. While we wait for them to arrive you might tell me how it is that you have come home on the wings of a gryphon." Looking past her granddaughter, she said to Medafil, "Welcome, old friend. It is good to see you again."

The gryphon bowed his head. "Greetings, Amalia Flickerfoot. I had heard news of your transformation. Even so, it is strange indeed to find that the girl I once knew as the Wanderer is now queen of the unicorns."

"No stranger, I suspect, than it is for me to *be* that queen. Thank you for returning my granddaughter safely to our midst. Now, come. We must be about business."

Though Cara had been rehearsing the story of the Whisperer in her head as she traveled, she felt a wave of panic at the prospect of telling it to an audience. "It's not about you, it's about the story," she murmured, repeating Grimwold's advice, and felt a bit calmer. Still, she continued to fret as the Queen sent out messages to those she wanted to join them.

CHAPTER LVI

THE EMPTY CAVE

Lightfoot had lost track of how many days he had been traveling when he came at last to the edge of the Dimblethum's territory. He quickened his pace, his limp now completely vanished. An hour later he sighed with relief when he spotted the clearing that fronted the Dimblethum's cave. Rushing forward, he whickered a greeting, hoping his friend would be home and not out foraging.

He received no answer, which saddened him. Even so, he continued toward the cave, hoping that if he waited till nightfall his friend would return. But when Lightfoot entered the cave his hopes were dashed, replaced by a cold rage.

The interior looked as if it had been attacked by vandals. The Dimblethum's few possessions were strewn about, shredded and shattered. Saddest of all to the Prince's eyes was the wooden furniture, which had been so carefully and lovingly crafted by the Dimblethum's own clumsy paws. Every single piece of it had been pulled apart and completely destroyed.

At first Lightfoot assumed the devastation was the work of delvers, and new fury filled his heart. But when he looked more closely he began to wonder, and his anger turned to fear. The marks on the wood were not those of delvers, but rather of great claws — claws like those of the Dimblethum himself.

What has happened here? Lightfoot asked himself in horror.

The silent stone walls made no answer.

Feeling as if the world were crumbling beneath his feet, the Prince stepped outside again. He scanned the ground for any clue as to what might have gone on. To his surprise, though he saw nothing, his sensitive ears caught the sound of the Dimblethum's voice in the distance.

He nearly called out to his friend. Then, thinking of what he had seen in the cave, he decided against it. Moving with the silence that only a unicorn can manage, Lightfoot trotted toward the Dimblethum's voice.

As he moved, he glanced up. A sudden, icy fear seized his heart. He had not been able to see the moon in the forest. On those nights when he had been in the open, there had been heavy clouds. So he had not kept as close track of time as he should have, and he hadn't realized that so much time had passed.

The moon was rising.

It was full.

And it was the color of blood.

CHAPTER
LVII

AT THE CENTER OF THE WORLD

It was dusk when the Geomancer came to the clearing at the center of the world.

In the center of that center stood the great world tree. Seeing it now, after so long, M'Gama was awed again by its size and its beauty — and even more by the sense of something ancient and sacred that she felt whenever she stood in this place. It was as if here, at the heart of the world, she was close to its truest and deepest secrets. The tree pulled at her own heart, and she yearned toward it as an infant yearns toward its mother.

The vast tree was so perfect and so beautiful that it was hard to imagine evil coming here. Perhaps she had been wrong that this was the spot at which Beloved would make her attempt.

Moving slowly, the Geomancer crossed the clearing. The grass grew barely higher than her ankles, though no one ever trimmed it. At last she stood at the base of the towering tree. Placing her hands against the smooth bark of the massive, silvery-blue trunk, she felt herself longing to merge with it.

Night drew on. Slowly a new light began to fill the clearing, as the red moon edged into the sky.

With its appearance, M'Gama felt a nameless dread rising within her. Something bad was going to happen, and she didn't know if she had the strength to prevent it.

She began to circle the tree, intending to draw a magical ring of protection. It seemed a small, foolish act, since the tree's power was so much greater than her own, but it was all she could think of. She was halfway around when she came to a kind of altar, a crude cairn of stones that rose almost to her breast.

"This does not belong here," she muttered. "This must not stand!"

She took off a stone and flung it away. Immediately a band of delvers came rushing across the clearing. M'Gama was prepared to fight. Reaching into the pouch at her side, she pulled forth one of the magical stones she had packed at her home. Flinging the stone at the approaching cove, she cried, "Akel ama anna dinna!"

The stone exploded in a burst of fire.

Screaming delvers scattered in all directions.

M'Gama smiled. But her sense of triumph was brief. In

just a moment another cove burst from the woods. She withdrew a second stone from her pouch, hurled it with the same great cry, and achieved the same satisfactory result.

She had thought herself well prepared. But there were more coves of delvers than she had magical stones and all too soon she was out of weapons. How many of the creatures had been set to watch here, anyway?

The altar of stones she had wanted to pull down was still standing. More delvers poured from among the trees. She had but seconds before they would overwhelm her. Digging into her pouch once more, M'Gama pulled out the four pieces of rootwood that had been taken from the trees at the great resting places.

"Anna alla makka hyadim," she muttered, passing her hands over them. "Anna alla makka hyadim!"

The wood began to glow.

She pressed the first of the pieces against the world tree, where it stuck at once, as if the bark were absorbing it. As soon as she saw that, the Geomancer raced a quarter of the way around the tree. She pressed in another piece of the rootwood, and chanted the same spell. She managed to set the third piece, and was just pressing the fourth into place when the delvers swarmed over her, and she fell to the ground.

CHAPTER LVIII

THE WOMAN IN THE TREE

Ian moved in a state of near terror all the while that he was following Felicity, prickly with fear that she would betray him simply for the pleasure of it. At the same time he was desperately using his Hunter's skills to remember all the jumps, so he could lead Fallon and Rajiv back once he had rejoined them.

As if sensing his desire to remember the route, and consciously trying to thwart it, the Blind Man's wife began making her shimmers faster and faster. "After all," she teased, "It's not like you're going back."

Ian didn't deny it, fearing to tell her an outright lie. But neither did he want her to know he had others with him. She was not the sort of woman to whom it was safe to give that kind of information — or any information, for that matter.

At last they reached a stand of old trees. Here their

jumps became shorter, since they could leap ahead no farther than he could see. With massive trees blocking his view,
fifty feet was often the most they could accomplish.

As they moved ever deeper into this scarlet forest, he
tried to brand each new spot into his brain.

Suddenly Felicity stopped. Pointing to an enormous oak
she said, "Inside you will find the one you seek."

Hardly daring to breathe, Ian circled the red tree. On
the far side the trunk was split, creating a deep hollow.
Dropping to his knees, he peered into the tree's heart.

Sitting serenely in the dark enclosure, eyes closed, face
unmoving, was his wife. Her red hair — its color oddly flat-
tened by the red light of the Rainbow Prison — cascaded
over her shoulders. The tip of her slender nose, the fullness
of her lips, was so like that of her daughter that it made Ian
ache to see them. His heart pounding as if it would beat its
way out of his chest, he lifted his hands. "Martha!" he whispered, his voice filled with joyous longing. "Martha, it's me!
Ian! *Ian!* I've come for you."

His joy turned to ash. Though it was indeed his wife
who sat before him in the hollow of the tree, her eyes did
not open at his words, nor at his increasingly desperate
shouts, nor even at his touch, which passed right through
her insubstantial image.

Scrambling to his feet he turned to Felicity. "What's
wrong? Why won't she answer me?"

The woman shrugged with infuriating casualness. "I have no idea. I knew she was here. I brought you to her, as you so sweetly asked. What else do you want of me?"

"Oh, I can ask nothing else of you," he said bitterly. "You've done as you promised. You can go now."

"I'd rather stay and watch. It's . . . amusing."

The trace of a smile that played about her lips made Ian long to grab the woman and shake an answer out of her. But he could no more touch her than he could his trance-bound wife.

He decided to shimmer back to where he was supposed to meet Fallon and Rajiv. He needed to reconnect with them anyway, and he wanted to get the smirking woman out of his sight. It gave him unexpected pleasure to see the look of surprise that crossed her face when he vanished — though he did feel a twinge of worry that she might use his absence to do something that would complicate the situation.

Waiting for Fallon and Rajiv to return nearly drove Ian mad. He began to shimmer back and forth between their meeting place and Martha's tree, choosing a spot about fifteen feet behind where the Blind Man's wife had been standing when he left her.

Felicity had moved slightly, and was now sitting beneath one of the other trees, staring at the space where Martha was hidden. Ian had the sense that she was waiting to see if he would reappear and what he would do when he did.

His own waiting was made more difficult by the fierce hunger that gnawed his belly and the powerful thirst that had made his lips dry and cracked, his throat sticky and painful. The hunger he could deal with — a man can go for days without eating, and his training with Beloved had taught him to endure pain and deprivation. The thirst, though, was of deep concern, for he knew it wouldn't be much longer before his body began shutting down. And it was harder to ignore either of these pains now that he was not focused on his search and could only wait for the others to return.

When they do come back, then what? Once I've led Fallon and Rajiv to the tree, what do we do? I don't know how to wake Martha, and she was the key to leaving.

He realized with surprise that he was desperately hoping Fallon would have some answer. He didn't like that; he was used to solving his own problems, and didn't want to start depending on anyone else.

Don't be a fool, he told himself fiercely. *It doesn't matter how we do it, or who comes up with the answer. The point isn't to be the hero. The point is to stay alive!*

With a start he also remembered that Fallon had his own agenda, his own quest, and there was no guarantee that he would continue with them if — not *if,* but *when,* he corrected himself fiercely — when Ian had awakened Martha and they managed to escape this scarlet hell.

Rajiv was the first to return, arriving during one of the brief periods while Ian was off checking on Martha's tree. Ian shimmered back to the meeting place to find the boy lying on the red grass, his eyes barely open.

"Sahib!" he whispered, when he realized Ian was there. "I hoped you would return soon! I cannot go on any longer, and I did not want to die alone."

It was clear that every word was an effort for the boy, and a wave of guilt washed over Ian. "We'll find our way out," he said, knowing even as he said it that he had no idea how to wake his wife so she could bring them back to Earth.

Rajiv shook his head, the movement slow and painful. "I have been hungry many times, sahib. Thirst is different. I have never gone without water this way. I do not think I will last much longer."

Ian longed to reassure the boy, tell him that all would yet be well, but the words would not come. Nor did he think Rajiv would want that. Lowering himself to the ground, he lifted the boy's head and placed it in his lap. He put a hand on the boy's brow. It was hot, and dry.

"I'm sorry, Rajiv," he whispered, cursing himself again

for acceding to Fallon's decision to let the boy come with them.

"I begged to come," whispered Rajiv through cracked lips. "And I have seen marvelous things, sahib. I only wish I had more time to . . ."

The sentence trailed off, and his eyes closed.

His own heart pounding with fear, Ian checked Rajiv's pulse; it was weak, but he was still alive.

Several minutes went by. Ian began to feel an urgent need to check the tree to make sure Felicity hadn't done anything, to confirm that Martha was still there.

"Rajiv," he whispered, not expecting the boy to actually hear him, "I'm going to shimmer away. It will only be for an instant. I'll be right back, I promise."

"Sahib, don't leave me." The words were barely audible through the boy's cracked lips.

"Only for an instant," repeated Ian. Then he shimmered back to the tree where Martha was imprisoned.

To his astonishment, Rajiv came with him.

Ian would have laughed, save for the fact that he did not want to alert the Blind Man's wife to his presence. What a simple, unexpected solution!

Rajiv started to murmur his own surprise, but Ian shimmered back to the meeting place before the boy actually made a sound.

"Sahib, what happened?"

"We just learned something very useful. If we are touching one another, we can shimmer to the same place simultaneously." Ian shook his head. "I wish I had known that *before* I nearly broke my brain trying to memorize the jumps I would need to lead you and Fallon back there."

"Very useful indeed, sahib. This way, we can show each other all the sights we have seen, right up to the moment when we die."

"Where the hell is Fallon?" muttered Ian.

Rajiv did not answer. He had lost consciousness again.

CHAPTER
LIX

THE BETRAYER

"Now! Now is the time! Do this thing, and your heart's desire shall be yours."

The Dimblethum stared at the ball of wire cupped in his burly paws. Light flowed over its surface, and it pulsed with energy, tingling against his skin.

His heart pulsed with energy, too, with desire, with an aching need that he could not understand, could not even name.

What *was* his heart's desire? Why could he not even remember what he wanted more than anything, anything in this wonderful, wonderful world?

How he loved Luster. He felt that love now, felt connected to this world in a deep and powerful way, yet separated, too — separated by the strange wall of fog that hid something from him, some distant memory, some ancient loss.

I want . . .

He could not finish the sentence. He did not know *what* he wanted, only that the voice, the voice that would not go away, that came at him night and day, had promised it would give him what he longed for, would give him his heart's desire.

He saw the pile of stones ahead of him.

Such a simple thing. Just put the wire on the stones. Yet deep inside him something was screaming out against it.

Something else, nearly as deep, yearned toward it.

As he stood there, wavering, the voice whispered in his ear, "Your heart's desire!"

The tones were sweet, rich, seductive.

"Your heart's desire! Such a small thing. Just put the wire on the stones, and you will have your heart's desire."

The Dimblethum started forward.

"Friend!" cried a voice in the distance. "Friend, don't do this!"

Who was that? He recognized the voice. Maybe this was a bad idea after all.

"Now," whispered the other voice, the one so much closer to hand. "Do it now! Do it, and you shall have your heart's desire!"

The Dimblethum reached forward.

CHAPTER
LX

THE TOUCH OF A CHILD

Though only minutes passed before Fallon arrived, to Ian's tortured mind it seemed as if hours had dragged by. The big man started to speak, but cut himself off when he saw Rajiv slumped against Ian's side.

"Is the boy sleeping?" he asked softly. The edge in his voice indicated that he suspected this was not the case.

"He is unconscious," said Ian. Placing a hand atop Rajiv's head, he murmured, "What a bitter ending to our journey, Fallon. I have found my wife, yet we remain trapped in this infernal prison, tottering at the edge of death, with no way out."

"You have found your wife? Congratulations, my friend! But then why cannot we escape? And why is she not here with you?"

Quickly, and leaving out the part about how he had been forced to beg, Ian recounted his meeting with

Felicity and what he had discovered when she led him to the tree. When he mentioned what he had learned when he shimmered there with Rajiv at his side — that by staying in contact, they could move to the same place together — Fallon brightened. "Let us go to the tree at once."

"Yes," agreed Ian. "Let's go."

Fallon came to stand behind him, and in only a heartbeat Ian had shimmered the three of them to the spot he had chosen to observe from. They arrived as they had departed: Ian sitting, Rajiv held tight against his side, Fallon standing behind them, his hand on Ian's shoulder.

Felicity stood about fifteen feet away, her back to them.

Fallon quickly crouched so that he was close to Ian's ear. "Is that the woman you spoke of?"

Ian nodded.

"Do you mind if I speak to her?"

"I don't see why not," said Ian, struggling to ignore the fear that she would gloat to Fallon over the way that he, Ian, had begged for her help.

Fallon walked to the woman's side.

"Ah," she said, turning at the sound of his approach. "I knew that young man must have others with him. I don't know why he wasn't willing to admit to it." She studied Fallon for a moment, then said, "Well, aren't you a big fellow?"

"About the right size to have my feet reach the ground. What can you tell me about the woman in the tree?"

"Why should I tell you anything?"

"Because I asked, and because it would be courteous."

Felicity snorted. "Ask your friend over there what he had to do to get information from me."

"I am not my friend, though I would not hesitate to do anything that he has done."

"It's not much fun if you're so willing," she pouted. "Even so, there's not much I can tell you. She appeared there some time back —"

"How long back?"

Felicity shrugged. "It's not easy to keep track of time in this place."

"Days? Months? Years?"

"It would have been months, at least. Years, maybe. It's not as if I saw her arrive."

"How did you find her, then?"

"Word gets around. Things are pretty dull in this place, so even the smallest bit of news is worth gossiping about."

"And what does the gossip say?"

"Nothing of substance. She's an interesting mystery, but no one really knows anything. I even have an outside source —" she paused here to peer past Fallon and wink at Ian, which made him shudder "— who has been looking for information about her. But all he has come up with is the name 'Beloved.'"

"Is there any way to escape this place?"

"None that I know of. Not for prisoners, and certainly not for the three of you who were fool enough to bring your bodies here."

"Is there any way we can find food or drink?"

Felicity shook her head. "There is no food or drink in the Rainbow Prison. Those of us without bodies don't need it, of course. It's convenient, but also one of the things that makes life here so boring." She looked at him more closely, and for an instant Ian thought he saw a flicker of empathy in her face. "You won't last much longer, will you?"

"No," said Fallon, "we won't."

As if to emphasize the point, Rajiv moaned. To Ian's surprise, he opened his eyes. "Is the memsahib here?" he asked, his voice little more than a husk.

"She is in the tree," said Ian. "But we cannot rouse her."

Rajiv sighed. "May I see her, sahib? We have come a long way to find her, and I would like to know what she looks like."

Ian carried him to the tree, and knelt before it.

"She is very beautiful," said Rajiv. Reaching out, he placed a trembling hand against her cheek.

Ian's heart trembled, too, when Martha opened her eyes and whispered, "There you are!"

CHAPTER
LXI

THE STORYTELLER

It didn't take long for the word to spread. All too soon Cara found herself at the center of a half circle of eager listeners, standing in the very place where Grimwold had stood when he first announced the mystery of the Whisperer. As she looked around, she realized that most of the faces, both unicorn and human, were familiar. She almost wished they were not, thinking it would be easier to tell her story to complete strangers.

"Go ahead, child," said her grandmother, her voice soft but insistent. Blushing, trying not to stammer, Cara launched into the strange tale she had learned from the Chiron. She was interrupted several times by indignant exclamations, until the Queen snapped, "There will be silence until the story is complete!"

After that her discomfort began to fade as the story took hold of her. Soon she was lost in the telling, trying to remember the details as she had heard them from the Chiron, while at the same time stretching her own imagination to find words and phrases that would make it more clear and vivid to her listeners. To her surprise, she found that in telling the tale of how the unicorns had unknowingly created the Whisperer, she experienced it even more deeply than she had when hearing it.

When she finished, a burst of voices clamored around her, some questioning, some belligerent and unbelieving. All were cut short by a another command for silence from the Queen.

"Well, granddaughter," said Amalia Flickerfoot, once the group had settled again. "You warned me this would be an uncomfortable tale, and I must confess that you were right — it is as strange a tale as I have ever heard, and even more disturbing than it is strange. The question is, What shall we do about it?"

"I say we do nothing!" said Moonheart, his voice sharp. "What? Shall we send a messenger to the King of the delvers, saying we're sorry we helped make them what they are? The whole thing is nonsense — probably something the centaurs made up out of their own bitterness."

A hooded figure stepped forward. Cara recognized it as that of Alma Leonetti. The unicorns fell into a respectful silence. Raising her withered hands, the old woman pulled back her hood. In her papery-thin voice she said, "This story has the ring of truth, Moonheart. It is easy enough to reject a story because you do not like what it says, but wiser to examine it first, to see what can be learned from it."

"What can we learn from this?" snorted Moonheart.

The old woman spread her hands. "Perhaps that the unicorns need to try to recover some of what they have lost?"

"What do you mean?" asked the Queen.

"You are not without strength and power. And clearly some, like Moonheart and Belle, still have a degree of fierceness. But you face a dedicated enemy who has shown no mercy, one who will stop at nothing to destroy you. And what have you done? Gathered together, which is good. Prepared to defend yourselves, which is good, too. But is it enough? How fiercely are you willing to fight to save your lives? How strong can the unicorns be?" She paused, then said softly, "Maybe you need to take in some of that darkness you once released."

"What do you mean?" said Amalia Flickerfoot once more.

"Perhaps you need to reconnect with the delvers."

And above them, the red moon rose.

CHAPTER
LXII

THE BETRAYAL

A dread he could not completely understand filling his heart, Lightfoot picked up his pace. It wasn't long before he found himself at the edge of a large meadow. The meadow, which was flooded by the reddish light of the ascending moon, formed a perfect circle. The grasses that filled it grew scarcely above the top of his hooves.

In the center of the meadow was a knoll.

From the center of the knoll grew the most enormous tree the Prince had ever seen, enormous in girth, but even more in height, its branches stretching so high they seemed to challenge the reddening heavens.

At the base of the tree, his great form visible in the red moonlight streaming from above, stood the Dimblethum.

The shaggy creature was facing a cairn of stones that came up to his shoulder. Even from where Lightfoot stood, he could see that his friend's face was twisted between fear and longing.

What was going on?

Just as Lightfoot was about to step forward, the Dimblethum raised his huge paws. Light flashed off whatever he was holding.

Without knowing why, Lightfoot sensed that something very bad was about to happen.

"Friend!" he trumpeted. *"Friend, don't do this!"*

He was too late. With a roar of desire and despair, the Dimblethum placed the shining, intricately woven ball of wire atop the stones.

What followed was not an explosion, exactly, just a burst of brightness, and a ripple of power so intense it knocked Lightfoot to the ground, momentarily blinding him.

Blinking, filled with a sense of horror, the Prince heaved himself to his knees, then back to his feet.

The Dimblethum had vanished.

Dazed, Lightfoot called out for his friend. He received no answer. Instead, a strange humming filled the clearing. Lightfoot started toward the cairn, but found he could get no closer than about ten feet. It was as if some protective wall of light, or magic, surrounded the thing.

He heard a deep sob to his right. He whirled, started toward the sound, then turned again as he heard another sound, this one a high-pitched whine.

The whine came from the ball of wire the Dimblethum had placed atop the stones.

Suddenly the Prince remembered M'Gama's description of the anchor. This had to be what she was talking about! But why would the Dimblethum have placed it here? He did not love the unicorns. But surely he did not hate them so much as to perpetrate such a betrayal.

The whining grew higher, louder, a horrible piercing sound that was like spikes being driven into his ears.

Lightfoot threw himself at the invisible barrier again, but could not pass it. He backed away, thinking to get a longer start, build more speed. But as he did the air itself began to shimmer, as if a great magic was in the making. He charged forward in a desperate attempt to reach the cairn. He wanted to knock it apart, then stamp that ball of wire into the ground, to shatter the magic that was taking place.

It was useless. He bounced away as if he had struck a wall.

Three times the Prince flung himself at the unseen barrier.

Three times he was repelled.

As he was staggering to his feet for a fourth attempt, Lightfoot felt a wrenching in the air around him, almost as if reality itself was being rearranged.

Struggling to stay on his feet, the Prince looked up, then cried out in horror.

CHAPTER LXIII

A HOLE IN THE WORLD

Beloved shivered in an ecstasy that almost erased her pain as the voice she loved to hear, the voice that meant so much, delivered the news she had been waiting for: "The arrangement of stones has been made at the base of the Axis Mundi. Though it was attacked, my delvers have repaired it."

"And the other thing?" she asked. "The most important thing of all?"

She could almost hear the smile in the voice as it replied, "You mean the betrayal that will give your spell the power to crack the walls between the worlds? Yes, that too has been taken care of. The anchor was set in place by hands that should never have done such a thing."

"Who?" she asked eagerly. "Who has betrayed the unicorns for me?"

"Not for you," breathed the Whisperer in sultry tones.

"It was done for me, for what I could offer. But I gladly share the results with you, for do I not love you? Now go. Go and open the way!"

Beloved swept down the castle stairs, passing, as she did, the room where Martha Hunter's body lay sleeping while her spirit was trapped in the Rainbow Prison. She glanced in at the door, a smile of contempt twisting her lips, and then continued down the curving stair.

When she reached the main room on the ground floor, which was lit by torches, she strode purposefully toward the doors. They swung open at her approach. The gathered Hunters cheered, then drew aside and bowed as she stepped into the courtyard.

In a protected circle within the Hunters' ranks stood two dozen young women clad in white — the virgins they would use to tempt unicorns to their doom. Some were daughters of the Hunt. Most, however, were orphans, or the unwanted children of starving peasants, born in lands where girls were not much valued.

Beloved mounted the platform she had had built for those times when she wanted to speak to her assembled children. A pair of torches, held aloft by curling metal stands, blazed on either side of her.

She stood for a moment, gazing out at her personal army. When all were silent, when every eye was fixed on her, she cried, "My Hunters! My children. This is the night we have waited for, worked for, yearned for — the night the Hunt can begin anew, in earnest. No longer must we content ourselves with seeking the single unicorn that may be here on Earth at any time. Tonight we carry the Hunt to Luster and move to end forever the blight that has deceived the eyes of mankind, the false dream, the lie of the unicorns. No longer will their threat be allowed to continue. No longer will they be a danger to innocent young girls. Because *we* see clearly what they are, and know we have a duty. And that duty is to eradicate, without pity or mercy, the evil of the unicorns."

She paused, as a great cheer erupted from her listeners.

"Once we enter Luster, all you have trained for, waited for, planned for will be waiting for you. Once we enter Luster, you can Hunt as you were born to do, trained to do. Once we enter Luster, we can finally — *finally!* — drive the unicorns to their well-deserved extinction.

"Are you ready to follow me to another world?"

Again her Hunters roared their approval and their readiness. The bloodlust in their voices made Beloved shudder with anticipation.

She stepped down from the platform.

The Hunters shifted to make a passage for her. Then, as had long been planned, they moved to the castle side of the courtyard, leaving Beloved alone in front of the gate, save for four men who stood beside her, holding torches.

The ancient woman drew a deep breath, then raised her hands. Her silver hair lifted around her, stirred by currents of magic. The light of the torches grew brighter. Her hands moved in strange gestures as she called on all the arcane knowledge she had gathered over the centuries. Using all the mystic power she had accumulated in that time, she began to sing the great magic that would transform the wooden gate into a World Gate.

Now she muttered deep in her throat, a chant that grew in intensity until it was a howl, then a piercing scream. Some of the virgins cried out and covered their ears.

Beloved spread wide her arms. *"Now!"* she cried, flinging the amulet into the air. *"Now! Pierce the wall between the worlds, now let the gate be open!"*

The earth seemed to rock around them. The air was filled with a crackle of energy. She felt a seismic shift, not in the ground, but in reality itself.

The amulet, floating in midair, spun and grew, shooting off fire. Then it struck the wood and exploded.

The men cried out as the castle gate shimmered. In the center of its rough wood, an opening appeared. The opening grew higher and wider, forming a new kind of gate, a gate that was nothing less than a hole in the world.

Beloved uttered one more cry, a strange and appalling sound that pulsed with pain and desire, satisfaction and fury, and above all a deep, eternal hatred.

Then she plunged through the opening.

Swiftly and silently, eager for blood and ready to kill, her well-trained Hunters followed.

The last hunt of the unicorns had begun.

THE LEGEND CONTINUES

What happened after Beloved and her Hunters entered Luster — how the unicorns resisted, and how Cara discovered the truth about Luster itself — is another story altogether.

It is recorded, like all such tales, in the Unicorn Chronicles.